DARK STAR RISING

DAVE SLADE

Zebulun Publishing

Zebulun Publishing
2719 Bosque Del Sol Ln N.W.
Albuquerque, N.M., 87120

ISBN: 9780985475024

Praise for Dark Star Rising

"Dave Slade's new book brings biblical prophecies of the final Antichrist to life, draping them in human flesh and artfully weaving them into current events in a realistic, riveting story. This book is engrossing. However, you will not just read a gripping story, you will also get an accurate picture and profile of the main traits of the coming world ruler as presented in Scripture."

Dr. Mark Hitchcock, Senior Pastor Faith Bible Church; Associate Professor of Bible Exposition at Dallas Theological Seminary and bestselling author of *The End: A Complete Overview of Bible Prophecy and the End of Days*

"From the ancient prophets to the New Testament apostles, the Scriptures have predicted the coming of a malevolent leader disguised as a liberator. *Dark Star Rising* presents a scenario that is uncannily possible in current international geopolitics. Author Dave Slade is engaging and captivating as he unfolds this leader's ride to world dominance within the construct of today's Middle Eastern tensions. There's not a dull moment in this book."

Skip Heitzig, Senior Pastor Calvary Church and Author of bestselling *The Bible from 30,000 feet: Soaring Through the Scriptures in One Year from Genesis to Revelation*

"Dark Star Rising is the chilling story about the rise of a Last Days leader who will be the most compelling figure in history since Jesus Christ. Author Dave Slade brings to life prophetic scripture about the man whom the Apostle Paul called the 'lawless one'. Readers will find this fast-paced story less fiction than reality as it projects from today's disturbing headlines toward a time of great chaos and hopelessness that will provide the perfect setting for his rise."

Joel Richardson, New York Times Bestselling Author of *Mystery Babylon: Unlocking the Bible's Greatest Prophetic Mystery*

*To my son Max, who struggled with darkness
but now lives in the light.*

I have come in My Father's name, and you do not receive Me;
if another comes in his own name, him you will receive.
John 5:43

List of Characters

Ahmadreza Abassi	President of Iran
Dr. Moshe Abrams	Professor of ancient languages
Abu Bakr	First Commander of ISIS
Bibi	Chief of Police in Beersheba
Randy Camp	Member of archeological team
Luke Chavez	Leader of Christian church
Rabbi Eli Cohen	Founder of Temple Institute
Daniel Ben-David	Prime Minister of Israel
Deena	Fashion editor of Jerusalem Times
Farid	Terrorist
Gadi El-Hashem	President of the United Emirates
Scooter Fensky	American archeologist
Colonel Saul Ganz	Shin Bet officer
Courtney Gattis	Commercial real estate agent
Mike Glickman	Israeli journalist
Goldstein	Editor of The Jerusalem Times
Brian Hansen	Member of archeological team
Usama Hussein	Friend of Yasin Mohammed
Jude Hyman	Jewish archeologist
Hank Jackson	American journalist
Kat Jackson	Wife of Hank Jackson
Jamal Jaffari	President of Egypt
Kamal	Terrorist
Lieutenant Kaplan	Detective
Al-Kassab	Supreme leader of ISIS
Abdul Khalid	Saudi Crown Prince
Corporal Levinsky	Soldier
Nadir Mehmed	President of Turkey
Mendel	Shin Bet official
Yasin Mohammed	Turkish billionaire businessman

Oma-Murshid	Friend of Yasin Mohammed
Salaam Nahid	Hamas military leader
Zoe Nash	American missionary
Johnny Naziri	Antiquities dealer
Andrei Primakov	President of Russia
Lance Senoski	CIA agent
President Vadim	President of Iran
Zedekiah Zukerman	Member of the Knesset, MK

Abbreviations: MK – Member of the Knesset
IDF – Israel Defense Forces
ISIS – Islamic State in Iraq and Syria
UAE – United Arab Emirates
UME – United Middle East

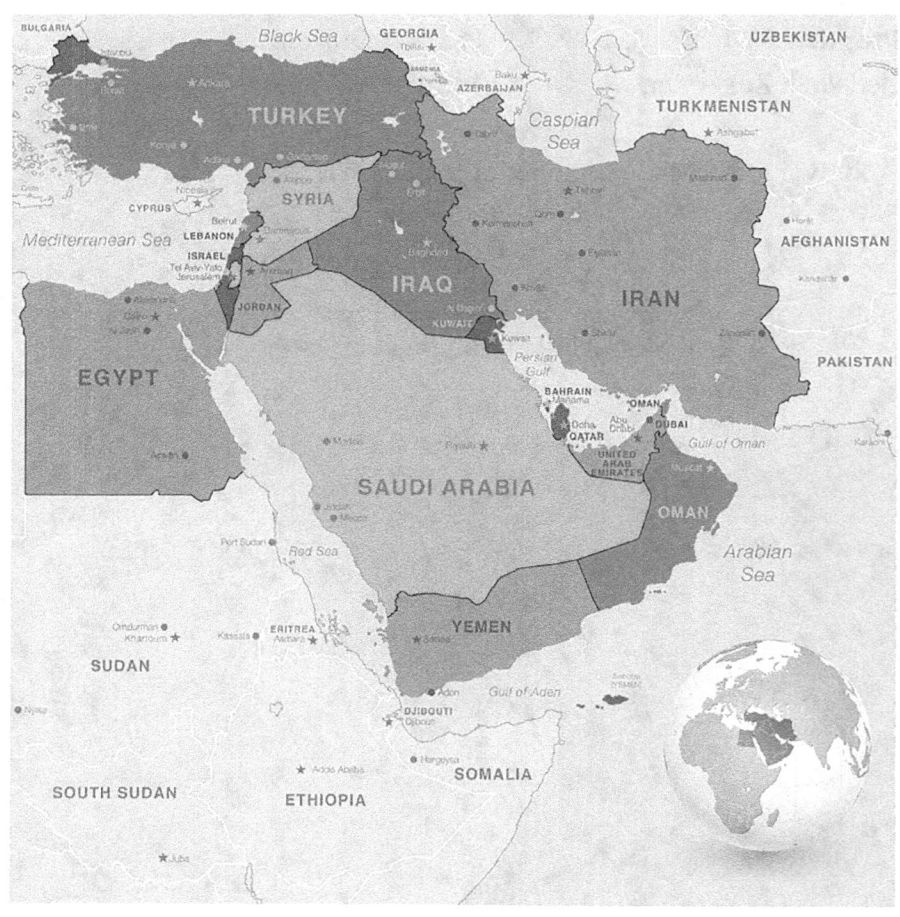

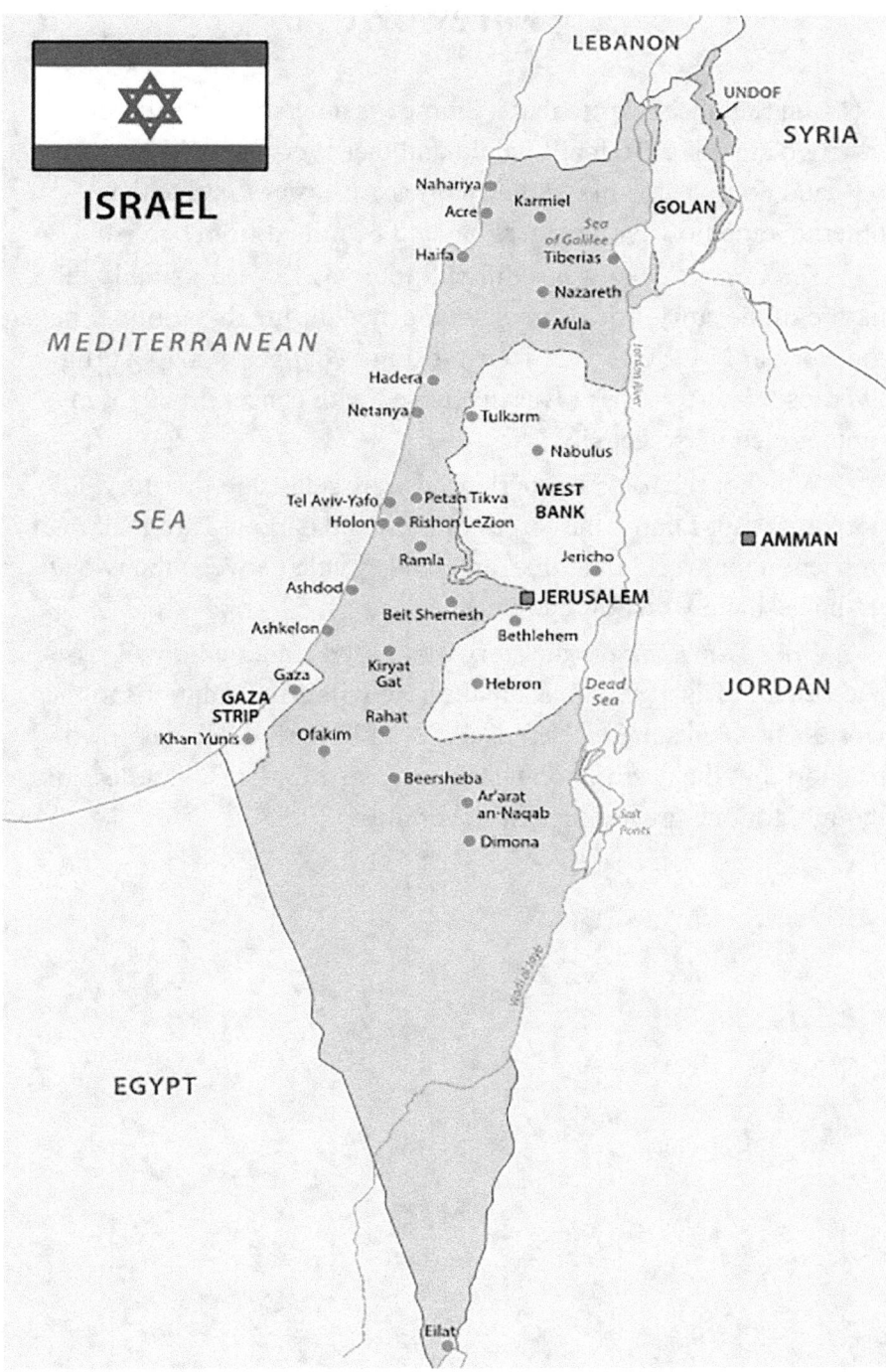

ISRAEL

Foreword

John Steinbeck wrote that a journey is a person in itself, and no two are alike. To that I would add that every book is a journey and no two are alike. Some stories are easier to write than others. Some flow while others have to be mined from hard soil.

Dark Star Rising was a difficult journey. It wasn't simply the nature of the story, but also what happened during its writing. I began the story in 2013. One year later I lost my youngest son to a drug overdose. Shortly after, I was diagnosed with cancer. In 2015, my mother died unexpectedly.

Whether the trials I experienced were related to the story, I do not know. But I know the forces of light and darkness are real, their impact on the world indelible, and the struggle between the two alive in the best and worst of mankind.

Dark Star Rising is the story of a gifted leader who will arise and be hailed as a great peacemaker. He will bring solutions to the world's problems, and all of his plans will succeed. His reign will be short, but the destruction he brings catastrophic. Do not despair though, for one greater than he is coming.

CHAPTER ONE

Raqqa, Syria, November 28, 2023

Commander Abu Bakr stood in the battle-worn minaret scanning the sky after the recent shelling. A brown haze hung over the white city. The strike by Iran was not intended to destroy Raqqa, only to remind ISIS that Persians were the real power in the Middle East.

It was good to be back in the ancient city. No one thought it possible only a few years ago. But nothing remains the same, not even the moon and the stars. Americans had tired of war and left. Everyone was tired of war—except the mujahideen.

Abu squinted at the late morning sky. The sun was trying to peek through gray clouds. It looked more like rain ahead than snow. He would have preferred snow. When it rained, the white wet blanket covering the city would disappear, revealing a scarred, dull landscape of gray and brown.

Tinny steps tapped against rusted metal, winding their way up the staircase. Oma-Murshid emerged from the stairwell. "Any sign?"

"Not yet."

The imam adjusted the black cap on his head that had shifted backwards. He placed his hands together as if he were about to pray, glanced at the sky, then looked at Abu. His dark eyes were filled with apprehension, but he said nothing.

"Our destiny is in Allah's hands. He will protect us." Abu said this for the imam and not himself.

Oma looked toward the east, still uneasy. "Where is it?"

Abu raised his field glasses. A stealth drone, distinguishable only by the hole in the layer of smoke covering the city, swooped down like a hawk in search of prey. He checked his watch. Al-Kassab would be headed through a tunnel toward a restaurant that had been closed for his arrival.

Abu walked down the steps of the minaret as Oma's rich tenor voice rose in prayer. "Allah Akbar, Allah Akbar."

*   *   *

Raqqa, Syria, November 31, 2023

Abu sat in an underground bunker with his black shepherd, Achilles, by his side. The table between him and the other three men was cluttered with rolled maps and coffee cups. Their faces were drawn and haggard. It appeared they hadn't slept in days. On their minds no doubt was how ISIS would survive without the charismatic Al-Kassab. On the television screen mounted to the wall, Iranians danced in the streets of Tehran at news of the ISIS leader's death. Financial markets surged as the whole world seemed to exhale.

The three men before him were members of the Shura Council and had been with ISIS longer. Some since the beginning with Al-Kassab. During his reign, the caliphate had regained control of Raqqa, and its former territory in Syria, Iraq, and Libya. It had also made significant gains in Jordan, Egypt, Afghanistan—and most recently, Pakistan.

"Our leader knew this day might come," Abu said. "He prepared for it by—"

"How did the Americans know his location?" The deputy and commander of Iraq, whose face was flat like a boxer's, studied his dirty fingernails. He was known for developing the barbaric tactics abhorred by the world and feared by the caliphate's enemies.

"We don't know if it was American," Abu said. "If it was, they will pay dearly."

The deputy of Syria waved his hand dismissively. His long oily beard was braided into several rows, like the ancient Babylonians and Assyrians. He was hated by the Syrian people but seemed to delight in his infamy. "Someone betrayed him. Someone close to him."

The deputy of Pakistan, an Egyptian, was the third commander at the table. He looked at Abu. "Weren't you supposed to have lunch with him?"

"Yes."

The Egyptian looked like a quiet, studious man with oval wire-rim glasses. But he was the most ruthless of the three, a legend among ISIS fighters for orchestrating the Vatican Easter massacre that killed hundreds and injured the pope. He had recently forged an alliance with Tehreek-e-Taliban or TTP, the largest of Pakistan's terrorist organizations, which had shaken the military. Many of the soldiers had defected to ISIS. Pakistan was the nuclear prize of the Middle East. If it fell, everything would change.

The Iraqi waved his hand across the table. "We were the only ones who knew of the meeting, besides the owner of Saladin's. I doubt it was him, since he's dead."

"Probably not." He knew where the questioning was headed.

Frowns descended on the men's faces.

"Did Oma know about the meeting?" asked the Syrian.

ISIS leaders had never accepted the imam. His brand of Islam was too mystical. Even Al-Kassab had been suspicious of him.

"He knew nothing."

"How can you be so sure?" The Syrian massaged his braids between his fingers.

"The only way Oma would have known is if I had told him," Abu challenged. He had fought by the side of each of these men during the last three years, but loyalty and allegiance were to the caliphate, not each other. It was Al-Kassab's wish.

"Did you tell the imam?" the Pakistani commander said.

"No," Abu said letting his left hand slip to his side.

The Syrian commander rose. "Where were you when the drone attacked?"

"I was on my way to meet with our leader."

The Iraqi also stood and leaned on the table. "You should have been at the restaurant." He raised his voice. "Why weren't you?"

Achilles growled as Abu stroked his shepherd. "I was late."

"Get that dog out of here," the Syrian said.

Abu continued to run his fingers through Achilles's thick hair.

The Egyptian remained seated, comfortable with letting the other two do his bidding. His left hand was below the table, probably wrapped around his gun. He wrote something on the tablet in front of him. His eyes rose. "You had the most to gain Abu."

"Get that dog out of here," the Syrian shouted, pointing at Achilles.

The shepherd leapt at the man's throat. The Iraqi pulled his gun to shoot the dog, but Abu stood and fired. The Pakistani unloaded his gun from under the table but only grazed Abu's leg. He squeezed a clean shot at the Egyptian's head.

Guards pounded at the door.

The Pakistani commander hit the ground, a look of utter surprise stamped beneath his cock-eyed glasses. The Iraqi was also dead. The Syrian was still alive and screamed as Achilles ripped at his throat. A crack resounded in the concrete bunker. The dog shrieked.

"Achilles," Abu yelled, running toward his dog.

The Syrian struggled to remove his 9mm trapped beneath the dead dog, but couldn't. He fired through the dog as Abu approached. The shot struck the ceiling.

Abu placed his boot on his dog, pinning it against the commander so he couldn't move. The Syrian's beard was entangled in the dead dog's mouth.

"Allah's curse on you traitor," he gurgled as blood flowed from his torn throat.

"This is for Achilles." Abu pumped three rounds into the man.

He limped to the door and opened it as several soldiers stood with their rifles drawn at him.

"They plotted our leader's death," he said sliding his gun into his belt. "Feed them to the dogs. They don't deserve burial. "

CHAPTER TWO

Chicago, April 4, 2024

Courtney Gattis was late for the most important appointment of her life. She honked her horn but it only elicited a jutting finger from the cabbie in front. Thursday was the worst day to get anywhere in Chicago. Everyone was leaving for the weekend. Her driverless black Mercedes coupe inched forward coming to a stop on North Michigan Avenue. She glared at the red light, willing it to turn green. *Come on, come on.* Her appointment was only a few blocks away, but it might as well be twenty miles.

She had never gotten use to driverless cars, although admittedly, they had a better record at avoiding tickets and fender benders. She glanced at her watch. *Forget it.* She stepped out of her car and shut the door.

A policeman on the corner looked puzzled.

She walked to the curb and removed her pumps.

He pointed at her car. "You can't leave your car in the street unattended."

Courtney flipped her blond hair to one side. "It driverless."

"You know the law. Someone has to be in the vehicle."

She reached in her purse and placed an extra set of keys in the officer's mitt-sized hand. "Tow it."

The bewildered man stared at her.

With shoes in hand, she sprinted down the River Walk toward her appointment. A drone hummed overhead with a package. She glanced upward to make sure the merchandise was securely in the machine's grip.

A few minutes later she stood in the shadow of the Chicago Spire. Early morning light gleamed in the silvery glass of the cloud-piercing tower. She checked her watch again. Eight minutes behind. She couldn't remember the last time she had been late for an appointment. Polished red toenails poked through tears in her Wolford stockings. She slipped on her shoes, straightened her suit jacket, and adjusted her posture.

Standing in the empty marbled foyer was Li Meng. He was frowning. Punctuality was important to the Chinese. But thankfully she was less than ten minutes late. Anything beyond that was considered extremely disrespectful.

She smiled, and bowed. "Zaochen hao."

He dipped his head. "Good morning." His creased forehead relaxed, but his lips still formed a thin, hard line. She would have to work to regain his favor.

She gestured toward the elevator. "Shall we?"

The Chicago Spire, completed in 2021, was still largely vacant. The twisting 2,000 foot tall skyscraper was originally scheduled for completion in 2012. But the financial crash of 2008 and lawsuits against the principals had locked up development for years. The architect said he found inspiration for the building's radical design in the spiraling smoke of a campfire. The unconventional edifice certainly added a distinct flair to the skyline, but it should have never been built. There weren't enough high-end tenants to occupy Chicago's other towers, let alone three million square-feet of new space.

Courtney pressed 150 on the panel, then punched in a code supplied by the listing broker.

"I hear developer in trouble." His eyes were expressionless.

Everyone is in trouble. Especially me if I don't make this sale. "I heard that also."

"How much you think I should offer?"

It was a tricky question—and a test. Mr. Meng knew exactly what he was going to offer. If she provided a figure too high, he would think she was soft and unqualified to represent him. But if she gave an estimate too low, she would doom the negotiation from the start. "The construction cost was four billion. The developer owes three. You couldn't build it for that today."

A slight smile revealed a dimple in the businessman's right cheek.

The elevator door opened to 30,000 square-feet of concrete. Not an interior wall in sight. The only interruption of space was a gray, plastic trash can tucked into a corner. The tops of Chicago's grandest buildings peeked through fluffy clouds far below. The sight made her a little dizzy.

Behind her were voices. She and Mr. Meng turned to see two men speaking in Arabic to each other about fifty feet away. The listing broker knew she had an appointment with Mr. Meng. Why would he schedule another showing? Was it a deliberate ploy to create competition?

The men were dressed in ill-fitted, off-the-rack suits, which might work in Vegas, but not Chicago. At least, not if they wanted anyone to believe they were legitimate investors. Everything about them was wrong. How did they get in? And what were they arguing about?

One of the men caught her looking at him and glared. She looked away.

Mr. Meng walked toward the east side of the building, a route directly past the two strangers like he wanted to get a closer look, size them up like a sprinter at the starting blocks does his competition, and determine whether they were legitimate players.

As Courtney walked past the two men, they switched from Arabic to what sounded like Farsi. She understood Arabic and Chinese. Both were a must for a career in high-end commercial real estate. Also critical, was an understanding of Middle East politics where the most complicated alliances in the world existed. Why had the men switched to Farsi? What were they trying to hide? Her skin tingled.

One of the two, a stocky man with a wide face, said something that sounded like *be-l-an-be*. He repeated it. She looked at Mr. Meng to see if the word had registered. It hadn't. Apparently, he didn't understand Farsi either. The men fell silent, and she could feel their eyes stalking her.

Mr. Weng stood at the side of the building, looking out toward Lake Michigan. "They're not buyers." With a dismissing wave of his hand, he eliminated them as a serious challenge.

"I know…" Courtney lowered her voice. "That's why I think we should leave now."

Mr. Meng looked puzzled for a moment, then seemed to understand. He walked swiftly toward the elevator, his eyes focused on the barren expanse of floor. Courtney followed, careful to avoid eye contact with the men.

As the door to the elevator began closing, she looked up. The two men were staring at her. She took a deep breath as the doors shut. Mr. Meng's puffy eyes studied her. He seemed unaffected by what had just happened. Perhaps he was right, and there wasn't anything to fear. But even if he were afraid, he wouldn't show it. The Chinese were masters at self-control, an invaluable discipline in negotiations.

As the elevator opened, she stepped into the lobby and finalized her lunch arrangements with Mr. Meng, then bowed. The investor exited the Chicago Spire. She spoke into her smart watch. "Be-l-an-be."

She shuddered at the translation.

CHAPTER THREE

Jerusalem, April 4

The flashlight probed the distant, arched ceiling dimly revealing elaborate mosaics.

Brian whistled softly.

"Turn that off," Scooter whispered.

But the sight was magnificent, Scooter thought. A tapestry of red and gold, pearl-shaped tiles arched overhead. Sixteen stained glass windows encircled the base of the dome. Slivers of moonlight slipped through dark glass bringing to life arabesque figures of scrolls and trees. Part of him hated to see the light switched off.

"Who's going to see?" Brian said. "It's the middle of the freaking night. No one here except us and the mice."

"You know the instructions."

Brian turned off his light, returning the ceiling to darkness, but lamps hanging far below the dome glowed, casting their light in yellow arcs. He tossed the flashlight toward the duffle bag. It missed, rolling across the plush Persian rug, until it smacked against a marbled pier. Scooter shook his head but didn't say anything.

"Can you smell the history?" He breathed deeply.

"Musty, dude," Brian said.

Scooter ran his hand over one of twelve marble columns in the middle of the shrine. The gray polished pillar with twisting black veins was cool. The columns, which varied in width and color, had been looted from the ruins of Roman and Byzantine temples. The stories they could tell.

He wanted to linger, but he had not been invited to study one of Islam's most revered sites. His work lay below the El-Sakhra, a massive slab of limestone rising six feet from the floor and stretching sixty feet across the Dome of the Rock. The sacred rock still bore the scars of crusader swords. Muslims believed it was from here that Mohammed ascended to heaven on his night journey. For Jews, it was even more significant. Early Jewish writers claimed it was the foundation stone, the very spot where Adam was created and where Abraham offered his son Isaac as a sacrifice.

"Let's go," Scooter said, waving at Randy and Jude, the rest of his crew, who were on the other side of the shrine studying relics. He walked toward the stairs near the sacred stone. The steps, cleaved from bedrock that once supported Herod's Temple, led downward about ten feet toward the Well of Souls, a cave beneath the holy rock that according to Islamic legend was where the dead awaiting judgment gathered.

A light set in the ceiling cast an ivory net that illuminated the center of the room but left the perimeter in shadows. A thick rug of red and gold covered the floor, beneath which was another chamber according to Jews. One that once housed the inner sanctuary of the first temple. Scooter hoped they were right.

On the far side of the cave, an eerie image formed from holes and niches in the rock glared at the intruders. A curtain hung from ceiling to floor. Scooter walked closer. How odd. It was black and white, completely unlike the bright green, a color favored by Muslims.

"Behind here." He pulled the drape back revealing steps down to a narrow steel door with rusted hinges set flush in rock.

The sound of footsteps behind startled him. He turned. A man dressed in a suit with dark glasses descended the stairs, his hand sliding down the handrail.

"Are you ready?"

"You must be Kamran?"

"And you are Scooter?" The long *oo* in his pronunciation sounded Indian or Pakistani.

"I'm in big trouble if I'm not."

The man didn't acknowledge his humor.

"You look different than your photo," Kamran said.

"My grandma told me it wasn't good manners to have your picture taken with your hat on." He removed the cowboy hat. "How's that?"

He hoped his second effort might lighten the man's mood, but he remained all business. His eyes were impossible to read behind the dark lenses.

"Your phones." Kamran extended his right hand. Scooter and his three assistants, reluctantly placed their phones in the man's hands, who slipped them inside the pockets on each side of his jacket. Not that they would work 25 feet underground anyway. But Kamran's demand for secrecy was understandable. The mere mention of Jews digging on the Temple Mount would set Israel on fire. Every Arab big enough to throw a rock or pull a trigger would consider it their sacred duty to retaliate.

"Remember, no one knows about this except for us and your employer. It must remain that way. If something happens, no one will save you. And one last thing: the door will be locked tomorrow."

He removed a key from his pocket and handed it to Scooter.

"Will I ever meet the man who hired us?"

"No. I have never met him or spoken to him myself."

Scooter studied the tarnished key, then enclosed it in his fist.

"All right, then. May Allah watch over you," Kamran said as he turned and left.

Jude snorted once Kamran was far enough away not to hear. "That's the last person I want watching over me."

Scooter ignored Jude's remark and faced the lock. He inserted the key and turned it, but it wouldn't budge. The tumblers in the padlock were either rusted, or it was the wrong key. He glanced back at the stairs but Kamran was gone. Scooter jiggled the key again searching for a connection. No luck.

"Any graphite in the bag?" He turned toward Randy. The archeologist was a former minor league baseball player with short brown hair and ears that looked suspiciously elfish.

Randy rummaged through one of the tan camouflage bags. "Sorry boss."

"Lend me some of your grease," he said handing him the key. "What?"

Scooter pointed at the man's crop of shiny hair.

Randy chuckled and ran his hand through the stubble, rubbing the key between thick, oily fingers. He handed it back.

Scooter massaged the key back and forth in the lock until it finally clicked. He opened the door to a waft of cool wet air and motioned for his crew to enter. Flashlights illuminated damp walls. Silently, his men descended steep wooden steps, using the walls to steady themselves.

At the bottom, some 15 feet below, his crew waited. He took a breath before descending, trying to contain the excitement coursing through him.

"Can you believe this?" Jude said.

The curly, dark-haired American, a rabbinical school dropout, had read his mind. It was unbelievable. They were standing on ground where few had in the last 2500 years. Even more unbelievable: two Jews were here to see it. And he was certain that somewhere in the expanse of forgotten rock lay the greatest of all archeological treasures, greater even than the Rosetta Stone. But even if he found it, his name would never be associated with the discovery. Kamran had made that clear. His employer, who he presumed was a Muslim, would possess Israel's greatest treasure. Few archeologists would take a job on such terms, except those who needed money and had few offers.

The shaft opened to a large natural cave, which was directly beneath the Well of Souls. *So it's true.* The cave's existence had been the speculation of archeologists for decades. No complete archeological survey had ever been conducted on the Temple Mount. The Islamic Waqf wouldn't permit it, which made his mission all the more remarkable.

But the Well of Souls was empty. Their path lay in the opposite direction. Scooter pointed to the right, down a passageway barely wide enough for Randy's shoulders. Scooter checked the map scrawled hastily on a piece of white paper. Green timbers braced the ceiling and thick upright beams spaced every six feet supported the tunnel. Along the top of the walls were lights connected to an extension cord, which he plugged in before venturing farther.

Evidence of digging was everywhere from exploratory offshoots chopped into the walls to rubble strewn across the stone floor. He shuddered at the priceless artifacts being lost. Another team had preceded them. Kamran had never said why they quit.

A glint of something near his feet stopped him. He stooped down, picked up a rock with a spot of gold embedded in it. He removed a small hammer from the duffle bag and lightly tapped at the rock. The curved outline of a golden nose ring emerged. He chipped away the rest of the stone, then placed the ring in his pocket. All artifacts were the property of the Waqf, except for what they had come for and—the ones they didn't know about.

Scooter led his crew deeper into the labyrinth. The men trailing behind were a motley crew: Jude the scholar, Randy the jock, and Brian, the tech junky, who was forever connected to something. Only Jude was trained as an archeologist. Randy and Brian were here, because they were reliable workers, and could be trusted to keep their mouths shut. He had known them for years.

They silently pushed deeper into the maze, their flashlights probing the dim light ahead.

"You sure this is the way?" Brian asked.

Scooter waved his men forward, but he was beginning to wonder if he had taken a wrong turn. Too bad he couldn't access the file with the map Kamran had sent. It had erased itself within five minutes of arrival, leaving barely enough time for copying. Had he made a mistake?

The tunnel came to an end. The digging halted abruptly leaving carved clefts in the rock that looked like the frenzied marks of a wild animal. The string of lights illuminating the tunnel had stopped short of the end leaving this section in darkness. Scooter leaned down and removed an aluminum suitcase from the duffle bag. Inside was a ground-penetrating radar unit that would reveal if there was anything behind the wall. He switched on the GPR. A bright amber light flickered, then turned green and glowed in the dim light. He lifted the flat, square 18-inch instrument up and placed it against the rock. Slowly, he slid the unit in a horizontal direction across the stone as he watched the screen below. If there was a chamber adjacent to the tunnel, it would show up as a light area. But each sweep of rock revealed nothing but dark gray lines.

Scooter checked the map. They should be very close to the Al Kas Fountain, almost underneath. The very spot where the artifact was supposed to be and where thousands had died during Babylon's destruction of the first temple and Rome's destruction of the second.

"What was that?" Jude said his voice breaking. He pointed back at the tunnel.

"Keep your voice down," Scooter said staring back into the passageway.

Kamran had issued strict instructions about talking. He said Jews were monitoring the Mount for any activity. That might be true, but what difference did it make? Muslims had been digging up the sacred 35-acre plot for years, destroying artifacts, and dumping the broken remnants in the Kidron Valley for archeologists to sift through. Israel had never done anything to stop the destruction. Why would they care now?

"I saw something," Jude said.

Scooter laid the GPR down and pointed his flashlight into the dim corridor. "I don't see anything."

"What did you see?" Randy studied the area illuminated by Scooter's light.

The crying of a child echoed through the chamber.

"Sounds like a little boy," Jude said.

Scooter stood up and walked back into the tunnel with his three men close behind. A shadow disappeared around a turn. He took a step back.

"There he is," Jude said pointing.

Scooter shrugged his shoulders and walked back to end of the tunnel. "We've got a job to do."

But Jude lingered, staring into the tunnel.

"Snap out of it." Scooter picked up the GPR and started scanning again. Still nothing. "Get out the pick axe. We need to dig." The thought of excavating an archeological site with a large pick was like telling an artist restoring a priceless painting to use a four-inch brush. But he didn't have the luxury of time.

Randy pulled the tool from duffle bag. He stripped down to his tee shirt and laid into the wall like he was at batting practice. Chips of rock exploded.

"I suspect the last crew didn't dig far enough," Scooter said, standing at a distance to avoid splinters of flying rock.

"But you said the map showed the chamber was under the Al Kas Fountain," Jude said.

"Maps can be wrong."

Randy kept pounding at the rock, making steady headway. A fine white dust covered his glistening, muscular arms. "Man, this limestone is hard." He stopped for a moment and wiped sweat from his brow.

"Turonian period," Scooter said. "It was more favored as a building stone."

"Thanks for the history lesson professor."

"If anyone is listening up there, they know the Arabs are remodeling again," Brian said.

After an hour, Randy had carved a two-foot deep by two-feet wide channel in the stone wall in front. It was about waist high. Scooter's idea was not to remove any more rock than necessary. "Stop. Let's check it."

Brian grabbed the GPR and slid it into the recess.

Everyone craned their necks for a glimpse of the screen.

"Anything?" Scooter said.

"Nothing." Brian slapped the rock with his hand.

"Randy get the sledge hammer." Scooter handed a chisel to Brian. "Hold this."

"Just keep your eye on the ball, Babe Ruth," Brian said.

Randy smiled as he swung at the steel shaft driving it into the stone.

It took another hour to chip away two more feet of rock.

"Let's check gain," Scooter said."

He slid into the hole and placed the instrument at the very end of the niche. The dark gray lines on the monitor faded to light gray.

"Boy howdy. I think we have something."

"The last crew missed it," Randy said.

"If Howard Carter were here, he would tell you there is a lot of luck in archeology," Scooter said. "Every archeologist before him missed Tutankhamen's tomb. But don't get too excited. This may be nothing more than an empty room."

Randy picked up the axe.

"Not yet," Scooter said. "No telling what's on the other side of the wall. Use the drill. All we need is a hole big enough to slide the camera through."

He grabbed a 12-inch mortar bit and inserted it into the drill, then tightened it down.

As the drill hummed, boring into the limestone, a hazy curtain of fine dust filled the tunnel. Brian pulled the drill bit out of the wall and inspected the hole, then removed the bit and inserted a longer one. He resumed drilling.

Several minutes later the four-foot bit punched through the other side of the wall. Scooter fed an optical cable fitted with a night vision camera through the quarter-sized hole. His crew strained to get a look at the monitor attached to the cable that Scooter held. The luminescent green screen yielded nothing distinguishable. He rotated the cable. The distinct lines of a large, ghostly green room took shape.

The ground rumbled.

"What was that?" Jude asked.

Scooter ignored the question, still fixated on the screen. He pressed the zoom function for a closer look.

"Felt like a tremor," Brian said.

"Maybe it's a terrorist attack," Randy said nudging Jude. Everyone knew Jude didn't like to be teased, which encouraged Randy to do it all the more.

The ground shook again rattling the timbers overhead. Slips of dirt streamed down between the planks overhead.

"That definitely felt like an earthquake," Brian said.

"It's a sign," Jude said. "We shouldn't be here."

Randy scowled. "If you knew you weren't supposed to be here, why did you sign up for the dig?

Jude said, "To be the first to see it."

"Try to remember that."

The ground shook again, this time violently, throwing his crew to the ground. Scooter stumbled backwards, falling on a sharp stone that stabbed his back. Flashlights rolled across the tunnel's floor. His men tried to stand but the ground continued to shake.

"We've got to get out of here before the tunnel collapses," Brian said.

A crashing sound in the distance sent a thick, brown cloud rushing toward them.

Scooter covered his eyes, choking on dust.

The shaking stopped. He stood up unsteadily and dusted himself off. It was dark except for shafts of light along the tunnel's floor from the flashlights. The overhead lights along the wall were out. He picked up one of the flashlights and walked down the tunnel to where it made a dogleg. At the bend an impenetrable mound of massive rocks and beams snapped like matchsticks blocked the exit.

They were trapped. No one knew they were here—except their mysterious employer and Kamran.

And his warning was clear. No rescue.

CHAPTER FOUR

Jerusalem, April 4

Hank Jackson leaned forward on the Tower of David, an ancient citadel near the Jaffa Gate, last rebuilt five hundred years ago by the Ottomans. The stones were worn smooth from countless hands. To the east, lay Jerusalem's Old City, compacted nearly as tightly as Herod's ashlars on the Western Wall. The sun glimmered on the golden Dome of the Rock as a blue and white flag fluttered nearby in a rare, cool afternoon breeze.

A piquant, citrus fragrance wafted over him as delicate hands slipped around his waist from behind. Hank grinned as he turned around. A radiant Kat Rodriguez stood in a long, lacy white dress, her raven hair draped over shoulders covered with a white shawl. A current of excitement shot through him. He was still in awe that she had agreed to marry him.

"Thank you for making my dreams come true," Kat said, her dark eyes sparkling.

He wrapped his arms around her. "I made more than one dream come true?"

"Jerusalem."

"What if I could have only afforded a wedding in Las Cruces?"

Kat grew up in the college town just north of El Paso and southwest of White Sands. Once known for its pecans, the orchards outside the city were now twisted, bare reminders of the historic drought.

Kat playfully swatted his arm. "I would have still married you. But Jerusalem makes it even more special."

Kat had always longed to see Israel. So Hank went one better and emptied his bank account to give her a wedding in Jerusalem.

"A bride should wear a veil."

The thin reedy voice startled Hank. A stooped man with dull gray eyes and a cane stood behind Kat.

He looked up from under the brim of his black fedora. "Bad luck to see her before your vows."

Kat turned around. "We're not superstitious."

The stooped Jew nodded thoughtfully. "One shouldn't believe in superstitions, but it's wise to be heedful of them. But above all on this day be vigilant."

A sonorous blast interrupted their unexpected encounter. A shofar.

Hank and Kat glanced upward at the trumpeting blast that seemed to coming from the sky, then back to the old man. He was gone.

"Where did he go?" she said.

"I don't know."

"Come on guys. You're going to miss your own wedding." The deep, familiar voice rang from below the fortress wall.

Hank and Kat peered over the south parapet at Pastor Luke Chavez who stood thirty feet below in front of a white satin-draped chuppah. He waved at them. Rabbi Lemuel Mezvinsky stood next to Luke. The rabbi looked frail compared to the broad-shouldered former boxer. Friends and family were seated, but everyone was looking up into the sky, searching for the source of the blaring trumpet.

Then, the shofar stopped.

Kat lifted the hem of her dress and held it in her left hand. "How strange."

"If you guys don't hurry, your guests might think you changed your mind," Luke yelled from below.

"Never," Hank said. He took Kat's hand. Together, they ran down the fortress path toward the garden where torches planted every four-feet lined an aisle separating the twenty guests into two groups of ten.

*   *   *

An hour later the ceremony was nearly over. Jewish and Christian customs had been combined to create a service steeped in ritual and meaning. Rabbi Mezvinsky supervised the Jewish part of the wedding, while Luke read from the New Testament. Kat wasn't Jewish, but anyone who knew her, could attest her heart was.

As Kat walked around Hank seven times to symbolize the importance of the groom to the bride, he was struck by the oddity of Hakafot. The bride's encircling served to protect him from demons. It should be the other way around. But perhaps there was something to the tradition. He felt stronger and more confident with Kat beside him.

Hank took a ring of white gold with a single round diamond from his pocket and held it up. "Behold, you are consecrated to me with this ring according to the law of Moses and Israel." He placed the band on Kat's finger.

Rabbi Mezvinsky removed a hammered gold band from his suit pocket hidden beneath his long gray beard. He handed the ring to Kat.

"I am my beloved's and my beloved is mine," Kat said smiling. She slipped the ring on Hank's finger.

Lines around Mezvinksy's eyes pinched together as he nodded.

Hank kissed Kat to the applause of the guests.

Only one thing remained—the breaking of the glass.

"The shattering of this glass should remind us of the destruction of the second temple." Mezvinsky held up an empty wine glass in his right hand. "It should also remind us that the world is imperfect and everyone should participate in Tikkun Olam, the mending of the world."

Hank looked at his wife. She was beautiful. Her eyes had always entranced him. But they weren't looking at him. He noticed Luke had turned his attention in the same direction.

The rabbi stopped wrapping a napkin around the glass.

Hank turned toward the stone parapet. Looking down at the wedding party from the precipice were two men.

Luke pointed at the exit. "Run!"

The glass slipped from the rabbi's hand, shattering against the ground, as a loud bang rang from the wall.

CHAPTER FIVE

Jerusalem, April 4

"If only I could have lived a few more years to see the Temple rebuilt. I prayed everyday for God to grant this request, but he wasn't willing. It wasn't my destiny. It will be yours ZZ." The ashen, sunken face of Rabbi Eli Cohen was tired.

Zedekiah Zukerman leaned down a little closer toward the old man, who was slipping in and out of lucidity. More and more his thoughts veered toward eccentric ideas.

The light in Eli's room was dim. A few rays of amber peeked through curtains that were yellowed and stained. Night would arrive soon. The smell of decay and eucalyptus hung in the air. Green and yellow prescription bottles competed for space with framed black and white photographs on top of the dresser in the small room. Stacks of dusty books crowded the floor.

Eli coughed and clutched his chest as he tried to sit up. The deep rattle sounded painful. Zedekiah helped the rabbi into a sitting position as he spit bloody mucus into a tissue and rested his head against Zedekiah's chest. "God promised there will be another temple that will usher in Messiah's reign and turn our people's hearts back toward him. Do you believe that?"

The question startled ZZ. "Of course." But the notion wasn't realistic. At least not now. The Temple Mount was occupied by the Dome of the Rock and the Al-Aqsa Mosque. Besides, the mere mention of building a third temple could start a war.

Zedekiah eased the man back down onto his back.

Eli seized ZZ's hand. The old man's paper-thin skin was cold. "You must believe. Without faith it is impossible to please God." Eli's rheumy eyes held a plea.

ZZ wanted to reassure the old rabbi, tell him he agreed, but Eli had already seen through his answer.

He had met few men who had real faith. Eli was one. There weren't many like him left. Maybe that wasn't a bad thing. Such unyielding faith whether Jewish or Muslim had incited riots and spilled untold blood. Today's world required compromise, not faith.

Eli licked his lips and glanced sideways at a water bottle on his nightstand. He was too weak to reach for it. ZZ pressed it to the rabbi's lips. He sipped.

The rabbi's dull eyes brightened. "I know where the Ark of the Covenant is."

ZZ smiled. *Of course you do.*

"So does the government."

"If they know, why haven't they recovered it?"

Eli chuckled, but quickly lapsed into a hacking cough. He took a deep raspy breath. "Who can understand politicians? They say one thing, but mean something else. Why did our soldiers fight so bravely in 1967 to secure the Temple Mount only to have General Moshe Dayan give it back to Jordan?"

Orthodox Jews were still livid all these years later. But Dayan did the right thing. If Israel had claimed the Temple Mount as spoils of war, it would have united Muslims across the world to wage a relentless war against Jews. Eli wasn't the first rabbi to insist he knew where the ark was. It was a fantasy of every old-timer and archeologist. "So where is it?"

Eli pointed a shaky finger at the floor.

ZZ smiled. "It's buried under your house?"

Eli closed his eyes and shook his head. "Under the rug. I have a safe. There's a map."

Many had claimed through the years to know where the ark was. A few had even said they had seen it. Some believed the ark was buried beneath the Temple Mount. Others believed it was hidden away in Ethiopia. And there were maps. Lots of maps but something about Eli's claim disturbed ZZ. Eli was one of the world's foremost experts on the first temple. Could he have an actual map of the ark's location?

"Where did you get the map?"

ZZ bent down close to Eli. The old man's voice was fading into a whisper.

"The late Rabbi Shiller, God rest his soul, was the only person to ever see the ark before Muslims closed off the tunnel. All the others were fakes. Shiller made a map and entrusted it to me before he died. And now I'm giving it to you."

"Why not give it to Rabbi Mezvinsky? He's your best friend."

Eli coughed. "No, not Lemuel."

"Isn't he your friend?"

The rabbi's tired eyes fixated on ZZ. "You must be careful. There are many powerful people who don't want the temple rebuilt."

"Who?"

Eli pointed again at the floor. "The map."

ZZ bent down and pulled back the matted rug revealing a safe set in the wooden floor. "What's the combination?"

"Two right…two left…three right." The numbers rolled out slowly.

ZZ spun the dial a few times. His hand was shaking. He rotated the disk.

"The numbers," Eli whispered. "Isaiah."

ZZ stopped spinning the dial and concentrated. "Chapter 2, verses 2-3?"

Eli nodded slowly. "Just as God re-gathered his people and brought them back to this land, so will he build a new temple."

The rabbi's words triggered ZZ's memory: *And it shall come to pass in the last days that the mountain of the Lord's house shall be established at the top of the mountains and shall be exalted above the hills; and all of the nations shall flow unto it. And many people shall go and say, "Come and let us go up to the mountain of the Lord, to the house of the God of Jacob, and he will teach us of his ways, and we shall walk in his paths: for out of Zion shall go forth Torah and the word of God from Jerusalem."*

He was surprised he remembered the passage. It had been a long time since he had read the scriptures. The dial clicked. ZZ flipped open the top and peered down into the deep box.

Eli smiled. "Rabbi Shiller entrusted the map to me when he was dying. Now, I'm giving it to you." He paused to catch his breath. A time is coming soon when the people will cry out for their temple again."

"There's nothing in here."

"What?" Eli gasped, struggling to push himself up from the bed. But he was too weak. He sank back.

"Are you sure you put the map in here?"

"I'm not senile," he snapped. "Someone has stolen it." The words were barely audible.

"Who has access to your safe?"

"No one." He paused. "A young woman comes to clean once a week."

"Does she know the combination?"

Eli shook his head. "No. No. She would never take it."

"Anyone else?"

Eli stopped and stared up into ZZ's face. "Lemuel."

"Rabbi Mezvinsky?"

"Yes," he said weakly.

"Why would he take it?"

"I don't know…" Tears flowed down the weathered face onto his matted gray beard. "What is the temple without the ark? Where will God meet us now?"

The question seemed to sap the rabbi's waning strength.

ZZ sat down on the bed next to Eli. "Don't worry. We'll find the map."

Eli's accusation against one of Israel's most respected rabbis was troubling. What had happened between these two men who used to be the best of friends?

Eli's gray eyes stared at ZZ as if searching for something. The intensity was uncomfortable. "Find the map." He gasped for air as he reached for ZZ's hand.

He took the rabbi's cold hands in his and held them tightly. Eli's breaths were slow and shallow but his eyes wouldn't let go.

"Vow before God that you will find it," he whispered.

ZZ shifted on the bed. He didn't believe in oaths, particularly to God. The scripture was clear about God's view of broken promises. His view of God differed from Eli's, but still, an oath was serious. Yet, he was inclined to say anything to comfort this old friend.

"In Jehovah's name I swear to find the map."

Eli nodded. "Good. What day is today?"

"Thursday."

"Pity. I always wanted to die on Shabbat," he whispered exhaling slowly.

CHAPTER SIX

Chicago, April 4

"What are you looking at lady?" The thick Indian accent of the dark-haired cab driver swung Courtney around in her seat. The man peered nervously into the rear view mirror. A hint of curry hung in the air.

"Mind your own business," she snapped. But it took all her resolve to not check the rear window again, scanning each car for any sign of the two men. The more distance between her and the Chicago Spire, the better. Perhaps, there wasn't anything to worry about. She could have misunderstood what the two Iranians said. But she hadn't. The Google translation was clear—bomb. But the argument between the two men could have been about a bomb somewhere else. There were plenty of bombings these days. But what if wasn't?

The thought sent acid roiling in her stomach. She reached in her purse and discreetly retrieved an antacid tablet and chewed it. She should alert the Chicago Police Department and tell them what she had heard. But what if she was wrong? If she called the police, the report might make the evening news. The CPD was as leaky as an eighteenth century frigate. Such a story, whether real or not, might be enough to make Mr. Meng reconsider an offer. That would be disastrous.

Courtney checked her watch. Less than 2 hours to pick up lunch and meet Mr. Meng at her office next to the River Walk, write the offer, then pick up her little sister at the airport. *Whew.* She had plotted the course on her wrist phone. It would take 15 minutes if traffic were light, which it never was. First stop was Lao Sze Chuan in Chinatown, known for its excellent Szechwan. The businessman was fond of spicy dishes, the hotter the better according to his assistant. Her recommendation: spicy sole fish, crispy chili shrimp, and steamed vegetables. Her Midwestern roots preferred something simpler like a good roast beef sandwich with fiery horseradish. But that would have to wait for another day.

The cab stopped at the unassuming restaurant with large black Chinese characters scrolled across the yellow awning.

"Be right back," she said to the driver.

He pushed his Chicago Bears cap back on his head and stared at the meter.

A homeless man wrapped in a blanket sat near the front door with a bucket at his feet. They were everywhere, and these weren't the bums of a few years ago. Many of the new homeless were educated and wanted to work but couldn't find jobs. She walked into the packed restaurant toward the cashier.

The young woman nodded. "Ms. Gattis, we've missed you." She placed the order on the counter. "$700,000."

The devaluation of the dollar still took a few seconds to register. Courtney passed her hand under a scanner. The world had been forced to adopt a universal, digital currency after the U.S. declared bankruptcy. That combined with the fear of touching bills that had passed through countless hands after the 2019 pandemic, made paper money a relic.

"Thanks for putting this together so quickly. I know you're busy. Tell Lin I appreciate it."

The cashier bowed slightly.

Courtney walked outside.

The homeless man stared at the take-out bag she held. His eyes were hidden in deep recesses. He shook his bucket. It was empty.

Written in crude black letters across the dirt-smeared plastic was *hungry* and underneath: *will take anything to trade.* A worldwide barter system developed after the pandemic, but the new currency system had eliminated most trading, except among the homeless. He shook his bucket again.

"Do you have a phone I can transfer a few dollars into?"

He shook his head, then removed the surgical mask. "Had to sell it." She dug into her purse for anything of value.

Courtney shook her head. "I'm sorry. I wish I had something."

The man's leathery face, which had brightened as she opened her purse, fell.

The fountain pen in the bottom of her purse stared up at her. She had won it in a sales contest and used it exclusively for signing contracts. She pulled it out. A pang of remorse stabbed her. *But it's my good luck pen.*

"You've got to promise me something," Courtney said extending the pen.

The man shook his head eagerly, the loose skin on his neck mimicking agreement.

"This pen is worth a lot of money. It's a Montblanc. 18-carat gold. I want you to promise me you'll get top dollar for it. Okay?"

The man grinned, then clamped his hand over his toothless mouth.

As she extended the pen, hands from behind scooped her up and swept her backward.

Someone yanked her inside a van. The beggar stood reaching for the pen as the door slammed shut. The driver gunned the engine.

Courtney drove the pen she still clutched backward. A man screamed.

"Crazy slut," he croaked, backhanding her.

She flew against the sliding door. The handle stabbed her back. Her cheek burned. She jammed her stiletto into the man's shin. As he clutched his leg, she swung her shoe upward into his chin. He slumped to the van's floor.

She grabbed the door handle, prepared to lunge from the van that wove in and out of traffic. But it wouldn't open.

"Help! Help!" She beat her fists against the van's panel.

Something hard slammed against the back of her head. She fell forward, dizzy. She rolled over and looked up at a 9mm pointed at her.

"Let's kill her now."

"No," said the driver. "We still have too far to go. If we get stopped with a dead body, it will threaten everything."

The lanky man kneeled beside her. "Put your hands behind your back and shut up."

Courtney placed her hands behind her. The man cinched the plastic tie so tight it cut into her wrists. Were these the men from the Chicago Spire?

The man she stabbed groaned and tried to sit up. The Montblanc lay at his side. He pressed his hand against a crimson-soaked ski mask, cursing under his breath. Blood streamed between his fingers. Too bad she hadn't planted the pen a few inches higher.

Her hands shook and the back of her head ached. The biggest deal of her life was on the line. Millions. The first big break she'd had in three years. And these thugs weren't going to take it from her. She glanced at her purse. But it was too far away.

"You'll never get away with this. People saw. They'll call the police." But would anyone call? Kidnappings were as common as burglaries. The financial collapse had turned honest people into thieves, which is what these men probably were. Hoping someone would pay a fat ransom. Good luck. Her once sizable bank account was as low as Lake Michigan.

"I said shut up," the man with the gun said.

"Is this about money?" Courtney did a quick mental calculation. "I'll give you $140 million if you'll let me go." About $10,000 in pre-collapse dollars.

The kidnapper laid his gun down, grabbed a role of duct tape and tore off a strip with his mouth. With his other hand, he punched numbers on his phone. "You think we're gang bangers looking for a quick score?" He fixated on her ring.

Aren't you? she thought, tucking her right ring finger into her palm.

He yanked the near perfect two-carat from her finger and slipped it on his pinky.

If only she had left it home, but she wanted to impress Mr. Weng.

"What do you think guys?" he said holding up his left hand?

"Gay," the bleeding man snapped.

The lanky man with her ring grabbed his gun and pointed it at the other terrorist.

"Knock it off," the driver said studying the rear view mirror.

"Okay. $1.4 billion." *That's $100,000. That should get their attention.*

"Your life isn't worth very much, is it?" The lanky man chuckled.

"$3 billion?" At least, they're willing to negotiate.

"Surely, a rich lady like you is willing to pay more?"

"All right. $15 billion. That's more than one million in pre-collapse dollars. All I have. Think of what you can do with that." She had no idea where she would get the money.

She waited for someone to say something. "Final offer."

The driver fired back, "It's not about money."

Acid rushed into her mouth "It's not?" Courtney had never met anyone who couldn't be influenced by ten digits.

"Money. That's all that matters to Americans."

"And sex," the lanky man added.

"The United States is evil. Its days are numbered," the driver said.

The man she stabbed fired a short burst of Farsi at the kidnapper holding the tape. He was angry about something.

Oh my God. They were the same men she had encountered earlier.

The lanky man slapped tape across her mouth. His gun lay so close its barrel touched her leg. If only she could grab it.

The bloodied man pulled his mask off and stared at her. A trickle of blood oozed from a dark red hole in his cheek. A red swath was smeared across his face and his right eye was bloodshot and swollen. He was the same man she had seen in the building, the one who said bomb; a stocky man with a wide face and eyes set so far apart he looked like a frog.

"What are you doing?" the driver asked looking in the rearview mirror.

"The mask is soaked with blood. What difference does it make? She won't be able to identify us." He placed the wet hood over Courtney's head and turned it backwards so she couldn't see. "Does that make you feel better?"

The driver grunted.

She gagged on the metallic smell of blood.

"She doesn't like it either."

"What's for lunch?" the driver asked.

The man next to her opened the bag.

"Smells good. Thanks for bringing lunch." The frog laughed.

Courtney closed her eyes and tried to check the panic seizing her. If only she had contacted the police. Gone straight to the closest precinct. Her captors wouldn't have tried to abduct her, and it might have persuaded them to abandon whatever they were planning. She pushed the thought from her mind only to have a vision of Mr. Meng frowning at his watch as he waited in her office.

Surely, her broker would recognize something was terribly wrong. Courtney had never stood up a client, and if she were late, she would call. But her broker would focus first on writing up the transaction, then on why Courtney wasn't there.

They were headed somewhere outside the city. It seemed they had been driving for at least an hour, but she couldn't tell anymore. Her bottom was numb from the metal floor, her cheek ached, and she needed a restroom. She tried to think clearly, but all her concentration was focused on bladder control. To make matters worse, she was nauseous and couldn't breathe well inside the bloody hood. The metallic smell mingled with the fishy odor of Mr. Meng's lunch in air thick with cigarette smoke. Each bump in the road stained her limits of control.

The van slowed and stopped. A garage door opened, and the vehicle pulled inside. The door rattled as it descended. The van's door slid open. A hand shoved her from behind. She scooted out and stood up on shaky legs. Someone yanked her into the house, shoved her down on a couch, then ripped the tape from her mouth.

"Ouch." Her lips stung. "Please remove the hood. I'm sick."

The mask slid upward. A cool rush of air hit her face. She took a deep breath and tried to keep her breakfast down.

"You don't look so good," the frog said.

"I have to go the bathroom."

"Shut up."

"Let her go," the driver said.

"I can't with my hands tied."

"Untie her."

"Are you sure?"

"Afraid she'll stab you again?" The lanky man laughed.

"No," snapped the frog.

The man removed a knife from his pants and flipped it open. He carelessly clipped the plastic tie nicking her wrist. Probably did it on purpose. He escorted her down a hallway to the bathroom, prodding her along with the nose of a gun. She walked in and closed the door, but he pushed it back open.

"Can I have a little privacy?"

He grinned, exposing a mouth with too many teeth crowded into too little space.

She closed the door again, sat down and relieved herself. Nothing had ever felt better. But her stomach was still queasy. She flushed the toilet and hung her head over it for a moment. *Deep breaths*. She stood and studied a visage in the mirror she hardly recognized: a blood smeared face with a large, red lump on her cheekbone and tangled hair. She washed her face, then surveyed the room for anything that might make a useful weapon. Nothing but a bar of soap. She quietly opened the vanity cabinet next to her and looked inside. Empty.

As she walked back into the great room, she made a quick visual accounting of its contents. A breakfast table stacked with newspapers, ashtrays, and a McDonald's bag. Dirty dishes in the sink. But nothing useful. The men were pigs but careful ones.

"Sit down." The frog pointed at a sagging sofa. "Put your hands behind your back."

As she placed her hands behind her, the top button on her blouse popped open, exposing cleavage. The frog stared down at her.

"American women dress like whores," he said.

"This isn't Iran."

The driver laughed. He removed his hood. She didn't recognize him. He was older with gray sprinkled throughout his short beard. He appeared to be the leader.

"You speak Arabic?" he asked.

"A little." She lied.

"A little too much I guess?"

She nodded. If only she had done a better job of pretending she didn't understand what the men had said, perhaps she wouldn't be here now.

"Did you tell anyone about us?"

"Yes, I called the police. They are probably searching the Spire right now."

The driver studied her. "You're lying."

The frog grabbed the driver's arm. "What if she isn't?"

"I'm telling the truth. What are you planning?"

The driver shook off the frog's hand. "The fulfillment of a dream."

"You'll never get away with blowing up the Chicago Spire?"

The three men looked at each other and laughed.

A cold chill descended down her back.

The driver opened her purse and grinned. "You're full of surprises." He removed her gun and tossed it to the frog.

"A pea shooter," he laughed, tucking the 9mm in his pants.

Ugh.

"You're quite a fighter," the driver said. "Did you study martial arts?"

She nodded.

"You have the instinct of a killer. In another life you would have made a good terrorist."

She spit on the floor.

The frog chuckled.

The driver checked his watch. "Won't be long now. Allah be praised. I'm going to get some cigarettes."

"Pick me up something. I'm hungry," said the frog.

"You're always hungry. If you want something, get it yourself."

"I'll watch her. Go get something to eat," said the lanky man.

"Keep an eye on the hooloo." The frog winked.

He frowned at Courtney as he left with the driver. He wanted revenge. Thank God he wasn't staying.

The lanky man sat down in a chair across from the couch. He removed his hood. He was the other man she had seen in the skyscraper. He had a long, pointed nose and scraggily hairs above his lip and chin that reminded her of a rat.

"What's your name?" Courtney asked.

The man said nothing but glanced at her cleavage.

A plan was forming in her mind, a distasteful one. But the rat had a gun and was too far away to reach. She was short on options.

"Is your name some big secret?"

"I'm not supposed to talk to you."

"Your friend did."

He grunted.

"Why won't you?" Courtney crossed her legs, exposing plenty of thigh.

"My name is Kamal."

"I'm Courtney. That wasn't so bad. Are you married?"

"No."

"Do you have a girlfriend?"

"No."

"Been awhile since you've had a woman?"

The man frowned. "It's not proper for a woman to ask such things."

"Just thought you might want to have some fun while your friends were out."

"What do you mean?"

"You know what I mean. But you have to untie me first."

"I can't do that."

"I'll bet your friend wouldn't say no. He called me a *hooloo*. Doesn't that mean hot?"

"Farid is better with girls."

"This is your chance to show him. Isn't it?"

Kamal walked to the window and looked out. "Farid thinks American women are prostitutes."

"So we're not the marrying type. But we're a lot of fun." She wasn't going to argue the point and destroy a potential opportunity. "How long before they return?"

"I'm not sure."

"We better hurry."

Kamal walked over to her and stared down at her. He pointed a 9mm at her. "Do anything stupid, and I'll kill you."

"Who can argue with that?"

He walked around to the back of the chair and untied her hands. He pushed the gun to the back of her neck.

She stood and walked toward the bedroom. The bed was unmade. She sat on the corner of it and took a deep breath.

The terrorist closed the door.

She removed her suit jacket.

The man kept his gun trained on her. "Take off the rest."

She began to unbutton her blouse but stopped.

The man's breathing quickened as he stared at her.

"Nice Glock, but it's ruining the moment." She pointed at the gun. "Put it away."

The man paused, then his small eyes darkened.

"No."

"Have it your way, but it won't be the same."

The rat glanced at the gun as if reconsidering. She swung her Manolo Blahnik pump into his groin.

"Ahhh." The man dropped the gun and doubled over grabbing himself.

Courtney removed her four-inch high-heel shoe and swung it down into the man's head, burying it to the shank.

He rose, his eyes wide in disbelief as a stream of blood trickled down between them. He reached for the shoe embedded in his head, then pitched forward.

She shuddered at the dead man at her feet. She plucked the shoe from his head, wiped the blood off with the bedspread, and dressed quickly. Then, she slipped her ring from his finger and put it on. She grabbed the gun from the floor as the man's phone rang. She pulled it from his pants. The caller ID indicated an international call. She placed it in the pocket of her suit jacket.

My purse. It was in the living room. As she opened the bedroom door to retrieve it, voices approached the front door. She shut the door.

"Kamal, where are you?" It was the driver's voice. "Where's the woman?"

"Maybe Kamal isn't gay after all," Farid said. "Let's check the bedroom."

Her heart pounded as she ran to the window and struggled to open it. It wouldn't budge. Decades of paint had glued it permanently shut. She shattered the glass with the gun's butt and knocked away the remaining jagged edges. Voices at the bedroom door. No time to climb out. She ducked into the closet, her heart pounding so loudly she was sure they could hear.

The bedroom door opened.

"Be tokhamn!" the driver yelled. "She's gone."

"The whore killed him," Farid said.

"Hurry. Through the window," the driver said.

Glass crunched as they climbed out.

The phone rang again. Adrenalin surged through her as she fumbled for the power button. She pressed it. Had they heard? She waited a minute.

She opened the door—and gasped.

The driver stood looking at her. A devilish grin spread across his face.

Without thinking, she swung the Glock up with both hands and fired.

The blast thudded into the man's chest. He staggered backward and crumpled to the floor. She shot him again.

Courtney leaned against a wall. She felt light-headed. Had Farid heard the shots? If he had, he would think the driver had killed her. He would head back to the house. She had little time. She walked to the window. The thin curtain flapped in the breeze. She peered out, searching surrounding homes. No sign of the terrorist, which was both good and bad. It would be better to know where he was.

Her purse. She ran back into the living room, grabbed it, and returned to the bedroom.

She knocked out one small piece of glass in the window frame and slipped her leg out. As she was about to swing her other leg over the sill, a blinding flash of light stunned her. The ground shook so hard she fell backward onto the floor. A roar like a train barreling down on the house shook it. Dishes in the kitchen exploded against the floor. Light fixtures swayed.

What was that? She stood up and climbed out the window and ran as fast as she could toward a nearby house, scanning the street. The ground continued to rumble.

Cars stopped. People stood transfixed in their front yards. A balloon slipped from the hand of a child. Courtney watched it rise.

To the northwest a dark mushroom rose into the sky.

"Taylor! No, not Taylor."

CHAPTER SEVEN

Jerusalem, April 4

"Run," Luke yelled as the rocket's fiery tail propelled it toward the wedding party.

Broken glass crunched beneath Hank's feet as he grabbed Kat's hand and ran.

A blur of people whirled around him amid an old woman's cry for help.

Someone slammed into Hank from behind. He fell, Kat's hand slipping from his. A group of people tumbled over him, as he lay sprawled on the grass looking up at his wife. Her silky dark hair swung forward as she reached for him. Behind her, ribbons of burnt orange stretched across a sky of ebbing light.

The rocket's hiss grew loader.

Hank reached for his wife's hand.

If only he could stop time.

Save us Lord.

The ground ruptured like an angry volcano, belching everyone into the air.

*   *   *

The faint sound of sirens. The smell of smoke.

Someone lay on top of Hank.

Slowly, his eyes caked shut, cracked open.

It was Kat. Her head lay on his chest as if she were asleep.

"Wake up honey." He shook her lightly. But she didn't stir.

Her white dress was crimson. Hank hugged his wife tightly as he shook.

"Wake up baby. Please wake up. I've got you. You're going to be okay."

A man in a bright yellow vest and yarmulke bent down and tried to take Kat. His mouth moved but Hank couldn't hear anything. The man tried again. But Hank wouldn't let go. Another man joined him and leaned down next to Hank's ear.

The words were distant. "Ana, ten lenv aveth."

Hank shook his head. He couldn't understand.

The man nodded. "Please let us take her. We might still be able to save her."

Hank kissed Kat's bloodied hand and let go. *Please God don't let her die.* But his words lacked conviction as he watched the two men lift her limp body onto a stretcher and rush her toward a waiting ambulance. He had seen the face of death too many times as a reporter. A man inside the van pulled the stretcher inside and closed the doors. The vehicle sped away.

"Why did you allow this to happen God? Why? Why?" Hank pounded his fist into the wet, red grass again and again until he was too tired to scream words he could not hear and hit a God he could not see.

He stood and shook uncontrollably. A smoky haze hung in the air. Kat's white calla lilies lay crushed on the blood-drenched grass behind him along with torn and twisted bodies, many unrecognizable. Hank scanned the carnage for any sign of his mom and Kat's grandfather but didn't see them.

Where was Luke? He would know what to do.

Hank struggled to his feet and stumbled past two paramedics working frantically over a young woman. One of her white pumps was missing. The ringing in his ears was subsiding. In the distance, wails of a broken heart grew like a crescendo. A woman was bent over the body of a man. Her body expanded and contracted in great sobs. Mrs. Worthington? He wasn't sure.

He stumbled forward into the nightmare. A paramedic grabbed his arm and tried to escort him to an ambulance, but Hank wrenched it free, nearly losing his balance.

"You're injured."

"Where's Luke?"

"Luke who?"

"Luke Chavez. The pastor." The words stumbled out of Hank's mouth.

The man pointed toward a paramedic hovering over a man.

Hank limped toward them. It was Luke.

He lay on his back. His face drained of its rich caramel color. The paramedic held a compress against a gushing wound in the pastor's stomach. His eyes were shut.

"Luke, it's Hank."

The paramedic looked up. She shook her head. "He can't hear you."

He persisted. "Luke, it's Hank. I know you can hear me."

The pastor's eyes opened slowly. He studied Hank as if he wasn't sure who he was. The lines around his eyes closed into small fans. "I saw Cindy and the Lord."

Hank's eyes watered. What would he do without him?

"They're waiting for me."

Fight Luke. Fight. But how could he implore his friend to stay when he was so lonely without his wife. Hank understood. He felt hollow, like much of him had vanished in the last few minutes.

Luke grabbed Hank's hand. His grip was firm. "Take care of Kat and the church."

Then he let go.

CHAPTER EIGHT

Sixty miles southeast of Chicago, April 4

Somewhere in the neighborhood Farid was watching, waiting. But Courtney's eyes were focused on the horizon. A dark fireball rose in the sky, inhaling Chicago until it towered like a gluttonous monster about to burst.

She wanted to cry. Cry for the all the things left unsaid, for all the things unfinished. For her little sister Taylor, who had just flown in for a girls' weekend; for her mom who was waiting to see them, for her reconciliation with her ex, Jeff; for the deal with Mr. Meng. None of it would happen now. Everything had changed in an instant. Tears would be too easy.

She could have prevented the attack. That was the inconsolable truth. A phone call to the police, so simple, could have changed the fate of millions. But her fear of being penniless like the homeless man had driven her to think of money first. It was the creed that had ruled her adult life. She had sacrificed everything to it: a relationship, children, even family. She told herself that one day there would be enough money and time for everything else. Oh God, she was so wrong.

A light rain began to fall. Cries of disbelief rose around her as more people poured into the street, wondering whether their family or friends had survived. In their hearts they knew. And she knew… Taylor, her mom, Jeff, Mr. Weng were all gone. Everything was gone.

Courtney froze. Through the crowd Farid stared at her, his back to the devastation. The smug look on his face contrasted with the masks of mourning around him. No one seemed to notice. Their eyes were fixed on the devastation, their thoughts turned inward. Would the fallout reach them? Had Washington been hit? Was there even a government left?

Her hand tightened around her gun. If she could get a clear shot, she would wipe the smirk from his ugly face. But he slipped into the crowd and disappeared.

She stared numbly at the people in the streets until they were gone. The sun was setting. She kept replaying the moments in the Chicago Spire and the cab ride as if rewinding the events could somehow change the outcome. But no matter how many times she replayed the scenes, they always ended the same.

Then, a simple idea cleared the stupor: The phone was still in the pocket of her skirt. It contained the number of whoever had called Kamal.

CHAPTER NINE

Jerusalem, April 5

A brown haze hovered above the twisted wreckage of timbers and rock. Scooter covered his mouth to keep from inhaling any more dirt than he had already as he searched for a way out. There wasn't one. The rocks blocking the entrance were enormous and weighed thousands of pounds. Scooter and his team were entombed as tightly as a dead pharaoh and just as forgotten.

He turned back to the wall and patted the cold stone. Finding the artifact was no longer a priority. They needed water. Their supplies wouldn't last more than a day. There were several cisterns on the Temple Mount, and if they could locate one, it could sustain them until they found another exit—if one existed.

Brian grabbed the pick. Everyone seemed to understand the only hope lay behind the wall. He swung. It bounced off the stone, leaving a small nick.

"It feels more like granite than limestone." He swung again. His body shook as if seized by an electric current. Another splinter flew.

"Let me do it," Randy said yanking the tool from Brian who offered little resistance. Shards of rock exploded as he hit the wall. He kept at it for several minutes until he punched a hole the size of a softball through the rock. "That's the way it's done."

Scooter bent down and slipped his flashlight through the opening and peered into the room. No water in sight.

He stood up and motioned for Randy to continue. The man's axe bit into an area above the hole, knocking out another chunk. He kept at it for two hours, trading off with Scooter when he needed a rest, until an opening big enough to crawl through gaped in the wall. Dark veins of sweat wound down his chest and arms.

A tingle shot through Scooter as he crawled inside. It might be nothing more than a forgotten room, but what if this was the inner chamber of the first temple? "Watch that," he said flashing his light down at rubble from the digging.

When everyone was in, he swung his light around the room. It was roughly 35 by 35 feet, the exact dimension of the Holy of Holies. The far west wall showed signs of a previous entrance. He walked closer. A three by five-and-a-half foot section had been sealed like the east gate of the old city. The wall was blackened. He rubbed his hand across the stone and illuminated the other walls. Scorched as well.

Jude stared at the patched wall. "We aren't the first."

"Maybe the same people who saw the ark," Brian said.

"Muslims probably discovered the tunnel and closed it off," Scooter said. "It happened once before. A rabbi discovered one of the original entrances to the first temple and tunneled under the Dome of the Rock in hope of finding the ark. The tunnel was discovered and quickly closed."

"It wasn't God's timing," Jude said. "The ark won't be found until there is a temple for it."

"There will never be a temple as long as Muslims control the mount," Randy said.

"Let's focus on finding water," Scooter said. "Jude, see if you can find anything behind these walls."

He removed the GPR from the duffle and placed it on the sealed entrance and began sliding it along the rocky face.

Scooter leaned against a wall. He removed the map, and studied it under his light. They were beyond the Al Kas Fountain above, but still close to where the map indicated the Holy of Holies was. Other possible sites were the northern location under the Dome of the Tablets and the central location directly under the Dome of the Rock. But if this was the Holy of Holies, where was the Ark of the Covenant? The room had been plucked as clean as a chicken and lit up like a Sunday barbecue.

Brian and Randy walked around with their lights inspecting the walls. A sharp aftershock rattled the room. The GPR slipped from Jude's grasp and hit the floor.

He bent down and flashed his light on the broken pieces and looked as if he would cry.

Brian walked over and examined the wreckage. "We're screwed."

Scooter sighed. "We'll figure it out." But without the GPR, they had no way of finding water or a way out.

Randy stood near the far wall studying it.

Scooter put the map in his pocket. "What is it?"

"I don't know. This looks like a seam." He pointed at a faint line.

Scooter walked over and added another light. Randy was right. There was a vertical line in the wall that was too straight to be a crack.

Randy removed a knife from his belt and ran it along the vein that stretched five-and-half feet from the floor. Then, he probed an area perpendicular to the top of the seam. His knife slipped into a crevice. "I think we have something here, captain." He placed his knife back in the sheaf and pushed against the wall. It didn't budge. He moved his hands toward the edge of a vertical line and pushed again. Nothing. "Give me a hand guys."

Everyone pushed. The stone began to shift inward, slowly rotating on an axis like a revolving door. They continued pushing until an opening emerged behind the door.

Scooter flashed his light into a long narrow tunnel. The air was damp and dank. He ducked and entered the passage. He walked for at least fifty feet before he saw an opening. He emerged into a small rectangular room. A pool of dead, still, black water lay before him.

He lapped some water into his mouth. It was good. Slightly sweet. *Thank God.*

Randy and Brian, who were right behind him, rushed to the cistern and dunked their heads, leaving a brown film that drifted across the surface like an oil slick.

The pool, which was tucked against a wall, stretched the length of the room, which was wide but not very deep. Steps led down into the water, which appeared to have had one use: a cleansing pool for priests. But why the secrecy and a separate tunnel? Scooter bent down and scooped up some more water, swished it around in his mouth, then spit it out. The grit from the cave-in was still in his teeth but the water tasted wonderful. Could this be from the Ash-Shafa spring that Edward Robinson, an early biblical geographer, said was located 80 feet below the Dome of the Rock?

Brian stood up and ran his hands through his long wet hair. Jude entered the room and knelt down at the pool and washed his face.

"I'm tired," Scooter said. He checked his watch. "We've been at it for hours. Let's eat and take a nap. We're going to need our strength if we have to dig our way out."

Randy tossed him a protein bar. He took a bite, lay down, draped his coat over him and fell asleep.

*   *   *

Scooter opened his eyes and tried to remember where he was. It was cold. He slipped on his jacket. How long had he been asleep? He sat up and checked his watch. Was that right? Had he been asleep for seven hours? He turned on the flashlight. Randy was stretched out flat on his back with hands behind his head; Brian had an arm draped over his eyes; Jude was curled up on his side.

Scooter stood up and walked over to the pool and lapped some water into this face, then took a drink. He was still groggy. He looked up and coughed. Staring down at him from the wall above the pool was the carved image of a two-headed serpent. Its four eyes were black in sharp contrast to the grayish stone. How had they missed it?

The ground trembled, sending a ripple through the dark pool.

Scooter glanced back at his crew.

Brian sat up and rubbed his eyes. "Looks like something from Dungeons and Dragons."

Jude jolted up. "Looks like a variation of the Nehustan."

Randy brushed dirt from his arms, sat up and grabbed one of his protein bars. "What's the Nehustan?"

"When serpents attacked the Hebrews in the wilderness, Moses had a brass serpent fashioned to hold up on a pole. Anyone who looked on the image was healed. According to the biblical record, the serpent eventually became an object of worship, forcing King Hezekiah to destroy it."

Scooter leaned over the pool and flashed his light up at the image. Through their long history the Jews had worshipped various animals, even the Canaanite god, Baal, but rarely snakes. The exception was the Nehustan. It appeared as old as the pool. The mouths of the two snakes were open wide as if they were about to strike.

"It could also be an image of Leviathan, the ancient sea monster described in Job," Jude added. "Isaiah wrote about it."

"What does he say?" Brian asked.

"In that day the Lord will take his terrible, swift sword and punish Leviathan, the swiftly moving serpent, the coiling, writhing serpent. He will kill the dragon of the sea."

Jude was a walking compendium of biblical archeology, which came in handy when reconciling an archeological site with the biblical record. His dad wanted him to become a rabbi, but he chose archeology, which seemed to satisfy a personal need to prove the Old Testament was more than myth.

"What does it mean?" Brian asked looking at Jude.

"There are several views, but the one I agree with says that in the day of the Lord, when Messiah arrives, he will crush Satan, the serpent of old."

Brian frowned. "So this is an image of the devil? What's it doing above a cleansing pool for priests?"

Randy turned to the two-headed snake and stuck up his middle finger. "That's what I think of the big, bad monster."

His petulance did little to lighten the mood.

"All right, we've got water, so we're not going to die of thirst," Scooter said. "But our food supplies are limited and before long, we'll be too weak to dig out if that is our only alternative. We need to keep searching for another way out."

Scooter flashed his light into the water, which was impenetrable. The pool must be several feet deep. He reached into the duffle bag and removed a bundle of rope. "Randy, we need a rock."

He walked back through the tunnel to the other room and returned with a hefty stone. He hauled it over and laid it at Scooter's feet. "What do you have in mind?"

Scooter slid a length of a rope under the rock, then pulled it up and twisted the rope and wound it in the opposite direction. He tied it. "Give me a hand."

They lifted the rock over the pool and eased it down while holding tight to the braided nylon.

"Let's see how deep this is." The rope slid quickly through their hands. Ten, twenty, thirty, forty... It kept dropping. The reservoir was much deeper than he had expected. Had it once been an escape tunnel? Dug to evade Babylonian conquerors in 597 B.C.?

The line went slack with about twenty feet left.

Randy peered into the pool. "I have an idea. The water is coming from somewhere and there might be an opening large enough to swim out. I'm going down to check it out."

"It's at least sixty feet deep," Scooter said. "That's crazy."

"We're short on options here, captain. No one is going to rescue us. It will take days to dig out and we'll starve before that happens. I've done some free diving. I can hold my breath for at least three minutes, which is more than enough time to get to the bottom and back up. Do we have anything water proof that I can wrap a flash light in?"

Jude said, "Are you serious?"

"No risk, no gain," Randy said.

"I can't let you do it," Scooter said.

"Since when are you averse to taking risks?"

Scooter coiled the end of the rope around his hand and looked at Randy. "You sure you want to do this?"

Randy picked up a rock that looked about twenty pounds. He sat it down on the pool's ledge and cut a six-foot length of rope. He wrapped it around the rock, made a large loop at the other end, then slid his legs through the loop and cinched the cord around his waist.

He walked down the steps into the pool, holding the rock in one hand and a flashlight in the other. He grimaced at the water's cool temperature as he grabbed hold of the rope Scooter held and sank below the surface. The light from his flashlight cast an eerie green glow as he disappeared into the deep.

CHAPTER TEN

Istanbul, April 5

"The situation in the Middle East is untenable. We must come together as one to fight ISIS or succumb to them." Yaser Mehmed, the aging leader of Turkey, stood before twenty-one men in the Ottoman room of the Ciragan Palace Kempinski in Istanbul. "ISIS is threatening to destroy everything."

Yasin Mohammed glanced up at the chubby angelic figures on the hand-painted ceiling looking down. They were smiling. But the leaders gathered around the long table were not. Grim faces attested to the gravity of what faced them. War was on their minds. The Middle East was caught in a crossfire between Sunni-led ISIS and Shiite Iran that threatened to destroy the tenuous balance of power that had sustained the region for the last 80 years.

At issue was the very survival of the Middle Eastern nations. ISIS now controlled the majority of Syria and Iraq. It had successfully expelled Russia from Syria except for its base at Tartus. Syria's president was gone. He had narrowly escaped Damascus before it fell. ISIS had also made significant inroads into several other countries including Libya, Yemen, Egypt, Jordan and Afghanistan. Arab leaders had unfortunately been more worried about Iran than ISIS.

But that was before Pakistan. The Pakistani army had suffered significant losses in recent battles with ISIS raising fears that the country with the largest cache of nuclear weapons in the Middle East was vulnerable. And many in the room believed the terrorists already possessed at least one or two nukes.

The door to the room opened and a diminutive man with dark circles under his eyes walked in. The president of Iran. The air in the room seemed to disappear. Had he really come? He had been invited, but no one thought he would attend, particularly since much of the discussion would revolve around Iran's aggressive behavior. He took the only remaining seat.

Yasin had been invited to the conference by Turkey's President, whose rise to power was largely due to his father. He had used his considerable influence to elevate the one-time mayor of Ayvalık, a small city on the Aegean Sea, to the presidency.

The corpulent crown prince of Saudi Arabia, said, "ISIS is attacking our mosques. We are under siege. We need to do something to stop them." He glared at the Iranian president. Iran had recently stopped and searched Saudi tankers as they passed through the Strait of Hormuz.

The fleshy Saudi leader knew as much about war as the Turkish president, which was next to nothing, Yasin thought. Neither had ever been in battle, heard the hiss of bullets zinging by or fired an AK47 until the barrel glowed.

He stood. "May I say something?"

Mehmed rubbed his index finger across his dyed mustache as if he was unsure, then motioned for Yasin to speak.

"The only thing ISIS respects is power," Yasin said. "Sending your ambassadors to Raqqa will not stop them."

The Saudi prince lifted his chin. "And who are you?"

"This is Yasin Mohammed," Mehmed said. "My guest. You all remember his father Abbas Mohammed?"

The leaders nodded.

"Aren't you the one who recently escaped from an ISIS prison?"

"I am." The story of his capture and recent escape had been on every network and made him somewhat of a celebrity. "A nuclear war is looming gentlemen. ISIS has its sights set on Pakistan. If it is successful, it will possess an arsenal larger than Israel and Iran combined."

The Iranian president shifted uneasily in his chair.

"The Persians can't let this happen, which means they will use any means necessary to stop the caliphate, including nuclear war." He glanced at the Iranian leader who nodded silently.

"And once they strike ISIS, they will hit Israel," Yasin said. Many had expected Iran to retaliate against Israel for an attack against several of its nuclear facilities last year, but it didn't.

Several of the representatives groaned at the mention of the Jewish state. They were torn between a desire to see Iran stripped of its nuclear capabilities and Israel destroyed. The enmity that began between two brothers 4,000 years ago was now embedded in the DNA of every Arab.

Yasin glanced out the windows stretching from floor to ceiling and gazed out onto the Bosphorus on the hotel's edge. The channel was an important shipping lane that connected the Black Sea with the Sea of Marmara and provided a natural division between the European and Asian sides of Turkey. It was dusk. Dark ribbons encroached on blue-green waters in the dwindling light as a wake of gold and silver shimmered behind a slowly advancing cargo ship. He turned back toward Khalid.

"We must act now. But a coalition is not the answer. We don't need a reincarnation of the Arab League. We need a united Middle East, a nation empowered to destroy any country or entity that threatens us." The league was more of a fraternity than a political union with little ability to enforce agreements or punish wayward members. It stemmed from centuries of tribal mentality.

The Saudi prince took a long drag on his cigarette. The conference room was nonsmoking, but the crown prince boasted to the hotel's manager that if he didn't like it, he would buy the

Kempinski Hotel and change the rules. "No one will ever agree to give up their sovereignty." He swept his hand around the members at the table and chuckled. "We are Arabs."

"Gentlemen, our prophet Mohammed believed in one nation," Yasin said. "When he began sharing Allah's message, Arabs were nothing but nomadic tribes. He organized them into one people. And he prophesied that Islam would one day rule the world and that a leader would arise who would unite all Muslims, both Sunnis and Shiites. What better way to usher in this age than consolidating our countries into one great power."

Jordan's leader, a Sunni, glanced at Bahrain's Shiite President and frowned. The division between the two factions had fractured and weakened Islam, much as the split between Catholics and Protestants had Christianity. After Mohammed's death, disagreement arose over who had the authority to guide Islam. And centuries later the division had given birth to Iran and ISIS.

"How do you propose to accomplish such a feat? Defeating a formidable enemy while uniting Muslims?" Mehmed asked. He stood at the front of the long walnut table leaning against his chair with a smug smile like a game host who knew the answer his contestants did not.

"The real question is what happens if we do nothing." Yasin looked at each member around the table. "You are the decision makers. This is your opportunity to save not only your nations but write a new history for the Middle East. Only a strong centralized government will be able to defeat ISIS. If you don't act, you won't survive. No one can save us except ourselves."

The Turkish President frowned. He was not in favor of any government that would remove him from power unless he was the president of the new nation. His selection of Istanbul for the conference and specifically, the Hotel Kempinski, was no accident. The conference building was once the palace of the last caliphate,

Abdülmecid II. And Istanbul was the former capital of the Ottomans, an empire, which during its height was one of the largest ever forged.

Mehmed said, "Are you proposing a democratic form of government?"

Yasin said, "It will strengthen our case with the people, but at this point the most important thing is to act. Do something." *But democracy has never succeeded in the Middle East.* "We also need the authority to conscript soldiers from all member states. Imagine if you all pooled your country's resources into one nation. We would have a formidable military that would rival any in the world. A united Middle East would also make us an economic power. We are falling behind the world's economy. We cannot compete against the trading relationships with those nations in the economic zones. We need to join them."

The President of Egypt stood up, "What makes you so sure we can contain ISIS? The world's powers couldn't, nor could they stop Iran from acquiring nuclear weapons."

Yasin leaned back in his chair. The president's point was valid. The West had brokered a nuclear deal with Iran that supposedly made the world safer. In exchange for $150 billion dollars and the lifting of sanctions, Iran agreed to not pursue the development of nuclear weapons. But it did. Everyone wanted to believe the Persians were reasonable and didn't want war, just as England had about Nazi Germany in 1938. But they weren't and neither was ISIS.

"Diplomacy won't work with ISIS just as it didn't work with Iran," Yasin said.

The Iranian president smirked like he was enjoying it all but said nothing.

"Then, how will you get them to back down?" The Egyptian president said.

"I think that ISIS, as well as the mullahs, are not seeking the end of the world as much as they want everyone to believe. There is only one thing wild dogs respect—and that is a bigger, meaner dog."

CHAPTER ELEVEN

Jerusalem, April 5

Z Z stepped into the bright afternoon sun and tipped his straw hat forward. The rabbi had a quaint courtyard filled with gorgeous sprays of violet, red, and yellow flowers, most likely all native. He had been an early advocate for Israel's flower industry, which now was one in the largest in the world.

ZZ sat down in a wicker chair surrounded by long, pink flowers which reminded him of flamingos. He knew little about flowers with the exception of the most common ones like roses and tulips. He needed to think. The idea of finding a missing map was ridiculous, but he had made a vow before Jehovah and even though he questioned God's existence at times, a vow was no trifling matter.

A vehicle with a rumbling exhaust pulled up outside the courtyard. The high wall and gate blocked any view. The bell at the gate rang.

ZZ unlocked the gate. Two soldiers stared at him. One was little more than a teenager with red tracks of acne across his face; the other man was considerably older, with steely brown eyes.

"May I help you?"

"Are you Zedekiah Zukerman, the one who called about Rabbi Cohen?"

"I called a funeral home, not the military."

"We're not here for the body. This is Lieutenant Kaplan. He is a detective. He needs to ask you some questions. I am Corporal Levinsky."

ZZ sighed. "About what?"

"Let's go inside." Kaplan gestured toward the front door.

ZZ removed a key from his pocket and tried to unlock the door but tremors in his right hand made it difficult. He steadied his right hand with his left and opened the door. They walked into the dimly lit house.

"Where is Rabbi Cohen?" Levinsky said.

"In his bedroom." He pointed toward a dark hallway. ZZ couldn't bear seeing his friend's lifeless body again. The soldier disappeared down the hall.

"Have a seat," Kaplan said.

ZZ sat on an elaborately ornate Persian sofa that was too soft in the middle. Hand-carved flowers burst from the frame in dense dark bouquets against emerald green velvet upholstery. The sun had reduced the top edge of the fabric along the frame to pale green. The detective sat opposite in one of two matching chairs. A table with a light brown water stain separated them.

The air conditioner was running but the room seemed hot. ZZ wiped his forehead again as he glanced toward the hallway. Had he remembered to spin the lock on the safe and replace the rug? Kaplan said something.

"I'm sorry, what did you say?"

"Were you and Rabbi Cohen close friends?"

"We attended rabbinical school." At one time they did everything together. They married and started families at the same time, spent holidays together, even worked together for a while. ZZ served under Eli at the Belz great synagogue, the largest in Jerusalem, before he received his own synagogue.

"How many years ago?"

"Forty, I think."

"So you knew each other for a long time. Were you close friends?"

"I hadn't seen Eli for several years."

"Why not?"

"When I left teaching, we drifted apart."

"When was that?" Kaplan wrote something in a little notebook.

"About 20 years ago."

"That's a long time. When did you last speak?"

"Before yesterday?"

The detective nodded.

"I can't remember. It's been awhile."

Kaplan glanced up. "Did you have a falling out?"

The truth was simpler. After ZZ resigned his position at the synagogue, he separated himself from his friends of faith. Eli had reached out, but ZZ didn't want anyone trying to convince him to remain in a profession that no longer meant anything. He simply quit believing. "Our lives took different paths."

"So why would he call you after all these years?"

"I was surprised to hear from him. But he was dying, and I think he wanted to see old friends."

"Are you aware of anyone else he called?"

"No."

"Why did he appoint you executor of his estate?"

"I don't know, but...how did you know?"

Kaplan crossed his leg. He scratched something else in his pad. "It doesn't add up. You suddenly get a call after 20 years and are appointed the executor."

"I didn't say twenty. We talked through the years. I just can't remember when the last time was."

"Okay, is it safe to say it's been a long time?"

"Yes."

"Have you made an inventory of his estate?"

"No, he just died," he glanced at his watch. "Nine hours ago. Why are you so interested in the rabbi's possessions?"

Kaplan ignored the question. "Why did you wait so long to call?

"I didn't. I called shortly after he passed."

"Did he have a safe or a safe deposit box?"

ZZ shifted to a firmer section of the sofa. *Should I tell them?*

"I'm not aware of either." He patted his forehead and wanted to remove his jacket, but he could feel sweat running down his sides. His shirt was drenched. But Kaplan seemed unaffected by the warm room.

Levinsky walked back into the room. The lieutenant turned toward him. The two stared at each other and even though neither said a word, a conversation was taking place.

Kaplan turned back. "Were you aware that Rabbi Cohen was involved in a radical organization to rebuild the Temple?"

"The Temple Institute?"

"No. An underground organization that was plotting to destroy the Dome and Al-Aqsa mosque so the Temple could be rebuilt."

"Ridiculous," ZZ said shaking his head.

"He said nothing about this before he died?"

"Of course not."

Kaplan removed a pack of cigarettes and took one out. "Do you think the Rabbi would mind?"

Levinsky chuckled as the detective lit a cigarette.

ZZ frowned. He wanted to tell the detective to put the cigarette out, that it was rude to smoke in someone's house, particularly someone recently deceased, but a cigarette sounded good right now and the smell of tobacco would be pleasant. He'd been trying to give up smoking most of his life. He breathed in the smoke and leaned back in the sofa. "Why would the government care about Eli's desire to rebuild the Temple?"

Kaplan took a long drag on his cigarette, exhaling a plume that hung in pungent air that reeked of mothballs.

"Did the rabbi ever say anything about a map of the Ark of the Covenant?"

ZZ wiped his forward with a handkerchief. "The government doesn't really believe the Ark exists, does it?"

"Whether it exists is not the issue. Perception is what's important. If a credible map were to surface, it could start a war—particularly, if it placed the ark's location on the Temple Mount."

"I don't think there are enough Jews in Israel who believe in the ark to start a scuffle, much less a war."

"You didn't answer my question. Did the rabbi ever mention a map?"

"Never."

Kaplan cocked his head and looked up at the cove ceiling. "I've spent a lot of time during the last five years interviewing Hamas, Hezbollah, and PLO. I've developed a unique skill. Would you like to know what that is?"

Who does this guy think he is? He clearly didn't understand he was talking to the chairperson of the Foreign Relations and Defense Committee for the Knesset.

ZZ didn't answer.

"I can tell when someone is lying, almost one-hundred percent of the time. The clues vary from person to person. Some shield their eyes or cover their mouth. Others lick their lips or touch their face. Some clear their throat or swallow before answering a question. Some sweat during questioning, which isn't a problem until they wipe their forehead or neck. That's a sure sign." He paused. "I don't think you've told us everything you know Mr. Zuckerman."

ZZ shifted on the sofa and resisted wiping his sweaty brow. "I've answered your questions. I'm sorry my answers aren't what you expected." He stood and slipped on his coat. "I have pressing matters at the Knesset. If you want to speak with me anymore, you'll have to make an appointment." *But this is the last time we'll speak, because next week you'll be in the Negev interviewing the Bedouin if I have my way.*

ZZ motioned the two soldiers toward the door.

As Kaplan reached the door, he stopped and pointed at ZZ's perspiring forehead. "Your brow. It needs attention."

*   *   *

ZZ stood at the entrance to Matcal Tower in Tel Aviv, home to several governmental departments including IDF, the Israeli Defense Forces. The 17-story contemporary building formed a protective wall on three sides around a cylindrical tower that rose above the building. The structure's design reminded him of IDF's mission: protect the Jewish people, a nation that had risen from the ash heap of history. Perhaps that's what the architect hoped to convey.

The drive from Jerusalem had taken an hour. It was early afternoon.

A security camera mounted above the door drilled down on him.

"What's your name?" A young woman's voice projected from an intercom.

"Zedekiah Zuckerman. I have an appointment to see Colonel Saul Ganz." He still called him colonel even though he was now a high-level officer in Shin Bet, Israel's internal security agency.

"Really? Please wait."

There was a note of incredulity in her voice. The colonel had graciously agreed to fit ZZ into his afternoon schedule without even asking why he wanted to see him. Had he forgotten about their appointment? Saul was an old friend. They had fought side by side in the 1973 Yom Kippur War when they were only kids.

The door buzzed and ZZ walked in. One of the two guards standing inside patted him down. "Do you have a phone?"

"Yes, I do."

The soldier held out his hand. "Please give it to me."

"Is that necessary?" ZZ handed his cell to the soldier.

"As long as your phone has a power source, it's never really off. Those with the right technology can tap into it and overhear sensitive conversations.

It was beyond ZZ just how that could happen, but if the IDF believed it was possible, then it must be.

The guard escorted ZZ down a long hallway to a waiting room. The cool, refrigerated air was a relief from Tel Aviv's recent heat wave, which was even more intense than Jerusalem's. Even Haifa was roasting, its ocean breezes strangely vanished. He pushed his hat back and skimmed sweat from his forehead. Where was his handkerchief?

As he waited for Saul to arrive, he tried to make sense of what had happened a few hours earlier. The detective believed Eli had a map and what was worse, that ZZ knew where it was. Even more troubling was the government wouldn't search for a map it didn't believe existed. Hadn't Eli said the government knew where it was?

If there were any truth to Eli's claim, Saul would know. Shin Bet knew everything.

Colonel Ganz walked into the room. The lean man had a distinctive star-shaped scar that looked like it had been stamped into his leathery cheek with an awl. He received it sometime after Yom Kippur. Saul had never volunteered what happened, and ZZ had never asked.

He stood up and extended his hand.

The colonel embraced him. "Good to see you old friend. How long has it been?"

"Too long." The last time their paths crossed was two years ago when Saul appeared before a committee ZZ chaired on the government's practice of spying on private citizens.

"Did you hear about General Heller?"

"He was a good soldier." ZZ nodded.

"We're getting old my friend. Too many of the patriots who made Israel great are gone."

"We couldn't have won Yom Kippur without Heller."

"It was simpler back then." Saul stared down at his black shoes shined to a high gloss. "Much of the world believed we deserved our own nation. Now, everyone has abandoned us, even the U.S." Ganz looked up. "You sounded a little worried when you called."

"Rabbi Cohen died this morning."

"I heard. You two went way back."

"We didn't talk much through the years, but I feel a strange loss now that he's gone. I didn't know I would miss him so much." Memories of intimate dinners and long conversations when they were young flooded his thoughts. "I was with him when he took his last breath."

Saul motioned toward the chairs. "How can I help?"

ZZ removed his wire rim glasses and wiped his eyes with a tissue. "My eyes water all the time these days." He put the tissue in his pocket. "Two soldiers showed up at Eli's house today asking questions. Do you know who sent them?"

"What did they want?"

"They believed the rabbi had a map, and they wanted it."

Saul frowned and rubbed the scar on his face. He pulled his cell from his shirt pocket and dialed.

"General Lansky this is Ganz. I'm with Zedekiah Zukerman. Yes, MK Zuckerman, a member of the Knesset. He said two soldiers showed up at Rabbi Cohen's house today asking questions about a map. Did anyone order an investigation?"

Saul glanced at ZZ. "What were the two soldiers' names?"

"Lieutenant Kaplan and Corporal Levinsky."

Saul nodded. "All right. Thank you General."

He hung up. "Not ours."

"If they weren't IDF, then who were they?"

"I don't know."

The news thudded into ZZ like a punch. Eli said there were many people who didn't want the temple rebuilt. Were these men part of that group?

"Before he died, Eli said the government knew where the Ark of the Covenant was located. Is that true?"

Saul's eyes flashed. "What else did he say?"

"He said he had a map showing where the ark is located."

"Did he tell you where it was?"

Sounds like he believes. "In his floor safe."

"Do you have it?" He leaned forward a little too eagerly.

"The safe was empty."

Deep furrows creased Saul's brow. "Empty?"

"Does the government know where the ark is?"

Saul flicked his fingers at the guard. The soldier closed the door as he left the room.

The colonel turned back and shook his head. "Did Eli have any idea who might have taken it?"

"No. He told me a maid cleaned his apartment once a week. Perhaps she took it." ZZ paused. "The only other person who knew about the safe was Rabbi Mezvinksy."

Saul's eyes narrowed. "Lemuel Mezvinksy?"

"Yes, but he was Eli's closest friend. Why would he take it?"

"Mezvinksy is dead."

"Lemuel?"

"Didn't you see *The Times* this morning?"

ZZ shook his head. There hadn't been time.

"There was a bombing at the Tower of David last night. Rabbi Mezvinsky was officiating a wedding there. He was killed along with many others. We think Mezvinsky was the target. The others were unfortunately in the way."

"Why would anyone want to kill Lemuel?"

Saul cleared his throat. "I don't know."

But eyes that had been trained to betray nothing avoided ZZ's gaze. Did Saul know? "Could the attack have anything to do with the map?"

Saul rubbed his clean-shaven chin as if he were evaluating whether to answer the question. He fidgeted with his uniform pocket, finally opening it. He removed a pack of cigarettes. "Mind if I smoke?"

ZZ shifted in his chair. "Go ahead."

The colonel took a long draw on the cigarette. "Can you imagine what would happen if the map fell into the wrong hands? Think what the PLO could do to us if they found the ark."

Saul's pronouncement of Israel's fate was disturbing. It conjured up all kinds of distressing scenarios. There would be a war to get the ark back. Or possibly, a humiliating negotiation that acquiesced to the PLO's demand for establishing Jerusalem as its capital. Or worse yet—they might destroy the ark. ZZ shuddered at the thought.

The colonel leaned back in his chair and took another puff on his cigarette. Smoke flowed from his nose as he studied ZZ. "What's your involvement in this?"

There was an accusatory edge to his question.

"Nothing. I thought you should know what happened today." A moment ago, he would have shared the promise he had made to Eli, but now he wasn't sure it was wise.

Saul leaned forward toward ZZ. "Forget about the map. I don't want to see anything happen to you."

An icy chill rippled over ZZ's skin.

The colonel's phone buzzed in his pocket. He pulled it out and looked at. He stood up and extended his hand. "I'm sorry I have to end our meeting so abruptly. But I have an urgent matter that needs my attention. Shalom my friend."

ZZ shook Saul's hand. "Shalom."

*　　*　　*

The black Ford Focus stopped across the street from the Tower of David. It was nearly dusk. A sign posted on the gate announced the historical site and museum were closed for the day.

He walked toward Jaffa Gate winding his way down David Street in the Old City toward Chain Street. He stopped at a vendor's booth that sold Jewish souvenirs: miniature brass menorahs, Star of David pendants, and baseball hats with Israel embroidered on the front. An Israeli solder with an M4 stood near the store and scrutinized the people walking along the arched stone corridor. ZZ paid for a newspaper.

There on the front page was the bold headline: *Wedding Massacre* and a photo of last night's gruesome scene. The article said the IDF was actively searching for the terrorists. Among the dead was Luke Chavez, leader of the world's largest Christian church. The article speculated that the pastor might have been the target of the terrorists. A story and photo of the American couple whose wedding had been attacked appeared below the lead news story. The groom, Hank Jackson, was an investigative newspaper reporter. But most knew him as the only person in the world who had been immune to a deadly virus that had killed millions four years ago. Once again, he had survived.

ZZ tucked the newspaper under his arm and walked back toward his car. He struggled to clear his head, but questions about the attack kept intruding. Why Mezvinsky? Eli had intimated he didn't trust the rabbi. Had Mezvinsky stolen the map? And if so, why? Saul probably knew the answers.

Just as troubling was why he had promised Eli and even sworn before Elohim to find the map? It was foolish to have made such a commitment. He should have refused the rabbi's plea. But how could he? The old man was already brokenhearted. At least, he died believing the map would be found, and the ark returned to Israel.

Eli was gone. And ZZ wasn't even sure if he believed in the Elohim of scripture anymore. He only attended the synagogue, because voters expected it of a former rabbi. Yet, the idea of breaking an oath made him nervous. Call it superstition, but he couldn't shake the notion that breaking an oath made on a friend's deathbed was worse than the consequences of trying to fulfill the pledge. All he could do was try. If he failed, how could God punish him for that?

He unlocked the door to his car and climbed in. He tossed the newspaper on the opposite seat. The photograph of the couple whose wedding was attacked stared back at him. Hank and Kat Jackson. ZZ had no idea of how to find the missing map or where to start, but an investigative reporter like Jackson might.

And wouldn't he want to know why his wedding was attacked and how the map might be involved?

CHAPTER TWELVE

Istanbul, April 5

The first hour of the Air France flight from Detroit to Istanbul was hellish. The jet rocked and bounced its way through a storm. Courtney leaned back in her seat and tried to relax, but the last 48 hours kept replaying, assaulting any thought. The drive from Gary, Indiana to Detroit had been the longest of her life. Total gridlock. People were acting crazed as they fled cities near Chicago. Many were armed and desperate to escape a follow-up attack. But the worse part was the haunting image of the dark cloud above Chicago and the questions: *Why didn't you call the police? Why didn't you at least call the listing broker and ask her about the two Iranians?*

Why didn't she? She knew the men weren't buyers. How much clearer did it need to be? She pressed a pillow against her face and tried to squash her thoughts, but she couldn't suppress the terrible truth that she could have stopped the attack on Chicago.

She popped a Xanax and Ambien, closed her eyes and descended into darkness.

Candles flickered along a long corridor. It was dim. Menacing shadows skulked along walls, moving just out of sight when she approached. Was someone following her? She turned around and looked for an exit but couldn't see anything. It was too dark. She was in what appeared to be a cave. Water trickled down the sides of slick rock that was as black as coal. Wet gravel crunched beneath her pumps. The sound of voices slowed her steps. Soon, the form of a man standing over a young woman emerged.

His back was turned, preventing Courtney from seeing his face or the young woman's. Something was branded into the back of his hand. It looked like a snake.

"I know who you are," the young woman said sitting up.

"And who is that?"

"The evil one Daniel prophesied about."

He chuckled. "What's evil to a Jew is not to an Arab."

"You won't win."

"It's unfortunate you trespassed. I have nothing against you, except I can't allow you to slander me."

What are they talking about? If only Courtney could see their faces. She stepped closer. Neither appeared to notice.

A flash of fire and a deafening bang filled the cave. She jumped back. The woman slumped to the floor, her face still hidden.

Courtney woke with a jolt as the jet bounced against the runway. She was shaking. What a horrible dream. The blackness of the cave still crawled across her skin. She raised the window shade and squinted at the sharp morning light.

*　　*　　*

Customs took thirty minutes to clear. She had no luggage so she headed outside to catch a taxi. The ride took 60 minutes. The last half through the city was slow and tedious. She checked in at the Hotel Kempinski and headed to the Ciragan Bar.

The walls of the bar were covered in panels of rich mahogany, which along with the low amber lights, felt like a cavern. Perfect for private conversations and forgetting the outside world. Thick cigarette smoke filled the air.

Courtney looked again at the international phone number on Kamal's phone. It had led her to Istanbul and the cab driver to the

Ciragan Palace Kempinski. He said the buzz was several Middle Eastern leaders were meeting at the hotel and Iran's president might be among them. No one had taken credit for the attack, but everyone knew it was Iran. Who else had nuclear weapons and hated the United States enough to use them?

Courtney stared down into the near empty glass. Now that she was here, the task before her seemed overwhelming. What was she thinking? She tried remembering the advice of her real estate coach Tom Kane, the author of *Kamikazee Selling*. *Go for broke. Burn the bridges. Sacrifice everything. When you do, your real potential is unleashed.*

But words that had strengthened her in the past provided no lift. She understood going for broke. She'd done it many times. But this was different. She didn't have the faintest idea of how to assassinate someone, let alone a head of state. The sum total of what she knew about international intrigue she'd learned from Jason Bourne and Jack Reacher and they weren't real. Even if Iran's president showed up to the conference, he would be surrounded by bodyguards. The only advantage she had was surprise—and she was a marksman with a handgun.

Courtney finished her drink. It was time to leave. She was tired. The thought of flying back to the states, most likely New York, and starting all over again was exhausting. The mood in the bar had also shifted. A group of loud men were celebrating. How could anyone be happy when millions had just died?

"Dry martini for the lady." A man next to her leaned against the polished ebony bar and smiled.

"Yes, Mr. Mohammed." The bartender went to work on the drink.

She was in no mood for conversation. "Thank you, but I'm leaving." She stood.

His smile faded. "I am very sorry."

The depth of his sincerity stopped her. "For what?"

"The bombing of Chicago. You are an American?"

Courtney took a deep breath and swore not to cry. But something about the pronouncement made the tragedy more real. Suddenly, she felt very alone in a strange country and missed home. She brushed her eyes. "Yes. How did you know?"

"Americans are not hard to spot."

She lifted her chin. "Is that so?"

"You have a slight accent. Midwestern. Are you from the Chicago area?"

He was handsome and familiar looking. Mid-forties. Arab but with none of the heavy features. More European with a lean, angular face and cleft in his chin. Very tall and well built. Suit was flawlessly tailored; the Breitling chronograph rare. He had money. But she wasn't in the mood for being picked up. Never had been. Whenever she frequented a bar, it was for business or meeting friends.

"Impressive," she said gathering her purse. "If your day job doesn't work out, I'm sure you can land a job in the circus." She regretted her comment almost immediately. She hadn't intended to be mean, just to ensure he left her alone. Subtle didn't work with most men. She turned toward the lobby.

"Forgive me for poor my manners and not introducing myself. I'm Yasin Mohammed. What is your name?"

This guy can't take a hint. But remember you're a guest in a foreign country, and he is trying to be kind. She turned around.

"Would you accept my apology and be my guest tomorrow night at a dinner I'm hosting?"

Any excuse for avoiding an airplane flight was tempting but accepting an invitation from a stranger was something she never did.

"Thank you for the kind offer, but I don't know you."

The bartender finished the martini, placed it on the bar. "Mr. Mohammed is a very important man in Turkey. He escaped from ISIS. Everyone knows him."

That's why his face was familiar. He was everywhere on the Internet and cable shows. He had escaped from an ISIS prison. And he was one of the world's richest men. She walked back to the bar, took a sip of the martini, never losing eye contact. He seemed like a decent man. At least her radar said so. Call it intuition or instinct, it had faithfully guided her through the years by providing a quick assessment of which investors were serious and which weren't.

"Why invite me? You must have dozens of female companions who would be more culturally appropriate shall we say for such a dinner?"

"You flatter me. But, it's a fair question. I would like to do something nice for an American. Consider this a small token of gratitude for your country, and all it has done for the world. What happened is a terrible tragedy, and I know the other dignitaries, regardless of their political views, share the same opinion. Won't you be my guest? I would consider it an honor and privilege."

His dark eyes were earnest, entreating and difficult to refuse. "What is the occasion?"

"Just a dinner to thank my friends for considering an historic union."

"The United Middle East Union. I read about it." She froze as the Iranian President's face flashed before her.

"It's been the dream of Arabs since the prophet Mohammed to have one nation united with one soul."

"I understand there is considerable opposition."

He feigned a smile. "Name one great accomplishment that didn't face resistance."

She couldn't think of any, especially in her life.

"Please, tell me you name?"

"Courtney Gattis."

"What a beautiful name. It is a formal dinner. I'll pick you up in the lobby at 6 p.m."

He smiled and turned to rejoin his friends, before she could accept or refuse.

Assumptive close. She had used it many times in real estate by sliding a pen toward a buyer or seller without ever asking them to sign the contract.

She had just been closed.

CHAPTER THIRTEEN

Jerusalem, April 5

Hank's body cried for sleep, but he refused to give in. Every time he closed his eyes his thoughts returned to the wedding, to the seconds before the attack when everyone was alive, to the time when he might have been able to save his wife, but didn't.

The Jerusalem Times sat untouched along with his dinner on a table in Kat's room at Bikur Cholim Hospital. Someone must have delivered the paper during a shift change, someone who hadn't made the connection between the story on the front page and the still body in the room. Hank sat up and folded the paper without looking at the headline and tossed it into the trashcan. A first. He had never thrown a newspaper away without reading part of it.

He got out of bed and pulled a chair next to Kat's bed. There were so many tubes and machines connected to her he was afraid to touch her for fear of disturbing some piece of equipment. She hadn't regained consciousness since the attack, which her surgeon said was a blessing. The loss of blood had deprived her brain of oxygen. It needed time to heal which a coma provided.

"Mr. Jackson?" The voice startled him. A nurse stood at the doorway. He hadn't heard the door open. She was young like so many of the people in Jerusalem.

"These are Mrs. Jackson's personal items. We removed them before surgery." She walked in and handed him an envelope. In a softer voice she added, "Here are Mr. Chavez's. He listed you as an emergency contact person. I'll need you to sign for his belongings."

Hank nodded and scribbled his name across the hospital form. "Thanks." He laid Luke's envelope on the metal tray along side the untouched dinner. He opened the package containing Kat's items. Inside, were her watch and wedding ring. He removed the ring. Someone had cleaned it. He slipped it on her delicate finger, carefully avoiding the IV threaded into her hand.

Had it been only a few hours ago that he had held her hand and slid on the same ring? Hank raked his sleeve across his eyes and reached for the envelope containing Luke's items. A cross with a chain slipped out. Crimson splatters marred the large silver crucifix. Someone had forgotten to clean it. He went to the bathroom and dampened a cloth. He wiped the chain and started on the blood-spattered cross, then stopped. Luke would have preferred it this way. Hank slid the chain over his head and clutched the crucifix.

I'm not as strong as you Luke. How did you go on without Cindy? Hank wasn't an optimist. Most hard news reporters weren't. They didn't have the benefit of writing feel good pieces about cancer survivors. Their world was dirty politics, terrorism, tragedy. All the bad stuff that sold papers. They were trained to doubt everything, which left little to believe in. But even Luke whose faith grew a small church into millions was never the same after his wife's death. The bullet that took her life, took part of him as well.

A light rap at the door. Hank turned around. A man in a dark suit stood at the half-opened door.

"Come in."

A white-bearded man wearing a kippah stuck his head through the opening.

"I'm Zedekiah Zukerman, a friend of Lemuel Mezvinsky. I'm so sorry about what happened."

Hank motioned him in as he walked back to his chair at Kat's side. "Have a seat."

The man sat down on the opposite side of the small room crowded with machines. "Forgive me for intruding. I knew Lemuel for many years. He was a good rabbi. How did you know him?"

Hank glanced at Kat. "We didn't really. Our pastor, Luke Chavez, recommended him."

Zukerman nodded, then looked at the floor like whatever he had to say would be easier without eye contact. "You and your wife weren't the target. It was Lemuel."

Hank sat up in his chair. "Rabbi Mezvinsky?"

Zedekiah looked up and nodded.

"How do you know?"

"A friend of mine told me."

"Who?"

"A high ranking intelligence officer."

"Why would terrorists want to kill the rabbi?"

"I don't know."

"Does the IDF?"

"Shin Bet."

"Do they know?"

"My friend didn't say."

"Why are you telling me?"

Zedekiah cleared his throat. "I thought you would want to know."

Hank rubbed the back of his neck. His head ached. Kat's doctor had insisted he have an MRI, but he refused. It could wait until Kat was better.

He studied the man across the room. A large head set on narrow shoulders. Squinty eyes framed by wire-rimmed glasses underscored by puffy folds of flesh.

"It doesn't add up," Hank said. "Why attack a wedding party if the target was Rabbi Mezvinksy? They could have shot him in some dark alley instead of blowing everyone..." He stopped. "There must be more."

"There probably is."

"Is the IDF looking for those responsible?'

"The killers are probably safe in the West Bank by now, which means the case is closed. Israel is no longer permitted to enter Palestinian territory even in pursuit of terrorists."

Hank said, "Even if by some miracle the IDF find the people responsible, it won't bring anyone back."

Zedekiah rose slowly. "Shabbat is in a few hours. I should go."

But as he turned for the door, he glanced at the empty envelope with Luke's name on it, then the cross hanging from Hank's neck. "Your friend's?"

"Yes."

"The newspaper said Luke Chavez was a professional fighter. A contender at one time for the heavyweight championship."

"Yes, before he entered the ministry."

"His wife was killed by a terrorist?"

Hank nodded as Zedekiah left.

CHAPTER FOURTEEN

Jerusalem, April 6

Two tugs on the rope signaled Randy had reached the bottom of the pool.

"He made it," Scooter said. "Now, let's hope he finds a way out."

The rope tugged again. What did he want? Randy continued to pull on the line. Scooter loosened his grip and let the remaining twenty feet of rope slide through his hands until only five feet remained. What was up?

Brian leaned over the dark pool as if searching for the bottom. "How long will it take people to rescue us?"

"No one knows we're here except our employer, Kamran, and I presume the Waqf. It will stay that way."

"What if Randy finds a way out?"

"If he finds a way out, maybe there will be a rescue, maybe not. I don't know. If he doesn't, we're digging. Those are the only choices."

"We could swim," Brian said. "Just like Randy."

"I can't swim," Jude blurted out, his dark eyes fixated on the cistern.

The announcement was news to Scooter. Couldn't all adults swim? It was a right of passage like learning to read.

"You don't have to swim. Just sink." Brian chuckled.

Scooter checked his watch. Randy had two minutes before he was out of air. The rope jerked downward, nearly pulling Scooter into the pool.

"Is something wrong?" Brian said.

"The guy doesn't know his own strength."

A ripple disturbed the dark veneer of the water's surface. Then another. Slowly, the water began to churn. The only sound in the chamber was water slapping against stone.

Scooter glanced at his men. Jude couldn't take his eyes off the pool. Brian stood speechless, fixated on the water spilling over the edge transforming his dusty boots into dark, wet leather.

What's in the pool? From the look on Brian and Jude's face, they were thinking the same thing.

The waves of undulating waters sloshed over the pool's edge.

"Help me. We've got to get Randy out of there." Scooter leaned back against the rope and braced his feet against the pool's edge.

Brian and Jude grabbed the rope, and pulled. But it wouldn't budge.

Something small bobbed on the surface like a cork. Scooter flashed his light at it.

"What is it?" Jude dropped the rope and leaned over the water's side. His legs buckled.

Brian caught him. "Sit down."

Scooter's stomach roiled at what looked like a finger. He let the rope slip from his hands.

Jude sat on the ledge of the pool and looked up at the carved serpent. "You should have never let him go down there."

"No one could have stopped him. And how could anyone have known there was something in there?"

"We may still have a chance." Scooter picked up the rope again. But it had been more than three minutes. Brian and Jude joined Scooter but the rope appeared anchored to something immovable. *Why wouldn't it budge? Is Randy tangled in it?*

"How long has it been?" Brian asked.

Scooter was almost afraid to check his watch again. Four minutes.

A chill swept through the cavern, which suddenly felt more like a tomb.

Jude broke the silence. "He's gone."

"Let's try one last time," Scooter said. "Give it everything you have."

Brian and Jude grabbed the rope and strained. It moved a few inches upward.

"It weighs a ton," Brian said.

Scooter took anchor. He wrapped the rope around his waist and leaned backward, and drove with his feet. But the stone floor was slick from water, and the fine layer of dirt had turned to sludge, making a secure footing difficult.

After what seemed like hours, a large rectangular box covered with moss broke the surface. Scooter wanted to shout at the discovery. But he was exhausted, and Randy was gone.

"Careful." Scooter secured the end of the rope through an iron ring embedded in the wall near the entrance. "We have to lift it onto the ledge. Brian, you and Jude take one side."

Scooter cast fear aside as he reached into the dark water. "Lift."

But the chest was too heavy.

A dark shadow flitted beneath the water.

"What was that?" Jude asked.

A scraping noise behind swung Scooter around.

The iron ring securing the chest was pulling free from the wall.

Scooter grabbed the rope. "We're losing it."

Brian and Jude grasped the rope.

The anchor broke. The nylon slid through Scooter's hands, slicing into his flesh. The chest sank out of view.

"Hang on."

A blue vein bulged in the middle of Jude's forehead as his feet braced against the base of the pool's wall. Brian leaned backward, his teeth gritted, his face reddened.

Hope faded with each foot of sharp line slipping through Scooter's bloodied hands. It might be nothing more than an ossuary, containing the bones of some dead priest. Maybe they should just let it go? But how could they? Randy had thought it important enough to risk his life. What if it was the ark? What better place to hide it than beneath 60 feet of water.

Scooter summoned what little strength he had left and drove his feet into the hard surface. "For Randy."

The dead man's name ignited Brian and Jude.

The chest's descent stopped and slowly rose.

CHAPTER FIFTEEN

Istanbul, April 6

A black, armored limousine with a police escort rolled to a stop in front of the Ciragan Kempinski Hotel. Courtney watched from the lobby as the general manager waited outside. He wiped his hands on his pants.

A slight man in a baby blue suit emerged from the limousine. The manager pumped the man's hand. An icy chill swept over Courtney's bare arms. It was Ahmadreza Abassi, Iran's president.

A warm hand brushed her chilled arm. Courtney jumped.

"I startled you. I'm sorry," Yasin said.

"It's okay. I'm surprised Iran's President is here."

"We were all surprised to see him yesterday, but he was invited."

Abassi approached, extending his hand toward Yasin. In Arabic he said, "Interesting speech yesterday. You're not really serious about uniting the Middle East?"

"I believe it will happen."

Abassi grinned.

"Allow me to introduce my guest. This is Ms. Courtney Gattis. She's an American."

The Iranian acknowledged her with a slight nod and forced smile. It was inappropriate for a man to shake hands with a woman unless related by family. *Thank God for that.* The thought of touching hands with a butcher was revolting.

She tried to smile back, but her face wouldn't respond like someone injected with one too many Botox shots. At least a stony expression was better than betraying her real feelings.

The Iranian appeared not to notice except for the glint in his small, dark eyes.

"Gattis. Is that Jewish?" Abassi asked.

Yasin frowned.

"Yes," she responded a little too abruptly. "Would you excuse me for a moment? I forgot something in my room."

She left the two men and walked toward an open elevator. Abassi's arrival changed everything. She stepped inside and took a deep breath. Her hands shook as she pushed the button to her floor. *You can do this.*

The elevator stopped at the third floor and the door opened. She walked to her room and waved the back of her hand across the door's sensor. It clicked. She walked in and opened her suitcase. Farid's phone lay on top of her clothes. She searched the room for a place to hide it. The top of the ceiling fan above her head caught her attention, but it was too high. She looked at the lamp sitting on the desk. Might work. She removed the backing from the bottom of the lamp. Good. She placed the phone inside the lamp, then taped the cover back in place.

She pulled packing tape from around a small box in her suitcase. To an x-ray camera it resembled a small Rubik cube. She removed the cube from the box. Mechanically, she snapped it apart and reassembled the plastic pieces into a 9mm. She selected three hollow points from a small box of shells she had purchased after arriving in Istanbul and loaded them. She was an experienced marksman and at one time, licensed to carry a concealed weapon until the United Nations made owning firearms illegal. *Screw the law. A woman needed protection.*

She tucked the small gun inside her bra, grabbed a shawl and draped it across her chest—and tried not to think about what came next.

Courtney couldn't remember the ride down.

Yasin was waiting when the elevator door opened. "Ready?"

She took a deep breath. "I didn't realize you were friends with the president?"

"President Abassi?"

Courtney nodded.

"I'm afraid you may have confused politeness with friendship. You don't like him." His eyes probed for more than an answer. "But why would you. I should have been more considerate of your recent loss. Forgive me. These are complicated times."

As they walked onto the veranda, a guard met them. In the distance the Iranian president stood surrounded by a small crowd.

A soldier approached and waved a wand over her. It beeped. Her breathing quickened.

"I need to check your purse," the soldier said.

"Ms. Gattis is my guest. Is this necessary?"

"Protocol, sir. I'm sorry."

Courtney opened her clutch containing a small make-up kit. "I'm afraid these evening purses are only good for a tube of lipstick."

The guard waived them in. The sun was setting in a perfectly clear sky. Cool air rose from the Bosphorus. Palm trees hovered over white linen tables set with illuminated ice sculptures of a crescent moon and star. A slight breeze picked up the sweet scent of fresh sprays of green and yellow tulips as a string quartet played. The music floated over the chatter of guests.

A sheik in a white robe waddled toward them, holding a plate of falafel and skewered meat. "Yasin, my friend. Are you going to introduce me to your beautiful guest or are you planning to keep her to yourself?" His puffy eyes crawled up and down her as if she were a prized Arabian at auction. Courtney had no shortage of responses to men making unwelcome overtures and was tempted to shoot him a zinger, but she had more important concerns.

"Courtney, this is the crown prince of Saudi Arabia, Abdul Khalid. Next in line for the throne." Yasin nodded but his eyes flashed a warning at the Saudi prince.

The leader smiled. The introduction seemed to please him.

"Yasin." Someone waved at him. He turned to see who it was.

The crown prince leaned in, his breath meaty. "You are very beautiful. We don't see many blonds in this part of the world. Would you like to be my wife? I am very wealthy." He tried sucking in his gut.

Courtney smiled. *A real charmer.* "I'm sure it would be a privilege, but I'm not the marrying kind."

"Every woman needs a husband."

"I had one. It didn't work out very well." She glanced at Abassi who was engaged in a conversation with a man who looked like the President of Egypt.

"Oh, I see. We don't allow divorce in my country."

"I'm not a fan of it either." *Time to switch subjects.* "How is the conference?"

"Very interesting. Are you familiar with the discussion?"

She smiled and refrained from saying: *men aren't the only ones who read newspapers and follow the news.* Instead, she said, "Yes, I think a united Middle East will have a great impact on the world."

Yasin glanced her way. He was close enough to overhear their conversation and seemed surprised the crown prince would consult a woman for an opinion.

The Saudi prince looked past Courtney at some of the other guests. The novelty had worn off, and he was ready to move on.

"A united Middle East is the only real chance you have of stopping ISIS and preventing a war with Iran. The union would also create a formidable economic power."

"Sounds like Yasin shared his thoughts with you."

Courtney smiled. "Those are mine."

A man approached the lectern as guests began to sit. Yasin shook the prince's hand, then escorted Courtney to her seat. Her heels sank into the turf soaked from last night's rain, making it difficult to walk. She sat down at a table with two men who nodded at her, then returned to talking.

A jet flew overhead, its red lights blinking in the dimming light. An imam opened the evening with a short prayer. *Thankfully*. Nothing worse than an endless soliloquy from someone no one came to hear.

Yasin whispered, "This is Yaser Mehmed, the President of Turkey." He approached the lectern slowly, looking very pale. He said, "Welcome my friends and honored guests. Tonight is Laylat al-Qadr, the night of destiny..." The president touched the side of his head as if he were trying to remember the rest of what came next. Then, he collapsed.

Yasin ran to Mehmed and bent over him and appeared to be speaking to him.

Another man rushed forward and began checking the leader's vital signs.

Within minutes, two paramedics wheeled a stretcher down the aisle. One of them gave the president an injection before securing an oxygen mask over his face. They lifted him onto a gurney and hurried out.

Yasin stood at the podium, gripping its sides. His tanned skin was flush. "Honored guests, I am Yasin Mohammed. President Mehmed assured me he will be fine, but please pray for him. He also asked me to finish his speech." He glanced at the President's notes. "I will do my best to honor his wishes."

"The president said that tonight is Laylat al-Qadr, the night of destiny," he paused. "It is a night when Muslims throughout the world look back and give thanks for the Qur'an. Fourteen hundred thirteen years ago the holy prophet Mohammed received the first five verses of our holy book and with it a vision of the day when the whole world would worship Allah. So it's fitting on this night that we gather to consider a union that elevates our strengths and transcends our differences. The world has never been the same since that night of destiny many years ago. And I promise you this: it will never be the same if we unite."

Courtney's skin tingled as clapping broke out. Yasin's silky baritone was hypnotic.

"The world needs hope. The pandemic four years ago and the financial collapse that followed left many in despair. Chicago is in ruins, and the shadow of war is upon the Middle East."

Courtney glanced at Abassi to see if the mention of Chicago elicited a reaction. Not a blink. A speech on the plight of the world's vanishing reefs would probably have provoked more reaction. *Psychopath.* He sat two tables away flanked by four men who appeared to be bodyguards.

"There is a vacuum of authentic leadership in the world today. Will we rise and fill a role that is rightfully ours, or let the world descend further in hopelessness and chaos? My friends, destiny is in our hands."

He continued to speak about the challenging issues facing the world and what a nuclear war would do to the Middle East. When he finished, Courtney checked her watch. Forty-five minutes had passed, and yet it seemed like only a few. Yasin had transformed the evening's sullen events in a mesmerizing display of oratory.

As he made his way back to the table, shaking hands and stopping to chat, she regretted what she had to do. It would overshadow his cogent words, and tomorrow, no one would remember anything. Yasin's association with her might even derail his plans for a united Middle East.

She stood and took a deep breath. The salty air felt thin the way it did after a strenuous mountain hike. Her head was fuzzy, but she couldn't wait until it cleared. She had to act now.

While the crowd was focused on Yasin, she walked toward Abassi.

CHAPTER SIXTEEN

Jerusalem, April 6

The top of the dark green chest broke the pool's surface. With strength he didn't know he possessed, Scooter and his men hoisted the container onto the ledge surrounding the cleansing area. They were exhausted and sat down on the stone ledge to rest.

After a few minutes, Scooter slid his hands under the chest. "Ready?"

Jude and Brian bent down and slipped their hands under the box.

"Careful. It's slick."

The three men lowered the moss-covered case to the ground.

They stood silently around the chest as if to honor the man who had given his life for it.

"I guess we should open it," Brian said.

Scooter felt conflicted. What if the chest didn't contain the ark? What if it was nothing more than an ossuary with some dead priest's bones? Randy's life was worth more. But either way, they needed to know. Unwrapping the chest would require patience. It was ancient. Probably hidden at the bottom of the pool since its disappearance. "If only we had the GPR, we could see what's in it."

Jude dropped his head and rubbed his forehead with both hands, then stopped. He bent down over the chest.

"What is it?" Scooter said.

"The letter Tav." Jude pointed at a small spot on top of the chest not obscured by moss. He removed a knife from his pocket and scraped at the green sheath. Each movement of the blade revealed ancient Hebrew letters. He kept at until all the characters were visible.

"Give me some light," Jude said.

Scooter handed him his flashlight.

Jude moved his hand from right to left across the dark carvings. "Classical Hebrew."

"What does it say?" Scooter said.

One of the reasons Jude had been selected for the team was because he could read an ancient language comprised completely of consonants. Few could. Vowels were an invention during the Middle Ages designed to make Hebrew easier to read.

He shook his head and stood up. "Don't open it."

Brian said, "Why not?"

Jude pointed at the engravings, which looked more like claw marks than letters. "It's a warning."

"What kind of warning?"

"Only the high priest can open this chest."

"Where are we supposed to find a high priest?" Brian asked. "Didn't the last one die 2,000 years ago?"

Scooter stooped and studied the etchings. Whoever chiseled the warning did so to scare away looters. He didn't believe in curses. "You were almost a rabbi."

"Almost doesn't count. Besides there's a big difference between a rabbi and a high priest."

No amount of coaxing could persuade Jude to open the chest. Scooter stood up and looked at the young archeologist. The skin between the bridge of his glasses was permanently pinched, which made him look like he was thinking too hard. Maybe he was. He saw the downside in everything, which wasn't necessarily bad, because he often provided the counterpoint needed in an archeological exploration. Many a priceless treasure had been destroyed by unchecked exuberance.

"Well, I'm not afraid," Brian said.

He took a chisel from the tool bag and approached the lid.

"Easy with that," Scooter said. "Take it slowly."

Brian tried to wedge the end the chisel between the top and the lip of the chest, but the lid was recessed into the box, which made removing it intact almost impossible.

"The craftsmanship is amazing," Scooter said. "Probably not a drop of water inside." He inspected the top's perimeter searching for a chip in the stone or an imperfection he'd missed earlier. But there weren't any. He hated the idea of damaging the chest, but the real value was what was inside.

Brian handed Scooter a hammer. "Thanks."

He placed the chisel near the corner of the chest's lid.

Jude shook his head. "Don't do it."

"It's just a chest," Brian said.

Scooter slammed the hammer into the chisel. A chip of stone flew upward.

Somewhere in the darkness surrounding them a child began to cry.

A sense of foreboding gripped Scooter.

"Sounds like the same little boy in the tunnel," Jude said. "I think he's trying to warn us like he did before the cave-in."

"I told you I don't believe in the supernatural."

"Well, how do you explain this?" Jude pointed toward the direction of the crying. "We should forget the chest and find a way out before it's too late."

"I'm not going anywhere until I see the ark with my own eyes," Scooter said. He slammed the hammer into the chisel again. This time knocking a hole in the lid large enough to pry it open. "Get the crow bar."

Brian handed it to Scooter.

He pried the top up as Brian grabbed hold of it. Jude stood and watched.

"It's heavy," Brian said as the top began to slip from his grasp.

"Give us a hand Jude." Scooter said. But Jude wouldn't touch the chest.

Scooter threw the crow bar down and grabbed the front of the lid as Brian and he continued to struggle. They heaved the top from the chest, but it slipped from Brian's hands and crashed into the stone floor splitting in two.

"Thanks a lot, Jude" Brian said stretching his back.

"I told you to leave it alone."

"Stop it," Scooter said as he sank to his knees.

Two golden angels stretched across the interior of the chest. They were bent down with wings spread upward as if they had just descended upon the Ark of the Covenant. Their wings shined as if they had just been polished. A braid of gold ribbon encircled the top of the chest and two golden poles were set in two rings on each side.

Scooter placed his hands on the golden cherubim and closed his eyes.

"No!" Jude shouted.

But Scooter didn't care what Jude thought. Despite being trapped underground with no exit and the loss of Randy, he felt a profound sense of peace, as if everything in his life had led to this moment. Someone else would take credit for discovering the ark, but it didn't matter. He knew. He had been the first to see it after 2500 years. No one could take that from him. "We're in tall cotton men. Tall cotton."

Jude bent down and rested his forehead against the outer box but did not touch the ark.

Brian whooped, "We're rich."

They had each received $10,000 at the beginning of the mission and been guaranteed $2 million with a bonus double that for Scooter if he succeeded in finding the ark.

The water in the pool churned.

Brian backed toward the tunnel while Scooter and Jude bolted upright.

Suddenly, a black scaly column burst upward spraying the entire room with water.

Brian ran into the tunnel with Scooter and Jude close behind.

CHAPTER SEVENTEEN

Istanbul, April 6

Courtney slipped her hand under her shawl and grabbed the plastic 9mm. Her hand shook so badly she could barely grip the gun. It felt hot like it had already been fired.

The Iranian President stood in front of her, his head tipped toward one of his guards who was saying something.

A distinct crack followed by a long echo pierced the chatter.

People dove to the ground.

Abassi's guards turned toward the river, their automatics in full view.

The Iranian President fell forward like someone had shoved him.

In the panic, someone rammed into Courtney. She slipped on the wet grass, tumbling forward.

She lay only inches away from the Iranian leader.

Eye to eye.

He was dead.

Her gun lay on the grass.

CHAPTER EIGHTEEN

Jerusalem, April 8

Z Z peered down into the eyepiece of the telescope on his patio. His high-rise apartment provided a perfect view of the old City of David, which was awakening. A few tourists milled about checking their guide maps. An Arab vendor pushed a cart filled with fresh bread, a scene that hadn't changed much in 2,000 years. The sight of the bread made his stomach growl. He had forgotten to buy any yesterday and nothing sounded better than a warm roll.

The glint of the morning sunlight caught the golden cupola of the Dome of the Rock. ZZ adjusted the focus. Where were the tourists?

People should be lined up for several hundred feet at the Dome waiting for it to open. Mondays were always busy at the shrine after being closed for three days. But the only person at the entrance was a guard. Nothing in the news indicated any incidents that would require closing. Normally, he wouldn't care, but the events of the last few days had heightened his awareness of anything unusual.

ZZ picked up the phone. His first instinct was to call Saul and find out why the shrine was closed, but the last encounter with his old friend had ended with a warning. Instead, he dialed Gill Silverman, a lower ranking intelligence officer, but nonetheless, one who kept close tabs on Temple Mount activities.

"Must be important." Gill's deep, scratchy voice sounded like he had just awoken.

But it was the unmistakable trademark of a lifetime smoker. ZZ crushed his cigarette in the ashtray and watched a trail of smoke twist upward.

"I thought all my calls were."

"Your kippah must be a little tight today. What do you want?"

"Why is the Dome closed?"

"Repairs. It has been closed for four days. The Waqf posted a bulletin. Why?"

"When was it posted?"

"Late Wednesday."

"Seems like an awfully short notice, especially for Muslims who traveled to see it."

"Since when did you care about the travel plans of Muslims?"

"I guess it's nothing."

"You've got too much time on your hand MK. Get a real job."

"I'll keep that in mind. Thanks Gill."

The line went dead but not ZZ's concern. Eli had been adamant the ark was buried somewhere in the bowels beneath the mount. The rabbi's steadfast insistence on the location had been puzzling, since as a scholar he rarely took an intransigent position unless he was absolutely certain. People chalked up his dogmatism to eccentricity.

The sight of Islamic buildings on the Temple Mount used to bring Eli to tears when they were young. God's judgment for Israel's idolatrous past he said. But he believed the temple would rise again and Messiah would enter it, which spurred him to help with the establishment of the Temple Institute. The organization was dedicated to raising money for the re-crafting of all the required sacred vessels, like the menorah, the table for the showbread, and the incense altar. Even a replica of the ark had been made.

But many, like Eli, believed only the original ark with the tablets of law written by God could return the Temple Mount to Israel. The sacred chest's discovery would be Jehovah's sign that

Israel's wait for the Messiah was over. And somehow God would orchestrate the return of the land that belonged to Israel so the temple could be rebuilt.

It was clear now though, the rabbi's resoluteness had less to do with faith and more with a map.

ZZ pushed back from the telescope. His hand shook slightly. He searched his pockets for cigarettes. Where had he put them? Was he out? He eyed the crushed cigarette in the ashtray. It was still smokable. He picked it up and straightened it the best he could, then relit it. He needed to quit before he sounded like Gill. He drew the smoke in and let it slip from his nose.

Was it possible the Dome of the Rock was closed because something was happening inside that the Waqf didn't want anyone to know about?

CHAPTER NINETEEN

April 8, Jerusalem

There would be several funerals today. But Hank wouldn't be at any of them—even his mother's. Her body and Kat's grandfather would be flown back to the U.S. Luke would be buried in Belize near the church; Rabbi Mezvinsky entombed in Jerusalem.

"How could I leave you?" Hank leaned over Kat and kissed her lips. They were cold and dry. He rubbed some of her lip-gloss on them, then stroked her thick dark hair. The nurses complained how long it was and wanted to cut it. Too much work they said. But he convinced them he would brush it daily, which he did.

"Don't worry honey, no one is touching your hair."

The effort probably seemed pointless to the staff, since Kat might never wake up. But that was exactly the point: if she didn't make it (but she would, she had to), then it was even more important for people to remember her as she was, not the broken, shorn victim of a terrorist attack. She would want it that way. And he loved her hair.

"Your color is good today, sweetheart." He ran his fingers across her smooth skin. The deathly pall was receding, her skin returning to the color of coffee with too much cream. She was still in a coma, and her doctors weren't willing to offer much in the way of hope. Unlike American physicians, they preferred unvarnished honesty. Maybe it was because Israelis had seen so much death and were more accustomed to it than Americans, who tried hard to pretend it didn't exist.

Hank was heartened by Kat's improvement, yet something was gnawing at him. Was it missing his mother's service? The family said they understood. Or the memorial today for the other victims? Or missing Luke's funeral? Hank winced. Of all the services, it was Luke's he wished he could attend. Some people were harder to say goodbye to than others. He would miss the old fighter.

But no, it was something else.

The friend of Rabbi Mezvinsky, what was his name? Zedekiah Zuckerman. Something he said. He had asked if Luke's wife was killed by a terrorist. Why? Everyone knew she was killed by Sulaiman Hadid, the head of a terrorist organization. So why the question?

Was he insinuating Hank lacked Luke's courage? It was true, even though the death of his friend's wife had nearly destroyed him. Luke had confided that he wanted to end his own life after Cindy's death.

He searched Kat's vacant eyes. What would she say about pursuing the men whose grenade had ripped her body apart and slaughtered so many good people? She supported Israel's position of zero tolerance toward terrorism. But she was also quick to forgive those who wronged her.

Jesus told his followers to forgive their enemies, to turn the other cheek. Yet, he also said he would return one day and destroy all those who opposed him and persecuted his church. There was a time for forgiveness but also a time for justice. Sometimes anger was justified.

Hank held Kat's hand. It was colder than normal. He looked at the monitors, which he had learned to read. Her blood pressure was plummeting. An alarm sounded.

Hank's heart pounded in his chest as he pressed the button on the bed for a nurse. *Oh, Father, please help. Please. Please.*

The fingers of Kat's hand squeezed his. Her eyes blinked. Had he imagined it?

Her lips moved. She was trying to say something.

Hank leaned down. "What is it sweetheart?"

Kat's lips moved again.

I love you.

CHAPTER TWENTY

Jerusalem, April 11

The screen on his phone read $60 billion. Scooter did the math. About $4 million in pre-collapse dollars. He had expected to feel differently. More like Brian who sat across from him in the back of the moving van. He was giddy, checking his phone every few minutes. He shook his head as if he still didn't believe the screen.

"I'm rich," Brian said tapping his foot against the truck's floor in time to the music pounding in his ear buds. "Richie Rich man."

Scooter needed the money as much as anyone, maybe more. His ranch in Denton, Texas was in a deep hole largely because of poachers and a lack of water. People were desperate. He had hired a security team to protect his herd, and that wasn't cheap. It would have made more sense to sell the cattle, but he couldn't part with the long horns.

But money wouldn't eliminate the guilt he felt about delivering Israel's most prized relic to a Muslim. Selling the artifacts he gleaned from digs had never bothered him much. It helped compensate for the pathetic wages archeologists were paid. But this was different. This was the Ark of the Covenant, which contained the tablets of the law. For an American, it would be like handing over the original Declaration of Independence to the President of Iran.

"You okay?" Scooter said. Jude sat sullenly staring at the large crate that contained the ark. He hadn't spoken much in the last few days. He glanced up, but said nothing. From his demeanor, it appeared he was battling the same feelings, probably more so because he was a devout Jew. Scooter shared the same blood, but not faith.

He looked at his hands. They were chafed and still raw in places. The last six days had been hard. First losing Randy, then being trapped and nearly dying. They never found another way out other than the way they came. It took four days to dig out. The only thing that kept them alive was the pool's water. The team after them that recovered the ark didn't believe Scooter's account about the snake in the pool or whatever it was. They found no evidence. It was as if the beast had acquiesced and relinquished the ark to its new owner.

The truck veered off smooth pavement onto a rough road. Where were they headed? There were no windows in the back of the vehicle. The squat man driver, whose brow bore the imprint of a perpetual scowl, had said little except the ride would take an hour. Scooter guessed it was Ben Gurion International about 60 kilometers from Jerusalem. That would make sense. The ark would be flown to its final destination, wherever that was, and then he and his men would catch a flight back home. But now he wasn't sure.

Jude pulled his phone from his jacket and began tapping.

"No messages," Scooter said. "Not a word." Those were Kamran's orders when he returned the phones.

Jude looked up, but his thumbs continued in rapid motion.

Scooter snatched the cell.

A message had been sent to a local phone number. The text vanished from the screen.

"What did you say?"

"Nothing that matters."

"Come on Jude. What's wrong with you?"

He wrapped his arms around himself and tucked his hands under his armpits. He looked at the floor. "Give me my phone back."

"Look, I don't want to act like your dad, but you know the rules. We all swore silence before we began. I've got a hunch the guy who hired us takes promises very seriously. I don't want to piss him off."

Scooter handed Jude the phone. He grabbed it and tucked it into his shirt pocket.

Brian seemed oblivious to the exchange.

The road became rougher, bouncing them and the crate. One of Brian's ear buds fell out. A faint, pulsating rhythm issued from the small white earpiece. This couldn't be the way to the airport. Were they headed to an obscure airstrip?

The truck slowed. Scooter sat up straight. He checked his watch. Forty-five minutes had passed.

"Where are we?" Brian said removing the ear buds and turning off the music.

"I wish I knew."

Jude hadn't moved or said a word since his phone was returned. He sat with eyes closed.

The truck stopped. A door opened and closed.

The lock securing the cargo door was removed. The back door rolled up.

"Get out," the driver said. The man of few words pointed an AK47 at them.

They climbed down. It was dark, except for a smattering of stars scattered across cloudy skies. They were in a deserted area thick with scrub brush, which could be just about anywhere in Israel.

"Over there," the driver pointed toward a dry riverbed. "Kneel down."

"What the...?" Brian said.

"Shut up," said the driver.

Jude kneeled next to him, his face expressionless.

Scooter felt sick. "Why are you doing this?" Were they in this mess because of Jude's text? What had he said? Or had his employer always intended to kill them, to ensure no one ever talked?

The driver snorted as if the question didn't deserve an answer.

Scooter had always imagined if he found himself in such a situation, he would rush the shooter or slip the knife from inside his boot, and throw it at the killer, sinking it between his eyes. But he was shaking. All he could do was kneel obediently and do nothing. He had wondered why Jews let the Nazis line them up in front of ditches and shoot them. They did nothing when they could have at least fought back, maybe even killed a few Germans. Now he understood.

The man walked around behind them and raised his rifle.

"God's judgment," Jude said.

Scooter smelled urine. He glanced across at Brian.

The driver pulled the handle back on his rifle and chambered a round.

It had been empty.

CHAPTER TWENTY-ONE

Jerusalem, April 11

Hank sat across from ZZ in his apartment. It was early morning, and the reporter looked tired. Dark circles that looked more like bruises underscored his bloodshot eyes. His red-orange, wavy hair was tangled like knotted rope. And his wrinkled shirt and pants were the same ones he had on five days ago.

"I'm glad you came," ZZ said. "I know it wasn't easy. I heard about your wife. I'm very sorry."

Hank closed his eyes momentarily as if trying to forget. His hands shook. "I buried Kat Sunday…in Jerusalem. She would have liked that."

ZZ nodded, unsure of what to say. "You're welcome to stay with me, until you decide what to do." It was the best he could come up with.

Hank looked up. "I'm staying with a friend right now. But thank you Mr. Zuckerman."

"Call me ZZ." He tore a piece of twisted challah from the loaf and spread a dollop of fig jam on it. You should eat something. The bread is still warm." He pointed toward the shiny, golden loaf.

"No thanks. I'm not hungry."

Hank's cheeks were sunken and his hair considerably shorter than the photos that had filled magazines, newspapers, and virtually every other media five years ago.

When was the last time Hank had eaten? ZZ extended a piece of bread. "You need to eat."

"You sound like my mother," he said taking the bread and staring at it with little interest.

"We don't have to talk about Mezvinsky or what happened."

Hank grimaced as if he were in physical pain. "It's okay. That's why I'm here. I need to focus on something else." He buried his face in his hands. "Sometimes I feel like I can barely breathe."

ZZ stood and walked over to Hank. He wished he could say something to comfort him. But what hope could he offer? He was so young to have lost so much. His whole world had collapsed and everyone he loved with it. He placed his hands on the man's head. *What am I doing?*

"Adonai, not a tear escapes your notice," ZZ said surprised at his own words. "You hear the cries of a broken heart. This young man has suffered great loss, and I pray that you will save him from his troubles and comfort him and in time, heal his broken heart. Thank you Father."

Hank grabbed ZZ's hand and squeezed it.

ZZ's face felt flushed. That was the first time he had prayed in years. He walked back to his chair and sat. His heart was beating rapidly. He tried to gather himself. "My dear friend Rabbi Eli Cohen died a few days ago." He paused to catch his breath. "We were young rabbis many years ago earnestly seeking God. He continued his pursuit, but I did not. Eli was a man of great faith who insisted the temple would be rebuilt someday." A tinge of regret stabbed ZZ. Had he made a mistake in forsaking teaching for politics?

Hank nodded as he picked at the bread. "I'm sorry about your friend. He was right about the temple. The Bible promises it will be rebuilt before Christ returns."

"Yes, that's what many believe. Eli was convinced the first temple was underneath the Dome of the Rock or very close to it, which is a popular view. Others believe the original temple was north of the Islamic shrine while a smaller number believe it was south."

"I'm familiar with the different views. But what does this have to do with me?"

"Before Eli died, he told me about a map identifying where the Ark of the Covenant is hidden."

Hank sat back in his chair. "A lot of people have made similar claims."

"True, but none were made by a respected scholar of the first and second temples."

Hank rubbed his whiskers. He was still skeptical.

"I visited my friend Colonel Saul Ganz who works for Shin Bet. While he didn't confirm such a map existed, he warned me to drop the matter. And two men posing as IDF soldiers visited Eli's house looking for the map just hours after he passed."

Hank took a small bite of bread. "Who sent them?"

"I don't know. The colonel said he doesn't either. In my mind, this all but confirms the ark exists, as unbelievable as that is."

Hank stared at him. "Sounds like you don't believe the ark is real."

"I'm beginning to."

"Maybe you should take your friend's advice and forget the whole matter."

"I wish I could, but I made a promise. It's not that I haven't broken promises in the past, I have. But not to Eli. He was my friend." ZZ shook his head. "On his deathbed he asked me to find the map. I swore before God I would."

Creases lined Hank's freckled forehead. "Is that what this is about? You want me to help you find this map?"

"I believe that Rabbi Mezvinsky was involved in its disappearance. It may even be why he was the target. I don't know. But if we can find his killers, we might be able to locate the map."

Hank leaned forward. "Don't you think the police are capable of figuring this out?"

"They won't waste time investigating this, because they believe those responsible are long gone, either to Gaza or Egypt or wherever they are from. Finding them would require a military raid into Gaza, which is no longer permitted. And crossing Egypt's border is out of the question."

Hank spread some butter on the challah and took a bite. "I did some digging of my own. I stopped by *The Jerusalem Times* and visited an old acquaintance, Mike Glickman, who wrote the story about the attack..." Hank's words trailed off as his eyes darted toward a pigeon pecking at something on the patio wall. "He invited me to stay at his apartment."

It was surprising Hank considered *The Times* reporter a friend given the lurid headline and photos the newspaper ran. But perhaps Glickman had little control of either.

"He shares your opinion that Mezvinsky was the target," Hank said. "The police aren't saying much."

"Does he have any evidence?"

"No." Hank stood and walked toward a bookcase and scanned the titles. "Mike wanted to interview me for a follow-up article about the attack, since the police aren't talking. But I wasn't up for it."

"I can't believe he asked." ZZ brushed crumbs from his robe and tore off another piece of bread.

"Reporters get desperate when the only news they have is a missing archeologist."

ZZ was about to take a bite but stopped. "What did you say?"

Hank turned around. "About what?"

"A missing archeologist."

"Mike said a woman contacted the police yesterday and reported that her nephew, who is an American archeologist, was missing. Well, not exactly missing. Overdue. He was supposed to stop by and see her three days ago. She's afraid something has happened."

ZZ stood up and walked out to his patio overlooking the old city. "I spend every morning when I can peering through my telescope at the Mount of Olives and the Old city." He touched the telescope. "It's beautiful in the early light."

"I noticed the shrine was closed the other day. I called a friend in the IDF and asked him why. He said it was being remodeled. But the notice was posted only a day before the work began, as if it were a last-minute decision. If the shrine were being remodeled, don't you think the Waqf would have known weeks in advance and provided an appropriate notice for tourists?"

Hank walked toward the balcony, searching ZZ's face.

"When I came home later that night, sometime after midnight, I looked out my telescope. I hate to say it, but the Dome of the Rock is stunning at night. I noticed the outline of a truck parked out in front. The back of it was open and men were loading a large crate. It might have been nothing more than remodeling trash or a shrine artifact being moved. But what if it contained something else?"

"Like what?"

"Did anyone at *The Times* find the shrine's closing unusual?"

"Mike didn't mention it."

"Probably nothing. Jerusalem is full of archeologists. The fact that one of them didn't check in with his aunt, may mean nothing." ZZ walked back to his chair and sat down heavily. He was tired. He leaned forward and tried to steady his right hand, which was trembling.

He studied Hank's face. *Should I share with him what I know?* "Eli appointed me to handle his estate. It was modest, mostly old books, rare coins and a handful of Krugerrands. Some of the books though, were first editions worth some money. I thought it was unusual he didn't appoint Lemuel, since he was Eli's best friend. But he also didn't want him to have the map. He was concerned Lemuel would use it for the wrong reasons."

"Wrong reasons?"

ZZ held up his hand. "In a moment. The only person named in Eli's will was his housemaid, Sonia. I called her, and we met. A pretty Arab girl. Probably no more than sixteen years old. I told her Eli had given his entire estate to her. Once his possessions were sold, I would send her a check."

"That was generous." Hank sat down.

"That's what I thought. When I met with her, she seemed uneasy. At first I chalked it up to distrust of Jews, but the more we spoke, I sensed something else. I asked her if she or Lemuel knew about Eli's safe or a map. When I mentioned his name, her eyes welled up. She couldn't even speak."

Hank leaned toward ZZ. "Were they close?"

ZZ motioned for patience again, which produced a frown.

"I probed a bit further and asked what was troubling her. She clearly didn't want to talk about it. Then I noticed her arms folded over her stomach, like she was trying to hide it."

"She's pregnant?"

ZZ nodded.

"Was Eli fooling around with her?"

"Of course not."

"Rabbi Mezvinsky?"

"Perhaps."

Hank jumped up. "He raped her?"

"She claims it was not consensual. But keep in mind, this is the word of a 16-year old Arab girl against one of Israel's most respected rabbis."

"Do you believe her?"

"She said Lemuel arrived at Eli's house one day when he wasn't home. He forced himself on her. She was so ashamed of what happened, she didn't tell Eli. I don't know what to believe."

Hank grunted. "He married Kat and me. It can't possibly be true."

"It may not be." But ZZ wasn't convinced.

Hank paced around the small apartment.

"Sonia said she didn't know Eli had a safe," ZZ said.

"That's seems a little hard to believe if she was his maid. Where was it located?"

"In the floor under the rug in his bedroom."

"Didn't she ever clean his rugs?"

"By the look of his house, it didn't look like she did much cleaning." But it was a valid point. "She said Eli was in love with her, but never touched her. He paid her generously. They shared meals and many nights together. She would read to him and rub his cold hands and feet. But nothing more than that."

"Did Eli ever learn about Lemuel?"

"She doesn't think so, but shortly after she said it happened, he stopped inviting Lemuel to his house." He tore off another piece of bread. He wasn't hungry, but he took a bite anyway. "There's more."

He studied Hank again. The reporter had a right to the truth, particularly about the attack, but it was going to hurt. "Eli's maid told her mother what happened. She has a large family in the West Bank—and two brothers."

Hank's face turned red. "The attack had nothing to do with the map. It was in retaliation for Sonia." He snapped, "Right?"

His question had the tone of a challenge.

"No one knows for sure." His heart ached for Hank. "She swears her brothers had nothing to do with it." He rubbed his forehead.

"Right. What could be more motivation than the dishonoring of their sister by a Jewish rabbi?"

"I'm sorry."

Hank sat down again and cradled his head in his hands, rubbing his temples. "You don't need me. If Mezvinsky took the map, call the police and have his place searched."

"It's more complicated than that." He removed his glasses and cleaned them with the hem of his robe, then put them back on. "If Mezvinsky did take it, I doubt it's still among his possessions. Before Eli died, he said there were powerful people who didn't want the temple rebuilt. Perhaps whoever took the map wanted to ensure it would never be found so the temple could never be rebuilt."

Israel had changed so much in the last ten years. Most Jews didn't attend a synagogue or even read the Torah. And people were tired of war and clamoring for a peace deal with the Palestinians—most at any cost.

ZZ said, "Liberal, centrist, and Arab members of the Knesset are jockeying to form a new government based on a peace coalition. Any talk of rebuilding the temple based on a convincing map would jeopardize this."

Hank said, "That's why Rabbi Eli wanted you to have the map, to ensure it never fell into the wrong hands. He was wise to choose you."

A sense of failure enveloped ZZ like a shroud as he recalled Eli's impassioned plea. Whoever had the map, had probably already destroyed it. Thank God Eli was not alive. ZZ supported peace with Palestine, like most Israelis, but not this way.

Hank placed his hand on ZZ's shoulder, which startled him. "Is that everything?"

ZZ hung his head and nodded.

"I'll do whatever I can to help you."

CHAPTER TWENTY-TWO

Unknown Prison, April 11

A blurred face hovered above Courtney.
"She's waking up girls." The hot breath reeked of onion.
Fuzzy features slowly sharpened into a large, slack face with hungry eyes. The hefty woman bent over her, stood up towering over everyone. She had cropped bleached hair, bad teeth, and tattoos snaking down arms so thick it appeared she had no wrists. Courtney tried to sit up, but it hurt. Everything hurt. It was difficult to breath. She touched her ribs. "Ouch."

"The guards kicked the crap out of you. You'll be sore for days," she said in a thick accent that sounded Russian.

The tips of Courtney's fingers were black, several of her nails broken. She scrubbed her fingers against the dark blue jump suit but the ink was indelible. A thick, pasty copper taste coated the inside of her mouth.

"No way off unless you skin yourself like rabbit." Three other women sitting against the walls laughed, except for one.

The dimly lit room was humid. Flies crawled across walls weeping dark stains covered with Arabic graffiti.

"Where am I?"

The Russian smirked. "In a prison that doesn't exist. No name except the choice ones we've given it like Hotel Bok because it smells. This is where they send you when they want to forget about you."

A foul stench wafted from the toilet in the corner. "How did I get here?"

"In an unmarked van like all of us, cookie. The guards said you're Mossad."

All of the women, except one, glared at her. She was young and thin and sat with her head bowed on the far side of the cell. Courtney took a deep breath and pushed herself into a sitting position. Stinging needles pricked her sides.

Mossad? The Israeli intelligence agency? "That's ridiculous."

"You couldn't kill Abassi by yourself." The Russian checked the wall behind her; swatted a cockroach to the floor, crushed it with her foot, and leaned back.

Did she? Didn't the president fall before she pulled the trigger? She couldn't even remember drawing the gun. "I'm glad he's dead. He killed my family."

One of the women, middle-aged with dark hair, coughed up something. She looked at Courtney, pursed her lips like she was going to spit in her direction, but instead, spat a phlegm ball at another bug crawling up the wall opposite her. "Bulls Eye."

The Russian said, "Iranians didn't like Abassi, but they hate Jews even more, particularly Mossad." She tipped her head toward the dark-haired woman. "She's Iranian."

"I'm not a spy," Courtney said.

The young woman raised her head. Her face was bruised, a dark abrasion on her cheek. Her eyes were too small for her face, but they were kind. She stared at Courtney, then turned to the Iranian. "She didn't kill the president."

How would she know? I'm not even sure myself.

The Russian scowled at the young woman. "Did I ask you?"

"She thinks she's a prophet," one of the women cackled. The others laughed.

The Russian turned back to Courtney. "The guards said there was another shooter. A sniper. The Mossad work in teams. You're going to need a better story, cookie."

Someone else shot Abassi? She hadn't imagined it. Had she stumbled into the middle of someone else's assassination and was now a convenient scapegoat?

"The guards said Iran wants you to stand trial in Tehran."

Extradition? Courtney closed her eyes. Acid erupted in her mouth. She had never considered the aftermath, because she assumed she would be killed. But now, Iran would make her trial an international event, particularly since she was an American. Iranians would demand revenge for the murder of a president they didn't love. The U.S. would do nothing.

Dear God. How could she endure it? Why would she? Why prolong the inevitable? No, there would be no extradition, no trial. If she was going to hang, she would do it herself.

A hand touched her shoulder, startling her. She opened her eyes. It was the blue-eyed waif from across the cell. "Can I sit down?"

"Go ahead."

"I'm Zoe," she said sitting down.

"Courtney."

"I kind of know what you're going through. But it's going to be okay," Zoe said. "God will take care of you."

"It's going to take more than God to save your butt," bellowed the Russian.

What crime could this woman, who looked like she was just out of high school, have committed? Courtney shook her head. "I'm not religious."

The Russian chortled. "You'll fit in just fine here."

"God isn't interested in religion. He wants a relationship with you."

"Here she goes, girls."

God wasn't real. If he were, he wouldn't have let her mother and little sister die and millions of others. How could a God who is love allow such a thing to happen? "I didn't believe in God before Chicago was bombed and I especially don't now."

Zoe lowered her eyes and in a whisper said, "I lost family too."

"In Chicago?"

She looked up. "My brother lived there—my only brother."

Courtney put her arm around the young woman, something she would normally never do with a stranger, but she felt an immediate bond. She hugged Zoe, who reminded her of Taylor, her little sister. They were about the same age. "I'm so sorry."

"I don't know why God allows terrible things to happen, but he promises that he will make all things work together for good for those who love him."

The Russian said, "Isn't that convenient."

Courtney released the woman. "What are you in here for?"

"I'm a missionary. I was sent out to share the gospel with Muslim women."

The frail woman barely looked old enough to date, let alone preach Christianity in a totally Muslim country like Turkey.

"You're lucky you've still got a head," the Russian said.

"I'd rather lose my head for helping oppressed women than smuggling heroin."

The barrel-shaped Russian bolted upright and thrust her enormous chest out. She was as big and tough as any bouncer Courtney had ever seen. Puffy eyes narrowed into slits. She balled her hand into a fist and stared over white knuckles straining through cracked, red skin.

"Remember, what I did last time. I'll do it again."

The missionary said nothing, but her eyes signaled defiance.

Courtney tensed for an attack.

The Russian waved her hand in dismissal and leaned back against the wall.

Courtney turned back to Zoe. "How long have you been here?"

"Six months without a trial."

"And you'll never get one," the Russian said.

"What's the punishment for proselytizing?"

"Beheading," the Russian said.

A shiver rippled across Courtney's balmy skin.

Zoe's eyes studied the floor, tracing dark veins winding their way through the concrete. A bloom of black moss, which looked like a tiny copse of mushrooms, spouted at a juncture where several cracks converged.

"Hasn't anyone tried to get you out?"

She looked up. "I'm sure my family and church have, but this is where Turkey puts its worst criminals. People disappear here."

"I can see why I'm here, but not you."

"It doesn't matter. If and when God wants me released, it will happen. And if not, then he'll give me the strength to face whatever happens."

Courtney reached for Zoe's hand and placed it in hers. She was just a kid facing death but unlike her, not afraid. She had courage even though it was misguided. "We'll help each other."

"How?"

"I don't know yet."

CHAPTER TWENTY-THREE

Sixty kilometers outside Jerusalem, April 11

Brian fell forward, face first into a bed of gray river rock not unlike the oval stones Scooter's grandfather had used to build a fireplace for his mountain home.

The driver pointed his AK47 at Jude who was mumbling something and rubbing a pendant hanging from his neck. Probably a prayer. If ever there was a time to pray, it was now. But what good would it do? They were going to die.

A loud crack shook Scooter. Jude collapsed next to him, his blood splattering the dry riverbed. The acrid smell of sulfur filled the air.

Scooter closed his eyes and clinched his jaw as acid rushed into his mouth.

"Lousy Russian gun."

Scooter turned to see the man fighting with the rifle's bolt. It was jammed. He removed the clip and slapped it against his leg.

Scooter grabbed a fist-sized stone and hurled it at the man's forehead.

It sailed past.

The man snarled, throwing the clip to the ground. He grabbed the gun by the barrel and swung it like a bat.

Scooter ducked, scooping up another rock. He slammed it into the driver's knee.

"Ugh." The man bent over, clenching his right knee.

Scooter smashed the stone into the man's head.

This time he didn't miss. The driver slumped to the ground as if overtaken by deep slumber. Scooter slammed the rock into the man's head again and again until his skull collapsed like a soft pumpkin.

His heart pounded as he sat down on the rocks. He was splattered with the man's blood. He yanked the truck's keys from the dead man's pocket.

He glanced at Jude and Brian. Jude lay on his back, his lifeless eyes staring upward at stars peeking through dark clouds. His mouth was half-opened, as if his final thought was not one of terror, but of amazement. Brian's face was hidden in rocks. Ear buds draped over his neck.

There was nothing he could do for them now. Whoever had hired the driver, perhaps the same man who had employed Scooter, would be looking for him and the ark. He had to go. Time was against him. He jumped into the van and started the motor, revving it.

He eased the truck backward into the highway. It was past midnight. The road was deserted.

He drove. Where he was going, he had no idea.

CHAPTER TWENTY-FOUR

Unknown Prison, April 12

The Russian stared at Courtney. She was sizing her up. It was only a matter of time.

Zoe had fallen asleep against her shoulder.

"Isn't that sweet," the Russian said. "Mother hen and little chick."

She walked across the room and stood a few feet in front of Courtney. The cell became quiet except for the Russian's heavy breathing, which sounded like a dull saw laboring through tough wood. "She's mine. I don't share."

This isn't your fight. It will only make things worse. You don't need any more problems. But wasn't this exactly the same logic she had followed in Chicago? And look where that led. No, Zoe clearly could not defend herself against a woman who outweighed her by more than a hundred pounds.

Zoe stirred and sat up, rubbing her eyes.

"Don't move," Courtney whispered.

The Russian glared at Zoe. "Get over here."

"No."

The big woman's face turned red. "What did you say?"

"No." Zoe nudged closer to Courtney.

There wasn't time to stand and fight. This would be on the ground. She visualized the attack: side kick to the Russian's left knee, which she favors; axe kick to the back of the neck when she bends to grab her knee; finish her with front kick to the nose.

"Get over here now." The Russian yelled. She reached for Zoe.

Courtney struck while the big woman was focused on the missionary.

It was over in five seconds.

CHAPTER TWENTY-FIVE

Hebrew University, Jerusalem, April 12

Mike Glickman, a reporter *with The Jerusalem Times*, insisted the place for the meeting be secure. He hadn't said why or what the rendezvous was about, which led Hank to speculate the reporter had either nailed a lead on the terrorists or found a connection to Mezvinsky.

Glickman sat at a table with Hank and ZZ at a cafe at the Mt. Scopus Campus of Hebrew University, a location suggested by ZZ. The school certainly looked impregnable. Its clean limestone walls, rising like a fortress, overlooked a hillside of olive trees in northeastern Jerusalem. The Romans had used the mountaintop in 70 A.D. as a staging area to launch their fatal assault against Jerusalem, according to ZZ.

Hank introduced ZZ and Glickman to each other. In order to find the map, he would need them both. They nodded curtly. Did they have some history?

"Now, what's this about?" ZZ said as students buzzed past.

Glickman warily eyed a table of students nearby.

ZZ said, "They're more interested in their phones, which makes this the perfect place."

The reporter leaned in and looked at Hank. Large, black-framed glasses sat on a curved nose. His dark hair was probably longer than his editor liked.

"My source at the police department called yesterday. Remember, the aunt whose nephew was missing?"

Hank nodded.

"She contacted the police and told them he sent a text."

"What did it say?"

"The police couldn't make any sense of it."

"Well, tell me."

"*We're cursed.* Not an unusual statement for a Jew mind you." He smirked. "We are the guiltiest people on earth. We have a whole book telling us everything we shouldn't do."

Hank smiled weakly; the best he could manage. He sipped his Americano. The first decent cup he'd had in days. He turned to ZZ. "The archeologist said *we're*, which indicates he had company. Did you see anything else provocative at the Dome of the Rock besides a crate being loaded into a truck?"

"Just some movers who got into the back. Three of them, I think."

"One of them could have been the missing archeologist," Glickman said. "Could you identify any of the men from photos?"

"I don't know. There wasn't much light."

Glickman removed a photo from inside his notebook and placed it before ZZ.

He squinted as he studied the photo, but he always looked that way, as if he were staring into the sun.

He pointed at the man and nodded. "He looks familiar. I think he was one of the three men. But I'm not positive."

Glickman poked the photograph. "That's the missing archeo-logist."

"Does he have a name?" Hank said.

"Jude Hyman."

"Khayim. It means life," ZZ said.

Hank slid the photo over. The man had dark curly hair as unruly as cotton candy with a kippah perched on top. "Did the police ask the woman who contacted them why her nephew was in Jerusalem?"

"They tried," Glickman said. "My contact at the police department said the Shin Bet paid her a visit. Somehow the agency intercepted Hyman's text. They confiscated the police department's main server, the backup drive and deleted the records in the Cloud." He paused, taking a deep breath. "The woman, who called, is missing. My source tried contacting her after Shin Bet left, and got a disconnected number. He drove to her residence. She's gone. The next door neighbor said she never saw her leave."

Hank said. "Sounds like we have a credible lead."

ZZ looked worried. "Shin Bet wouldn't be involved unless natio-nal security was at risk, which confirms my suspicions that the ark's discovery is real. And I fear, our involvement in this could be very dangerous."

"You really think the ark exists?" Glickman said. "I don't buy it."

ZZ stared up at the juncture of arches above. Light poured through clerestories encircling the ceiling. His eyes dropped on Glickman like a hawk. "Do you believe in anything Mr. Glickman?"

"I believe in what I can see."

"When you look at Israel, what do you see? Do you see the miraculous? A nation that should have never been? A nation with unique laws that sets us apart from all others. The ark is part of that heritage."

The MK's fervor surprised Hank. A few days ago, he didn't believe in the ark. Now, he seemed its newest proselyte. Hank had researched ZZ's background: he was known for being an independent in the Knesset, taking positions that rarely gave liberals or conservatives what they wanted. Liberals argued his compromises weakened the path toward peace while conservatives claimed his positions undermined Israel's influence. Some thought the former rabbi clever for his middle-of-the road stances, but Hank's experience was people who rarely took sides did so, because they lacked passion for either. Maybe, his faith had been resurrected.

Glickman adjusted his glasses and glared. "The law may run through your veins, but it doesn't in mine."

A florid glow spread across ZZ's face. He shook his head and seemed too exasperated to say anything.

Hank said, "I don't know Mike. I think ZZ may be right. The evidence is mounting that the government believes the ark is real. And what happened the other night at the shrine suggests it may have already been found."

"Perhaps," Glickman said frowning. "I also found that Hyman often worked with Scooter Fenksy, another archeologist. When I called his office, the message said he was on a dig. And guess what his expertise is?"

"The Temple Mount?" ZZ interjected.

"Close. He's been involved in the excavation of several of Israel's tells. So there could be a connection."

Glickman leaned back in his chair and ran his hand through his long hair. "The question is why Hyman thought he and whoever else was with him were cursed."

Hank said, "If Hyman found the ark, maybe he felt guilty for robbing Israel of it."

"We're presuming Israel doesn't have it," ZZ said.

A bell rang dismissing class. Hank jumped.

"This would be a blockbuster story if any of it could be proved," Glickman said.

"The story will never make it into print," ZZ said scanning the students pouring into the little restaurant.

"Why not?" Glickman said.

"You should know this Mr. Glickman. The government will impose a gag order on any story that threatens the nation," ZZ said. "There is strong political sentiment in Israel for peace with Palestine.

The discovery of the ark on the Temple Mount would complicate the process by proving the land belongs to Israel. Whether it's true or not, even a rumor the ark had been found, could cause a political tsunami."

"Israelis have a right to know," Glickman said. "For that matter, the whole world. We can't let Shin Bet cover-up such an important discovery—if it's true."

"How can we prove any of this?" Hank said. "We don't have any hard evidence."

"We've got to find the man who sent the text," Glickman said.

"Whoever sent it is as missing as the woman who received it," ZZ said. "Shin Bet or whoever is involved is several moves ahead of us."

Hank scratched the stubble on his chin. He hadn't shaved in a few days. "All right, so we're playing catch up. But the call can be traced. If he still has the phone with him, GPS can identify the location. Mike, do you have any contacts who can get that information?"

He nodded.

"Be careful using phones or the internet."

ZZ's cell phone buzzed. He pulled it from his pants pocket and studied the number. A ghostly pall fell over his face.

"Who is it?" Hank asked.

"Saul Ganz from Shin Bet."

CHAPTER TWENTY-SIX

Hebrew University, Israel, April 12

"I'm going to visit Kat's grave." Hank quietly examined his empty cup. "Nothing we can do until we hear from Mike. Hopefully, his contact can locate the signal."

ZZ nodded blankly. He was a million miles away.

A stooped figure dressed in black entered the coffee shop, which had emptied out. He appeared to be an orthodox Jew, but his hat was a black fedora, with a little gray feather in the band, and he wore a van dyke instead of the traditional beard. He tapped his silver cane against the floor as he advanced across the room in Hank's direction.

"In a field where there are mounds, talk no secrets," the man said. His eyes were cloudy and gray. The man's voice was like a rustling of wind through trees. He was the old man at the Tower of David. A cold breeze rippled across Hank's skin.

"In the Valley of Elah where David conquered the giant, is where you will find what you are seeking."

The man turned and disappeared around a corner.

ZZ's eyes followed the stranger. "Do you know him?"

"Kind of."

"What did he say again?"

"Something about finding what we are searching for in the Valley of Elah."

"Is that all?"

Hank jumped to his feet and ran after the stranger, but when he turned the corner, the man was gone. And something inside said it would be pointless to look any further.

*   *   *

"This is crazy," ZZ said. "We have no idea where we are going or what we are looking for. I thought reporters were supposed to be guided by facts."

Hank gripped the steering wheel of ZZ's car as he followed Highway 38 south and resisted common sense urging him to turn back. They had been driving for nearly an hour and Glickman still hadn't called.

"The old man spoke to Kat and me before our wedding. I think he was trying to warn us." He winced at his own statement. "I know it sounds insane." Sometimes, all a reporter had were his instinct and his told him that whoever the blind man was, he had a special gift. Maybe he was an angel. He certainly came and went as one. "Somehow he knew we were looking for something. How do explain that?"

"Not everything in life can be explained."

A road sign announced *Valley of Elah*. Beyond it were hills lined with pine trees.

"Highway 38 is the same road the Philistines used when they returned the ark to the Israelites in Beth-Shemesh." ZZ said.

Hank turned the car onto a two-lane road and drove only a few minutes before he noticed tire tracks. He stopped the car and got out. The impressions in the road could have only been made by a truck. "Dual rear wheels."

Something else caught his attention. Something out of place. A pile of dirt had been shoveled onto an area not far from where the tire tracks stopped. Fresh cuts into the nearby riverbank pointed to recent digging.

ZZ kicked at clumps of dark earth, overturning rocks underneath.

A dark sticky substance clung to the tip of his shoe.

Hank grabbed a dead branch lying nearby and turned over stones exposing layers of crimson. He pried up more rocks. Beneath them lay a dark pool like a hidden cistern.

"We're too late." ZZ's voice trailed off into a whisper.

Something glinted in the afternoon sun. Hank reached down and picked up a chain with a small medallion caked in blood.

"What is it?"

"Looks like a coin." He handed it to ZZ.

He removed a handkerchief from his pocket and wiped the blood from the coin. He turned it over in his hand. "One silver shekel. Minted during the first year of the Jewish revolt in AD 67. "Just the kind of artifact a Jewish archeologist would appreciate."

The blood at their feet and abandoned pendant had the fingerprints of murder.

Hank walked back toward the road where the tire tracks began. "Another vehicle was here." He directed ZZ's attention to the second set of smaller tracks.

"Perhaps someone intercepted the truck and there was a battle?"

"Maybe."

The evidence before them held few clues. They had a pendant that might belong to the archeologist, tire tracks from a truck and another vehicle, and blood. But none of this proved a connection to the ark—except the mystic. Somehow, he had known they were searching for something and where to guide them.

A group of ten fighter jets passed overhead flying in a loose horizontal line. Shortly after, another group flew by in a similar configuration.

Hank looked up into the cloudless blue sky marred only by white contrails. "Unusual. Jets generally fly in formation."

ZZ studied the sky, covering his squinty eyes. "They are in formation. That's battle formation."

CHAPTER TWENTY-SEVEN

Highway 12, Israel, April 12

T he money was gone. Every last dollar promised to him.
Scooter glanced in disbelief at the pitiful balance on his
phone as he drove. The Arab had somehow retracted the wire.
Scooter threw his cowboy hat on the seat and wiped his hand against
his wet brow.

It was only 9:30, but already hot. Temperatures everywhere
were ten degrees warmer than normal, whatever that meant anymore.
The most tragic consequence were the fish dying in record numbers.
A friend had sent him a video of thousands of catfish and bass
bobbing on their sides in Trinity River near Denton where he had
fished many times.

Scientists blamed the scorching heat on the United States. In a
desperate attempt to eradicate the deadly virus sweeping the country
four years ago, the military had nuked dozens of quarantine camps
crawling with the pathogen, which sent enough debris into the
atmosphere to damage the ozone layer. And the bombing of Chicago
was sure to make things worse. Scooter headed south on highway
12. He had stopped in Idhna, a Palestinian town and ditched the van
for another. The men who rented the truck to him struggled with
the crate. It took four of them to move it. While he waited for the
crate to be transferred, he used a pay phone to call Johnny Naziri, an
antiquities dealer he had used through the years to move many of the
pieces he had acquired. He never thought of the artifacts as stolen.

They were compensation for work that paid little. He didn't tell the dealer what the cargo was, only that it was priceless and worth the trip from Damascus.

Scooter studied the rearview mirror. A white Toyota trailed about two cars behind. It might be nothing. But every passing vehicle, every open window, every stranger who stared at him was a potential threat. The new vehicle provided some cover, but he wouldn't breathe until he reached the Egyptian border. Johnny would have already paid off the border guards. All he had to do was make the border. He had taken Highway 90 on the eastern side of Israel, which was less traveled to avoid scrutiny. But he was back on the main road only five miles from the border.

By now the death of Brian and Jude in the Valley of Elah had been discovered, probably by a tourist hunting for five round stones as David did 3,000 years ago. The police would be combing the scene for clues. He glanced down at his blood-splattered pants. He was wearing all the evidence they would need. Sure, the rifle at the riverbed would have the killer's fingerprints on it, which would exonerate him, but it was unlikely the gun would be found. Assault rifles had been banned by the United Nations three years ago due to death squads shooting anyone suspected of the virus. An AK47 carried a hefty price on the black market.

Connecting him to his crew wouldn't be difficult. Customs would confirm four Americans had entered Israel about the same time. But he was more afraid of whoever had hired him than the Israeli police.

The white car slid in behind him. Was it his imagination or was the driver leaning forward studying his license plate?

The answer awaited 100 feet in front. A barricade of white police cars.

His heart pounded. They had found him. Had they located the van in Idhna? He couldn't stop. If he did, he'd be just as dead as his friends. He had to make it past the barricade. He punched the accelerator to the floor and headed toward the blockade of police cars. A plume of blue smoke coughed from the engine as the truck fishtailed through traffic.

He braced for impact.

CHAPTER TWENTY-EIGHT

Unknown Prison, Istanbul, April 13

Shouts exploded from beyond the cellblock. Courtney stood and walked to the rusted bars. The clamor didn't sound like women arguing or fighting. This sounded more like a celebration.

A door opened at the end of the long corridor. A guard yelled something in Turkish.

The cellblock broke into a cacophony of whooping and laughter.

"What did he say?" Courtney shouted above the noise to the caged woman in the cell opposite her, who was pumping her fist in the air as if the news constituted a personal victory.

"Iran declared war against Israel," she shouted.

Courtney's legs felt weak. She found the wall and slid to the floor. She covered her ears as the Russian and other women rushed to the bars, banging their shoes against the metal. They joined in a chant making its way through the cellblock: death to Israel; death to Jews.

Zoe stood up and walked across the cell and sat down next to her. "You okay?"

She said nothing.

"You think Iran is attacking Israel because of you?"

Courtney uncovered her ears and looked up into Zoe's pale face. She didn't feel like talking but it was difficult to ignore the missionary. "I made things worse."

"They've been planning to attack Israel for years. The assassination gave them an excuse. You just happened to be in the wrong place at the wrong time."

"But I planned to kill Abassi, wanted to kill him, and would have if someone hadn't done it for me. The gun the police found on me was all the evidence they needed. Now, I'm despised."

"I don't despise you. And I'll bet Americans are cheering back home."

Home. She would never see it again.

A guard walked up to the cell grinning like he'd just won the lottery.

He switched to English. "It's a special night ladies. We're going to celebrate."

"What did you have in mind?" The Russian pressed her large chest against the bars.

The guard in dark glasses stepped back, frowning. He looked at the rest of the women. "We're going to break the rules...just a little."

The women stood up. "How?"

Courtney and Zoe remained seated.

He unbuttoned his dark green uniform and slipped a bottle from inside. "Raki. There's enough for all of you, except them." He gestured toward Courtney and Zoe.

It was no secret they were disliked by the guards, Courtney, because she was supposedly a Mossad agent and Zoe, a Christian missionary. They routinely received less time outside than the others and were given the worst jobs like cleaning toilets.

The guard took a long drink, then passed the bottle through the bars to the dark haired woman, whom he favored. The Russian's scowl prompted the woman to give her the bottle. She gulped.

The guard slammed his club against the bars. "That's enough. Pass it around."

The bottle made its way around the circle of women with each imbibing of the anise-flavored liquor.

Zoe said, "The Bible predicted this would happen to Israel. But God will defend her."

Courtney looked at the missionary. Her faith was admirable but naïve. How could a tiny country defend itself against Iran, which was sure to marshal its proxies in Lebanon, and Gaza, maybe even Russia. And if it looked like Iran would prevail, the rest of the Middle East might join them.

A disheveled guard ran up to the cell with his shirt untucked and hat askew. He was out of breath. He shouted to the guard standing near their cell waiting for the return of the Raki. "You'll never guess who's here?" He straightened his hat and tucked in his shirt.

The guard turned abruptly, fear gripping his face. "The warden?"

The guard laughed. "Burak, you're paranoid." The two bantered back and forth excitedly in Turkish.

Courtney recognized one word. *Yasin*. Had she heard correctly? She turned to Zoe. "What did they say?"

"Yasin Mohammed is here."

A hot flash swept over Courtney. Why would he be here? Had he come to express his support for her extradition? Maybe, even brought a television crew to record the drama? The reality of what awaited her in the next few days was setting in—the extradition, the trial, the certain guilty verdict—the execution.

The guard pointed toward the bottle the Russian had just passed to Burak. He tucked it inside his shirt.

A trail of applause and whistles proceeded up the corridor, growing louder as footsteps approached. The guard removed his sunglasses and both men stood at attention. Yasin walked up to the cell dressed in a dark blue suit and peered inside.

Courtney wanted to disappear.

"Greetings gentlemen," Yasin said in English.

"Mr. Mohammed, have you to come celebrate with us?" Burak asked. The other guard standing behind Yasin shook his head in an apparent attempt to keep his fellow guard from saying anything stupid. The guard blushed. "I mean, isn't it great that Iran has attacked Israel?"

Yasin turned to the man. "We will be fortunate if there is anything left of the Middle East when it's over."

Burak's eyes dropped toward his boots as a hush fell over the cellblock.

Yasin's dark eyes found her. "Will you please release Ms. Gattis?"

Courtney's heart pounded. *Did he say release?*

"The assassin?" Burak protested adjusting his belt.

The description as an assassin still seemed surreal. But even more bizarre was Yasin asking for her release. Why?

Zoe grabbed Courtney's hand and squeezed it. Her blue eyes were moist.

The guard pulled his radio from his belt. "Open cell 129. We're releasing inmate #67. You heard me. Just do it." He slipped the radio back into his belt.

The other guard behind Yasin placed his hand on his gun as if one of the inmates might be stupid enough to bolt from the cell. The steel door jerked slowly open as metal screeched against the rusted track.

Courtney hugged Zoe, then stood. "I'll do everything I can to get you out."

"Thank you," Zoe whispered back.

Courtney turned to the Russian. "Touch her and you know what will happen."

The big woman smirked.

Courtney had no idea why she was being released or whether she would be able to help Zoe or muscle the Russian into good behavior. But she felt a small glimmer of hope.

CHAPTER TWENTY-NINE

Outskirts of Beersheba, April 13

"Israel is under attack." The tremulous voice on the radio delivered the devastating news. "Tel Aviv and Haifa are being shelled by Hezbollah. Gaza is launching hundreds of missiles into Beersheba and Asdad." The announcer paused. "And the Iranians are advancing through Iraq toward our border with heavy tanks and more than 100,000 troops. Pray for Israel."

ZZ turned the radio off as the white tail of a missile streaked overhead exploding in the hills beyond the highway.

Hank ducked.

They were on route 12, only a few miles from the Egyptian border. They had been driving all night. ZZ was exhausted and conflicted about chasing a truck that might contain the ark based upon a riddle from some mystic. His time would be better spent in the Knesset, helping his country. Had he not already honored Eli's request to find the map? There was nothing more he could do.

The traffic in front came to a halt. An endless line of cars stretched before them. Hank slammed his hands against the steering wheel. "This is going to take hours to clear and we're sitting ducks for another one of those rockets."

ZZ opened the car door and stepped out.

"Where are you going?"

"To see what's happened." But it was more than curiosity summoning him. He walked past several cars. In the distance police cars swarmed around what looked like an overturned truck, while an impenetrable row of white vehicles separated the accident scene from an endless procession of cars. As he approached the barricade, a man stood near the overturned vehicle with his hands up as police surrounded him.

"What's in the van?" one of them shouted.

The man appeared dazed and said nothing.

A police officer near the blockade motioned ZZ backward, "You can't go any farther."

Flames exploded from the truck's underbelly. Orange fingers quickly wrapped themselves around the truck's hull.

A terrible realization rocked ZZ: he knew the man. He was one of the three he had seen at the Dome of the Rock. "The ark is in there!" He screamed. "The ark is in the truck!"

A police officer swung around, his gun aimed at ZZ.

"Back away." He planted his feet and thrust his gun forward. "Now."

"Stop the fire before it destroys the ark. Please do something." He pointed at the back of the vehicle, which was difficult to see through waves of heat and smoke. His eyes were clouded with wetness.

Hank ran up and tried to get ZZ to return to the car.

"No, the ark is in that truck," he said as he struggled free of Hank's grip.

"How do you know?"

"That man was with the other two at the Dome of the Rock." He pointed toward a catatonic figure. "I'm sure it's him."

The officer, his gun still trained on them, said, "Who are you?"

ZZ's tongue was thick, his mouth as dry as the desert around him. He tried to speak but nothing came out.

"He's Zedekiah Zukerman, a member of the Knesset." Hank said.

"And you?"

"Hank Jackson, an American journalist. We believe the Ark of the Covenant was stolen and it's in the back of that truck."

The policeman shook his head. "The Ark of the Covenant? Is this a joke?"

"It's going to blow." Another officer on the far side of the truck shouted.

Several policemen ran for cover behind their vehicles.

ZZ and Hank crouched behind a police car as the ground shook and the truck exploded, blowing the back door and top off.

ZZ buried his face in his hands. *Jehovah, why, why would you allow this?* It didn't make any sense.

He stood up on shaky legs. Fire swirled inside the three remaining sides of the cargo area. Jagged white rocks, blackened from fire, were scattered inside. Several more rocks were strewn outside. Metal bands groped for the crate they once bound, which was now nothing but embers.

CHAPTER THIRTY

Ataturk International Airport, April 13

The countryside streaked by covered in a veil of darkness. Courtney sank into the car's plush leather. She had no idea where they were headed. Yasin had been on the phone for nearly an hour speaking with the ailing Turkish President, who was still hospitalized. He spent most of the conversation listening but when he spoke, it sounded like the two were weighing the advantages and disadvantages of supporting Iran in its fight to defeat Zionism.

The limousine stopped next to a sleek white Gulfstream on the tarmac at the airport. The private jet shimmered under terminal spotlights as a crescent moon peaked through long, thin gray clouds.

She was dressed in a new dark blue suit, about the same color as Yasin's. In the shuffle of paperwork and protocol surrounding her release, he had said little other than presenting her with the new wardrobe. The fit was perfect and felt tailored.

Yasin said goodbye and put the phone down. He looked at her. His dark eyes were probing. Why did he ask for her release when such a move was sure to cost him politically? What drove him to take such a risk?

"Thank you. I am beyond grateful for your kindness."

"You are most welcome."

An awkward moment of silence followed, which Courtney felt compelled to fill. "I overheard you discussing the war with Israel. Why would Turkey support Iran?"

"The president believes that if Turkey helps Iran, it might share in the massive oil fields on the Golan Heights, which would eliminate our need to import oil." He lit a cigarette and rolled the window down. Fumes, redolent of kerosene, wafted from outside. He rubbed his chin. "But what you really want to know is why I interceded for your release from prison."

Exactly. She nodded.

"You're not a Mossad agent. Any competent attorney can prove that. You had a gun, but you never removed it, nor threatened Abassi with it. Yes, I presume you wanted to kill him, but you didn't. So, the case against you is based on the assumption of intent, which is not enough to convict. No one liked Abassi, even his own people. Whoever killed him, did the world a favor."

The kindness and support from a man she barely knew was unexpected—and overwhelming. A few hours ago she was facing extradition and certain execution. Courtney turned away and brushed at her moist eyes. "The mullahs won't be happy."

"They never are. Have you ever seen a photo of one smiling?"

She turned back and attempted to smile, the first time she could remember since the bombing. Abassi was dead. But she felt no satisfaction. Her mother and sister were gone and the redemption she had hoped would follow was missing.

She glanced at the jet. "Where are you headed?"

"Prague. But it's we who are leaving. There is this great little restaurant. I suspected you might be hungry."

"Why are you doing this?"

"Do I need a reason?"

She smiled again. "I guess not."

CHAPTER THIRTY-ONE

Prague, Czech Republic, April 13

Courtney looked upward at the curved beams arching across the ceiling 80 feet above. They looked like great ribs plucked from a whale. Tall, blue-stained windows of long forgotten saints looked down on the patrons of Bartolotta's Ristorante like the eyes of God.

"It's beautiful, but having dinner in a church feels a little sacrilegious."

"Oh, this was more than a church," Yasin said. "This was St. Vasily Cathedral, one of the grandest and most important in Europe. But there weren't enough parishioners to fill its pews anymore, like many of Europe's great cathedrals. The buildings fall into disrepair until some enterprising entrepreneur is inspired by a vision and buys the property, or it's torn down."

"Still, it's a little sad."

The sommelier walked up cradling a bottle of wine like a new born child. "Good evening Mr. Mohammed. We have the bottle you asked for: 1997 Domaine de La Romanee Conit Richebourg."

Yasin put on a pair of reading glasses and inspected the label. He nodded, and the sommelier uncorked the bottle and presented the cork. Yasin drew in the aroma like a sweet rose. "Wonderful bouquet." The man poured a small amount of the dark purple liquid into a glass. Yasin swirled the wine, took a sip. "Excellent."

The sommelier finished pouring the wine and left. Yasin removed his readers and raised his glass. "To new beginnings."

Courtney raised her glass and wanted to believe that such a thing was possible. The crystal let out a small high note as their glasses touched.

"Domaine de La Romanee comes from one of the finest vineyards in the world. Let it linger on your pallet."

The flavor was complex and unlike any wine Courtney had ever tasted. She had been exposed to many fine wines though the years but never one as extraordinary as this.

"At one time in my life I wanted to be a vintner."

"Really? Why didn't you?"

"I love everything about wine, but I wanted something bigger."

"Like uniting Sunnis and Shiites into one nation?"

He smiled. "When my father died, I had no choice but to take over the family business. I was the only heir to his shipping business. I expanded into leasing cars, jets, apartments, and commercial properties. If a customer desired something, I found a way to acquire it and lease it."

"You must have some very good people running your businesses to give you the freedom for politics."

"I do." He rubbed his dark beard as if the question triggered some deep thought. "And you, why did you choose real estate as a career?"

"My mother knew one of the city's top agents. She told me there was a lot of money in selling houses, and I should consider it as a career. So I did. I worked as a real estate assistant for five years while I attended college and then got my license. I also wanted something bigger. So I chose buildings—very tall buildings."

"You are very driven."

"I had to be. My father left us for another woman when I was twelve. My mother didn't have an education and was forced to clean houses. We lived off food stamps and wore clothes from second-hand stores. I don't ever want to be poor again."

Courtney's candor with a near stranger surprised her.

"I feel certain you are very good at what you do."

"Was. My business is gone along with the city."

"I am very sorry about your loss. Your mother gave you good advice."

Courtney's throat tightened, and she turned away. "My mom and sister died in Chicago."

He reached across the table and took her hand in his. Her instinct was to draw back, but she let him touch her. He had an ugly scar on his right hand, but his touch was soft and warm.

"I'm sorry. Truly sorry." Yasin fell silent for a moment as if he were searching for something to say.

"Have you ever been married?"

"Once."

"But you're not now?"

"No." She didn't want to talk about Jeff or what happened between them. It wouldn't be right. He would have been at the Chicago Theatre rehearsing for his new part when the bomb exploded.

"What about you?"

"Never married."

"That seems odd for a man of your charm."

"I never found the right woman, I guess. When I was younger, I never thought of settling down or needing anyone. But now, I see things differently."

"What changed?"

"A plane crash. Everyone died except me."

"My God, really?"

He nodded.

"Is that what happened to your hand?"

He drew it back from her. "Yes." He studied the dark liquid in his glass. "Do you like the wine?"

"I love it. It's truly the most interesting wine I've ever tasted." She took another sip, and regretted mentioning the scar.

"Wonderful. What are you plans now?"

"I don't know. I have some connections in New York. I'll probably start over there." Her stomach churned at the sudden dose of reality. She hadn't dared consider the future while in prison. One day at a time was enough of a challenge.

He slipped his hand back into hers and caressed it. It felt good and sent a shiver through her.

"I would like you to stay for awhile. Be my guest at my home on the Bosphorus. The sea air will be good for you. You have been through so much. Take a little time to relax before you make any definite plans."

Her head felt a little fuzzy. She had never been able to drink much. But she tried to enjoy the moment. She was drinking an exquisite wine in Prague with a handsome, complex man, who seemed interested in her.

"That would be nice."

"Good. Now I have a favor to ask."

She tensed. "What is it?

He finished his glass of wine. "A small trip."

"What kind of trip?"

He motioned for the waiter. "Bring us another bottle and a menu."

CHAPTER THIRTY-TWO

Beersheba, April 14

Z Z shielded his eyes from the bright desert light. He was exhausted. He and Hank had spent the night in jail. Neither had slept much after a three-hour drive to Beersheba and hours of interrogation. His legs felt rubbery and heavy as he tottered across the street toward his car.

"You okay?" Hank reached to steady ZZ.

"Just old."

ZZ rubbed his eyes, which felt dry and scratchy. A lean man with a head of closely-shaved white hair stepped from a white compact car. He had been waiting. As he approached, he looked like Saul Ganz in civilian clothes.

"Is that you Saul?" ZZ said. He couldn't ever remember seeing Saul in anything but a uniform.

"Let's take a ride."

"A friend of yours?" Hank studied the man as he unlocked the car door.

ZZ whispered, "Shin Bet."

"I'll ride in back."

ZZ slid into the front seat with Hank behind the wheel.

Saul motioned Hank forward. "Head south."

He eased the car into traffic, glancing in the rear view mirror. "Where are we going?"

"Just drive."

"I don't like this," Hank said.

Neither did ZZ. Saul's unexpected appearance wasn't for a cup of coffee. Shin Bet never made social visits. And the colonel's decision to sit in the back wasn't a random impulse but one drawn from years of experience. It was the high ground. He would ask the questions and control their route.

"What's this about?" ZZ asked.

"I left you a message. You never called me back."

"I've been a little busy."

"Too busy for an old friend?"

Hank glared into the rear view mirror. "We just went through hours of interrogation. We're not up for more."

"I heard."

"Can't you see ZZ is exhausted?"

He was. More tired than he could ever remember. Every movement was mechanical, requiring too much thought and effort. It was as if he had become an old man overnight. All he wanted was to lie down in his own bed and close his throbbing eyes. He patted Hank's arm. "It's okay."

ZZ turned around to Saul. The man had lived most of his life in shadows. His deeply plowed brow bore the imprint of years of strain. "Why are you here?"

Saul said, "You've waded into something far deeper than you realize. I told you to forget the whole thing." His dark eyes pleaded. "Why didn't you listen? I've been trying to protect you, but I'm not sure I can anymore."

"Whom have you been protecting us from?" Hank stared in the mirror.

"You'd be dead by now if I hadn't."

A sharp pain stabbed ZZ's chest. He struggled for breath and turned away from Saul, hiding his discomfort.

"Who wants us dead?" Hank said.

"I can't tell you that."

Saul's dress in civilian clothes now made sense. He wanted a low profile to ensure he wasn't spotted, which meant even he might be in danger. Few things ever worried him. Once during the Yom Kippur War, overcome with exhaustion, he dozed off—with bullets whizzing past them. Who could do that?

"What should we do?" ZZ said.

"First thing you both need to do is remove the chip from your hand. You're being tracked."

Nearly everyone had a chip implanted in the back of their hands. The pandemic of 2019 had necessitated a chip whose original function was to scan a person's blood and determine whether they were infected. But its applications were expanded soon after the pandemic to include financial transactions, identification, and tracking.

Saul pulled a small pouch from his pocket and passed it over the seat to ZZ.

"What is this?"

"Small first aid kit."

"I don't have a chip," Hank said.

"Is this really necessary?" ZZ said. "I have everything on this chip."

"If you want to live, I suggest you remove it."

ZZ frowned but opened the bag and removed a small blade, a bandage and some antiseptic. He cleaned his hand, then held the razor near the chip, but couldn't steady his hand enough to make an incision.

"Let me do it." Saul leaned over the seat and took the razor from ZZ. He located the nearly imperceptible bump on the politician's hand and removed the chip."

"That didn't hurt at all. You should have been a doctor."

"Toss it out the window," Saul said.

ZZ rolled the window down and threw out the grain-sized chip."

"The next thing you need to do is leave Israel. I can't protect you anymore. Besides, missiles are raining down on our cities. And the Iranians are headed here. It's going to get ugly."

"Why are we such a threat?" ZZ asked.

Saul looked out the window. "It's the ark. You know too much."

The landscape had gone from parched to burnt. They were about fifteen miles outside of Beersheba headed south on highway 40 toward Ramat Hovav, an industrial compound of chemical plants, the principal dump site for Israel's hazardous waste. The city's jagged profile loomed in the distance. An odious thought flashed through ZZ's mind: was Saul's talk of protecting them just a ruse? Had he received other orders? Was that why he was pressing them deeper into a wasteland? But how could he think such a thing? Hank's skepticism was rubbing off on him. Saul was his friend. They had fought side by side.

"We don't know anything about the ark. Not even enough for a small article in the newspaper."

It was true. Everything he and Hank knew was based on speculation. The truck they had followed contained a crate full of rocks.

Saul grunted. "You reporters are all alike. You think your stories make a difference. But all you do is screw everything up by revealing sensitive information. Remember, this is Israel. A little knowledge here can be very dangerous."

Saul pointed toward an exit. "Turn there."

The car slowed. "Where are you taking us?" Hank said.

"Just drive," Saul snapped.

They turned onto Sderot HaDkalim and headed west. Dozens of smoke stacks spewing white, vaporous clouds lined both sides of the road. The cool air flowing from the air conditioner turned sour. A sharp acidic smell filled the car's interior. ZZ would have turned it off, but outside temperatures were already boiling.

The only access to Ramat Hovav soon turned into a thin, dirt road as they continued west. The compact car bounced across the dusty, rutted surface.

A deepening sense of gloom descended upon ZZ. The ache in his chest made each breath difficult.

"You okay?" Hank glanced sideways. "You look pale."

Saul leaned forward on the back of ZZ's seat. "What's wrong?"

ZZ fought the urge to grasp his chest. "I'm okay. Just a little short of breath."

"We're almost there," Saul said.

"Where's there?" Hank said.

Saul pointed toward a lone grove of palm trees in the distance, which surrounded a house and barn.

Hank stopped the car in front of a white, flat-topped house.

"Why have you brought us here?" ZZ asked.

Saul got out of the car and walked around to ZZ's door. He opened it. A blast of hot air rushed in.

"I can do it." He waved off Saul's offer. The colonel's sudden shift toward concern reeked of insincerity. A true friend wouldn't commandeer his vehicle without any explanation and march them toward who knows what.

Hank stepped in front of Saul and helped ZZ from the car.

He plodded toward the house with Hank by his side. It was farther than it looked. As he approached the doorway, it swung open. A figure stood inside, his face obscured by the dark interior.

He braced for the worst.

CHAPTER THIRTY-THREE

Beersheba, April 14

Scooter woke with a splitting headache. He tried to sit up. An IV tugged at his arm. The room swirled. He lay back down. A policeman stood guard near the door. The room was austere: a single chair, bare walls, no toilet, no windows. If he was in a hospital, it must be military.

The door opened. A short, bull–of–a man with tight, curly black hair entered. The dark stubble on his face looked a day's growth. The policeman standing at the door stiffened, then turned and left.

"You've been out for a day." The hint of bad cologne surrounded him. Or was it alcohol?

"What time is it?" Scooter searched the room for a clock. There wasn't any, making it impossible to know whether it was the dead of night or crack of day.

The man said, "Ten hundred hours."

Scooter's mind was foggy. The conversion took a minute. 10 a.m.

"When can I leave?"

"I have some questions." The man pulled something from a wallet and studied it. "Thaddeus Fensky. Jewish?"

Scooter nodded. Hopefully, that helped since it was Israel. But the man looked Arab. "Who are you?"

"Chief of Police. Why didn't you stop at the barricade? Why would you risk your life for a truck full of rocks? We thought you had a bomb."

"Rocks?" Was this some kind of interrogation trick?

"What did you think you were transporting?" The man's dark eyebrows merged into a thick, dark line.

What should Scooter say? If he told him about the ark, a barrage of questions would follow that he couldn't possibly answer, at least not honestly. "I was hired to drive the truck. No one told me what was in back." A lame response, but the best he could come up with half-drugged.

The police chief crossed his arms. He wasn't buying the story.

The door swung open. A tall man with a slight stoop entered the room. He was dressed in a dark green suit, which hung from his bony frame, giving him the gangly appearance of a scarecrow. He studied the chief, his eyes descending toward the officer's dusty shoes. The man's thin, gray eyebrows twitched. The chief had failed inspection.

"I'll take over now."

The chief pulled his sloped shoulders back. The muscles in his jaw twitched. He stretched himself upward, but he still fell several inches shorter than the other man. "This is my case."

The older man's face barely registered the challenge. He leaned in and whispered something to the chief. The older man's eyes darted toward the entrance. Without a word or gesture, he ushered the chief to the door. The lawman stopped, turned around and glared, his eyes burning as he left.

The scarecrow closed the door, then turned back. Large, dark pupils set in pale green eyes, that belonged more to a cat, stared down at him through large glasses. "How are you feeling?"

The words dripped with insincerity. Whoever the man was, he wasn't here to take his temperature.

"I don't know anything," Scooter said.

"I haven't asked—yet." The words, which lacked any trace of Hebrew, were unhurried.

"One of you is missing."

The statement startled Scooter. His mouth went dry. How did he know about his team? "Like I told the chief, I was just a driver."

"Should I name your friends: Brian Hansen, Jude Hyman, and Randy Camp. You and your crew had quite a run stripping Israel of priceless artifacts. You're a thief and everyone knows it." He held up the gold nose ring that Scooter had found in the tunnel as proof of his thievery. He slipped the artifact in his pocket.

The man knew more about him than his mother. If only he hadn't taken the job. His crew would be alive, and he wouldn't be here. Even the promised payday that drew him to Jerusalem was gone.

The man grinned exposing a mouth of small white teeth. "You see Mr. Fensky. I know all about you and your crew. Where is Randy?"

Scooter's eyes took refuge in the thin white blanket on his bed. "Randy is…"

He stopped. Why did the scarecrow want to know? Obviously, he had spied on them. How, he wasn't sure.

"He's alive. Hiding." He glanced up.

The man's large pupils constricted. "Is he still in the tunnels? Injured perhaps? Or dead like your other friends?" A small smile tugged at the corners of drawn, pale lips that looked like an afterthought.

"Why do you want to know?"

The man leaned in toward Scooter, a stale, moldy smell rolling off him. "Don't screw with me, Mr. Fensky. I have never been fond of games."

Scooter's tongue clung to the roof of his mouth. All he wanted right now was a glass of water, but there wasn't one in sight. An image from one of his digs of a mummified servant buried alive with his master flashed before him. The young man's mouth wrenched open. A stone jar with claw marks on its side that once contained water stood nearby chronicling the final desperate moments.

"We were trapped with few resources." His tongue was thick, his words slow. "Randy descended through a water shaft searching for a way out and found one." The explanation was what Scooter wanted to believe, what he told himself, despite evidence to the contrary.

"He would have contacted you by now if he were alive. He didn't make it." The scarecrow ran his hand over the sides of his head. Short bristles of white hair fanned between his fingers. "I checked your phone. No messages." He held up Scooter's phone.

Scooter was beginning to understand. Whoever killed the members of his team, had to be positive every person connected with the discovery was dead. If anyone had escaped and leaked the story of how Jews had entered the Dome of the Rock in search of the ark, the Arab world would explode. That couldn't happen. Which meant one thing: this man intended to silence him.

CHAPTER THIRTY-FOUR

Black Sea, April 14

"**D**o you have any idea what this letter says?" Andrei Primakov said through an interpreter.

Courtney still couldn't believe she was meeting with the President of Russia. This was Yasin's small favor: to courier a letter. All she had to do was deliver the message and remember the talking points. She had not been told what the letter contained but from the talking points she had an idea. She told Yasin she wasn't a diplomat, which he said, was why she was perfect. He had saved her life. How could she object?

The Russian President's steely blue eyes bore into Courtney. No doubt a stare perfected during his days as head of the KGB.

"No, Mr. President." Her voice broke. "I haven't read it."

He seemed to mull her response.

Gentle turquoise waves unfurled into a rolling white carpet of beach beyond the 20-foot windows of the Russian President's Black Sea estate. Everything was larger than life. A fresco with biblical figures reminiscent of Michangelo's Sistine Chapel stretched across a ceiling 30 feet above. A gilt-drenched staircase wide enough for ten abreast greeted guests near the entry. And Primakov boasted that the huge chandelier in the main ballroom where they sat, once hung in Napoleon's Tuileries Palace.

But it would take more than gaudy opulence to transform a commoner into royalty. Much is forgiven because of beauty, but the president was anything but handsome. His hands were thick with stubby fingers more suited for a butcher; indentations marred a bald, bony head which looked like a piece of unfinished marble; and years as a boxer in the Russian Army had reduced his nose to a fleshy lump.

He held the letter Courtney had delivered up to the light pouring from a large skylight. "I don't understand. Why is Turkey opposed to Russia helping Iran? Israel is no friend of Turkey."

He threw the letter on the large coffee table of thick glass set on an ornate gold frame of winged lions. His face grew red. "President Mehmed can't blockade the Straights."

The letter was more of a bombshell than she had guessed. She lifted her cup of tea with both hands and sipped, the only thing she could do to steady them. *What am I doing here? Yasin must have been out of his mind. But I have negotiated with billionaires. I can do this.*

Primakov frowned and turned his attention to a chessboard sitting between them. He studied the pieces carved from ivory and onyx sitting on the table. He moved a white pawn. "Do you play?"

"A little."

"Do you know what the weakest piece is?"

"A pawn?"

"At first glance it looks that way. But if a pawn's advance is not checked, it eventually becomes a queen. It's the king. The least offensive of all pieces. I think a woman must have created the game."

"I'm not sure I follow you, Mr. President."

"President Mehmed has the appearance of power, like the king." He picked up the piece, examined it, then set it down. "But he is nothing. His navy is no match for Russia's."

"Mr. President, the 1936 Montreux Convention gives Turkey control over any warships entering the Straights." At least that's what the talking points stated.

The interpreter frowned, then rattled off in Russian.

"Humph. They think that will stop Russia?" Primakov bellowed in English overpowered by a heavy Russian accent.

"You're probably right, but can Russia afford to lose its aircraft carriers?" They had very few from what she remembered reading in *The Economist*. "And the law is on Turkey's side. Russia will be sued in international courts for violation of the treaty."

He waved his hand in dismissal. Russia had never worried much about international law.

The president's bald pate glistened in the early morning light, twitching as if stimulated by some invisible force. "Russia has a treaty with Iran to support it militarily."

Courtney nodded. "Your treaty was structured for defensive support. But Iran isn't being attacked." She tossed her hair back. "Mr. President, recalling your aircraft carrier isn't a retreat. It's an opportunity to play an instrumental role in a peace negotiation." The differentiation was hers and probably a generous interpretation of the Turkish President's intentions, a habit developed through years of reframing unappealing offers and counteroffers into something more palatable for buyers and sellers.

He looked up at his interpreter and chuckled. The fair, bespectacled man with blond hair looked more German than Russian. He grinned, like a mirror reflecting the president's sardonic humor.

But as Primakov turned back his bushy dark eyebrows pitched downward. "What do you know of peace? You're American, right?"

She nodded.

"The Middle East is in crisis, because the U.S. meddled in affairs that were not hers. If it had stayed out of Iraq, there would be no ISIS."

Time for redirection. "I brought you something. A very special gift from President Mehmed." She patted the top of the box on the floor next to her.

Primakov's loose face tightened into a broad grin. "What is it?" He reached for the box, his hands brushing against her calf.

"Please, open it."

Primakov ripped open the box and stared down.

"A gift to compliment your chandelier. One of Napoleon's clock."

"Oh, your president has outdone himself." He carefully removed the golden timepiece from the box and sat it on the table between them. The clock featured three bronze figures atop a timepiece overlaid in pure gold. His hand drifted down the length of the golden surface. "Magnificent. This calls for a celebration. Let's have a drink."

A servant approached with two small glasses filled with a clear liquid. No doubt vodka.

Courtney glanced at the clock. Drinks at 11 a.m.?

Primakov removed the glasses and handed her one. She couldn't refuse.

"Thank you."

He lifted his glass in salute. "To Napoleon and President Mehmed."

She lifted hers.

Primakov downed it. "Ah."

Courtney took a sip.

"No." Primakov motioned upward with his hand for her to empty the glass.

She did, lighting up her throat.

"You are a very beautiful woman." He reached across the table and removed her glasses before she could protest. "That's better. You shouldn't wear glasses that hide such blue eyes. They look like two pieces of lapis lazuli." His eyes fell to Courtney's legs. He had a reputation as a notorious womanizer even though he had been married for more than 40 years.

"Perhaps, you could extend your stay?"

His bluntness startled her. "President Mehmed is expecting me back today."

Primakov set his glass down, smacking it against the glass. "I want you to take a message back to President Mehmed or whoever conceived of this plan. I doubt it was Mehmed." He snorted. "Tell him I appreciate the generous gift and sending such a beautiful woman to deliver it, but if he tries to block my aircraft carriers, Russia will retaliate."

Primakov stood and canted his head. "Have we met before?"

She slipped her nonprescription glasses back on, the only disguise she had, and stood. "I hear that a lot, but no, we've never met."

He studied her. "I've seen you somewhere." He slid his hand across his head.

She tried steadying her voice: "I have a jet to catch. Thank you for your time. I will convey your answer back to President Mehmed." She extended her hand.

Primakov grabbed her hand and held it. "Where have I seen you?" He grinned exposing a mouth full of crooked teeth.

She wrenched her hand free, her heart pounding against her sternum.

Primakov studied her as he gestured for his guard to escort her out. "It will come to me."

As she walked toward the front door, she restrained herself from bolting toward it.

CHAPTER THIRTY-FIVE

Istanbul, April 14

"Could you slow down?" Courtney said.

The driver slowed the limousine as streetlights illuminated brightly colored murals of people at work beyond the rain-streaked windows. A bearded man conducted an orchestra, another stood in front of a canvas poised with an artist's brush; a woman with flowing black hair sat a potter's wheel, her hands cupped around a bowl.

What a sham. Hidden beyond the adorned walls, deep within the interior was a prison. Even its walls perpetuated the ruse. The public believed the notorious Bakirkoy women's prison, which once housed more than 1,000 women, had been converted into a cultural center, which was partly true. The outer buildings formed a rectangle with several more buildings inside the perimeter, which probably looked like a maze from above. All had once been part of the prison complex, until the cry for reform had shut it down. Converting the penitentiary into a cultural center and school for the arts was the government's attempt to erase the stain of decades of torture and abuse. But in the very middle, one building dedicated to misery remained with no record of its existence.

She had asked the chauffeur to drive by the prison after picking her up at Ataturk International airport. Zoe was in there. Still suffering abuse from the guards and most likely, the Russian.

Courtney had promised to help her, and the pledge gnawed at her. But what could she do?

In the distance the city lights of old Istanbul twinkled. The distinction between her departure and arrival was painfully evident. Yasin had accompanied her to the airport when she left for the Baltic Sea, but now he was missing. No doubt, he was disappointed in her failure to convince Primakov to recall his carriers, but then, she was disappointed that he had misrepresented the risk. The trip was supposed to be an unofficial diplomatic visit, not an amateurish attempt at high-level diplomacy gone wrong.

It was dark and still raining when the limousine approached a magnificent chateau descending a steep cliff like a terraced garden to the Bosphorus. The car rolled onto a cobblestone driveway as one of eight garage doors opened, revealing an enormous cavern packed with exotic cars. The driver opened her door and directed her toward an elevator. She stepped inside and took a deep breath.

Yasin was standing there as the door opened.

"Welcome," he said embracing her. "I'm so glad you're back."

The sudden contact startled her. It was the fourth time he had touched her. "Thank you."

He directed her through a long entry of polished plaster and marble to stairs that descended to a dining room with stunning views of eastern Istanbul, the Asian side of the continent. A deck extended out over the cliff.

"Are you hungry?"

"A little." Actually, she was famished.

"My chef prepared something special for you." He poured a glass of white wine and handed it to her, then, picked his up from the table and raised it. "Here's to your success."

They clinked glasses and took a sip. *What success?*

"I'm not... sur... sure... I... I understand," she stuttered. "Primakov's carriers are headed through the Turkish Straights. He's not going to back down."

A small corner of Yasin's mouth turned upward. "I knew he wouldn't withdraw them. His ego would never allow that. And Turkey won't intervene and block the Straights."

Courtney's face felt warm. "Then, why did you send me?"

"Turkey has not been able to breach Russia's intelligence network—until now."

"What did I do?" She sat her wine glass down.

"Napoleon's clock. It was coated with millions of microscopic transmitters. When Primakov touched the clock he transferred them to his hands. That's why I asked you not to touch its sides. The coating is like permanent ink and will take weeks to wash off. We will know every word Primakov utters and every move he makes before he makes it for the next few weeks. And the technology is undetectable."

Courtney stiffened. "Let me see if I've got this right: you sent me to deliver a Trojan Horse? Why didn't you tell me?"

"You would have been too anxious if you'd known, and Primakov's finely tuned antennae would have suspected something."

"If I had known I was delivering an espionage device to a former KGB chief, I wouldn't have gotten on the jet. You knew that. I appreciate the fact you got me out of prison, but I am not accustomed to being played." What upset her most, was the absurd thought in the back of her mind that he had rescued her because he cared for her. The betrayal stung.

Yasin stared at her for a moment, frowning slightly as if he were perturbed. "Did I get you back safely?"

She crossed her arms. "Yes, but things could have gone differently."

"I left nothing to chance."

"You had no right to put my life at risk without my consent. Primakov was only minutes from identifying me. If I hadn't left when I did, I might be headed to Tehran."

Yasin rubbed the back of his neck. "Please forgive me. I will do whatever is within my power to make amends."

Courtney thought for a moment. "I met a young woman while I was in prison that I promised to help. Can you get her out of that hell hole?"

"What's she in there for?"

"She's a missionary."

"Christian?"

"Yes."

"Well, she knew the risks of proselytizing Muslims."

"She will die in there if you don't intervene. I gave her my word I would try to help her."

"I'll ask my attorney what the chances are of getting her released. In some ways her case may be more difficult than yours. But I will try. You have my word."

"Thank you." She turned away and took a sip of wine. The key to being a good negotiator was knowing when to remain silent.

"I should have told you. I'm sorry. I am trying to stop a war that could blow up the entire Middle East. Turkey has never been able to penetrate Primakov's inner circle. It was vital to know what he's planning."

She turned back to him. "It seems pretty obvious. He's sending his carriers to the Mediterranean."

"Yes, that much is obvious. What isn't however, is how committed Russia is to war. What has Primakov promised Iran? Will he provide air support and get involved? Will he send Russia's stealth nuclear subs to the Mediterranean?

Yasin moved closer. She could smell his cologne and feel his breath. "I know what you're thinking: the only reason he got me out of prison was, because he needed someone beautiful to entrap Primakov." He took her hand and kissed it. "I didn't bail you out, because I needed your help. I bailed you out, because I admire you. I've never met a woman as strong as you."

His seductive eyes bore into her. He brushed her check with the back of his fingers. A hot flash swept over her.

She looked at him. He was tall, at least six-five, handsome, powerful, intelligent and surprisingly romantic. "I admire you too."

The cook arrived with their dinner. He bowed and smiled as he set their plates on the table.

"Chilean sea bass in a white wine butter sauce on a bed of jasmine rice with seasoned, grilled vegetables," the man said.

"My absolute favorite," Courtney said.

Yasin smiled. "It's mine too. The bass was caught today."

Her stomach rumbled at the slightly sweet smell of the fish and herbs.

They sat down as the cook filled their wine glasses. "Bon appe'tit."

She waited for Yasin to cut into his fish before doing the same. "Thank you for asking me to stay with you. But I need to tell you that I'm old fashioned in some ways. I don't sleep with a man unless I'm in love." And there had been very few men she had loved.

"I knew that about you and would expect nothing different."

"You did?"

"You do not trust people easily, especially men. Do you?"

A cool breeze slipped through the warm air and chilled her. How did he know so much about her? Trusting men had always been difficult, since her father left her waiting on a Friday night years ago at Chicago's Navy Pier. She was only twelve. They met each Friday after school to eat hotdogs and ride the Ferris wheel. But on this Friday, he never showed up. She was afraid something had happened to him and cried all the way home. But her mother explained later that he ran off with another woman. Courtney never heard from him again.

She brushed her hair from her eyes. "Are you the kind of man that can be trusted?"

"I am." Yasin leaned over the table and kissed her.

CHAPTER THIRTY-SIX

Dubai, United Emirates, April 15

The sky stretched for miles and for a moment Yasin felt as if he were flying through pale blue heavens. In a sense he was as he sat in the uppermost conference room of the Burj Khalif, the world's second tallest building. He and the heads of 17 Middle Eastern countries were gathered for a summit to discuss an idea as lofty as the 2717-foot edifice—the creation of a new nation.

Yasin had persuaded the leaders to meet again, but it didn't take a great deal of arm-twisting. The expanding war between Iran and Israel was threatening to engulf the entire Middle East and public support for the new nation was gaining traction. ISIS continued to besiege the embattled Pakistani army with daily defections weakening the last line of defense between the brutal terrorists and a nuclear arsenal.

Of course, even if the new nation became a reality, it would be anything but united. Missing from the second conference were Iran, Syria, Iraq, and Libya. The countries had joined Iran in its war against Israel. Even Turkey had declined an invitation. The death of President Mehmed had shaken the country and empowered Prime Minister Tamir Hussein to announce a new non-western direction for Turkey, threatening its EU membership.

Gadi El-Hashem, the President of the Arab Emirates, stood, "Our friend Yasin Mohammed is intent that the only way to preserve our sovereignty is to give it up. This is not new to the citizens of the United Arab Emirates. More than 50 years ago seven countries formed a federation with the idea that we were stronger together than apart.

"Look at what a united people can accomplish." He swept his arm toward the panoramic view of a diminutive skyline below that looked like glistening stalagmites.

Yasin nodded at the UAE President. It was a point well made, and one of the reasons he recommended Dubai as the site for the second conference.

Jamal Jaffari, the President of Egypt stood. "I fear we're all too late to stop Iran, not that any of us wouldn't like to see the Zionist state eliminated, but if the Persians capture the oil fields on the Golan Heights, they will become the largest producer in the world, which will convince the mullahs they really are a people of destiny. I don't want to go to war with Iran, but how do we stop them?"

Crown Prince Abdul Khalid, of Saudi Arabia, grunted as he hefted his girth to a standing position. "I must admit that I was cool to the idea of seeing my country absorbed into a new nation. We have one of the largest militaries in the Middle East and more resources than most of you, but I fear neither will be enough to stop ISIS if they obtain nuclear weapons. They are crazier than the mullahs."

Everyone sat down as Yasin stood. He looked at each of the expectant faces of the 17 men seated before him. He didn't have the power to vote, but he was in command. In a short time he had risen from political obscurity to center stage. His escape from an ISIS prison along with his public campaign to unite the Middle East had made him a media star. And the late President Yasser Mehmed's deathbed remarks that he was the most qualified person to guide Turkey had solidified his credentials as a rising political phenomenon.

"Iran's threat to destroy Israel is bluster," Yasin said. "All they and their allies really want are the oil fields. They know that if they threaten Israel's existence, the Jews will rain nukes down on them.

They don't want that. They have too much to lose even though they talk like they are willing to risk everything to usher in the return of the Mahdi. ISIS, on the other hand, believes everything they say. They have spread throughout the world and are on the verge of metastasizing like cancer. Their impact will be felt far beyond the Middle East."

"The first order of business for our new nation will be to bolster Pakistan's defenses and stop ISIS from obtaining the largest arsenal of nuclear weapons in the Middle East. Our second step will be unexpected."

"What is that?" El-Hashem said.

"Sun Tzu in *The Art of War* said, let your plans be dark and impenetrable as night, and when you move, fall like a thunderbolt. We will fall like a thunderbolt on Iran's rear flank and make them fight a war on two fronts."

CHAPTER THIRTY-SEVEN

Ten Miles west of Ramat Hovav, April 16

Z's hands shook as he held *The Jerusalem Times* and stared at the bold headlines: *Iranian Tanks Near Border.*

Hank scanned the article over ZZ's shoulder as he sat in a well-worn recliner. One hundred thousand troops were moving unopposed across Iraq and Syria. More were on the way and Russia said it would lend air support from its aircraft carriers headed to the Mediterranean Sea. And if necessary, Iran said it would use nuclear weapons to eliminate the Zionist state.

"Why is ISIS allowing the Iranians to cross their country?" ZZ said, "It doesn't make any sense. They are enemies. Why don't they stop them?"

Hank scratched his beard. It was a provocative question. ISIS hated the Persian Shiites almost as much Jews. "This wouldn't be happening if my country hadn't forced the treaty through with Iran. We gave them a license to build nukes. Now, they'll threaten to unleash them on anyone who interferes with their agenda."

"Will the US help Israel?" The MK's leaky eyes searched Hank's face for an answer.

"I don't know." But he did and so did ZZ. The mood in the US the last few years had turned isolationist. The recent bombing of Chicago, rather than igniting Americans to strike back against Iran, had psychologically paralyzed the country. The US would not get involved in the conflict.

ZZ leaned back in his chair and closed his eyes. The newspaper slipped from his hands and unfolded on the floor.

Hank stooped down and gathered the paper and placed it on the table next to ZZ. Slivers of light leaked from the edges of drawn shades and fell on the photo of a car's charred and twisted shell. The headline above the photo caught his attention: *Times Reporter Dies in Bombing*. The morning's bagel and cream cheese churned in his stomach as his eyes searched for the victim's name. *Mike Glickman*.

Hank gripped the paper tightly. No motive or suspects had been identified in the city's first suicide bombing in 16 years. *Poor Mike*. Was he killed by the same people looking for ZZ and him?

Hank eyed the cell phones on the kitchen table across the room. Useless without the SIM cards. Ganz supposedly had taken them for their protection. The forced drive south had been nerve-racking with the colonel sitting behind him. A reporter's mind was programmed to think the worst, which included anything from a bullet in the back of the head to entombment in a vault of toxic waste. But the Shin Bet official, although as approachable as a cactus, had not meant any harm. In fact, he had arranged for them to stay with his friend Jonas Cranston at his isolated ranch outside of Ramat Hovav, until a plan for their safety could be developed.

He and ZZ had been in hiding for three days, but already, it felt suffocating. The only tether to the outside world was Cranston, the plant manager of Chada Cosmetics. But he rarely came home. The manager kept a cot at the plant, where his work often stretched into the evening hours.

The colonel advised leaving Israel, but Hank couldn't just leave ZZ behind. He wasn't strong enough to travel. The MK moved slower each day like a clock someone had forgot to wind. He insisted there wasn't anything wrong with him, but Hank was worried. Even if ZZ were well enough to leave, there were no guarantees they would be safe anywhere. Borders posed little challenge for trained killers. And the MK said he couldn't leave the country, because he needed to return to his duties in the Knesset. But that was a fantasy.

"I have terrible news." Hank tossed the newspaper on the coffee table.

ZZ opened his eyes and bent over the paper. His hand quivered as he picked it up and read the article. "The ark has brought death to everyone connected to it."

They hadn't spoken much about what had happened, since the chase that ended with the shocking discovery that the crate contained nothing but rocks. A decoy truck had been employed to mislead any would-be suitors of the ark. The whole plan had been carefully scripted like an author who knew the end from the beginning.

ZZ sat slumped in the chair, lacking the energy to right himself—or maybe it wasn't energy at all, just the will.

"Mike may have tried to reach me," Hank said. "If I can access my phone records, I can see if he called."

"And if he did?"

"He may have left some indication about what he found."

ZZ frowned. "Saul forbade any outside contact."

"I know. I know," Hank said shaking his head.

"Saul risked his position, maybe even his life to protect us. He said we're being hunted. He knows these people. One call may be all they need to identify our location."

"If I can access the phone records from a computer, it will take longer to trace."

"But eventually they will find us?"

Hank nodded. "If we stay here—yes."

"It seems like an awfully big risk for a call that may never have been made."

ZZ was right. There was an equal chance, maybe even greater, that Mike didn't call. He had a seasoned reporter's nose for danger, and knew the more layers he peeled back in search of the truth, the more exponential the risk became. But Hank's gut, said the reporter's death was connected to something he found. And if he had discovered something significant, he would have wanted to share it.

"Jonas has a notebook computer," ZZ said. "I think he uses it to read at night. I saw him put in the drawer next to his bed. But even if Mike left you a message with the names of the people involved in this mess, what good will it do? They are powerful people. And Israel is at war. No one will care."

CHAPTER THIRTY-EIGHT

Beersheba, April 16

Scooter's jailers kept him so drugged, he was blurry-eyed. If there were a toilet in his room, he wouldn't be able to shoot straight enough to hit the bowl.

Why didn't the scarecrow just kill him? He had visited his room dozens of times, placing a gun against his temple each time and spinning the cylinder—then pulling the trigger. Minutes became hours as he waited for the inevitable. There were hundreds of ways to kill someone quickly, but the scarecrow seemed to relish never rushing death, savoring each click of the trigger, reducing his victims to babbling idiots. If the fate of the murdered left clues about their executioners, Scooter was sure the scarecrow's victims would reveal a soulless creature whose only friends were demons.

The door to his room eased open. Someone slipped in.

The fuzzy figure next to his bed didn't look like the scarecrow. Missing were bony shoulders poking up through his suit like tent poles. This man was stocky.

"I don't know why I'm doing this," a man who sounded like the chief said. "This is crap what they're planning."

"Who…"

"Shut up and listen. I'm going to create a diversion. When the station is empty, we'll leave through the back door. My vehicle is parked there. Got it?"

Scooter wanted to ask why he was doing this, but his tongue was so thick it felt like there wasn't enough room for words. He nodded. But thick fog wrapped around his thoughts, smothering any chance of clarity.

The chief left.

Within a minute, an explosion from somewhere shook everything so hard it felt like the building might collapse.

Feet pounded down the hallway outside the room.

The door swung open. Dark wild eyes belonging to a man who liked like the chief scooped Scooter out of bed. He reached for his hat on the table as the man carried him out of the room.

Scooter swooned from the sudden movement. The last thing he saw was the scarecrow with a gun.

CHAPTER THIRTY-NINE

Ramat Hovav, April 16

He'll be livid when he wakes up. Hank grabbed the keys lying on the kitchen countertop and placed a note next to ZZ. The MK was in no condition to travel and even if he were, the road ahead would be too dangerous. At least ZZ was safe here. Hank decided against using Jonas' laptop. It would put ZZ and Jonas in jeopardy. He wouldn't do that.

He opened the front door and shielded his eyes from the blinding light. A wave of heat rushed him. Jonas' old truck sat out front, a layer of dust covering the rusting hull.

Hank got in the truck, pumped the gas, and turned the key. The motor turned over, but died. When was the last time Jonas drove it? He tried again but the engine sputtered and died again. Hank winced. How would he explain this if ZZ woke up and found him in Jonas' truck? He didn't want to be dissuaded against leaving.

Hank laid his forehead against the hot plastic steering wheel. He wanted to ask God to start the engine, but he was afraid to. *Does he hear me anymore?* He certainly hadn't when he begged for Kat's life. Hank tried again. The engine coughed and roared to life. He pumped the pedal, revving the engine. It backfired, a sound resembling a shotgun blast.

He backed out of the driveway and turned down the dirt road. In the rear view mirror, ZZ stood peeking through the curtains.

I'll come back for you my friend when it's safe.

Hank kept driving.

CHAPTER FORTY

Somewhere southeast of Beersheba, April 16

The truck sailed over a dip in the road landing hard, bouncing Scooter off the rear seat onto the floorboard. The wheels whined against the pavement as the engine's hum slid into a higher octave. They were moving fast.

Scooter tried to sit up but the gray interior swirled. "I'm dizzy."

"Stay down," the chief said.

Scooter climbed into the seat and turned around. It was difficult to see anything through the truck's wake of brown dust. "Is someone chasing us?"

"Can't see anyone yet, but I'm sure they aren't far behind."

Scooter leaned back against the seat. His head spun. "I can't lie down."

The chief tipped a flask to his mouth as he studied the rear view mirror. "Why not?"

The sharp smell of alcohol made Scooter queasier. He belched.

"You sick?" He threw a white bag reeking of greasy falafel over the seat. "Don't puke in my truck."

Scooter rolled the window down and pressed his face into a rush of warm air. He took a deep breath and belched again. "Where are we going?"

"Somewhere they can't find us."

"Why are you helping me?" He rolled the window back up. The last thing he remembered was the scarecrow pointing a gun at him.

The lawman's dark eyes studied him through the mirror. "I'm not a murderer."

The rescue by the chief still seemed like a dream. The drugs were wearing off, but his mind still felt numb. No one had ever risked his life for him. But what the chief did went beyond that. His life would be as worthless as a bucket of spit. The chief would never be able to go back to his former life.

"What about the scarecrow?"

"Who?"

"The man who interrogated me. I saw him holding a gun before I passed out."

The chief stared into the mirror again and grunted. "Mendel. Shin Bet."

"National security?"

"Yeah, they're just trying to do a job. It gets tougher every year. But Mendel enjoyed his job too much. But he won't bother you…or me anymore."

"What happened?"

"The less you know, the better."

Scooter rubbed his face as if somehow the brisk massage could revive his senses. "What's your name?"

"Bibi."

"Egyptian?

"Iraqi."

"How did you land a job on an Israeli police force?"

He glared in the rear view mirror. "I grew up in Israel, fought against Hezbollah in 2006. My dad was Arab, my mom Jewish. When I was a kid, I saw him blown to bits by a suicide bomber. I don't have any love for the other side. I'm more Jewish than you."

"I'm sure you are." Scooter had never thought of himself as a Jew even though he was. "Did Mendel tell you why Shin Bet wants me dead?"

"I was hoping you could tell me. What kind of crap did you get yourself into?"

Scooter weighed whether he should answer truthfully. It seemed wrong to lie to someone who had given up everything to protect him. "I believe it's linked to the project I was involved in."

Bibi's eyes narrowed. "Project? Sounds like a clever name for breaking the law. What did you do?"

He leaned back against the seat. "I'm an archeologist. I was hired to search for the Ark of the Covenant."

"You're kidding, right?"

"No, the ark is very real."

Bibi looked in the rear view mirror again. "I don't believe you. But who wants it?"

"I don't know."

"Well, that's the first mistake you made. Never take a job unless you know who you're working for."

"He's Muslim and powerful enough to convince the Islamic Wafq to let me to dig underneath the Dome of the Rock. I know that much."

Bibi stared into the mirror. "Are you making this up?"

"I wish I were."

"Did you really find it...the ark?"

"I did." The statement still seemed surreal. "The most beautiful thing I've ever seen."

"No wonder you're in trouble. No telling how many people want you dead."

"I was the first person to see it in 2500 years." He closed his eyes and saw two golden angels kneeling in prayer over the chest.

"Where is it now?"

"I don't know. I thought it was in the truck I was driving."

"No one risks their life like you did for a crate of rocks."

Scooter shook his head and wished he hadn't. Everything swirled again. "Whoa." He took a deep breath. "So the rocks were real? That wasn't just a line to goad me into saying something incriminating?"

"Didn't need to make you say anything. SP-117 did it all."

"What's that?"

"A truth serum developed by the KGB. Mossad stole it and now our intelligence uses it. Pretty amazing stuff. You don't remember anything about the questioning do you?"

"No. What did I say?" His pulse quickened.

"I don't know. I wasn't there, but Mendel said you sang like a canary."

Another wave of nausea rushed up Scooter's throat. He rolled the window down and hung his head out. No wonder he was a dead man. He had given the scarecrow everything he wanted. Mendel knew Randy was dead and every connection to the ark gone—except for him. He probably even disclosed a Muslim had hired him. Was there anything more treasonous than turning over Israel's greatest treasure to an Arab? But Mendel didn't want him dead because he was a traitor. He wanted to ensure the ark's story never saw daylight. Its discovery under the Temple Mount made Israel's claim to the sacred real estate indisputable. If the truth leaked out, the Arab world would explode upon Israel like fire supposedly did upon Sodom and Gomorrah.

But Shin Bet had a bigger problem. A Muslim had the ark now. How would they silence him? If they even knew who he was. Maybe, he was just a collector who wanted the mother-of-all treasures and would keep its discovery a secret. But that was doubtful.

Bibi's eyes fixated on the rear view mirror. "Trouble. Big trouble."

Two white cars behind them were closing fast. Scooter rolled the window up.

A rapid series of cracks thudded into the truck's tailgate. Bibi winced.

"They're trying to kill us." Scooter ducked below the window.

"They are trying to hit the tires."

Bibi pushed a button on the dashboard. The truck rocketed forward, flattening Scooter into the seat. The cars following them faded into white dots as Bibi's hands tightened around the steering wheel. He struggled to maintain control.

"What do you have in this thing?"

"Insurance. 440 hp and a turbo charger. But unfortunately, now, that they know where we are, they'll call for backup. Maybe a helicopter. We don't have much time."

"What's the plan?"

He pointed left, toward a cluster of brown and black specks.

"What's that?"

"You'll see soon enough."

Scooter wasn't a big fan of surprises. Not the kind wrapped in a bow, but those that felt suspiciously more like an ambush. Bibi studied the mirror as he slowed the truck and pulled it off the road. He kept his eyes trained behind as he guided the truck onto a dirt road that was more of a trail. The tires spun in loose sand as the vehicle accelerated, fishtailing across the same stubborn land Abraham had traipsed across four thousand years ago. Small clouds trailed them, rising into the air like smoke signals. They wouldn't be hard to find.

They drove several miles northeast. In the distance unrecognizable shapes morphed into an outline of tents. Within minutes, it became clear the village of stretched canvas shelters belonged to Bedouins.

"This is your plan? Hiding with the Bedouin?"

"It's better than it looks."

Bibi stopped the truck in front of a group of wiry, bearded men, who seemed more interested in their camels than the new arrival.

"Come on," Bibi said getting out of the truck.

Scooter stepped out. A fine layer of dirt, the consistency of flour, clung to the vehicle, transforming the shiny black exterior into a dull tan that conveniently blended into the surroundings.

"Where's Zafar?" Bibi asked a leathery man wrapped in a long white robe that needed washing. The man pointed toward a tent.

Scooter followed Bibi toward a tent of sun-bleached, layered browns that matched the strata in nearby hills. Inside, a gray-bearded man sat cross-legged polishing an AK47.

"Sit," the old man said, motioning toward the rug.

Bibi and Scooter sat down on plush rugs of green, red, gold, and blue covering the floor.

"This is the man I told you about. Scooter Fensky."

The old man continued rubbing oil on the rifle. He picked it up and looked through the sights. "What kind of name is Scooter?"

"It's a nickname."

"What does it mean?"

"I don't think it means anything."

"A name is very important here."

"What does Zafar mean?" Scooter asked.

"Victory. My parents wanted me to be a leader. In order to be the chief, you must be more powerful than your enemies."

"My real name is Thaddeus. I never liked it."

Zafar laid the rifle down in his lap and for the first time, looked at Scooter. He smiled, revealing a mouth of gray teeth that looked like leftover coals from last night's campfire. A man walked to the entrance of the tent with a silver pot. The Bedouin motioned him to enter.

"Have some coffee Thaddeus," Zafar said.

Scooter had spent enough time in the Middle East to know that the leader's statement wasn't a request. To refuse would be an insult. The leader poured three cups of coffee that looked strong enough to make bricks with. He handed a cup to Bibi and one to Scooter. The old man's hands were as steady as a surgeon's.

Scooter squirmed and glanced at his watch. They didn't have time for coffee. There were people who wanted them dead.

"Thank you." Scooter sipped the hot coffee. Spicy cardamom and sugar softened the dark brew's bitter edge.

"To the Jews your name means courage. Thaddeus is a good name. Maybe you should stick with it."

Scooter focused on the hot coffee, sipping it gingerly.

Bibi fidgeted. "Zafar, the police will arrive soon. There will be trouble. Don't you think we should leave?"

He went back to his rifle, removing the loaded clip and re-inserting it. "The truck in trade?"

Bibi coughed. "Yeah."

"I'm the last of the Bedouins who travel by camel. Everyone drives a truck. I guess it's time I do as well."

Scooter looked at the police officer. It had never occurred to him that Bibi would travel with them. But where else could he go? His face was swollen, his eyes puffy, like he hadn't slept in some time. Was the impact of his decision to stop Mendel just hitting him? It must have been agonizing for a man whose world was built upon a chain of command. More than anyone, he knew what it meant for his career and reputation. Did he have a family?

"It's a good trade."

Bibi nodded. His eyes appeared to trace the intricate pattern of the rug beneath his feet. He didn't seem convinced.

Zafar stood and placed the rifle next to a long chest. He extended his right hand toward Bibi, who also stood. They shook. Bibi, who appeared to be left-handed, was careful not to shake with it.

"We should go," Bibi said.

Zafar stood and removed a dagger from his belt and pulled it from its sheath. "You both must remove the chip from your hands before we begin our journey." He handed the knife to Bibi, who skillfully wicked the miniscule device from his hand. Scooter took the dagger and repeated the procedure but not as adroitly. He handed the knife back to the Bedouin leader.

He nodded, walked out of the tent. Scooter and Bibi followed.

Zafar looked up into the late afternoon, pale sky. In the distance a cloud of dust kicked up by cars headed toward them. Scooter pointed toward the approaching vehicles "They'll be here in minutes. We shouldn't have waited so long."

The old leader seemed oblivious, still studying the sky. "They're right on time." He walked 15 feet beyond the tent and turned east. He motioned for them to follow. He pointed. "Haboob."

In the distant eastern plain an ominous mountain of sand and dirt several miles long approached like a tsunami devouring everything in its path.

CHAPTER FORTY-ONE

Negev Desert, April 16

Gusts of wind began bullying anything erect. Men and women leaned into the approaching storm as they shouldered their valuables. A gust of sand slammed into the camp, a portent of what the dark eastern sky held.

Scooter had seen dust storms in the Middle East before, but never one this size. Its dimensions were staggering: it stretched for miles with no end in sight, towering to the very limits of heaven and looked like a raging, swirling mass conjured from the depths of hell. Everything beneath the monstrous wave of sand felt small and insignificant. Arabs called it haboob, which meant blasting. But it was doubtful that whoever came up with the name had ever seen anything like this.

"How are we going to escape?" Scooter held his hat tight against his head. "That thing is probably moving 60 miles per hour."

"Probably faster," Bibi said. "Follow Zafar. He knows where to hide in these hills."

The Bedouin leader revved the truck's engine and looked back over the truck bed loaded with rugs. The compound was being disassembled with the systematic precision of an army corps of engineers. Everyone had a task and performed it efficiently without panic. Within minutes, the entire camp was packed and ready for transport.

Everyone lined up behind the truck. Camels loaded with sacks and possessions were guided by women, while children prodded goats. Men carried possessions on their shoulders that couldn't be strapped to the humped beasts. Zafar stuck his left hand out the window and motioned for everyone to follow him.

The double-cab Ford started toward the nearby hills. Scooter scanned the mounds ahead, which looked like layers of stacked cow pies, for any sign of caves. There weren't any. The unremarkable knolls of strata were probably significant to a geologist. They might even contain important scrolls like those found in Khirbet Qumran. But the only thing they were good for now, and the only thing that mattered, was shelter.

An old wooden chest sat alone in the sand. A casualty of the hurried exit. Its sides were covered with tarnished silver tacks arranged in a geometric pattern. The wood was a rich dark color, maybe teak. It was probably valuable at one time, but now its top was warped and marred by water stains. Bibi bent down and wrapped his thick arms around it. He glanced back at small brown clouds trailing two police cars that would arrive in minutes.

"They're persistent," Scooter said quickly picking up a sack of grain and hefting it onto his shoulders.

"I trained them well," Bibi said grimacing. "But I don't think they're coming to throw me a going away party. Let's get out of here."

The question of why Bibi had given up his job, his truck, everything, remained unanswered and probably would until he felt ready to shed some insight. He didn't seem like the kind of guy who welcomed probing questions.

They trailed the caravan northward toward the hills, trudging as quickly as possible through a landscape intent on making each step difficult. Scooter continually checked their progress against the approaching storm. By his calculations, they wouldn't make the hills before its onslaught. He tried not to think what sand traveling 60 to

80 mph would do to his flesh. He'd seen a far lesser storm strip a car to bare metal. He tugged his bandana up over his nose, adjusted the goggles Zafar had provided, and cinched his hat to his head before lowering it into the gathering wind.

As they approached the hills, a path wide enough for a vehicle became evident. It was difficult to see, because its entrance zigzagged between two hills. Two faint red taillights disappeared around a bend. Bibi quickened his pace as Scooter struggled to keep up. Behind them, the murky afternoon light faded into night as the storm descended. In the distance, four yellow lights punched through the dark like the eyes of nocturnal animals. Cops. An eerie howl moaned as the storm arrived.

A gust slammed Scooter to the ground. The sack split open. Pelting volleys of sand bit into his ears as easily if they were soft cheese. Bibi leaned into the storm, planting each foot securely, with his arms wrapped around the box. But the storm's ferocity stopped his advance, forcing him to make a stand. He spread his legs apart like two trees and struggled to keep from being uprooted. How could he even stay upright?

Something dark, the size of a gas can flew through the air and slammed into the side of Bibi's head. He crumpled to the ground, the chest tumbling from his hands. Scooter stood and leaned into the storm as it slashed his clothing and devoured his denim jacket and pants. It felt like thousands of jagged bits of glass were swirling about him. He plodded in the direction toward Bibi, but it was becoming impossible to see. He reached the chief and tried to rouse him, but he was out. He grabbed him with both hands by the scruff of his jacket and dragged him 30 feet around the hill's bend, beyond the storm's pounding.

Up ahead, the outline of what looked like remnants of Zafar's tribe disappeared around another turn as spinning dust devils followed them. The path appeared to snake through the hills. Scooter sat down and leaned against the mound and rested. The chief wasn't very tall but he was stocky and easily weighed more than 200 pounds. At least, they were out of the storm's ferocious blast, which was passing overhead.

Bibi lay next to him, unconscious. Whatever struck him, hit him in the temple, which was swollen. His scalp was cut and bleeding. The skin around his goggles, and bandana looked like a chemical peel gone bad. Scooter's face probably looked just as bad, but at least he couldn't see it. His clothes, or what were left of them, had been reduced to rags.

Bibi stirred. *Thankfully.* The thought of dragging him any farther was daunting and carrying him was out of the question.

He shot up to a sitting position. "What happened?"

"Stay down." He motioned. "The storm is in front of us. Give it a few minutes, then we can catch up with the others."

Bibi grabbed his wrist and drew Scooter toward him. "Something hit me."

"I think it was a can at about 60 miles per hour. You're lucky you've got a thick skull."

Even the fogged goggles couldn't hide the alarm in his eyes as he sat up. "Where is it?"

"What?"

"The chest."

"Out there where you dropped it." He pointed to the bend.

He stood up, a little wobbly and disappeared out of sight.

Scooter waited a few minutes for Bibi to return, lugging the old trunk, but he didn't. He stood and traced the wall's uneven contour back to the opening. The dark brown sky was growing darker. It was only about five o'clock with at least two hours of light remaining. As he cleared the wall, he heard Bibi digging.

"Where is it? I can't find it." He was talking to himself, his voice strained, a pitch higher than normal.

Scooter walked in the direction of his voice.

Bibi sat on his knees, his hands clawing at the sand.

There wasn't any sign of the chest.

Scooter dropped to his knees and began digging. The trunk could easily be buried under four-feet of sand. He had read that smaller storms like those that struck Phoenix periodically could suck up and drop more than 40,000 tons of dirt. No telling how much earth this one moved.

In the distance, the faint yellow glow of four headlights faded. The posse was retreating. They would be back, but they would find nothing. No tracks. No clues. The storm had made sure of that.

Scooter dug near Bibi, but couldn't shake the feeling that something mysterious was connected to this trunk and went far beyond its intrinsic value. Had Zafar stored something valuable in it that Bibi felt obligated to guard with his life? Bibi leaned into a hole a few feet deep, his hands scooping like a backhoe. A pile of sand formed on both sides around him.

"I found it. I found it. Help me dig it out."

Scooter dug furiously around the sides of the wooden cabinet until there was enough room for Bibi and him to wrap their hands around it. They lifted the chest from its sandy grave.

Bibi stroked the cabinet blasted to virgin wood in several places. He removed his goggles and wiped at the dark rings around his eyes.

"It was my mother's dowry chest. She was so proud of it. It's the only thing of hers that remains."

Scooter nodded.

When they turned back to the path through the hills, there was no trace of Zafar or the tribe.

"We're lost," Scooter said.

"There's only one way through these hills. We'll catch Zafar when he stops for the night."

Scooter followed Bibi as they pressed forward, walking for hours until exhaustion and blinding darkness stopped them. The storm had not only swept away everything in its path but the moon and stars as well.

And there was no sign of Zafar or the tribe.

CHAPTER FORTY-TWO

Istanbul, April 16

"I don't trust her," Rashid said.

"You don't trust anyone." Yasin pressed the phone to his ear to mute the wind.

"I trust Allah and you."

"Allah, I believe. I'm not sure about me," Yasin sniggered.

He leaned against the railing, and studied the blue-green water lapping against his dock. It was nice to be back home. The wind was picking up, forming white caps farther out. A large Russian tanker carrying oil moved through the channel.

He wished Rashid were here. It had been several months since he had seen him. But it wasn't possible. Someday, they would be united again.

"She tried to kill Abassi," Rashid said.

"She wanted to, but she didn't."

"How do you know she won't try the same with you?"

"Why would she? She had a reason to kill Abassi."

"She has a reason to kill you too. She just doesn't know it yet."

Yasin pulled the phone from his ear and double-checked the switch to ensure the security shield that provided a sophisticated layer of encryption was activated. "She won't find out."

"Why take the risk?"

"I enjoy her company." But it was more complex than that. He felt a connection to Courtney that Rashid would never understand.

He had from the first time they met. He wasn't sure he understood it. It was more than attraction. Like a bond, not dissimilar to what he felt when he met Rashid, the cousin of Sulaiman Hadid, the leader of Mahdi's Chosen. Hadid died in the pandemic, but through him, Yasin found Rashid. Destiny brought them together. Perhaps, it was at work again.

"Is she going to stay with you?" Rashid huffed.

"She's already here."

"You should have let the Iranians have her."

"Why would I give them the satisfaction of making a spectacle of her? I know you're looking out for me, and I appreciate it. But I'm not worried."

"She's a Jew."

"Is that what this is about? She's only half Jewish."

"A Jew is a Jew. Why pick a Jew when you can have your pick of the world's most beautiful Arab women?"

The phone seemed to empower his friend. He would not have made the statement if he were standing in front of him. "Careful. I gave your life back to you, but I can take it away."

The line went dead. Yasin put the phone in his shirt pocket. They were a good team, even when they disagreed. They complemented each other's weaknesses. Rashid was a spiritual man, who spent a great deal of time studying the Qur'an and Hadith.

Religion had never interested Yasin. He understood politics and war. But both power and religion would be needed to build a new Middle East.

CHAPTER FORTY-THREE

Jerusalem, April 16

A slender woman in a fitted green skirt, wide black belt, and white blouse stood in the shade of *The Jerusalem Times* building. She held a cigarette elegantly between her fingers as if she were posing for a photo. Her head was turned toward the outskirts of the city where smoke rose from the recent rocket attacks. Iran and its proxies in Lebanon, the Gaza strip and West Bank were pounding the edges of the city.

Hank crouched between two cars in the parking lot 100-feet away. He had met her once before when he visited Mike Glickman. She was the fashion and entertainment editor.

"Deena," he said loud enough to get her attention. "Over here. It's Hank Jackson." He wanted to wave, but it was too risky. The exterior of *The Times* was lined with security cameras.

His arrival at the newspaper would be unexpected, hopefully a move whoever wanted him dead wouldn't anticipate. No one would be crazy enough to walk into a lion's den crawling with agents. That was his theory at least.

He held his breath, waiting for a response. But she stood there oblivious, enjoying her cigarette.

"Deena, it's Hank Jackson." The second appeal worked. She dropped the cigarette and studied the parking lot. Hopefully, she wouldn't run back inside and alert security that someone suspicious was lurking among the cars. She walked cautiously in his direction.

"Over here."

She found him huddled near a car and stared down at him.

"Hank?"

"Yeah, I know this is weird." He handed her a note. "Give this to Mr. Goldstein."

"What's this about? Are you in trouble?"

"I don't have time to explain, but it involves Mike."

She closed her eyes for a moment. Mike had said they were friends, but maybe it was more. "Do you know who killed him?"

"I'm trying to find out."

"I hope you do. He was a good man and a good reporter." She sniffled and walked back into the building.

Hank made his way through rows of cars, keeping his head low enough so the cameras couldn't spot him. He slipped on a floppy hat that he'd tucked in his back pocket and pulled the brim low to conceal his face, then slipped on a pair of sunglasses. A red patchy beard, that represented a two-week sabbatical from shaving, added to his cover.

He stood and walked out to Romema Street and headed back to the bus station, where he had arrived only minutes ago. He had left Jonas's truck at the station in Beersheba and used the phone there to leave him a message of where the truck was and authorization for a $50 charge against his e-bank for gas. He apologized for taking his truck and told Jonas he was concerned about ZZ's declining health.

The bus station was only ten minutes away, and the best place for meeting with David Goldstein or Goldy, as his colleagues called him. He was the editor-in-chief of Israel's second largest English newspaper.

Despite even more security than *The Times*, Central Bus Station had one advantage: it was jammed with lots of people, which made identifying him difficult. Bus stations were always a bit frenetic, but the explosions rocking the city's perimeter had everyone on edge. Most of the buses were packed with people leaving Jerusalem, with few new arrivals.

Hank walked past the metal detector into the slick, modern structure that looked unlike any bus station in Charlotte or Belize and held his breath as he passed two guards at the entrance. He walked toward the coffee shop and tried to act normal.

"Americano with room," he said to the barrister.

The rich smell of brewing espresso eased his anxiety, which at the moment, swung back and forth between being identified by the guards or stood up by the editor. It was unlikely Goldstein would contact the police, although it was a possibility. As a rule, most newspaper people distrusted the government regardless of where they lived. It was in their blood. The exception was state controlled media. But the possibility the editor would sidestep a meeting with him to avoid any potential confrontation with authorities was very real.

The barrister slid the cup of piping hot espresso toward Hank. He leaned down and inhaled the rich brew. A little bitter. He took a seat where he could watch the entrance for any sign of Goldstein or trouble. It was still hard to believe Mike was gone. He had stepped on a land mine somewhere. What had he uncovered? Truth never came cheaply. It was a reality every journalist who had reported on war or the underworld understood. It was dangerous. Many good men and women died in pursuit of stories they believed the public had a right to know.

A few minutes later, the editor walked into the terminal looking perturbed. Hank removed a paperback from his jacket. He laid it on the table and pushed it to the center of the table where the title could be clearly seen. He had purchased the thriller in a bookstore at the station after his arrival. Goldstein's eyes zeroed in on it. They had only met once and even if the editor remembered him, he wouldn't recognize him with the hat, glasses and beard.

He walked up and took a seat at the table. "I'm on deadline. What's this about?"

Hank leaned in toward Goldstein and dropped his voice. "Do you know why Mike was killed?"

"Police said it was a terrorist."

"I think Mike was murdered, because of something he uncovered connected to the discovery of the Ark of the Covenant under the Dome of the Rock."

"Do you have any proof the ark has been discovered?"

"No, but…"

Goldstein held up his hand. "You're trying to connect random events and make them into something they aren't." He glared. "Mike was one of my finest reporters, and he's gone because someone convinced him to follow a ridiculous lead."

Hank took a sip of the espresso and tried to keep his cool, but the editor was indirectly accusing him of complicity in Mike's death. He sat his cup down. "Could I review Mike's notes?"

Goldstein smirked. "You haven't been listening. There's no story and you're not going to invent one." He pushed back from the table, checked his watch, and stood. "Are we finished?"

"I gave you the first chance."

"What's that supposed to mean?"

"It means I'm going to discover why Mike was killed and let the world know."

"It shouldn't be hard. Look in the mirror."

Hank watched the editor leave the terminal. He looked around. A young woman with long dark hair who looked like Kat passed through the crowd. He stiffened and fought the urge to follow her.

If only it were her. He bent over the coffee cup and tried to repress the grief swelling inside. *Oh God, why did you let Kat die?*

Everything seemed pointless without her—especially this investigation. Maybe, Goldstein was right, and he should abandon the whole idea.

CHAPTER FORTY-FOUR

Negev Desert, April 17

In the distance branches snapped. Scooter crouched and looked for something to hide behind, but the thin landscape offered little cover.

"What is it?" he asked.

"Shh." Bibi removed his gun.

More branches snapped as a jackal howled in the distance.

Bibi spat on the ground. "Bad luck."

The shadow of a camel's hump bobbed up and down. The animal was limping.

The chief stood slowly, his gun still ready. He walked toward the animal and ran his hand down its front legs, then back ones. The camel flinched and raised its left rear leg. Bibi's hand was dark and wet. "It's been shot." He grabbed the hackamore's lead dragging along the ground.

"Who would shoot a camel?"

"It wasn't the target."

Bibi pointed his gun at the animal and fired.

*   *   *

It took two more hours before they found Zafar's tracks. He had turned north at least a mile back at a rocky patch, which is why they had missed him. It appeared the leader had split the caravan into four groups and sent three in different directions. Bibi explained that the decision to split into four rather than three, or five was, because it was the square root of sixteen, which was two times eight, a number considered to be perfect. But beyond the superstition of numbers, the Bedouin wanted to protect his family. Smaller groups meant smaller targets and increased the chances of survival.

Bibi dropped the chest and ran toward a dark image about a hundred feet in front of them. His fists slammed against metal. Dull, hollow thumps broke the desert silence. "This should have been me."

A ruptured, blackened shell took shape as Scooter approached. Bibi's truck. Bodies and animal carcasses lay scattered across parched ground as if they had tried to escape the attack that likely came from above.

"I should have been here to help him," Bibi shouted.

"This is my fault. They wanted me." Scooter's eyes were wet. How many had died because he took a job he shouldn't have? A job that robbed Israel of its most priceless treasure. And now, cost these poor people their lives.

Bibi slammed his fist into the mangled wreckage again and strangled sobs trying to escape.

CHAPTER FORTY-FIVE

Jerusalem, April 18

The front door knob turned. Hank tossed the newspaper on the sofa and stood up. He hadn't seen anyone walk by the living room window. But they could have taken the other staircase and approached from the opposite direction. There was no window on that side of the door.

The knob twisted again. Had he locked it?

Deena stepped inside, the smell of cigarette smoke close behind. "You look like you've seen a ghost." Her eyes were red.

"Just edgy."

A thunderous explosion in the distance shook the apartment building.

"More rockets are getting through." She looked out the front window as air raid sirens screamed. "Just too many rockets for the Iron Dome System."

"It's the best missile defense system in the world," Hank said.

"It is. But it wasn't design to stop a hundred thousand rockets." She shook her head numbly.

"Did you notice anyone following you?"

"No." She sat her purse down on the coffee table.

Deena was mid-thirties with stylish oversized glasses. She looked like she just stepped out of Chanel ad. The chic small yellow and green butterfly tattoo on her arm looked real enough to fly away.

Hank walked to the window and peeked through sheer curtains and surveyed the parking lot below the three-story building. It was empty except for a few scattered cars, which was typical at midday. He had stayed at Deena's place the last few days.

A car pulled into the parking lot. The doors opened slowly. Two elderly women emerged, each carrying a bag of groceries.

Hank turned back to Deena. "Did you get the thumb drive?"

She nodded. "Mike was a bit of a slob. A lovely one, but messy. I had to rummage through his desk for quite sometime before I found it. I kept expecting him to walk in and ask me why I was going through his stuff. Touching his things brought everything back." She brushed at her eyes. "I miss him."

"So do I." But Deena's loss of Mike triggered thoughts of Kat. Thoughts of things he would never hear again until heaven—the rip-roaring laughs that doubled him over even when he didn't know why she was laughing or her goofy animal voices and a million other things she did.

Deena removed a thumb drive from her purse and sat down on the sofa. She slipped it into her notebook. "Let's see what's on it."

Hank sat down next to her. "I think you should leave town for a few days. Get out of Israel."

"Why?"

"This story is too dangerous. I don't want anything to happen to you."

"I have some friends in France."

"That will work."

A car door shut in the parking lot. Hank stood up and walked back to the window. Two men dressed like rabbis got out. He studied them as they walked toward the stairs.

"Do you recognize the men who just pulled into the lot?" Hank motioned Deena toward the window. "Any rabbis live here?"

She walked over and peered out. "Never seen them before."

"How about the car?"

"Don't recognize it."

"Is there another way out of this apartment beside the front door?"

"The balcony. Do you think I was followed?"

"I don't know. Maybe someone is watching your apartment and saw me." He walked back to the computer and removed the thumb drive and put in his pocket.

They walked through the galley kitchen to the balcony. He opened the sliding door and looked at the ground. He tugged the fire escape ladder, but it wouldn't release. And it was definitely too high to jump even with grass below. A tall slender cypress tree stood six feet away.

"Any rope?"

"No."

"Sheets?"

"Yes. "

"Get me four. Hurry."

Hank glanced at the front window. The two older women with groceries stood peering inside. His heart pounded.

"Get in the tub."

The women reached into the sacks and removed two round metal balls. Hank ran toward the balcony.

CHAPTER FORTY-SIX

Negev desert, April 18

Scooter and Bibi spent the entire next day digging graves. Seven of them.

Burying Zafar was the most difficult. Bibi was as tough as they came, but his dusty face was streaked as he placed what remained of his uncle in the ground.

"My men would never do this." He shoveled dirt over Zafar's body. "And it isn't Shin Bet. They would never attack Israeli citizens."

"Are you sure about that?"

"I used to be."

"If it not's Shin Bet, then who is it?"

"Someone who believes they are above the law. The only thing we have going for us is they think we're dead. But if they discover the graves, they'll rewind the satellite images and see us."

It wouldn't be hard, because they were working in broad daylight. But Bibi wasn't about to leave Zafar, his favorite wife, two children, and three servants for the jackals and hyenas.

"How long do we have?" Scooter said.

"Hopefully, long enough to get across the border."

They finished the last grave and turned their attention east. Bibi estimated they were approximately 35 miles from the border. They would have to walk.

"Are you going to carry that chest?" It would slow them down, and they needed all the speed they could muster to get to the border before they were spotted.

Bibi looked down at the scarred wooden box on the ground and seemed to consider the question. "No," he said carrying the set over to the only surviving camel. "He's going to carry it."

*   *   *

They rested for a few hours, then started for the Jordanian border. The sun had dropped bringing relief from the scorching heat. The cool air felt good. The only sound as they walked was the rhythmic rubbing of the chest against the camel's saddle.

"How are we going to cross the Jordanian border?" Scooter said. "I'm sure the border is tight because of ISIS."

"We're taking a different route, since the tribe was…" He coughed. "Since there are only two of us. There is a cave that leads to a tunnel extending under the border."

"How do you know about it?"

"The Bedouin have used it for years."

"And you remember where it is?"

"It's been a long time, but I think so."

"Any other options if we can't find it?"

"Sure. Capture."

CHAPTER FORTY-SEVEN

Istanbul, April 18

Z oe stared up at the vaulted bays in the interior narthex of the Hagia Sophia, her eyes wide in childlike wonder. "I didn't think I would ever see this again."

The former church was the first place Zoe wanted to visit after leaving the prison.

"The mosaics are so beautiful. Did you know these were once hidden under plaster for hundreds of years?"

"Why?" Courtney was pretty sure she knew.

"After Constantinople fell to the Ottomans in 1453, they plastered over them. The Muslims wouldn't allow any art depicting figures, especially of Christian saints."

"Who are the two people on either side of Christ in that picture?" Courtney pointed.

"That is Emperor Leo and the other is Empress Zoe."

"A distant relative?" Courtney smiled.

"The closest I ever got to royalty was when King William and Queen Catherine visited New York City while I was there preparing for my trip to Turkey. I saw them drive by in a limousine. The queen waved at me."

The fatigue of prison had faded from Zoe's eyes and with it the thin waif Courtney remembered. New clothes, some make-up, a new hairdo—and freedom had worked wonders.

"You've been so good to me." Zoe smiled at Courtney.

"It was Yasin." He had honored her request. Words were cheap, but he had risked his reputation on her. Not once, but twice. And she loved him for it.

"You fought for me." Zoe grasped Courtney's hand. "Where did you learn to fight like that?"

"There was a YMCA near my house that taught kick boxing. I studied it for many years. I was the only girl so I had to compete against guys."

"I couldn't believe what you did to the Russian."

If only Courtney could have seen the Russian's face when the guards unlocked the cell and told Zoe she was free.

"You're a good friend."

"So are you."

Courtney felt a bump at her shoulder as a slip of paper was pressed into her hand.

She swirled around and searched the crowd. But everyone was staring upward or taking pictures of the icons that still flashed brilliant colors of blue and gold. The basilica, now a museum, was packed. She opened her hand and stared at the slip of paper.

I have information about Yasin Mohammed you need to know. Tell your friend you have to go to the restroom. Come alone.

She looked around the room again. Was this a setup? Had Iran sent someone to kidnap her? Would they try it in a public place? Yasin said she would be safe, but even in this thick crowd someone had identified her. A chill swept over her bare arms. She folded the paper and put it in her purse.

"Are you ready to leave?" Courtney asked.

"We just got here." Zoe looked at her. "What's wrong? You look worried."

"It's nothing. Just a little restless."

"We can go if you want." Disappointment filled Zoe's eyes.

"No, you're enjoying this. I'll head to the little restaurant across the street. Call me when you're ready to leave."

"Are you sure?"

"Of course."

Courtney turned and retraced her steps, studying the face of each advancing tourist, but she couldn't shake the feeling the real danger was behind her. A few minutes later she walked into the Ottoman Palace Restaurant.

She asked for a table with a clear view of the entry. A large oculus poured light into the center of the room leaving the tables along the perimeter of the circular room dark, which was perfect.

A man, dressed in a light tan suit and cheap tie, entered. He was Arab with a nondescript face. A hostess seated him. The man searched the room as Courtney disappeared behind the menu. Had he followed her? Her stomach tightened.

"Can I get you something to drink?" A waiter looked down at her.

"Just a glass of water for now."

The man frowned and left.

As she lowered the menu, the Arab with the cheap tie was gone.

"Don't turn around. Listen carefully."

The voice from the table behind startled her. "Who are you?"

"What I'm about tell you, is to protect you."

"Why should I believe you?"

"Yasin Mohammed has ties to ISIS."

She shook her head. "I don't believe you."

"Keep your voice down." He passed a photo back toward her seat.

She took it and immediately recognized Yasin but not the other man. "Who is the other man?"

"Oma-Murshid, the supreme leader of ISIS."

CHAPTER FORTY-EIGHT

Jerusalem, April 18

Hank searched his pocket for the thumb drive. He emptied both pockets at Dublin's Tavern and found nothing but lint. He checked his shirt pocket. Nothing. He stood and immediately wanted to retrace his steps to Deena's, but it would too dangerous. His sat down and slapped the bar's counter. The bartender spun around and frowned.

"You got a problem?"

"No. Just a bad day."

"Have a drink."

"O'Doul's."

"Sorry. We only serve real beer here."

"Whatever you have on tap."

The bartender filled a glass mug. He placed it in front of Hank.

"This will help you forget," the bartender said.

The drive must have fallen out when he dove off the balcony toward the tree or more accurately, was blown into the tree. He snagged it a few feet short of breaking his neck. He was unharmed except for the ringing in his ears and scratches on his arms and face.

But what about Deena? The last thing he remembered was her diving into the tub. There hadn't been anything on the news about the bombing. That wasn't unusual. The only news anyone cared about was the war. And it wasn't going well. Many of Israel's jets had been lost trying to stop the relentless westward movement of Iran's tanks.

Hank stared down into his mug. He hadn't touched alcohol in years, but maybe the bartender was right, and he needed to forget. Judging by how packed *Dublin's* was, he wasn't the only one. The bar was an authentic looking Irish pub located in Zion Square about midway between the bus station and the Old City.

For once, he didn't care who saw him. A bullet might not be so bad. At least, he could be with his wife. Nothing remained in Israel for him. Without Mike's notes, there was no story. Tomorrow, he would catch a jet back home. Luke had asked him to watch over the church, which meant returning to Belize, but he couldn't. Too many memories. He would get his job back at *The Observer* and try to go on.

A man took a seat next to him. "Tough day?"

Hank lifted his head and glanced at the man. "You here to kill me?"

"What?

Hank took another drink.

"I knew Mike," the stranger said.

Hank set his mug down and turned to the man. "Glickman?"

"Yeah, but I suggest we move to a different place." He nudged his head toward a corner of the tavern.

They both walked to a table and sat.

"All right. You've got my attention. How did you know Mike?"

The man leaned in and whispered. "Not so loud." He was in his thirties with short brown hair and a day-old beard. "Mike was killed because of what I told him."

Hank's pulse quickened. "Who are you?"

"I'm Gordon Koslosky, a Rasab in the IDF, the equivalent of a sergeant major in your army. Two weeks ago when Jerusalem was hit with several suicide bombings, my unit found a tunnel more than a mile long that extended from East Jerusalem to a Palestinian settlement."

"A tunnel under the wall?"

Koslosky nodded. "I called my superior to tell him we were going to blow it. He agreed, but just minutes later before my unit could carry out the demolition, he called back and told me to leave the tunnel. I protested but was told to follow orders or face court martial."

"Why would the IDF want to keep the tunnel open?" Hank shook his head. "That makes no sense."

The soldier hung his head. "Thirty-five more people died because that tunnel wasn't destroyed. So, I did the only thing I could think of and called a reporter."

A loud boom shook the bar. A siren went off. A woman screamed and ran outside. Everyone else stood waiting for another blast that didn't come.

"The siren was a little late," the soldier said coolly.

"I'm getting used to the rockets. Can you believe that?" Hank studied the people in *Dublin's* and caught a man at the bar staring at him who quickly turned away. "How many people know about this?"

"Besides my officer and whoever he spoke with, just you and me. But what troubles me is that shortly after I told Mike about the tunnel, he was killed. He told me to contact you if anything happened to him."

"How did you find me?"

"I've been tracking you. I saw what happened at the apartment complex."

"Do you know if the woman who lived there survived?"

He shook his head. "I don't know."

Hank rubbed the scratches on his forehead. "I need to get you on the record. Are you willing?"

The soldier's deep brown eyes look tired like he hadn't slept in days. "I have a wife and two kids. I'm worried about them. I still can't believe the IDF would allow its own people to be slaughtered. But Mike's death wasn't a coincidence. There aren't any in Israel."

"I can keep your name out of the story, but that won't protect you. Your superior will know where the leak came from."

Koslosky studied his rough hands with dirt under the nails. "I'm not willing to see anymore of my people die."

"Good. Now, can I see this tunnel?"

CHAPTER FORTY-NINE

Istanbul, April 18

Courtney couldn't get the photo out of her mind: the dark bullets for eyes. She had run through a dozen different explanations for why Yasin would know Oma-Murshid, the ISIS leader. None were convincing. But then, anything could be photo-shopped.

The spy had spun an enticing promise like a glistening spider's web after a rain: *what I have to tell you will protect you.* But it had nothing to do with protecting her. What he really wanted from her was information on a man who showed no indication of being dangerous or having an affiliation with terrorists. A man who had done so much for her.

"Is this the Christian missionary?" Jakad said. He stood at the top of the stairs in Yasin's chateau.

Courtney shook off the daze. "Yes, this is Zoe."

Zoe stood next to Courtney. Yasin had invited the missionary to stay at his home until she flew back to the states in a few days.

"I hope you've changed your mind about being a missionary in Turkey." Jakad descended the stairs. He was Yasin's guest. Courtney knew little about him.

"What should I say?" Zoe whispered. She looked perplexed.

"The Bible and the Quran both teach that believers should obey the government's laws," Jakad said. "Didn't Jesus say render to Caesar what is Caesar's and to God what is God's?"

Courtney patted Zoe's arm. "She won't be proselytizing. She's leaving for the states in a few days."

Zoe glanced at her shoes and twisted a silver ring with an inlaid cross on her right finger. She said nothing.

"I hope we'll have time to visit before you leave. I'd like to share my faith with you. Who knows, you might even convert." He smiled as he reached the foyer.

Zoe raised her head. Her blues eyes flashed. "Jesus said no one comes to the Father except through me." The meekness of a moment ago was gone.

Yasin had gone to great trouble to get her out of prison, and she had stuck her own neck out as well. So what if Jakad was being confrontational. She frowned and hoped Zoe got it: *Don't say another word.* "I learned long ago to never discuss religion or politics in social settings."

"What else is there besides religion and politics?" Jakad said looking a little surprised.

"Plenty," Yasin said emerging from the elevator. His coal black hair was windswept. He ran his hand through it, brushing back a shock hanging over his eyes. "The Bosphorus is getting choppy."

The river was always choppy, but that never stopped him from zipping his jet boat across it at terrifying speeds. He had taken Courtney out once, which was once too many. She was sick for a day.

"There's art, architecture, literature, music. You'll have to forgive Jakad. His focus is rather narrow—he wants to convert the world to Islam and sharia law."

The man smiled as if pleased with the portrayal.

Yasin looked at Zoe. "You look even younger than Courtney described."

"I'm twenty-one."

"You're quite bold for your age. Traveling to the most Muslim country in the Middle East as a missionary is intrepid. Especially, since trying to convert a Muslim to Christianity is punishable by death here."

"Thank you for what you did. I'm very grateful."

"You're welcome. Now let's talk about something else. Have you seen my library?"

"I was just about to show her," Courtney said.

They all proceeded up the stairs toward the mezzanine. Courtney trailed her hand along the smooth mahogany bannister, polished to a deep luster by thousands of hands during the last 150 years. The chateau was a piece of living history. A Turkish shipping magnate built the estate in the late nineteenth century. Yasin remodeled the interior but preserved the architecturally significant features like the staircase, and rare marble floors. When he reached the top, Courtney and the others followed him through a doorway into a large room filled with books from floor to ceiling.

Zoe let out a low whistle.

"Ten thousand books, many of which are first editions. Yasin walked toward a glass enclosure in the center of the massive library. Under it, was a large book. "Do you recognize this?"

Zoe peered down into the enclosure. "It looks like an antique Bible."

"It's the Gutenberg Bible, the first book printed with movable type. The most valuable book in the world."

"Was it difficult to acquire?" Courtney touched the glass case. *It must have cost a fortune.*

He smiled. "One hasn't sold since 1978. The auction houses say it's worth at least $25 million."

"You have so many books," Zoe said. "Do you collect them as an investment or because you love books?"

"Both. Do you like to read?"

"My favorite thing is cuddling up with a good book on a stormy day."

"Who is your favorite author?"

"Without a doubt, Jane Austen."

Yasin smiled. "You're a romantic."

Zoe blushed.

"I have a first edition of *Pride and Prejudice*. Would you like to see it?"

"Can I?"

Courtney had read the book in high school but found the 19th century novel ponderous. Perhaps she would like it today.

Yasin walked toward a shelf near the entry and picked three books off the shelf. He knew exactly where they were. The library was divided by subject: literature, history, philosophy, science, and so on with each section organized by the author's name.

He handed the three-volume set to Zoe.

She opened the cover of the first book and ran her fingers across the page.

Yasin's charm had eased the tension. He had a way of making a person feel like they were the most important one in the room. But even his considerable charisma couldn't ease the gnawing inside that the agent could be right. There was so much she didn't know about Yasin, a man who was careful about revealing only what he wanted people to see.

Zoe pressed the books to her chest and walked along the library studying the myriad books. She stopped and stared up, scanning the titles. "You have a lot of books on war."

"It's the largest part of my library."

"Why?"

"Epic battles reveal the best and worst in men. What is more interesting than stories of courage, sacrifice and struggle? Did you know more books have been written on war than love?"

Zoe clutched the *Pride and Prejudice* volumes to her chest. "I find that hard to believe."

"It's true."

"How many of these books have you read?" Courtney asked.

"Most of them."

Zoe gasped. "When do you have the time?"

Courtney was wondering the same thing. She'd never once seen Yasin reading, since she arrived at his estate.

"I read a book a day and have for many years."

No wonder he could converse on such a wide variety of subjects. And unlike most people, he didn't seem to forget anything.

"Who do you think was the greatest leader of all time?" Zoe asked.

Courtney held her breath. Is she setting Yasin up? Is she going to say Jesus Christ?

"My, you are full of questions. Most Americans would say it's Abraham Lincoln. Certainly, a great leader. Europeans would say Charlemagne or Richard the Lionheart, maybe even Julius Caesar. They were all exceptional leaders and generals. Muslims would be split over Saladin and Suleiman the Magnificent, two of Islam's greatest leaders. Asians would probably agree on Genghis Khan, whose Mongol empire was the largest in history. There are many others."

"But who do you think was the greatest?" Zoe said. "You've read all these books on war. You must have an opinion."

"The majority of historians believe it's Alexander the Great. He conquered the known world by age 30 and was never defeated in battle. The other is Cyrus the Great, a lesser-known leader. I believe he was greater than Alexander."

Courtney recognized the names, but knew little of military history. Why was Zoe so interested in his answer?

"Cyrus was the king who allowed the Jews to return to Jerusalem and rebuild the temple," Zoe said. "He even gave them the sacred vessels stolen by Nebuchadnezzar."

"You know your history."

"Why do you think he was the greatest leader?"

"The Archaemenid empire Cyrus created was the largest in history until that time. His people called him father and the Babylonians whom he conquered called him the liberator. He believed it was only possible to rule people if they were willing. A very democratic idea when you consider he lived 2500 years ago. Many of his reforms in human rights, government organization, warfare strategies revolutionized the world and had a far more lasting impact than those of Alexander the Great, who by the way, left a fragmented empire after his death."

A cloud passed over the sun, darkening the light filtering into the library from its high windows.

Jakad cleared his throat. "The mullahs have aspirations of recreating Alexander's empire."

"I believe someone will succeed in uniting the world once again, but it won't be the mullahs," Yasin said. "They're cranky old men with outdated ideas. People want to be inspired, not put to sleep."

Jakad chuckled nervously.

"You're right," Zoe said. "They won't win."

CHAPTER FIFTY

Istanbul, April 19

Zoe sat up in bed and shuddered. The remnant of a terrible image still clawed at her consciousness. *What a terrible dream.* She looked out the window at the dark Bosphorus. A golden skin shimmered across the water as a cool breeze eased through the open window. Gentle waves rocked against the dock below. She glanced at the new phone Courtney had given her. It was 4 a.m. She got up, slipped into her robe and flip-flops and peeked out the door.

The bedrooms were on the third floor, ten of them, each with its own bathroom and view of the river. The living room, dining room, and ballroom were located on the main floor where most of the entertaining occurred with the exception of the library off the mezzanine. The kitchen was on the second floor. But the floors didn't go up as in most houses, but down, with each descending the side of a rocky cliff. The exception was the master, which was located above the library, and the study and observatory perched at the very top. The lower floors contained a wine cellar, gym, and pool, although she hadn't seen them.

Everyone was still sleeping. Zoe loved the early morning, before the sun rose, when she could be alone. That was the most difficult part of prison: people corralled like cattle, making a quiet thought impossible. But she was free now, and it felt good. Everyone was expecting her to leave Turkey. But was this what God wanted?

Hadn't she been called to preach to Muslims? Had anything changed? She hadn't contacted her supporters in the states to let them know she was okay, but what would they say? Come home, you're lucky to be alive. Some would. Others would remind her that Muslims needed to know how much God loved them. But if she were caught again, she would be executed.

She walked down the long hallway, the only sound the clip clop of the thongs. Drawings by Da Vinci of the human body lined the walls and seemed to twist and move in the dim light.

She stepped gingerly up the staircase, each movement producing a moan as if the ancient wood was not ready for her weight. She arrived at the mezzanine and walked into the library. A dusty, woody scent mixed with a hint of vanilla greeted her. She breathed in the welcome aroma of old leather. The glare of outside spotlights intruded through high narrow windows striking the dark wooden sentinels casting jagged shadows across the books like a claw. *Creepy.* Zoe turned on the lights and adjusted them to low.

As she stared at the endless rows of books, a section stood out. Religion and Philosophy. It was still hard to believe Yasin had read most of the books. If she began reading now, it would take a couple of lifetimes. There were dozens of Bibles. One of them looked particularly old. What if it was John Wesley's or maybe it belonged to Jonathan Edwards? As she removed the bible, the book next to it fell from the shelf, thudding to the floor, shattering the silence. She picked it up. *The Secret Doctrine* by H. P. Blavatsky. She replaced the book. Next to it was a book called *Confessions of Aleister Crowley.* She wasn't familiar with either. She replaced it and pulled another called *The Book of Fallen Angels.* She flipped through the pages. There was a note penned in the margin of one page: *Shemyzaz is real. I've met him.* She read down the page and shuddered. Shemyzaz was a powerful angel who was the leader of the watchers. Some claimed he was Satan. She closed the book and returned it to the shelf.

A draft of cool air brushed against the back of her neck. She turned toward the bookcase on the eastern wall. Was she seeing things? It appeared the cabinet was separated from the wall like a door someone had forgotten to close. She walked to the bookcase and poked her head through an opening. It was pitch black. In the distance, faint, strange words emanated. Where were they coming from?

She slipped behind the bookcase and groped for something to grab. She found a metal railing. It appeared she was at the top of a staircase, but it was too dark to know for certain. Maybe she should turn back? But echoes of alien verses beckoned. She descended the spiral staircase, carefully planting each foot on the metal steps, leaving behind the last vestiges of light.

"Lak shama abasha luk hora." Muted, guttural words floated through cool damp air. She reached the bottom. The ground was wet. Water trickled down walls on either side. She stepped gingerly on gravel, which sounded like broken glass, each footfall trumpeting her arrival. She stretched her hands out in front, like a sleepwalker, and moved toward the incantations and into a darkness that pressed her from all sides.

"Melahe maak ha hosha lama meh. Halo deshame."

The words were unfamiliar. She could generally pinpoint the origin of most languages. There were traces of guttural Hebraic overtones, and many of the words sounded Aramaic, similar to some of the prayers she had heard by Syrian Christians. But that's where the similarities ended. As she moved deeper into the cavern, the chanting became more intense.

"Lak shama abasha luk hora. Melahe maak ha hosha lama meh."

Ahead, dim lights flickered, and a sweet, smoky fragrance filled the air. She moved back into the shadow of the cave's wall. She should leave, but she needed one small glimpse. Crouching, she advanced slowly.

A haze drifted from what appeared to be a room carved from stone. She slid along the base of the wall to the opening. Glowing candles, dozens of them, seemed to undulate behind a smoky veil. The chanting intensified like a crescendo.

A shiver swept over her. *Get out. Get out now!* Something moved in the thick smoke, and as much as she wanted to run, she couldn't.

"Maak heh roja toleh." It sounded like Yasin's voice. Was she hearing things?

He kept repeating the phrase over and over, like a needle stuck on an old vinyl record.

"Maak heh roja toleh."

Roja was red in Spanish. But the rest of the statement was undecipherable.

Something in the middle of the room began to glow, revealing the luminescent outline of something very tall. Smoke swirled around it like bees buzzing a beehive. Then, a creature emerged from the haze clothed in a brilliant white robe. Light spun off him in radiant bursts like exploding flares from the sun. The whole cave lit up. The man, whose back was to her, threw himself to the ground before the angel.

Zoe was about to do the same, but suddenly, the angel turned and stared at her. He looked surprised at first. Then, a scowl fell across his face. His golden eyes, which looked like two pieces of scintillating amber, turned black as coal. She gasped. His beautiful face morphed into the scaly visage of a serpent, and a long, forked tongue slid out of his mouth and snapped back.

Zoe ducked back around the entry, her heart beating so loud it sounded like pounding at a door. She scrambled to her feet and sprinted blindly through the dark toward the staircase. Where was the staircase? Her lungs ached as she pumped her legs harder. Had she taken a wrong turn?

She stopped, pressing her body against the cool, wet cavern wall. Water trickled down her hot face. The staircase had vanished, and she was lost. And footsteps were approaching.

CHAPTER FIFTY-ONE

Near the Israel-Jordan border, April 19

"Is this it?" Scooter stepped around a lone tamarisk tree obscuring the entrance to a cave, which was easy to miss. The slim opening was a diagonal slit between two rocks barely wide enough for a man. He turned sideways and slipped inside. A slant of light from outside revealed a narrow tunnel ahead with smooth walls of striated, milky limestone, the work of an ancient river.

Bibi stood at the entrance with his arms wrapped around the chest. "It's a been a long time since I've been here, but this is it." The trunk would not fit through the cleavage in the rock or the tight tunnel ahead. Bibi knew this, but his eyes signaled he wasn't ready to let go of the heirloom.

He placed the box on the ground near the tree, ran his hand across the rough, sandblasted wood. "Mom loved this chest. It reminded her of happier times, when she was young and pretty." He opened the top and ran his hand across the wood inside. He fiddled with a side panel and finally removed it, revealing a hidden compartment. "This is where she kept her silver coins." It was empty. He took a deep breath and patted the chest. "I'll be back for you."

Bibi swatted the camel to leave, then squeezed himself into the opening, and grunted as he strained to push his body between the two slabs of stone. He stood and brushed dirt from his clothes.

"How many people know about this tunnel?" Scooter said.

"You mean besides the Bedouin?"

"Yeah."

"Thirty years ago it was just Zafar and a few other tribes. Who knows now? But it's obscure and remote, so probably very few."

The thought of being the first archeologist to visit an unknown tunnel spiked Scooter's endorphins. If only he had time to explore, but their provisions were meager and insufficient for the 120-kilometer journey to Amman. They had scavenged what they could from the victims: water, dates, nuts, some dried lamb, but it wouldn't last more than a few days. They also had gathered some batteries, flashlights, matches, rope, Zafar's AK47, and some ammo. And Bibi had his Sig Sauer automatic.

They crouched as they entered the tunnel, which was no more than four-feet high. A lizard zipped down the sloping path in front. "He knows the way," Scooter said.

The path declined for the next half hour and with it the temperature. "It's colder than a frosted frog down here." Scooter zipped up his jacket. The tunnel finally leveled out fifty to sixty feet underground before splitting into two passages. "Okay chief, which way?"

Bibi furrowed his brow as he looked left, then right. "Let's go this way. It looks like it heads east."

Scooter removed his Leatherman and unfolded a blade. He carved SF into the soft stone. He put the tool back into his pocket. "I feel a little bit like Professor Liedenbrock.

"Who's that?"

"A geologist who wanted to find a path to the center of the earth."

"Did he?"

"Yeah, but I hope we're not as lucky."

The right tunnel was even narrower and so low in some places they were forced to crawl.

Bibi said, "I've been in some tight spots, but this…"

"Is tighter than a frog's butt," Scooter said.

"What is it with you and frogs?"

"Come to Texas and you'll understand."

They traveled at least another hour until the tunnel divided again. This time into three paths.

"This is getting complicated," Scooter said. "Which way now?"

Bibi's dark unibrow buckled. "I don't remember any of this. Everything looks different."

"Well, I hope your memory improves soon, because if these tunnels keep multiplying, the odds of finding the right one out are slim."

They chose the left channel this time and continued forward. It was higher in this section and the ceiling gradually increased the farther they went, until they could stand upright. Scooter stopped and stretched his back. He ran his hand across the wall's rough edges. He looked closer. "This tunnel is man-made."

"This isn't the right way. I've never seen any of this."

"Chief, I'm beginning to think we've been going the wrong way since we crawled into this hole."

A broken clay pot lay on the floor near their feet. Scooter stooped down to inspect. The handle was missing. He picked it up. There was a hole in the center and another smaller opening at the opposite end. "The Jews poured olive oil in these and used them as lamps. Looks like someone was as lost as we are."

They walked a few more feet until the tunnel ended abruptly.

"That's strange. Why did they dig this far and stop?" Bibi said.

The real question was why anyone was down here? There was no evidence of mining. So what were they doing? And why did they suddenly abandon this section? They retraced their steps to the junction.

"Wait a minute," Scooter said. "Let's go back. I want to check something." They turned around and walked back to the dead end.

He flashed his light at the wall in front of them. He hadn't imagined it.

"What is it?" Bibi said.

"See these lines?"

Bibi squinted. "Kind of."

"We may have just solved the mystery of why the digging stopped."

Bibi scrunched his face up as he examined the cracks in the wall.

"They were finished," Scooter said.

"With what?"

"These ancients were clever people." Scooter pointed at the wall. "Help me push."

They both pushed against it, but it was as unmovable as it looked. "I think this is a wall of fitted stones, cut as cleanly as the pyramids' blocks. Someone blocked this area."

Bibi motioned Scooter away from the wall. "Let me give it try."

He backed away from the wall. He lowered his shoulder and ran at it like an angry bull, punching two blocks inward.

"You're right. There's something behind here."

Bibi took another run at it and this time, the wall collapsed into a cave below.

"Remind me, to never make you mad," Scooter said.

A cool, musty breeze wafted from the interior. Scooter's pulse pounded. He flashed his light down into a cavern. It reflected on a pool of dark water in the center, probably fed by an underground spring like the one under the Temple Mount. He moved his light slowly around the interior. There were dozens of large stone jars and several clay pots.

"What is this place?" Bibi peered around Scooter's shoulder.

"I don't know, but I intend to find out."

"We don't have time for this."

"Look chief, this could be an important discovery. It doesn't look like anyone has disturbed it since it was abandoned. I can't date it, but it's old."

"I should have known better to climb in here with an archeologist."

Bibi wrapped the rope around his waist and braced himself as Scooter climbed over the side and slid down. "Have you got me?"

"I got you, but just remember I have the rope, and I may decide to leave your butt down there if you take too long."

Scooter slid down the rope to the bottom, which was at least 20 feet. The cave was larger than it appeared. He stepped over rocks from the fallen wall and walked to what looked like a hole in the cave's ceiling and flashed his light upward. A shaft of some kind. He couldn't tell how far it extended, but he felt a breeze. *I'll be darned. A ventilation shaft.* Below it were charred stones. This is where they cooked their meals.

He removed the lid to one of the stone jars and pointed his light into it. Dark discoloration on the sides and bottom. A wine container.

He removed the top to one of the pots nearby. It was filled with small donut sized clay discs. "I wish grandma could see this."

"See what?"

Scooter held up a disc with cuneiform writing. "This has to be 2500 to 3000 years old." He walked to each of the jars. They were filled with the same round clay tablets. Hundreds of them. He checked his phone. *Dang.* The battery was low. He took several photos of the tablet, then swung his light around the room and stopped. What looked like a large vault was carved into the side of the cave. He walked closer. Unlike a tomb, this chamber wasn't filled with sarcophagi containing bones but dozens of neatly stacked scrolls. He scanned the cavern. "Do you know what this place was?"

"An archeological goldmine for Israel."

"It's an ancient library." Scooter pointed toward the stone tables along the perimeter of the room. That's where the scribes worked.

The cuneiform tablets are part of their collection. I'll bet those scrolls are as old as Qumran, maybe older. Which means they are worth a bloody fortune."

He removed a scroll and unrolled the stiff vellum carefully. He photographed several sections of it, then replaced the scroll.

Bibi said, "They belong to Israel. They aren't yours, and you can't sell them."

Scooter looked up at Bibi and glared. But he was right. This wasn't a nose ring, or bracelet, or cache of coins. This find could be as important as the ark. Scooter's attempt to cash in on the artifact had ended badly. What advice would his grandma give him? She was half Creek Indian and grew up in Oklahoma before there were cars. She'd been dead for 25 years but her words were still strong and true: *I want you to listen good, son. In my day they shot horse thieves. No good comes from stealing anything unless you need to eat. And you've got plenty of viddles. So get along.*

"You're right. They belong to Israel. But we need to find out exactly what they are. I know an antiquities broker in Damascus who can tell us and how much they are worth."

Bibi shook his head. "I'm not going to Damascus. The city is crawling with ISIS. Besides, we don't need to know what they are worth. Just turn them over to Israel."

Scooter still felt bad about not getting back to Johnny Naziri. He might still be at the Egyptian border waiting for him. But he didn't dare use a phone. Even turning it on to take photos was risky, but he needed to document the find.

"Okay. Once we get to Amman, I'll call Johnny and send him photos. He brokers antiquities for ISIS." Johnny would forward the photos to friend Moshe Abrams at Hebrew University, who would provide a translation and rough dating. And perhaps Israel would pay at least a finder's fee.

"You have some interesting friends. A broker for ISIS? No wonder trouble follows you."

"He can be trusted. I've worked with him many times through the years."

"I'll bet you have."

CHAPTER FIFTY-TWO

Istanbul, April 19

Footsteps drew closer. Zoe's heart thumped so hard she could barely breathe. Whoever was approaching, would surely hear. But the man walked past her like she didn't exist. *Thank you, Lord.*

His face was difficult to see in the dim light. He walked fast like he knew the way.

She shuddered. The serpentine visage still clung to her. What was it?

Zoe waited for the man to pass. But he stopped and turned as if he had heard something. She held her breath and didn't move.

He walked toward her. She bolted, running as fast as she could in the opposite direction. The candlelight of moments earlier has disappeared submerging the cave in total darkness. She slammed into a wall, knocking her down and the air from her lungs. She sat up trying to catch her breath.

"What are you so afraid of?" The voice was Yasin's.

"I'm not afraid."

But her entire body shook. She wrapped her arms around herself.

"I'm cold." The truth was she was terrified of what she'd seen and being trapped in a subterranean hideaway where no one would ever find her.

"How did you get in here?"

"The door was open."

"Do you always walk into a room if the door is open?"

"I heard strange chanting. I wanted to find where they were coming from."

"And did you?"

"Someone was speaking in what sounded like some dialect of Aramaic or Hebrew. I don't think it was either." *It was you.*

Her eyes were adjusting to the dark. A faint image of his face peered down at her.

"Why were you running?"

Should she lie? Her voice quavered. "I was lost and afraid of being trapped."

"And nothing more?"

She buried her face in her hands. "I just want to go home."

Was it possible it wasn't Yasin in the room with the demon? No, it was him. He knew. A cold waft of air swept across his skin as a scripture came to mind.

She needed to warn Courtney.

CHAPTER FIFTY-THREE

Jerusalem, April 20

The reflection of a stranger stared at Hank from the glass door of *The Times*. He pulled his hat a little lower and stared at the bearded image, which was still novel. As he reached for the door handle, an explosion in the distance shook the ground. He grabbed the knob and steadied himself. A crimson-stained wedding dress, crushed white calla lilies, and Kat's limp body swept before him.

"Hank, is that you?" The voice was familiar.

He opened his eyes to see Deena standing behind the glass door. He mustered a smile.

She opened the door and hugged him. "I've been so worried about you."

"I'm glad to see you too. I heard you were in the hospital and wanted to see you, but under the circumstances, it wasn't possible."

"You saved my life. That was enough." Her smooth olive skin was marred with scratches. The dark bruise on her right hand looked painful.

"The bathtub saved you."

She smiled. "Why are you here?"

"I came to see Goldstein."

"He's not in a very good mood today."

"Neither am I."

"Well, it should be an interesting meeting. He's in his office, kvetching over being scooped by *The Jerusalem Post*. Come with me."

The editor was standing, fixated on the front page of *The Times* spread across the top of his large desk. He was in his late thirties, young for an editor-in-chief. He wore oval-shaped glasses and a bow tie, reminiscent of Hank's editor at The Charlotte Observer. The glasses intensified deep-set brown eyes that were blood shot.

Bold headlines declared: *Golan Heights May Fall*. Hank had read the story. An anonymous high-ranking Israeli general said the burning oil fields, which could be seen 220 miles above the earth, and Russian tanks were making defense of the Heights especially difficult. He admitted the IDF might not be able to hold the ground much longer. The Times led with a story on the war as well, but completely missed the game-changing development to the north.

Hank stood at the closed door and knocked.

"Good luck," Deena said as she scooted back to her desk.

Goldstein looked up with a scowl on his face. Was he still seething over blowing a story or did he recognize Hank? The editor waved him in.

"Who are you? And what do you want?"

"Jackson. I wanted to give you another chance at an exclusive. It's only right that the Times publishes this story, since it cost Mike his life."

"Is this the same crazy idea you pitched before?" he growled.

"Mike's source is credible and on the record. I have photos to back up his claim." Hank opened his satchel and spread half a dozen photos of a tunnel over the top of *The Times* article.

"Mike found a tunnel terrorists have been using to launch attacks in Jerusalem. The IDF is aware of the passage, but has not destroyed it. According to Mike's witness, orders were given to leave the tunnel."

Goldstein studied the photos. "Who is Mike's source?"

"He's IDF."

The editor pointed at the photos. "This is East Jerusalem. Are you sure this is for real?"

"I have seen it with my own eyes."

The editor looked up and motioned for Hank to sit. "Go on."

"There are two wars being fought in Israel. The obvious one and the secret one, which may be just as destructive. This tunnel proves that people high up in the IDF and most likely, in the government, believe the sacrifice of innocent Israelis is justified."

Goldstein sat down, propped his elbows on his chair, and folded his hands. "Justification for what?"

"There is a hidden sector within Israel's government that believes the only path to peace is by breaking the will of the Israeli people."

"Seems like an odd time to try to convince Israelis to pursue peace when there is a war going on. Do you have any proof of this?"

"Not yet, but I know someone who does?"

"Same source?"

"No."

The editor stood and paced. "Does this soldier understand the crap this story is going to unleash, particularly against him?"

"He does."

"If we run the story, the IDF will deny the soldier's claim, destroy the tunnel, and fire some people. And that will be that. But if your assumption is true, then the real story is not the tunnel but the people behind it. If you find another source within the IDF or government who confirms the story—I'll run it."

CHAPTER FIFTY-FOUR

Istanbul, April 20

Z oe's bedroom was empty. The tattered suitcase that sat on the chest the day before was gone. A hastily scribbled note from the missionary lay on the dresser. It said her father was very ill, and she had to leave immediately. She apologized for not saying good-bye, but it was the middle of the night. She would call when she arrived in the states.

The sky was overcast and a light drizzle rapped at the window. She sat on Zoe's bed and tried to make sense of her sudden departure. Zoe wouldn't leave without saying goodbye regardless of what time of night it was. Just as troubling was she had never spoken of her parents, only her brother.

An empty feeling as bleak as the gray sky crept inside. Zoe reminded her of Taylor, the little sister she'd lost. They were about the same age with similar ambitions. Both wanted to change the world: Taylor by working with underprivileged kids and Zoe by saving souls. Zoe's disappearance was a fresh reminder of Taylor's loss. Who was responsible? Jakad didn't like the missionary. Was he to blame? Or was it Yasin?

Yasin peeked into the room through the cracked door.

Courtney jumped.

"Are you all right?"

She couldn't force a smile. "I can't believe Zoe would leave without saying good bye."

He glanced at the note on the dresser. "She left me one on the dining table. I'm just as surprised. She must have taken a cab to the airport. My driver would have taken her, if she had asked."

He walked over and sat on the bed next to Courtney. "I'm sorry."

He was too close. But moving away would be too noticeable. "Looks like you're headed somewhere important." He was dressed in a custom-fitted black suit, crisp white shirt and red silk tie.

"Headed to Riyadh. I have another meeting with leaders. We're close to finalizing details on the nation and framework for a constitution. We may even get to the subject of who will guide the government."

"Won't the people decide?"

"The first president will be elected by the members."

"When are you coming back?"

"I don't know. It depends on how quickly everyone agrees on the remaining issues. By the way, could you do me a favor and stop by the market and pick up some curry? A friend of mine has a spice booth with the best curry this side of India. His name is Momar and his stand is called *Spices of the World*. It's located in the middle of the Grand Bazaar. Do you mind?"

"Not at all. It will be nice to get out."

"When I return, I'd like to talk to you about a position with one of my companies." He reached over and pulled her toward him and kissed her lightly. "I'll see you when I return. By the way, Jakad is leaving today."

He stood and turned around. "Are you sure you're okay? You look a little pale."

"I'm fine. Good luck today. Hurry back."

Yasin walked out of the room. She stood and walked to the rain-streaked window. Below, a black limousine sat in front of the estate. After a few minutes, the driver got out with an umbrella and walked around and opened the rear door and waited as Yasin and

Jakad stepped from the house into the car. The driver shut the door and walked back around. Jakad stared up at her through the car's window as the vehicle drove away. An odd smirk was on his face as if he knew something she didn't.

Courtney shuddered. She needed to find Zoe, and she had a sense there wasn't much time.

CHAPTER FIFTY-FIVE

Grand Bazaar, Istanbul, April 21

A sharp aroma redolent of chili and saffron wafted through the Grand Bazaar. Crowds of people pushed through walkways lined with booths. Merchants stood in front of their leather goods, jewelry, ceramic bowls, carpets, and trinkets of every kind and beckoned shoppers.

"Here, come here." A bearded man with a belly, that strained the fabric of his robe, waved Courtney toward his display of leather purses and bags. "Look at this quality. Soft leather." He caressed the bag like it was his favorite cat.

She shook her head, but the man persisted.

"Bargain prices."

Won't hurt to look. She walked toward the booth.

"Touch it." He shoved a bag with an animal print at her.

"Look at the stitching. Nothing cheap. Only finest."

The purse reminded her of the knockoffs along Canal Street in New York City: all glitz and no ritz.

"No thank you."

The man wrapped his fleshy hand around her wrist and pulled her toward another rack of purses. He pressed his face close; his breath smelled of onions.

"The very finest. Italian." He removed a dark leather shoulder bag from an overhead rack with a pole and lowered it into his hands. He stroked the satchel as if coaxing it to purr.

Courtney patted her Louis Vuitton tote. "This is more my style." She regretted the pretentious statement, but the hawker had provoked it. She didn't like being grabbed and particularly by strangers.

She left the booth and pressed deeper into the undulating mass of people.

Buckets of green, yellow, red, and brown spices, some ground as fine as flour, filled a stand. A wiry man held a small cup of viscous Turkish coffee. He swept his hand over the display in a graceful gesture as if he were presenting royalty. She checked the booth's moniker. *Bombay Spices.*

"Finest spices in Turkey."

The vendor's gesture swept a waft of fiery red chili upward. It tingled in her nose. Most of the spices she recognized: mint, curry, saffron, and ginger. But some were new, like urfa chilies, which looked like shiny bits of purple coal.

Yasin said his friend's booth was about half way through the market. But she had no idea where she was in the sprawling complex.

"Do you know where *Spices of the World* is?"

He frowned, rubbing the scraggily hair on his chin. "We have best spices. What you want?" He picked up a handful of yellow turmeric and sniffed it. "You want the best, you buy here."

"I want to know where *Spices of the World* is?"

The vendor threw his hands up as if he had no idea where his competitor was located.

"Fine." She walked on passing several other booths. She had hoped a stroll through the market might provide time to sort things about, which were becoming complicated. There was no logical explanation for Zoe's disappearance other than the troubling conclusion that Jakad or Yasin were involved. But the press of strange people against her, the bitter smell of tannin, and the exhortations of vendors crowded her mind.

A young kid stuck an amulet in her face. "This keep you safe."

She took a step back.

"Protect against the devil," the thin teenager said in his best English as he dangled the amulet in front of her.

An eye in the shape of a teardrop was centered in a round, cobalt blue piece of ceramic. It swayed gently from a tarnished chain. Several necklaces hung from a rack behind the kid. She had seen a number of people in the market wearing something similar. Recent news of several murders in Turkey by allegedly demon-possessed people had everyone spooked. And a recent cable show reported the Catholic Church was being overrun by requests for exorcisms.

"I don't believe in the devil."

The kid glanced at someone behind her. She turned and caught a man in a suit and tie at a copperware booth staring at her. He abruptly turned away, denying her a look at his face. A shiver rippled across her warm skin. The temperature in the covered market was uncomfortably hot, several degrees warmer than outside, no doubt from the shoulder-to-shoulder crowd packed under thousands of overhead lights.

The dark young man, who was no more than sixteen, dangled the amulet in front of her. "Without this, someone will…How do you say…lanet etmek?" He paused, searching for the right words in English. Turkish, which most everyone spoke in Istanbul, sounded more Eastern European than Middle Eastern. "Put a curse on you."

She was exasperated. "How much?"

He grinned. "Good deal. Only $200,000."

Courtney knew without looking at her phone that her funds were low. "Too much."

The kid stared at her purse like he thought she was lying.

"Like I said, I don't believe in the devil—or curses."

The boy's dark eyes dropped.

"All right, how about $50,000? That's it." She was a sucker for kids selling things.

The boy's face brightened.

She hung the blue charm around her neck at the boy's urging. It looked tacky. But it put a smile on his face. She had never been superstitious or troubled by the idea of curses, never even thought about them. But given her track record the last few weeks, it would be hard to make the case she didn't need all the help she could get in the luck department.

The boy passed a small wand over the top of her hand. A moment later a wizened man tottered out from behind a curtain at the back of the booth and handed Courtney a receipt. He glanced at the amulet the boy had handed her and nodded, then glanced in the direction of a booth selling jewelry.

She turned around. A man in a suit left the booth and merged into the crowd. From behind, he looked like the same man she had seen earlier, but she couldn't be sure. Was she being followed?

She turned back to the old vendor. "Do you know where *Spices of the World* is?"

He grinned. His worn, yellowed teeth framed by dark lines looked like kernels of dried maize. He pointed down the crowded lane. "Very close."

"Thank you."

As she stepped into the throng, a policeman shouted. Suddenly, someone slammed into her, knocking her to the ground. A young man's wild eyes stared down at her. Clutching a purse, he sprinted away as the police pursued.

Someone helped her up. She felt faint and needed fresh air. Where was the exit? It was difficult to see anything with so many people. The tourists and locals who had momentarily deserted the main thoroughfare flowed back into it as quickly as water from a broken levee.

She searched for a way out, then gasped. The man she had seen at the copperware booth stood in front of her. She recognized him— he was the agent from the restaurant near the Hagia Sophia.

"We need to talk."

"You've been following me. What do you want?"

"Let's walk."

"Where are we going?"

"Just walk."

After a few minutes they emerged from the bazaar. The agent pointed toward a black Suburban across the street. "We can talk there."

CHAPTER FIFTY-SIX

Ten Miles west of Ramat Hovav, April 21

A shofar was blowing somewhere. The sonorous sound alternated between high and low notes. But as pleasing as the vibrant tone was, it was a warning.

ZZ startled awake. Was it a dream?

The room was dark, but he recognized the faint shape of the marlin on the wall, Jonas's prized catch. He sat up in the chair and pushed himself to a standing position. His legs were wobbly. The shofar blew again. Who was blowing it? He walked to the front door and opened it. The sun was setting and a dry breeze brushed his face. The sound was coming from outside, but there wasn't a person in sight. He closed the door. The trumpet's sound rang filled the house. He went back to his recliner and sat.

Only God could produce a sound that could be everywhere at once. The priests had used the shofar to announce festivals and at worship in the Temple. But there wasn't any festival to announce and no Temple for its use. This had to be a warning. ZZ's chest tightened, but it wasn't his failing heart this time.

He bowed his head. "Elohim, I hear the trumpet blowing. Is there something you want to tell me or have me do? I am an old and not much use anymore, but I will do whatever you ask."

ZZ looked up, his eyes sweeping the living room. Jonas was a man whose mantra was never buy anything new if something used will do. His furniture was a collection of worn pieces but comfortable. His vehicles were old but ran. His television was at least 30 years old and the picture a little dim, but it still worked. His t-shirts had holes but no one could see them under his shirt.

ZZ fixed on a calendar sitting on the kitchen counter provided by an insurance agent. Today was April 21. The Knesset's winter session had been extended because of the war. An anxious feeling gripped him. A prompting. He felt it 40 years ago when Jehovah God directed him toward rabbinical school. He couldn't explain the urgency then, and he couldn't now.

But he was certain of one thing: he needed to go to Jerusalem.

CHAPTER FIFTY-SEVEN

Tel Aviv, April 21

The windows of the Matcal tower, the Ministry of Defense building, seemed to turn from green to red, in the furnace of the afternoon's sun. How much heat could they absorb before cracking? Hank wiped the sweat from his forehead and moved into the shade of a store selling cell phones. Not even an ocean breeze today. He checked his watch. The colonel should have been here by now if he was coming. Asking for a meeting was a gamble, but he had nothing to lose. He had already lost everything.

A white sedan pulled into the parking lot of the strip center near Weizman Street. The window rolled down. It was difficult to tell who was driving. Hank was reluctant to move out of the shadows until he knew for sure. The headlights blinked on and off three times. He quickly walked to the car and got in.

"What's this all about?" Saul Ganz said.

"Get onto Route 1."

"If you wanted a taxi, you should have called one. We're not going anywhere until I know what this is about."

"I have irrefutable evidence the IDF knows the location of a tunnel terrorists are using to launch their attacks on Jerusalem."

Saul stared at him as if the statement meant little.

"Ready to take a drive?"

Saul grunted as he headed toward the expressway.

"I should drive your sorry butt to headquarters and turn you in."

"But you won't."

"And why's that?"

"Because you know about the tunnel. What I want to know is why the military is allowing innocent Israelis to be slaughtered. That would make quite a story."

"You're a dead man if you write that."

"Like Mike Glickman?"

"He was warned just like I'm warning you now."

"What do I have to live for? My wife and best friend are both dead."

"I'm sorry about your wife." The colonel's steely countenance faded, as if he were genuinely sorry.

Hank winced. The mention of Kat resurrected an emptiness that had no bottom. He saw her everywhere and sometimes, even followed women who looked like her from behind, until they turned around. Everyone said it would get easier with time, which meant forgetting her. But he didn't want that. He never wanted to forget anything. If that meant living with this level of grief the rest of his life, so be it.

He took a deep breath. "I've discovered that men without anything to live for are more dangerous." He removed a Glock from inside his pants pocket and pointed it at Saul.

"We're going to have an honest conversation and you're going to tell me the truth. ZZ still thinks of you as a friend, but I'm not sure of his judgment."

"You have no clue what's going on. ZZ is my friend. I've done everything I can to protect both of you. But it's out of my hands. You should have left Israel when I told you."

"I've written a story revealing the IDF knows the location of the tunnel the terrorists are using but has done nothing to destroy it."

"You don't have a story. Just hearsay."

"I have an eyewitness. One of your soldiers."

"I don't believe you."

"It doesn't matter what you believe. If my editor doesn't hear from me within the hour, his instructions are to run the story."

"You have no idea how much damage that will do."

"That's the difference between us. I believe the story will destroy the tunnel and save lives. It will launch an investigation into why the IDF is allowing terrorists to kill Israeli citizens when thousands of soldiers are fighting to save Israel."

"You'll get one or two officers fired. They'll be accused of being Palestinian sympathizers. The tunnels will stop for now, but you'll drive the people behind this more underground. Besides, there is a war that isn't going well. People are more concerned about that."

"Except those dying from the suicide attacks." The facade of limestone government buildings faded into the car's rear window. "Are you part of this group?"

"No."

"Then, tell me who's behind this so we can expose them."

Saul squeezed the steering wheel until his knuckles were white. "It's not that easy. These people are very powerful. What they want isn't bad, it's their methods that are wrong."

"Is this about forcing Israel into a peace deal with Palestine?" Hank touched Luke's cross hanging inside his shirt. Israel had just rejected a new United Nations peace plan before the war began. The Palestinians wanted all borders restored to pre-1967 and control of East Jerusalem. It was a proposal that the majority of Israelis rejected. But the more Israel's security was compromised, the more willing they would be to negotiate.

Saul glanced at Hank, then back at the expressway. "I don't agree with what they're doing. But peace is what everyone wants."

"Then help me stop them."

"They can't be stopped."

"And why not?"

"They're well organized, well funded, and at every level of government."

"A deep state?"

"Call it whatever you like. Where are we headed?"

"You're driving me to *The Times* so nothing mysterious happens, like my rental car blowing up." But Hank had another reason for forcing Saul to drive him back. He wanted Goldstein to see who his corroborating source was.

"I don't have time to drive you to Jerusalem."

Hank motioned with the Glock for him to continue. "Make time."

Saul frowned and grunted.

"Now tell me the truth about what's really going on. What the deep state wants."

Saul sighed. "I'll tell you this: the men who attacked your wedding weren't terrorists. They were hired to kill Mezvinsky. He took Eli's map to protect it from those who would use it for the wrong reason. He knew Eli didn't have much longer to live. Mezvinsky also intended to expose the deep state. Someone found out. I had nothing to do with it. And I'm truly sorry for what happened."

The revelation didn't soften the loss of Kat, and Luke, and the innocents who died that afternoon, but it helped Hank understand why it happened. "Thanks for telling me. I know we've had our differences, but you have to expose these people. They'll destroy everything you've fought for your entire life. You can't let that happen."

Saul scratched the scar on his cheek. "If you agree to not run the story, I'll tell you what I know."

"I can't commit to that. But I won't use your name."

CHAPTER FIFTY-EIGHT

Grand Bazaar, Istanbul, April 21

"Are you sure this is the man who kidnapped you?" Lance Senoski, a CIA operative, pointed to a photo on the screen of his computer.

"How could I ever forget?" Courtney said.

"Farid Al-Enzi has been on our radar for a long time. He's a psychopath, who murdered his daughter, because she allegedly dishonored him by kissing a non-Muslim boy. She was only 14 years old. He's one of ISIS's elite operatives. He and his friends, whom you killed, helped plan several terrorist attacks throughout Europe."

"Too bad I wasn't able to kill him."

"You killed two of ISIS's best. That's pretty good for someone with no experience in killing."

The agent selected another photo, this one of Farid standing next to another man. The photo was grainy, obviously taken from a long distance with a telephoto lens.

"I followed Farid to this abandoned shopping center in a rough part of Istanbul. And the weirdest thing happened. He looked right at me when I took this picture, almost as if he sensed someone was watching him."

Courtney glanced at the photo. The other man looked familiar. "Who is he?"

"Jakad Hussein."

She froze and looked at the photo again. He was right. It was Jakad. She felt sick.

"You see, your boyfriend is a very clever man who is good at covering his tracks," Senoski said. "We can't prove he is directly connected to ISIS, but his friends are. And if he knows Jakad, he knows Farid. And you can put two and two together. What we need is more evidence to nail him. We were hoping you could help us with that."

"You want me to spy for you? I told you at the restaurant I wouldn't. I still won't."

"You're the only one who can prove Yasin's involvement in the Chicago bombing. Everyone thinks it was Iran. It wasn't. It was ISIS."

Courtney's head was spinning and she was nauseous. "I need air."

The agent rolled the window down. "Don't stick your head out."

She bent forward and tried to calm her stomach. But her head still spun.

"Clearly there is a connection between the two men. What more proof do you want?"

"I can't do it. He'll know. I swear he can read my thoughts."

"We believe ISIS is planning something big in Europe. Our intelligence monitoring has been lit up for weeks. We need your help."

She shook her head again. "I can't."

"We're out of time." Senoski handed her a small golden chip, the size of bullion.

She sat up. "What's this?"

"If you change your mind about helping us and saving lives, just wave this over his cell. It will automatically capture all of the data."

"How am I supposed to get his cell? He never goes anywhere without it."

"You're a smart woman. Figure it out. You have a chance to save many lives, maybe millions if they explode another nuke."

The comment stung. The agent knew where to punch. "All right. But I need a favor."

"What?" The agent seemed indignant.

"A Christian missionary named Zoe Nash was staying with me. She left unexpectedly in the middle of the night without any notice. It's very odd. I'd like you to track down her relatives and missionary organization and find out if they have heard from her."

"Okay, we'll see what we can find her. In the meantime, get the data."

CHAPTER FIFTY-NINE

Riyadh, Saudi Arabia, April 21

C rown Prince Abdul Khalid had been talking for at least an hour. But the voices in Yasin's head were making it difficult to concentrate. *You can't trust her. She will betray you.*

He rubbed the scar on his right hand, which had become red and sore the last few days. He received it sixteen years ago when everything changed—when the voices began. He had been on his way to a New Year's Eve party in Monaco.

A spicy scent of frankincense tickled Yasin's nose. It was oozing from the long legged woman sprawled across two seats. She must have bathed in it. He reached across the aisle and ran his hand down her bronze leg. She didn't look familiar or the other people sitting behind him. He raised the window shade and squinted as blinding light pierced the dim interior. From the barren terrain thousands of feet below, they were over a desert. Which one, he had no idea.

The woman stirred. "Hey baby." Slurred words parted pouty, scarlet lips. She raised her hand. It hung in the air, then collapsed in her lap.

He strained to remember who she was, but his head hurt. In the back of the jet someone groaned. It must have been a helluva party. From his suit pants he removed a small box with a Krugerrand embedded in its lid and opened it. He tapped the container. White powder splashed onto the table in front of him. He swiveled the gold top and removed a blade and a telescopic straw. With the razor, he arranged the powder into two narrow lines. He leaned over and inhaled deeply.

"Ah." He pushed a button in the overhead panel. "I need a Bloody Mary. Where are we?"

"Good morning Mr. Mohammed," the captain said. "Crossing Libya now. We should be in Monaco within two hours. The attendant will be right out with your drink."

"Thank you."

Fragments from last night flitted for a moment before slipping away. He looked at his watch. Tonight was New Year's. That much he was certain of. He sank back into his chair. Thank God the year was almost over. The collapse of financial markets as a result of the American mess had drained trillions from bank accounts worldwide, ruining many of his friends. Some had even taken their lives. But he had shifted most of his portfolio into commodities before the crisis. He looked at the woman across from him. What was her name? Did he pick her up in Amalfi or had it been Amman? It was hard to tell. She could pass for Italian or Jordanian.

An ear-piercing alarm shrieked. The door to the bathroom flung open. A man ablaze ran out. From the back of the jet, someone screamed.

Yasin jumped up.

"Help me!" the man cried, his arms flailing as he ran up the aisle.

Yasin grabbed the blanket next to him and threw it over the flaming man, who clawed at it like a bagged cat. He threw the man to the floor and rolled him over.

A sulfurous, charcoal smell rose from his burned body punctuated by something sweet. *Freebasing. What an idiot.* He curled into a fetal position and moaned. His hair was gone leaving only a blackened scalp which looked as if it would slip from his skull with the slightest touch. Who was he? Yasin looked up at the other two passengers in the back. A wiry man rubbed sleep from his eyes. A gorgeous blond sat next to him. *Friends of the hottie across the aisle?*

The co-pilot emerged from the pilot's cabin. "What's going on?"

He stared down at the smoldering figure in the aisle, but his eyes rose toward the rear of the plane.

Yasin turned to see flames pouring from the bathroom, already snaking along the ceiling's belly. "The extinguisher," he yelled, pointing at the cylinder mounted on the exterior of the bathroom.

The wiry man grabbed the canister but quickly let go. "It's hotter than hell." The paint on the cylinder bubbled into dark blisters. An explosion repelled the man backward like a shotgun blast, enveloping the cabin in a white cloud. A series of explosions somewhere above the bathroom shook the jet, rolling it on its side. High-pitched screams and grunts pierced the cabin as passengers were thrown from their seats. A deafening roar sucked everything toward the bathroom. The blonde screamed as she clung desperately to her seat.

"The oxygen tanks must have blown," the co-pilot yelled above the thundering noise. He turned and clawed his way back to the pilot's cabin.

Yasin braced against the vortex dragging him down the aisle. He had to get to the woman. He gripped each seat as he made his way toward her. "Grab my hand," he yelled.

She strained to reach it. The jet righted itself but lurched downward. Yasin tumbled forward past her, missing her outstretched hand. Red nails, dug deep into the leather seat, began to slip. Her eyes pleaded for help. The centrifugal force of the jet's dive pinned him against the floor. In a flash she flew backward still reaching for the seat. She slammed into the frame of the bathroom's door with a thud, her arms and feet splayed on either side, her head wrenched backward by the relentless tornado. With a loud pop, she disappeared.

The fire had spread the entire length of the ceiling. The seat next to Yasin burst into flames. His skin sizzled. The jet shuddered as it pitched into an even steeper descent. He looked up from the floor to see his raven-haired beauty clinging to the seat above him. Lama was her name. It meant dark lips. He'd met her in Amman. Sheer terror twisted her unlined face into a desperate mask that shouted *I don't want to die.*

Neither did he. He closed his eyes and waited for impact. Then, everything went black.

*   *   *

Something sharp poked his forehead. With each strike, the pain spiked. It felt as if someone were trying to drive a nail into his head.

He opened his eyes. A blurry image emerged of a small black ball peering over a yellow cone dipped in red. Whatever it was, pressed against his chest, pinching his flesh, making it difficult to breathe. A putrid odor burned in his nose. Yasin gagged. He rubbed his eyes. Enormous pale golden wings spread outward. "Jeez." He slammed his hands into it. The bird shrieked and lifted off, landing a few feet away.

He sat up. A sharp pain stabbed at his lower back. Something warm trickled down his face. He wiped the cuff of his shirtsleeve across his forehead. Blood. His head throbbed. What had happened? Where was he?

He struggled to his feet on unsteady legs. The sun directly overhead was scorching. In front of him lay nothing but godforsaken desert as far as he could see except for a tower of black smoke twisting upward in the distance. A strong wind whipped up the rolling dunes in front of him. The swirling sand spun around and around like hypnotic, whirling dervishes. Yasin shielded his eyes and headed toward the smoke.

Several minutes later, he stood in front of twisted wreckage strewn across the desert floor. The storm had stopped. Small fires smoldered as thick billows of smoke rose from the broken fuselage whose top was missing. Heat radiated from the crash site like an over-stoked bonfire. He backed away. Sand near the jet had dissolved into chunks of murky quartz-like rocks. Blackened bodies or what was left of them, lay twisted into freakish positions among the debris.

The gruesome scene didn't trigger any memories. Why had the plane crashed? Who were the people?

He sat down in the sand. It was pointless to strike out for help until he knew where he was. His mouth was dry, his lips cracked. Without water, he wouldn't survive for long. Surely, a search party would arrive soon. Something caught the sun, glimmering beyond the plane's wreckage. A bottle of water? A cell phone? He stood up and walked toward the scintillating object.

Halfway buried in the sand was something that looked like a small glass pyramid. He reached down and picked it up the exquisite bottle. *Les Larmes Sacrees de Thebe* was etched into the crystal. The sacred tears of Thebe. It contained an interior chamber the color of amber. His stomach gurgled, rebelling. *Liqueur.* But any liquid was better than nothing. As he removed the amethyst-colored crystal top a complex, lusty scent drifted out. He brought the bottle close to his nose. *Frankincense and myrrh.*

His hands began to shake. The bottle slipped from his grip and fell, spilling its precious contents onto the sand. A sweet aroma rose, cutting through the charred smell of wreckage. It triggered an horrific vision: people on fire, screaming, bodies flying through the air. He shook his head to weaken the image's grip. But it didn't help. He remembered—Lama's perfume. He had spent $7800 for the bottle. The jet or what was left of it, was his father's. Today was New Year's Eve. He was supposed to be in Monaco for a party with his friends. How had he survived such a horrible crash? The utter destruction before him made it difficult to believe it was luck. He dropped to his knees and buried his forehead in the sand, as if somehow the searing heat against his flesh could provoke an answer from a God he didn't know.

Something deep within him groaned. *I should be dead like everyone else.* No one could have survived this crash. He sat up and glanced at the blackened bodies and tried for a moment to identify who they were, but it was impossible. They were no longer human.

He gasped. Standing in the middle of smoldering flames was a man in a long, white, radiant robe. Yasin rubbed his eyes. The encircling flames had no effect. He beckoned with his hand.

Yasin stood and walked toward him until the flames were too hot. "Who are you?"

The man was radiant; his face glowed like molten bronze.

"Remove your shoes."

Yasin bent down reluctantly and removed them, anticipating the scorching sands. But the ground was cool, even the withering heat from the wreckage from a moment ago was gone.

"Look around you. From the north to the south and east to west. All of it is mine." His words thundered and reverberated into the distance.

"What do you want?"

"Worship me, and I will make you great."

Yasin sank to his knees and bowed.

"Stand up and stretch out your hand." Yasin stood and extended his hand. Searing pain shot through his hand as the angel touched him. It traveled up his arm. He gasped for air as the molten pain reached his heart.

"I have chosen you above all men. You will be my son, and I will be your father. I have given you a new name written on your hand. Only you and I will know what it means."

"Mr. Mohammed, do you agree with the crown prince?"

The voice startled him and for a moment. Yasin didn't know where he was. "I'm sorry. Can you restate the position?"

Everyone laughed except Abdul.

Yasin tried to focus. This was his third meeting with Middle East leaders, this one at the Jeddah Tower, the world's tallest. The leaders were hashing out the structure of the new government.

Gadi El-Hashem, the President of the Arab-Emirates, explained that Abdul insisted the capitol of the new nation be in Mecca. What the crown prince really wanted, was to ensure the Saudi royals had control over the new nation. But placing the capital in Mecca would split the new nation between Sunnis and Shiites, the very thing the nation had to avoid. Many Shiites no longer made hajj to Mecca. Beyond that, the new nation needed to be founded on strength, not religion. It would be a nation inclusive of religion, but not exclusively religious.

The voices wouldn't stop. *You can't trust her. She will betray you.*

Yasin stood. "I'm sorry gentlemen. I have an emergency that requires my immediate attention. Will you excuse me?"

He hurried from the conference room.

CHAPTER SIXTY

Jordan, April 21

Scooter and Bibi stood just inside the Jordanian border with Israel, nearly blind from the bright light after two days in a matrix of dark tunnels. Buried in their backpacks were a handful of clay discs. Scooter had convinced Bibi they might need the cuneiform tablets for trade since they had little money.

"Any idea where we are?" Scooter said.

Bibi studied the terrain in front of him. "In the middle of nowhere."

"That's helpful."

"I'd say about 60 kilometers from the main highway to Amman. We need to head east toward highway 65. We should be able to catch a ride there."

"I thought we were farther north."

Bibi shook his head. "Still south of the Dead Sea."

Scooter took a GPS reading of their position and made a memo on his phone. It would be critical to finding the cave again where they left the scrolls and discs. Fortunately, they were outside again, and the sun would recharge the phone's near-dead battery.

If Bibi was correct, they were still 40 miles from Amman. The sooner they got there, the sooner the scrolls would be safe. The remote, hidden cave with its austere surroundings was certainly similar to the Qumran caves inhabited by the Essenes, an ascetic order believed to be the authors of the Dead Sea scrolls. And the cuneiform tablets could contain a prehistory of Israel.

Bibi studied the steep terrain in front of them. "No easy way down the side of this mountain, particularly with this backpack."

The loose shale made their footing treacherous. They wound their way down the side of the mountain slowly toward a faint dark line at the bottom, which undulated in the heat. After a couple of hours, they approached the highway.

Bibi pointed. "Someone's coming."

"Maybe our luck is about to change."

An amorphous image broke through a glassy barrier and coalesced into two trucks, which slowed. "I think the hounds have picked up our scent." Scooter said.

"Anyone ever tell you you're corny?"

"All the time."

Bibi clutched the AK47 and handed his Sig to Scooter. "You know how to use this?"

"Good enough."

The trucks came to a halt as a group of six bearded men dressed in black jumped out with AK47s.

"So much for luck," Bibi said. "ISIS. Don't shoot. There are too many, and we don't have any cover."

After a few minutes the fighters reached them.

"Where are you going?" One of the soldiers said.

"Amman," Bibi said.

"What's in the sacks?" A scowling soldier pointed his rifle at the backpacks. He had a French accent.

"Just supplies," Scooter said swinging the bag off his shoulder.

"Open it," the man said.

Scooter lowered the bag gently to the ground. His hand brushed the gun under his shirt. There were six rifles pointed at him. Bibi shook his head at him slightly as if he knew what he was thinking.

The man walked over and peered into the open sack and dug around in it. He poked the end of the barrel into Scooter's shoulder. "Where did you find these?"

Think fast. "We bought them from Bedouin."

"What are they?

"Clay tablets."

"Where did they find them?"

"I'm not sure."

The soldier frowned. "You lie." He swung the butt of the gun swiftly into Scooter's jaw.

A sharp pain exploded up the side of his face as he hit the ground. The end of the barrel was jammed into the side of his head. Another older soldier with gray patches in his beard waved the man off and stepped forward.

The soldier turned to Bibi and studied his dirty uniform.

"Who are you?"

"I was the police chief in Beersheba."

"Where are you going?"

"Amman."

"On foot?"

"The police are after us."

"The police are chasing the police chief?" The soldier laughed. "This is a story I'm looking forward to hearing."

He kicked Scooter in the side. "We'll see if a knife improves your memory."

CHAPTER SIXTY-ONE

Riyadh, Saudi Arabia, April 21

"Hello Momar," Yasin said. "How have you been old friend?"

"Mr. Mohammed?"

"Yes. I sent a woman by today to pick up some curry."

"What did she look like?"

"An American. Blond. Very good looking. Not easy to forget."

"She walked by about 20 minutes ago, but she didn't buy any curry."

"She didn't stop?"

"No."

"Strange. Maybe, she didn't see your booth."

"Maybe."

"Will you do me a favor and see if you can find her?"

"I'll try. But you know the crowds."

"You're a good friend. Thank you."

Yasin hung up and peered through the window at the minuscule landscape of buildings far below the 3281-foot tower. He felt as if he were staring down at another world beneath a clear lake. He leaned his head against the cool glass. He wanted to forget the warnings inside his head about Courtney. From his first meeting with her, he had felt a connection. He had only felt that bond one other time. His instincts had never betrayed him. Were they wrong this time?

His phone buzzed. It was Momar.

"Sorry to disturb you Mr. Mohammed. I found her."

"Did you remind her about the curry?"

"I didn't speak to her. She's in a car with a man outside the Bazaar."

"Did you recognize the man?"

"I've never seen him."

"She didn't look very happy about whatever they were discussing."

"What kind of vehicle?"

"Black Suburban."

"Thank you old friend. I owe you one."

"It's always a pleasure to help you Mr. Mohammed. What about the curry? Would you like me to have some delivered? It would be my privilege."

"That would be nice. Thank you."

He hung up again. The news could mean several things: she was meeting with Mossad or the CIA. His head ached. Both agencies had been following him ever since he proposed nationhood for the Middle East. Of course, there was an outside chance it was another man. That seemed remote. He sensed nothing unfaithful in her. The only one real possibility: the Mossad or CIA was trying to recruit her or she was already spying for them.

He pushed back from the window and slammed his fist against it and wished for a moment it would break.

CHAPTER SIXTY-TWO

Istanbul, April 21

Courtney glared at the tiny square in her hand that looked like gold bullion and placed it in her pocket. She dialed Jamal for a ride.

"Hello."

"Hi Jamal, it's Courtney. Can you pick me up?

"Are you at the market?"

"Yes, I'll be at the entry."

"Of course Miss Gattis. I'll be there in 10 minutes."

Courtney checked her watch as she waited, trying not to fidget, but suddenly she felt sick. *Oh my God, the curry.* How could she have been so stupid? She hurried back inside to the spice booth. A crude sign scrawled in shaky letters set among the spices. *Back in a few minutes.*

She looked at the open bins. A stack of bags lay nearby. It would be easy to dish out some of the red-orange spice. But if she was caught, the police would arrest her, and she would be in an even bigger mess. Thankfully, Yasin was not due back for a few days. She could return tomorrow and buy it.

*   *   *

Courtney stood on the upper deck of the villa peering at the Bosphorus below. She slipped her hand into the pocket of her coat and clutched the slender metal device. For a moment, she considered tossing it into the blue sea. She still didn't trust the CIA.

A black limo drove up the hill. It looked like Yasin's. He wasn't supposed to return for another day or two. Why had he cut short his trip?

Her heart pounded. Did Yasin suspect something? Did he have her followed? *You haven't done anything wrong—yet.* But she was about to betray a man who was fast becoming one of the most powerful men in the world.

Within minutes, the elevator opened behind her. She turned to see Yasin enter the house. She walked into the dining room. "Is everything okay? I didn't think you were due back for a couple of days."

He shot a glance upward, barely acknowledging her and said nothing.

Her stomach knotted.

Walking up the stairs, he said flatly, "Abdul will be president."

"What happened? I thought you were the favorite?"

Yasin ascended the stairs and walked to the deck. She hugged him, but he was stiff. She opened the refrigerator near the grill and removed a bottle of chardonnay along with two glasses and poured wine. A thin layer of ice formed on the exterior of the stemless glasses.

"What happened?"

"I had to cut a deal with Adbul to keep Saudi Arabia in the union. I told him I would support his presidency if his country remained in and the capital in Istanbul. He agreed and said he would lobby the members for me to be vice president."

"Is he even capable of running the UME?"

Yasin smirked. "Of course not. That will be my job." He took a sip of wine and squinted into the late afternoon sun. "Did you pick up the curry?"

She coughed. "I'm sorry. I forgot."

"How could you forget?" He sat his glass down heavily against the metal table. "What were you preoccupied with that was so important?" He rubbed the scar on his right hand. It was red and puffy and for the first time, she realized it was an image of a snake. He stood and walked back inside.

She took another sip of wine and closed her eyes. She had never seen Yasin angry before. And it wasn't over curry and probably not even because of the negotiation. Something deeper was troubling him.

There was a breeze blowing across the Bosphorus, but the setting sun felt hot. The back of her head ached as pain radiated up her skull. She had seen the serpentine scar before. Where? She sipped the wine. The dream on the flight to Istanbul. The man standing over the young women with a gun. The scar on his hand. The gunshot.

CHAPTER SIXTY-THREE

Istanbul, April 21

Yasin stared down at Courtney from the observatory at the top of his estate. She was still on the deck, leaning against the rail and staring across the Bosphorus. The wind was caressing her golden hair. Her back was turned so he couldn't see her brilliant blue eyes, but he knew they were wet. He had been so certain about her, about them. But he had been wrong.

He turned around and walked to the large telescope in the center of the room and peered into the eyepiece. The brightest star in the heavens had appeared in the northern sky, finding a home in the Draco constellation. Tomorrow the world would be abuzz about whether it was a comet or an exploding supernova and where it had come from. But he knew—it was the sign of his coming. And those who were expecting him would know as well.

CHAPTER SIXTY-FOUR

Jerusalem, April 23

Hank sat in Goldstein's office at *The Times* drinking a cup of bad coffee. It was early morning, the sun was out, the birds chirping, and no one had tried to kill him today. But he didn't feel like celebrating. Prime Minister Daniel Ben-David's appeal to the newspaper's owner had stopped his article from being published.

"What kind of Journalism is this?" Hank said it loud enough for the rest of the office to hear. "People are dying in Jerusalem because of a conspiracy and Ben-David wants time to resolve the issue internally?"

Goldstein frowned and stood up. "All right Jackson. The whole office heard. I understand your frustration. I don't like it either, but this is the Prime Minister. He believes Israelis can't afford anymore bad news. Public morale is already low. We're getting our butts kicked and may lose the Golan Heights. We don't need to read our own government refused to shut down a tunnel used by terrorists."

"I can't believe you're saying this. You said if I found a corroborating source, you would run Mike's article. I got one of the highest-ranking military officials in Israel. What more do you want?"

"I don't own the paper. Beckman does, and he and the Prime Minister go way back. He wants to give Ben-David time to make good on his promise to destroy the tunnel."

"That won't eliminate the deep state that is really running the government. Look, news organizations are supposed to protect the people. Israelis deserve to know the truth. How would Woodward and Bernstein have reacted if their editor told them that *The Washington Post* owner had struck a deal with President Nixon to drop the Watergate investigation provided the president promised to no longer spy on Democrats?"

"This is Israel, not the U.S., which you often forget." Goldstein fidgeted with the pen in his hand. "Ben-David believes the article will divide the country at a critical time."

"What Ben-David is really worried about is his job. This is about his neck. You know that."

"I know it stinks."

"Everything in my life stinks." Hank stood up and walked out of the building. He needed some air and decent coffee. The streets were quiet. Many had left the city to avoid the encroaching bombardment.

Heavy steps quickened behind him. He glanced over his shoulder. A heavyset man lumbered, his scuffed wing tips shuffling along the pavement. Was he being followed? His scalp tingled, the way it always did when trouble was near. The round man walked past him with a bag of donuts in one hand and a cup of coffee in the other.

The sidewalk behind was clear except for two individuals nearly a block away. No one appeared to be following him. But he couldn't shake the perception he was being watched. Was his radar malfunctioning? There was a coffee shop about 12 minutes from *The Times*. The safest place right now was inside where he could watch the people come and go, not out in the open. He turned toward *Landwer's Coffee*. As he quickened his pace, he called ZZ, who had returned to Jerusalem.

There might be another way to reveal the truth about Israel's deep state.

CHAPTER SIXTY-FIVE

Jerusalem, April 23

Z Z sat at his desk in the Knesset and watched the small screen in front of him. A text of the member's message scrolled across the display. He was scheduled to speak next. The Speaker of The Assembly had pressed him on what he wished to say, if he had a prepared speech. But ZZ said only that it was urgent news about Israel's war. How many times had he spoken before the Knesset in the last 20 years and taken pleasure in delivering soliloquies and sophistic essays that were more about hearing himself speak than a real message? Somewhere in his journey he had forgotten what he once knew was true. But God had reminded him, and now with time so short, he knew what needed to be said, what must be said.

The speaker sat down. ZZ stood and walked slowly to the front. He had missed being here, feeling the tension in this great room, seeing old friends and even rivals. As he looked out on the members, he wondered if those who wanted him dead were present.

"Thank you for indulging an old man. First of all, it is good to be back. As you know, I have been away, and I know it has caused some speculation about my health. I'm healthier than I deserve, praise be to God. But I am troubled my friends and colleagues, which is why I asked to speak." He paused and tried to dismiss the numbness in his hands. "We are engaged in a great war, which I am told we may lose. But we will not lose Israel. We are a great nation that has defied history. The fact that we have risen from the ashes is a testimony to God's existence and his promises to Abraham and David. God will protect us from our enemies."

The hall broke out in applause. MK Michaels, who sat in the front row, rapped the top of his maple desk with his hand.

"Who are our enemies? You may think this an inane question. Of course, it is Iran, Russia, and its proxies. But I believe an even more insidious foe is inside our borders."

Many look puzzled at the statement.

"A cancer is growing in our government that I would never have believed possible. It has the ability to destroy us faster than the missiles raining down on our cities."

Some members sat up straighter. MK Michaels searched ZZ's face. The soldiers standing guard at the doors glanced at each other.

"A secret coalition in our government, military, and intelligence communities plan to reshape Israel as we know it. To reduce it to a shadow of what Jehovah God intended. Many of you are aware of this. Some of you may belong to this group."

Murmurs rumbled through the room like distant thunder. MK Michaels glanced at the legislator next to him with a worried look.

"I have evidence this group is secretly negotiating with the enemy."

"That's a lie," shouted MK Michaels, who stood and pointed at ZZ. A wave of angry voices swept the room.

"Please, let me finish." But the rancor continued. ZZ raised his voice above the tumult, almost shouting. "Have we not learned from history? Did God not punish our nation for its alliances with Egypt and others? What is prompting these men and women who are entrusted with protecting our nation to such treasonous acts?" He looked upward and raised his hands. "A lack of faith. They do not believe God will fulfill His promises. They believe the only path to peace is through compromise, which is not compromise at all, but surrender."

He lowered his hands. "And yet, did God not say that when his people turn back to him, he will hear their prayers and forgive their sins, and fight for them? Turn back to the only one who can save you."

The whole room exploded. People shook their fingers at ZZ. Some shouted. Some at each other. Some even stood on their desks and shook their fists.

Pounding at the hall's great doors diverted the two soldier's attention to the entry. They swung their rifles into action and opened it. The uproar simmered as all eyes swept to Colonel Ganz who pushed past the two men.

His brow was plowed into furrows. "The Golan Heights have fallen!"

A stabbing pain pierced ZZ's heart. He clutched his chest and collapsed.

CHAPTER SIXTY-SIX

Jerusalem, April 23

Hank sat in the back of the cafe where he had a clear view of everyone coming and going. Taking refuge in the coffee shop hadn't shaken the sense he was being followed. Didn't the killers hunting him get the memo that Goldstein wasn't going to publish the story? Perhaps, it didn't matter. They wanted him dead regardless to ensure the truth died with him.

He still had the micro drive with the soldier and Ganz's statement on it. He had refused to turn it over to the editor. It was stored in a safe place just in case he or his sources disappeared.

Hank stared down into his empty cup. His third. He couldn't hide here all day. He walked back to the counter and ordered another Americano to go, then left. He walked southeast to Gan Sacher Park, the largest public park in Jerusalem.

He found a bench near a small lake under the shade of a tall eucalyptus tree. He leaned back. A breeze moved through the tree's great limbs coaxing susurrus replies. Flowers swayed in submission.

A woman sat down at a bench adjacent to his and glanced at him like she recognized him. He had never seen her. She was tall and thin like a model with short dark hair and carried a bag from the *Mahane Yehuda Market*. She sipped a drink and stared at the water.

She tossed breadcrumbs from a baggie to pigeons that pecked greedily at them. Then, she stood and left. His eyes followed her for a distance. She stopped and turned back as if she sensed he was staring.

He glanced at the bench where she had sat. She had forgotten her bag.

CHAPTER SIXTY-SEVEN

Istanbul, April 24

Courtney lay in bed wide-awake. She hadn't slept all night. She kept searching for some explanation for the photos, the dream, the sickening feeling gnawing in her gut that felt like fear.

The trilling sound of the call to prayer signaled it was 5:48. An engine revved. It sounded like the Bugatti. Where was Yasin going so early? He hadn't said anything about leaving. But he hadn't said much the last few days, since returning abruptly. It was unlikely he was headed to the mosque. He never attended morning prayers. She slipped out of bed and pulled the curtain back. A thin yellow line was emerging over the dark Bosphorus. She cracked the window and listened to the sports car descend the driveway. She couldn't see it, since her bedroom faced the channel, but the car had a distinct sound. And Yasin was the only one who drove it.

He was gone and so was his phone. She sat down on the bed. There was no chance of copying the data now. In a way she was relieved. The CIA's idea had never seemed tenable. Her phone buzzed. She picked it up from the nightstand. A text from an unidentified sender. *Parents deceased. No contact with mission team since prison release.* A wet chill crept in from the open window. Courtney stared at the message and sat down. Her eyes welled and her hands trembled.

Oh Zoe. Forgive me. Please, forgive me. It's all my fault. She buried her face in her hands and let her nails sink into the soft flesh of her face. What kind of sociopath had she climbed into bed with?

She lifted her head, brushed her eyes, and tried to still the voices screaming inside: *Forget the phone and get out while you can. You know what he will do if he catches you.* But the house was still quiet. The cook and maid weren't up yet. And Yasin was gone. She had time. *He needs to pay for what he's done. Fate placed you here for a reason.* She dressed and left the room.

She glanced at the stairs. *Too creaky.* The elevator was quieter and faster. She pressed the button on the door and waited. The door opened, and she stepped in. There were ten floors. Five below the main level and four above. They were all identified except for one, which was Yasin's. She pressed the button and held her breath. Perhaps he had left something behind in haste the CIA could use. He carried three phones. One for business, one for his political work, and probably one to connect with Jakad and Farid.

The elevator opened, and she stepped out. The door to his room was shut. She tried the knob. It opened. She walked in and closed the door. She was familiar with the room. It smelled like the man—citrusy. It was orderly. He made the bed every morning even though he had a maid. There were paintings, but no photos, which had always puzzled her.

She walked into an enormous closest. In the center of the room was a long island with drawers on both sides. She opened them. Socks, tee shirts, and underwear, all organized by color. Dozens of suits organized by season hung along one wall. The other side had casual wear. But nothing useful.

A door creaked. She froze. She peeked through the crack of the closet door, but saw nothing. She ducked back inside and picked up the pace. A large safe was set against the back wall, but it was locked. There were more drawers next to it. She rifled through them. Nothing. Then, she remembered something odd: a travel bag near the foot of the bed. She walked back into the room and saw it. Had he forgotten his luggage? Was he headed back at this very moment for it? She lifted the bag and set it on the bed. Inside was his passport, a gun and—a phone. It might be the right phone or wrong one. She didn't have time to check. She removed the gold wafer from her pocket and waved it over the cell and then, placed the thin device in her pocket. Done. *Now, get out of here.*

A toilet flushed in the master bath. She turned for the door, but the bathroom door opened.

Jakad stood there. She gasped.

"What are you doing in Yasin's room?" His face denied the incredulity in his voice. He looked more amused and pleased for having caught her.

Courtney stumbled for words. All she could think to say was: "I could ask you the same question."

He reached inside his robe and removed a pistol. He pointed at the bag on the bed. "What were you looking for?"

"Nothing."

"I told Yasin not to trust you. Maybe he will believe me now. Let's take a walk."

"Where?" Her bottom lip trembled as she scrambled for a plan.

"You ask too many questions. Take the stairs." His fingers tapped against his phone.

As she walked, she assessed whether she could reach Jakad with a back kick, but he was out of range and had a gun.

They reached the mezzanine. Jakad waved the gun, motioning her through doors to the library and toward the far north wall. He backed toward the bookcase, keeping a safe distance. He pressed something inside the shelf and the floor-to-ceiling bookcase creaked as it crawled from the wall, leaving an entrance wide enough for a person to slip through. Cold, stale air slipped from the opening.

Jakad pointed at the dark sliver. "There's a staircase just inside. Move."

"What's down there?"

"It's where you're going to stay until Yasin returns."

"I'm not going in there."

"You're not in a position to negotiate. Now move." He pointed the gun at her head.

She raised her hands. "All right. Just tell me if Yasin had anything to do with the bombing of Chicago." She knew the answer, but needed time.

"Where did you hear that? The Mossad or CIA?"

"The CIA approached me at the market, and told me Yasin was connected to ISIS, but I didn't believe them. I was in his room looking for something to prove he had nothing to do with them."

"Sure you were. Well, ask him yourself. He'll be here soon." He motioned with the gun toward the opening.

"If you're going to kill me, I prefer to die here, not down there. Is that where Zoe was killed?" She clenched her jaw and she stared into his dark eyes, daring him to make a move.

A scowl fell across his face.

There were footsteps below the mezzanine. He lunged toward her and swung the gun at her head.

She ducked and struck quickly: a front kick to the chest that knocked him to the ground. A hard heel to the groin. He doubled over still holding the gun. Another kick to the chin. He was out. She grabbed his cell and the gun.

In the distance, the throaty roar of the Bugatti approached.

CHAPTER SIXTY-EIGHT

Jerusalem, April 24

A phone was ringing somewhere or he was hearing things. Hank tried to sit up in bed but pain raked the back of his legs and buttocks. His head throbbed with every thump of his heart. And his eyes refused to focus. Where was he? The last thing he remembered was sitting at the park and staring at a shopping bag left behind by a woman.

A white image entered the room.

"You're awake." She moved toward his bed. "Your vitals look good. You're one lucky guy."

Hank knew the nurse was trying to be encouraging. But he didn't feel lucky. He felt confused. Why was he still alive? It was the same question he had asked a million times after losing Kat. Why didn't God take him instead of her? She was a better servant and far more useful.

"Paramedics found you in the lake face down. It's a wonder you didn't drown. A witness said you dove into the lake before the bomb exploded."

He didn't remember any of it.

"By the way, I noticed you don't have a chip. I hate to bring it up, but administration wants to know how to bill you for whatever your insurance doesn't pay."

"Tell me what I owe, and I'll have the balance wired from my bank."

"That's highly irregular, but I'll let them know."

The phone rang again.

"Your phone has been ringing nonstop the last hour." She pressed it into his hand. "Answer it and put us out of misery."

"Hello."

"Jackson?"

The gravelly voice belonged to Colonel Ganz.

"What do you want?"

"I heard someone tried to kill you."

"I bet it was a big surprise."

"Not really. I told you to leave."

"Are you the one who has been calling?"

"Our friend ZZ had a heart attack. He…" His voice faltered. "He asked for you."

Hank was in no shape to go anywhere. But he had to.

"Tell him I'm on my way."

CHAPTER SIXTY-NINE

Damascus, Syria, April 24

The raggedy man stared at random bullet holes spread across the wall, his lips moving silently. He tilted his head sideways as if a different angle might provide illumination. He was gaunt and even from 20 feet away, smelled. He face was as gray and dirty as his tattered dishdasha. Patches of white nested in his long, tangled, dark beard like small doves that had found a home.

It was early morning. The dirt floor was still cool. Rays of grainy light filtered in from outside, which was beginning to stir. Scooter rubbed his eyes, which felt scratchy after hours of being blindfolded. They had been transferred from Jordan to Syria. A flea crawled across his arm. He slapped it. The sudden noise seemed to remind the shabby prisoner he wasn't alone.

He turned slowly toward them, revealing half a face that sagged like wax down the side of a candle. "Once, I was handsome."

The prisoner had an English accent. "How did it happen?" Scooter asked.

He pointed at his disfigured visage. "Abu Ahmad Bakr, the first commander of ISIS, did this." He looked like he wanted to spit.

"Who's that?" Bibi asked.

Scooter had never heard of him either.

The man looked away as if the question resurrected difficult memories. "My name is Daoud. I was an assistant to Al-Kassab, the supreme leader of ISIS. He was everything to me. I should have died with him."

"He was killed in a drone strike by the U.S.," Scooter said.

"He was betrayed. Bakr had him killed."

"One of his own men?" Bibi scratched his leg.

The prisoner spit again. "Bakr deceived everyone."

"Does anyone else know this?"

"Everyone who did is dead. I'm the last."

"Why did this Bakr kill Al-Kassab?" Scooter said.

"So his imam, Oma-Murshid, could lead ISIS."

Scooter had heard the name. His followers claimed he had supernatural powers, but very little was known about him. "Where is Bakr?"

The man turned back. A wry smile tugged at the corners of his mouth. "Everywhere."

Bibi glanced at the barred window above the prisoner's head. "What is that supposed to mean?"

"ISIS was a stepping stone for Bakr. He still controls it."

"A stepping stone?" Bibi said. "To what? Who is he?"

The man waved off the question. "How did you end up here?"

Bibi glanced at Scooter as if the question was his to answer, since he was responsible for their predicament.

"We were on the run from Shin Bet and were intersected by ISIS fighters just inside the Jordanian border," Scooter said.

"Why were you running?"

"That's a long story."

"I've got plenty of time." He scratched his head. "Lousy fleas."

Scooter related how the chief rescued him from the scarecrow, what happened to Zafar, and their escape through the tunnel. He left out the discovery of the ark and scrolls.

"Are you rich or do you know someone who will pay a ransom?"

"Hardly," Scooter said.

"Then, you won't live long. ISIS only keeps prisoners who have money or friends who do."

"Why are you still alive?"

"Do I look alive? My family is dead, most of my friends gone. Death would be merciful. Bakr extended my life as a reminder of what happens to anyone questioning the death of Al-Kassab."

Bibi glanced at Scooter. They seemed to be on the same page.

Scooter lowered his voice. "We discovered a cave with ancient tablets. The soldiers found a few cuneiform discs in our backpacks."

"That will keep you alive as long as you can endure the torture."

Scooter dropped his head. He had feared as much. "Any chance of escaping this place?"

The prisoner snickered, then coughed so hard, he bent over and clutched his chest. "I have thought of a thousand ways and yet, I'm still here."

The man turned back to the wall and began studying it. He counted silently.

"What is so important about that wall?" Scooter asked.

The man pointed at it. "Each one of these holes represents how many days I was given to live. So I count them everyday."

"How many holes are there?"

"This morning there were 192. Yesterday was better. I counted 196."

"How many days have you been here?"

He smiled grimly and pointed to several rows of marks on the wall behind him. "One-hundred seventy-nine."

CHAPTER SEVENTY

Istanbul, April 24

The Bugatti was close. Courtney's heart fluttered as she examined her options. She could hide and hope Yasin wouldn't find her, abscond with one of his cars, or leave on foot. All of the choices had drawbacks. He knew the house better than she, so hiding was risky.

Taking one of his cars wouldn't work, because he would be entering the garage any minute. And trying to escape by foot wouldn't get her very far. She glanced down at the Bosphorus through the lower windows of the dining room.

She hurried from the library down the stairs to the main floor. The quickest way to the dock was the elevator. But it was already headed down to the garage. The outside terraced levels of the house were connected by a stairway on one side, but it was at least 200 yards to the bottom. She scooted past the kitchen on her way to the outer deck. She grabbed the rails to steady herself and bounded down every other step.

When she was halfway down, Yasin yelled from the top of the stairs. "Why are you running?"

She fought a sudden urge to look back. *Don't listen*. The boat was still a good hundred yards away. He would not take the stairs but the elevator, which was much faster. She tried estimating how many seconds it would take for him to reach the dock, but the only thing her mind could process was the command to run.

Her foot caught a stairwell tread and stumbled, nearly tumbling. She stopped the fall but wrenched her wrist. In the distance the speedboat rocked on blue green water unconcerned by the unfolding drama. As she reached the dock, the elevator door 100 yards behind her opened. She glanced back. Yasin was sprinting. She yanked the ropes from the two mooring posts and jumped on board, turned the key in the ignition and thanked God when the engines roared to life.

"Don't leave. I love you."

Her hand shook as it gripped the throttle. Was she making a mistake? Were the text messages from the CIA a setup? She released the throttle and looked back.

Yasin was only a few feet away. His arms were outreached, beckoning her to return; his countenance pained, full of regret.

"Goodbye Yasin."

She pushed the two accelerators forward. The front of the boat reared up like a spirited horse and jetted from the dock across the channel.

CHAPTER SEVENTY-ONE

Jerusalem, April 24

The overhead lights in the hall gleamed against glossy hospital floors. Hank was tired of hospitals, especially this one. Bikur Cholim was the same facility where Kat had died 17 days earlier. Had it only been that long? It felt like months since he had looked into her large brown eyes.

Guards stood outside ZZ's room in ICU. They motioned for Hank's hand so they could scan it, but he offered his driver's license instead, since he didn't have a chip. One guard checked his ID on their phones. He frowned as he looked up but nodded for the other guard to open the door.

ZZ was sitting up in bed as if he were ready to leave. The round face was sunken and a splotchy yellowish tint colored his skin. His thick white beard had thinned with whiskers shooting in odd directions like unruly alfalfa sprouts. But there was a twinkle in his eyes Hank had never seen before.

"I'm sorry to bring you back here," ZZ said. "I know it must be difficult and dangerous. But it was important I see you."

Despite his appearance, ZZ's voice was steady and strong.

"You look better than the last time I saw you," Hank said.

"My doctors tell me my heart is failing, but I feel better than I have in a long time." He motioned for Hank to come closer. "I know you question why Jehovah spared your life and not Kat's or your pastor's. I would ask the same question if I were you. But because of your faith something remarkable has happened."

"What?"

ZZ beamed. "Moshiah spoke to me in a dream."

"Jesus?"

ZZ closed his eyes for a moment as if trying to remember. "Yeshua's face was brilliant like the sun. I couldn't look at him. I fell on my face."

"What did he say?"

"He told me he is coming for his church and the day of Jacob's trouble is near. He asked me to tell the people. I spoke to the members of the Knesset, and I shared your message about Israel's deep state."

Hank nodded. "I heard you caused quite a commotion."

"Yes. I guess Mike's story made it into print in a roundabout way."

"It needed to. He died for it."

ZZ grabbed Hank's hand. "Don't you see? Jehovah preserved your life so that you could lead me to Moshiah, so I could share his message with Israel. He is about to do something special in this land."

"The Bible says there will be a great awakening in Israel in the latter days. It may be about to start."

ZZ nodded. "Moshiah also wanted me to share something else, but only with you."

Hank sat down on the bed. He had never received a direct message from the Lord. "Okay."

"He was very emphatic about one thing."

Hank leaned closer. "What?"

"He said to make sure you knew that Kat and Luke will be with Him when he returns."

"He said that?"

"He did."

Hank buried his face in ZZ's bed. Warm tears flowed.

ZZ placed his hand on Hank's head and stroked the unruly red hair.

CHAPTER SEVENTY-TWO

Istanbul, April 24

Courtney turned the speedboat into the choppy, afternoon waves, bounding over the tops. The sleek craft was doing 52 knots at half throttle. It was tempting to go faster and put more distance between her and Yasin, but she was struggling to control the craft. Besides, she had no idea where she was going, and little time to decide. Before long, authorities would be buzzing the speedboat.

As she sped along the curved shoreline, two large cruise ships emerged near the golden horn, a knob of land jutting into the Bosphorus.

Courtney cut the speed and idled toward the dock, about 200 yards west of the cruise liners. She moored the boat, then searched the cabin for extra clothes always kept for guests and a first aid kit. She found a long, light blue hijab with a white lace bodice and tucked it into her tote. She removed some bandages, antiseptic, and a razor blade from the kit, which she would need to remove the chip in her hand, and added them to her bag. She left the boat, hurried past the ships to a series of shops catering to tourists and found a restroom. Inside, she changed into the hijab and covered her face as she left. Police had already spotted the speedboat, which meant the cruise ships would be the first place they would search. A rusted freighter that barely looked sea worthy was docked just east of the vessels.

She quickened her pace without running. What she needed was luck, but how many times could she tap that well? A clipboard hung near the ramp to the freighter. She grabbed it and walked on board toward a door.

"What are you doing?" Someone asked from behind.

Courtney turned to see a young man with a blue cap and light beard. She glanced at the clipboard, which looked like a record of the ship's delivery. "Safety. Here to do a quick inspection."

"We've never had an inspection in this port before. Who ordered it?"

"Turkish Department of Safety. There was a report of a possible violation. I'm here to ensure compliance."

"What type of violation?"

"What is your name?"

"Aaron."

"Thank you, Aaron. I am simply doing what my supervisor asked me to do. Shall I leave and ask him to come and conduct his own inspection?"

The sailor scratched his chin. "The captain isn't going to be happy when he hears about this but go ahead." He opened the door for her, and she walked through.

"Thank you. When are you scheduled to leave?"

The man checked his watch. "Crew should be headed back now. Why?"

"I need to ensure this report is filed before you leave. You have been so helpful. I will make this is as brief as possible."

The man's countenance softened. "Where do you want to start?"

"If you please, I don't need an escort. I'll conduct my own review."

He waved his hand as if to brush her off and walked toward the stairs at the bow.

Courtney took a deep breath. She needed to find somewhere unobtrusive, where she could disappear. The freighter was a fifth the size of the cruise liners, spartan and smelled of fuel and something else foul. She glanced back over her shoulder to ensure Aaron wasn't watching and opened a door. Sleeping quarters. That won't work. She walked back to the hallway and proceeded farther into the ship.

At the end of the corridor, located at the stern, was a stairway that ascended and descended. There was also a window. She peered out. Police were gathered around the speedboat. Some people pointed toward the shops and restroom. Yasin stood in their midst listening to them. He began walking toward the cruise ships, but stopped and turned toward the freighter. He looked directly at her. She was too far away for him to identify her, but he knew. She ducked back behind the wall.

She grabbed the handrail to the stairs. The ship appeared to have seven levels, three above the deck, and three below. The bridge, where navigation occurred, at the top. The light in the stairwell was burned out and the nearer she came to the bottom, the stronger the foul smell permeating the ship became. She covered her mouth and nearly retched. Whatever was stored in the belly of the ship was putrid, and she didn't want to get any closer. She turned and headed back up the stairs.

"I think she went this way." It was the young man's voice. "I should have known something wasn't right. She told me she was here to do a safety inspection."

"Here's a picture. Is this the woman you saw?"

Courtney froze. It was Yasin.

"I can't tell for sure, because she was in traditional dress. But the eyes look familiar."

Courtney tiptoed back down the stairway and prayed they wouldn't creak. The men were only a few feet from the stairwell. At the bottom, there was a door with a round wheel. The foul smell invading the higher decks, was now revolting. She tried turning the hand wheel, but it wouldn't budge. She leaned all her weight into the wheel, and it squeaked as it turned.

"Did you hear something?" Yasin said.

"No."

"Let's check the storage tanks."

"It's pretty smelly."

"It's chicken crap. It's supposed to smell. I sell it to Israel."

The door creaked opened. Courtney bit her lip. A rush of rotten smell assaulted her so revolting she gagged.

"I heard something again. Hurry."

Courtney stepped through the door and grabbed the ladder attached to the wall. With one hand, she held onto the ladder, with the other she cranked the wheel handle to the right until it stopped. The smell was overwhelming. She vomited but descended the ladder until she reached what felt like quicksand grabbing at her. She vomited again.

There were voices above.

"Open it."

"No one would go in there."

Courtney's heart sank as the rusty wheel handle slowly moaned. She submerged herself into the revolting soup, clamping her eyes and mouth as tight as she could.

Someone coughed. "All right close it. Keep searching the ship. She's here somewhere. If you don't find her, make sure you post an armed guard when you dock at Ashdod. Tell him to be careful and watch her feet. She can be dangerous. But don't kill her."

*   *   *

Courtney held her breath as long as she could before exploding out of the putrid swamp, gulping in the foul air filling the tanker's belly. She wretched until there wasn't anything left in her stomach. If Yasin were waiting at the door, he could have her. She didn't care any longer. Everything that she cared for had been stripped from her, including her dignity.

But the room was dark and quiet except for the shifting of the slimy grunge clinging to her like glue. Engines churned. The tanker began to move.

CHAPTER SEVENTY-THREE

Jerusalem, April 27

ZZ looked up at the nine, crystal, pear-shaped chandeliers draped from the grand ceiling of the Belz Great Synagogue like jewels from a queen's neck. Every row was filled, even the galleries on each side. Ten thousand people. Such a crowd had not filled the enormous synagogue in many years. They had come to celebrate Passover, the holiday commemorating Israel's liberation from Egypt—and pray for Israel. The loss of the Golan Heights and the thousands who died defending the critical defensive barrier was on everyone's mind. Would God protect Israel the way he had in the past or would the Jewish state cease to exist?

The pew's hard wood pressed against the soft flesh of ZZ's round back. He sat in the third row from the front. It felt good to spend the Sabbath in a synagogue instead of hiding or in a hospital.

Rabbi Libni raised his hands and looked up as if he were searching for answers. He was a tall man with elongated features that looked plucked from an El Greco painting. But even his height was diminutive against the massive wooden ark behind him.

"Has God abandoned us?" Libni said. "Jews asked this question when the first temple was destroyed and our people were carried off to Babylon, and again with the destruction of the second temple and the diaspora. And we ask now. No people on earth have suffered as much as the Jew and yet we are still here." His gray eyes found ZZ and settled on him. They were old friends.

ZZ felt compelled to stand up and address the thousands at the service. That's a ridiculous idea, he thought. He couldn't and wouldn't interrupt the service. But the prompting to speak grew stronger. He battled with the force exhorting him but after ten minutes, he stood and made his way toward the aisle. Libni stopped speaking as thousands of curious eyes bore into ZZ. A guard seated in the front pew stood and started toward him but the rabbi waved him off.

"I know I'm breaking all the rules," ZZ whispered as he walked up the steps to the platform, "but I believe Jehovah God wants me to address your congregation."

"This is highly irregular." The rabbi whispered, leaning toward ZZ. His breath was sweet and smelled of mint. "Should I be worried?" News networks had branded ZZ as a religious radical who believed in conspiracy theories after his speech at the Knesset.

"Not in hope."

Libni stepped backward tentatively and offered his lectern, but he seemed unsure.

ZZ steadied himself as he leaned on the pulpit. He felt weak and the stinging heart pain was back. *Strengthen me, Jehovah.* A surge of energy flowed into him like a rushing river. Uncertainty filled confused faces searching for an explanation on the change of teachers. But in the audience he spotted two familiar faces. Hank was seated four rows back and behind him was Dr. Moshe Abrams, a professor of ancient languages at Hebrew University. The sight of his friends strengthened him.

"Thank you, Rabbi Libni for allowing me to speak to your congregation. I am Zedekiah Zukerman as some of you know, a member of the Knesset. For 20 years I was a teacher and taught at Menachem Zion. Rabbi Libni and I often spoke during those years. He is truly one of Israel's great teachers."

"We are all worried about the loss of the Golan Heights and what will happen. But we shouldn't be. God told Ezekiel he would restore Israel and he did. He promised difficult times ahead, but never again the loss of our nation. Even if the whole world opposes Israel, we have a great God who fiercely loves his people and will protect them. I believe that."

"I'm going to share something with you that the government doesn't want you to know."

People slid to the edge of their seats as Libni stirred behind him.

"The Ark of the Covenant has been found." ZZ turned toward the rabbi, whose mouth was agape. "It's true." He turned back to the people. "Unfortunately, it is not in Israel's hands, but I believe God will return it just as he did when the Philistines captured it. Soon, the temple will be rebuilt and Moshiah will appear."

"Although I believe in scripture, I have always been skeptical of miracles. I've always been a very pragmatic man, which made accepting the miraculous difficult. But the very fact Israel exists is one of the world's greatest miracles.

"Which leads me to a dream I had a few days ago, the most vivid of my life. Moshiah appeared to me. His face was burning bright like a hot coal." ZZ glanced back at Libni who looked worried. "He wanted me to deliver a message to you. That is why I am here. He is returning."

The last word slipped by the congregation, but not the rabbi. "You mean appearing," he offered.

ZZ turned toward the rabbi who was frowning. "No, returning." He turned back to the filled pews. "Yeshua is our Messiah, and he is coming soon."

Gasps filled the synagogue. An orthodox Jew in the back stood, his broad black hat slipping from his head and shouted, "You're a liar."

Libni grabbed ZZ's elbow and pushed him from the podium as other orthodox Jews screamed insults. As ZZ stepped from the platform a young man rushed forward from the aisle and pulled a gun from his coat and fired.

The force of the shot knocked ZZ backwards. He gasped for air as the lights overhead swirled. Shouting surrounded him as Hank bent over him.

"Well done faithful servant of God," Hank said.

Professor Moshe Abrams kneeled next to him and said nothing but held his hand.

ZZ gasped for air. With his fading strength, he took Hank's hand and placed it on Moshe's hand. "Protect the ark." Then, the great synagogue was dark.

CHAPTER SEVENTY-FOUR

Damascus, Syria, April 27

It was the middle of the night. Bibi was asleep as was the prisoner across the cell. He was snoring as if he hadn't a worry. Scooter couldn't sleep. Every time he closed his eyes, the distant sound of explosions jarred him awake. They were about 40 miles from the Golan Heights. The continual bombardment produced flashes like a lightning storm, revealing an ominous sky of towering dark gray clouds through the jail window. But it was more than noise disturbing his sleep. A question kept needling him: why hadn't the soldiers questioned Bibi and him since their arrest? Clearly, they didn't believe the story about obtaining the tablets from the Bedouins. So, why hadn't they pressed them for more information? And where was Johnny Naziri? He lived in Damascus. Surely, they would have called him and asked him to authenticate the tablets and what they might be worth?

The prisoner stirred as if he sensed he was being watched.

"You get used to the explosions." He sat up and pushed his back against the wall disappearing into the shadows. "Night is hardest. You wonder how you will make it through another day of torture. It never gets easier until you wish for death more than life."

"You said the only thing that will keep me alive is not revealing where the cave is," Scooter said. "Why haven't the soldiers questioned me again?"

He was silent for a moment. "They may already know."

"How could they? We were miles from the tunnel when they arrested us. And it was well hidden." His stomach churned. He belched.

"You okay?"

Scooter spit and wished he could rinse his mouth. "My phone. I made a note of the cave's location, and they have photos of the scrolls and tablets."

The man picked up a stick next to him and began drawing in the dirt. "I'm sorry."

A spotlight from outside shone through the window behind Scooter, illuminating the center of the room but leaving the opposite sides of the jail in shadows.

"You asked me today if I knew of any ways of escape. I lied. I know one. I haven't used it, because I don't have anything to escape to. Everyone I loved is gone."

Scooter looked at the barred window above the prisoner. "I'm listening."

The prisoner continued drawing in the dirt." He stopped and looked at Scooter. "If you make it, there is something I want you to do."

"What?"

"Tell the world who Bakr is?"

"Who is he?"

The man wrote a name in the dirt.

Scooter stared at it in disbelief.

CHAPTER SEVENTY-FIVE

Istanbul, April 28

Courtney lost track of time. How long had she been trapped in loathsome animal waste and perpetual darkness? Her head ached, she was dizzy, and weak from vomiting. The incision on her hand from removing the chip also hurt.

She had considered climbing out of the container and stowing away. But the smell clinging to her would be impossible to hide. If she were caught, Yasin would be contacted, and the plan now spinning in her head would never have a chance.

All she wanted was a shower and clean clothes. If only she could stand under a hot shower and wash the filth off, everything would be better. At least she had the wafer, Jakad's cell, and his gun. Hopefully, there was something on them of value. She slid her hand into a pocket to touch the metal sliver. She had done it a million times to make sure it was there. But where was it? She ran her sticky fingers through her pocket, but it was missing. She searched frantically and wanted to empty her pocket, but it was too dark to see. Her heart sank at the thought of it at the bottom of the container. If it were, she would never find it.

The tanker was slowing. After a few minutes, there was a sudden jolt, and the ship stopped. *Thank God.* Leaving would be tricky. She would wait until the ship's crew was gone, then crawl out, take a shower, and find some clothes.

*   *   *

Courtney peered out the porthole and searched for the guard. He was standing at the bottom of the ramp with his side arm. No chance of exiting that way. Of all the bad luck, she had picked a ship Yasin owned. And, the wafer was lost.

Dressed in baggy blue pants and a matching shirt she had found in the crew's quarters, Courtney spun her damp hair into a bun and tucked it under a blue baseball cap. She found a first aid kit, cleaned the incision on her hand, which looked infected and put on a fresh bandage.

She walked up to the main deck. The ship was docked on its right side, starboard if her memory was correct. She walked to port side. It was a long drop to the water. Too far to jump. A boat was suspended by a small crane at the stern, but she couldn't access it without drawing the guard's attention. But a life preserver attached to a long nylon rope was anchored to the cargo deck. She wrapped the preserver's rope around the hand rail a couple of times, then threw the remaining rope over the side. She slipped the preserver over her and grabbed the free rope and lowered herself down the side of the ship. Her arms shook from the effort. She was weak and light-headed.

The water was frigid and oily but it helped revitalize her. She maneuvered to the ship's stern where the propeller was located and peeked around the starboard side. The guard was still there. She removed the preserver and dove under the water and swam to the dock where she was out of view. From here, she moved slowly down the dock. When she was far enough away, she found a ladder descending from a pier and climbed out. People stared at her drenched clothes, but she smiled and asked where the nearest store that sold towels was located.

It took ten minutes to walk to the convenience store. The cashier stared at her and seemed reluctant to let her enter the store.

"What can I say? I was taking a selfie and fell into the water."

He laughed.

"I need a favor." She removed Jakad's cell phone from her pants. "My phone is ruined, and I had an accident that ripped the chip from my hand. I have no money. Would you please let me use a towel to dry off and give me a bottle of water. I hate to ask, but I need your help."

The cashier nodded. "It's a crazy story but you look honest." He removed a towel from a rack and gave it to her along with a large bottle of water.

"Bless you." She guzzled the water with one hand and dried herself with the other. The water tasted wonderful.

Next to the cashier, a newspaper's bold headlines declared: *MK Assassinated*. She glanced at the byline. Hank Jackson. She had heard the name before. She removed the paper and scanned the article.

According to the story, Zedekiah Zukerman, a member of the Knesset, was murdered by an ultra orthodox Jew during Passover because of his comments about Jesus. Zukerman said Jesus was the nation's long awaited messiah. She glanced at the reporter's name again. Hank Jackson. *The Jerusalem Times.*

She left the shop and looked for a taxi.

CHAPTER SEVENTY-SIX

Golan Heights, April 28

Deafening explosions shook the ground beneath Scooter, making it difficult for Bibi and him to even stand. The air was thick with the smell of burning oil, irritating their eyes.

"I can't believe we're walking into the middle of a war." Bibi kept his head low and crouched as he struggled to maintain his footing.

"What choice did we have?" Scooter said. "We can't go north, or east or south. West is the shortest route to safety." And if he had choose how to die, being shot or blown up was better than being tortured.

"A few days ago we were trying to escape Israel. Now we're sneaking back."

"A lot can change in a few days." Scooter looked up into a gray sky dawning behind dark clouds as rockets streaked across. Behind them, snow-capped Mount Hermon loomed like a silent witness of the battle. They had walked all night. By now, ISIS soldiers would know they had escaped through the loose bricks in the prion wall, and find Daoud complicit. They had tried to convince the prisoner to come with them, but he refused. He said he would slow them down and endanger them, but the real truth was that he had lost the will to live.

In the distance, diesel engines rumbled. A thunderous explosion rocked the ground as a jet tumbled like a fiery spinning wheel across the dark landscape. They climbed a rocky hill and crested at Nimrod's Castle, an ancient fortress built by the Muslims to defend Damascus against the Crusaders in the thirteenth century. Below, lay the Golan Heights.

Bibi rubbed his watering eyes. "I don't believe it."

The blackened hulls of Israeli tanks dotted the plain, while hundreds of tanks scurried across the land's skin like beetles. Fires burned everywhere.

"The Iranians and Russians have completely overrun the Heights." Bibi pointed toward the massing of tanks on the southern part of the region that were firing anti-aircraft missiles into the sky. "Those are Zulfiqar 5 Iranian tanks and the green ones are Russian Armatas. It looks like they are staging for another attack."

"There are so many of them." The only chance Israel had was to do the unthinkable and launch their nukes. They weren't going to win a conventional war.

Bibi pointed at troops moving toward the Golan Heights. "See the black flag. That's ISIS. They came just in time to stake a claim to the Heights."

Scooter shook his head. "It doesn't make sense. ISIS hates Shiites almost as much as Jews. They would never fight side by side with Persians."

He turned toward the chief. "Say, if we don't get out of here alive, I need to know why you saved my hide."

"We saved each other." Bibi coughed.

"How's that?"

"Mendel caught me drinking on the job. He was going to fire me. My wife had left and taken our daughter. She wouldn't let me see her." He shook his head as if trying to erase the memories. "I've spent my whole life fighting for what's right. Somewhere along the line, I forgot that. You reminded me of why I joined law enforcement. To protect guys like you."

Scooter wanted to express his gratitude, but words seemed insignificant given Bibi's sacrifice. He nodded.

A crackle of thunder lit up the early morning sky as a cold wind laced with rain began to blow. Scooter zipped up his jacket.

Bibi looked up. "Very strange to get thunder this early in the morning."

Lightning struck a tank. It exploded. "Did you see that?" Bibi yelled.

The wind blew harder and sideways, making it difficult to see. Scooter ducked under a crumbling portico. Lightening struck again, destroying another tank. "You better take cover."

Bibi's stumbled toward the portico, fixated on the heavenly attack.

"I don't believe what I'm seeing," Scooter said. "If there is a God, he's definitely on Israel's side."

At that moment, fire descended from the sky like molten spears repeatedly striking the invaders.

CHAPTER SEVENTY-SEVEN

Jerusalem, April 28

Dark plumes of smoke rose from Jerusalem as the taxi veered through streets crowded with cars and trucks leaving the city. A scratchy radio broadcast said the government had ordered all citizens to leave the holy city. Courtney leaned back in the stiff vinyl seat and tried to absorb the news.

The taxi stopped in front of a long rectangular building finished in limestone. "This is newspaper office."

"I'll be right back with payment." She got out.

The taxi driver frowned. "You better not stiff me lady."

The parking lot was empty. She peeked in the window of the building's front door. The office was empty. She brushed at her eyes. Her hands were red and itched, and the wound on her right hand still hurt. She had rubbed herself raw trying to rid her skin of the retched smell. She sat on the curb, buried her face in her hands as an explosion a few blocks away shook the ground. She didn't care.

"Are you all right ma'am?"

Courtney looked up. A man with a shaggy red beard stood in front of her. The sun was to his back making it difficult to see his face. She wiped her eyes on her sleeve. "No, I'm not all right. Not at all."

"It's not safe to stay here."

Courtney stood up and brushed off her blue trousers. She glanced at the men's boots she wore but didn't care how ridiculous she looked. "Why are you here?"

"This is where the story is. I'm a reporter."

"Do you know Hank Jackson?"

"Why?"

"I have a story he needs to hear."

"What kind of story?"

Another bomb exploded even closer than the last. Courtney jumped, but the man didn't flinch. "Sorry, I can't share it with anyone but him."

The reporter stuck out his hand and smiled. "I'm Hank Jackson." He flashed his press ID card. "Now, let's go inside and down to the basement where it's safer. I want to hear your story."

She glanced back at the taxi driver who was scowling at her. "I took a taxi here, and I don't have any money to pay for the fare. Could you pay it? I'm sorry to even ask."

The reporter nodded. "Sure."

She had never asked anyone for money before. It was difficult and humbling.

CHAPTER SEVENTY-EIGHT

Golan Heights, April 28

"I'm almost tempted to believe in God," Scooter said. Forget trying to blame the destruction on some freakish lightning storm. Not one strike missed its target.

Bibi rubbed his dark unshaven face. His eyes were glassy. He just shook his head.

Devastation littered the scorched Golan Heights. The ruptured hulls of tanks reminded Scooter of the tin garbage can he had blown a hole through with cherry bombs as a kid. A seething furnace of dark smoke twisted upward from the scorched plain. What was left of the Iranian and Russian tank armada, turned eastward toward home.

At the southern edge of the Heights, the Israeli army waited as if unsure of whether the lightning might return and destroy them next.

"I felt safer in prison." Scooter steadied himself as the ground shook again.

Bibi said, "I thought the fighting was over."

"That wasn't a bomb." An image of the collapsed tunnel beneath the Dome of the Rock flashed before him.

The ground shifted. Scooter glanced up at the stone blocks of Nimrod's Castle overhead. "Let's get out of here."

But before he could take a step, the fortress shook ferociously, throwing him to the floor. The whole structure began to shift and groan as stones competed against each other. A portion of the portico's roof fell, hurling large blocks down the mountain. The stone floor buckled in the middle of the room.

Scooter scrambled to his feet. The only exit was the stairs, but he would be crushed before he ever made it clear of the stronghold. He glanced at the window overlooking the plain. A ten-feet drop to a steep rocky hill.

"It's our only chance." Scooter glanced back at Bibi.

He stumbled toward the window like a drunken man.

The floor collapsed. Scooter was pushed through the window down the mountain. Rolling, rolling, until he his head struck something hard.

CHAPTER SEVENTY-NINE

Jerusalem, April 28

The woman sitting in front of Hank was like a Faberge egg wrapped in butcher paper—a regal woman with eyes like deep ocean blue, but attired in common laborer's clothes. They sat in a basement lined with forgotten boxes of information that should have been shredded years ago. A fluorescent light above flickered and hummed.

"Do you have any proof?" Hank asked.

Courtney said she was a commercial real estate agent from Chicago, which seemed plausible despite her appearance. But her story was another matter. Her eyes dropped to the floor. "The CIA gave me a device to download Yasin's phone, but I lost it."

"Do you have any idea what was on his phone?"

"Not really. I don't even know if the phone I copied was the right one. He had three. The CIA believes Yasin has ties to ISIS. I saw a photo of him and Oma-Murshid. The agent also showed me a photo of one of the Chicago terrorists talking to a friend of Yasin's, who was staying at his home. I have his phone." She pulled it from her trousers and placed it on the table.

A foul odor surrounded it.

"I took this from Jakad. But it doesn't work. I think the chicken crap I was submerged in for a couple days and salt water destroyed it."

"Maybe not." Hank was reluctant to pick up the phone. "I'll check with my editor and see if he knows of anyone who can retrieve the data. This may be all we need to substantiate your story."

"But if that doesn't work, doesn't an eyewitness testimony count anymore?"

"I'm certain my editor won't run a story incriminating Yasin Mohammed of terrorist ties without hard evidence. If he wouldn't publish a story about the IDF's refusal to close a tunnel, he sure as heck won't print a story that will get the paper sued or worse."

Courtney lifted her eyes and shook her head. "He also killed my friend."

"I'm very sorry. I hate to ask, but what kind of evidence do you have?"

"Just a text from the CIA that she never made contact with her missionary team after her disappearance."

"May I see the text?"

She shook her head, obviously frustrated. "My cell is in Istanbul, but I can access my messages through the carrier."

"I don't know if that will help much anyway. Unfortunately, your testimony as his girlfriend would be suspicious. We have to find something solid to go after a guy of Mohammed's stature."

Courtney leaned her head back and closed her eyes. Even without makeup, she was beautiful. She opened her eyes and sat up straight. "I forgot about Kamal's phone. He was one of the three terrorists involved in the bombing. I have his phone."

"Where is it?"

"Inside the bottom of a lamp in a room at the Hotel Kempinski. Someone from Istanbul called Kamal's phone shortly before the bombing. That's why I came to Istanbul. I'm sure there aren't any voice messages on the phone from Yasin. He's too smart for that. But one of phone numbers might match his."

"We need that phone. You can't call the hotel, because they'll contact Mohammed. That won't work. I'll figure it out."

Courtney rubbed her red hands together.

"Are you cold?"

"A little."

Hank removed his jacket and draped it over her shoulders. "How about something to eat? You must be hungry."

"Thanks. Maybe, after we finish talking." Her big eyes searched his face. "Isn't there anything else we can do?"

He sat back down and leaned toward her. "Why are you willing to risk your life to destroy this guy?"

She looked away. "My sister flew into town the day of the bombing. We had planned to visit my mom at the nursing home and then have a girl's night out." Courtney brushed at her eyes and looked at Hank. "That never happened. He robbed me of everyone and everything I loved." Her voice quavered. "Isn't that enough?"

Hank knew about loss and the desire for revenge. But there was no way to get even, because getting even required restoring what was lost and that wasn't possible. "Do you know if the CIA's suspicion of Mohammed's connection to the bombing is based on anything more than the photos?"

"I don't know. When I first saw the photo of Yasin's friend, Jakad, and Farid, one of the other Chicago terrorists, I was in shock. I didn't want to believe the connection."

"Why?"

"I'm embarrassed to say I was falling in love with Yasin. There is one other important thing: the agent I met with said there has been a high volume of communication between terrorists in the last few weeks indicating they may be planning a large attack."

"Another bombing?"

"I don't know."

Hank leaned back in his chair. "What if Mohammed really is a terrorist masquerading as a man of peace?" The more he ran Courtney's story through his mind, the more he began to believe her.

Who could think up something like this? She would have to be crazy, and she didn't appear to be.

He scratched his beard as he eased his chair down. "Look, I want to help you. I'll talk to my editor, but he's going to want more evidence before he goes up against Yasin Mohammed. We'll see if we can resurrect anything from this phone." He pointed at the cell on the table. "And somehow, we'll get the phone you left in Istanbul. In the meantime, I'll contact the CIA to corroborate your allegations."

"They'll want to know where you got your information. You can't tell them where I am."

"I won't. I promise."

The floor and walls shook.

Courtney grabbed the table between them to steady herself.

Hank fell out of his chair as the shaking increased. The stacked boxes toppled to the floor. He and Courtney ducked underneath the table as the shaking intensified.

"That bomb was close," Courtney said.

"I don't think that's a bomb. Felt more like an earthquake. A big one."

CHAPTER EIGHTY

Jerusalem, April 30

A steady stream of cars and buses jammed the streets outside of Jerusalem as the local transit Scooter rode plodded ahead inches at a time. Bibi was gone. Buried alive in the collapsed ruins of Nimrod's Fortress. Scooter stared out at the mass of cars exiting the city. Anxiety was etched into the faces of the fleeing drivers. He should feel something for these poor people who were leaving everything behind, but he was numb. It was as if the nerves between his head and heart had been severed like the electrical wires to a house. Maybe, it was because he had seen too much death and lost too many friends.

The bus driver adjusted the dial on the radio and turned up the volume. A reporter said ISIS was attacking what remained of the Iranian army and its proxies. They were in full retreat. One enemy was vanquished, but another had taken its place. And Israel was bracing for another invasion.

Traffic came to a standstill on a hill overlooking Jerusalem. Scooter gasped at the devastation below. The Dome of the Rock was missing.

He glanced at the man next to him holding his phone. "Can you call out?"

"Yes, I just called my wife. Jerusalem's cell towers seemed to have survived."

"Do you mind if I make call? I lost mine."

The man handed his phone to Scooter. "Don't be too long. I'm expecting a call from my mom to let me know she's safe."

He dialed Dr. Moshe Abrams from Hebrew University, one of the most respected scholars in ancient languages in the world. The phone rang. "Dr. Abrams? It's Scooter."

"So good to hear your voice. Are you okay?"

Each breath Scooter took hurt, and the side of his head was tender and swollen. "I've got a world class headache, but I'm still alive." But it should be Bibi who was alive. He had a daughter. All Scooter had were longhorns. And he wouldn't have them much longer given his current financial condition.

"Johnny Naziri called and told me about your discovery," Abrams said.

Should he tell the professor about ISIS and the scrolls? Not now. He'll find out soon enough.

"He sent a photo of a scroll. I'm excited to talk to you about it. Where are you?"

"Outside of Jerusalem in gridlock. I can't believe what I'm seeing. The Dome of the Rock is gone."

"And the Al Aqsa mosque," Abrams said with a ring of glee. "We have much to discuss. And there are two people I want you to meet."

"Who are they?"

"I can't say.

"All right. I can see the university from here, but I don't know how long it will take."

"We're not going anywhere. Call me when you're headed up the hill."

*   *   *

Scooter got off the bus at the bottom of the hill. The road hadn't been cleared and was still littered with rocks from the quake. As he reached the steps of Hebrew University, it looked like a bomb had ripped through the school. Blocks of limestone were scattered everywhere. A large section of the outside wall was collapsed, exposing the interior of the school. The parking lot was empty except for two cars. Dr. Abrams stood at the top of fractured steps along with two other people.

Scooter picked his way up through the obstacle course.

"Good to see you old friend," Dr. Abrams said.

Scooter had always liked the professor, who seemed unconcerned about his dubious reputation.

They shook hands and the professor made a quick introduction of Hank Jackson and Courtney Gattis. Two Americans.

"I'll explain why my two friends are here shortly. But first, let's descend to the bomb shelter where it will be safer. ISIS is routing what's left of the Iranians and Russians. And once they're done, they'll turn on Israel."

They silently made their way down several stairs to a large room crowded with over-turned chairs and tables. The room looked more like a storage facility hit by a tornado than a shelter. They cleared some space and sat at a table.

Abrams folded his hands. A small smile tugged at the creased corners of his mouth. "Now keep in mind what I'm about to say is with a large dose of caution. Until I personally examine the scrolls, I can't make any definitive statements. But from the photos Johnny sent, it appears the scrolls are older than Qumran. Let me show you why."

The professor removed a slim computer from his satchel and turned it on. He scrolled to an icon and tapped the tracking pad. "This is today's Hebrew alphabet. Do you see the alphabet next to it?"

Everyone nodded.

"And this is the Paleo-Hebrew alphabet. Like the original Hebrew alphabet it contains all consonants. Scholars believe it originated from the Phoenician alphabet because of the strong resemblance. The scrolls you found are in written in Paleo-Hebrew, which dates them to the first temple. The oldest example of this writing is the Zayit Stone discovered on a wall at Tel Zayit. It is the only fragment of writings from the first temple era—until now.

Scooter's skin felt warm and flush. "What's written on the scroll?"

Abrams took a deep breath and placed his hand over his mouth and closed his eyes for a moment. "The Torah."

"Well, bless Sam Houston." But by now ISIS probably had the scrolls.

"The cuneiform discs are even older. I saw a photo of one and couldn't tell much. But they could contain a prehistory of Israel. Where did you find the scrolls and discs?" Abrams leaned forward over his notebook.

"In the Negev," Scooter said. "They were buried in a cave that looked like an ancient library."

"This is wonderful news."

"That part is."

Abrams looked perplexed. "What's the other part?"

"I'm pretty sure ISIS has the scrolls and discs."

"No!" Abrams threw his hands into the air. "How did this happen?"

Scooter explained the story of his capture and escape. "I don't think ISIS will destroy them. They know the relics are valuable. They'll show up on the black market and perhaps Israel will be able to buy them."

Abrams covered his face with his hands and shook his head. "Those scrolls may be the greatest discovery in Israel's history and now ISIS has them. How could Jehovah allow this?"

"Not the greatest," Scooter said.

Abrams removed his hands from his face. "What aren't you telling me?"

"The ark of the covenant. I found it."

Abrams's mouth fell open. "Is this true?"

"Located would be more accurate. We had a lot of help from a map."

"My friend Zedekiah Zukerman was gunned down a few days ago." He paused and grimaced as if the recollection caused physical painful. "Before he died, he announced the ark had been found, although it was not in Israel's possession. He connected Hank and me as he lay dying. His last words were: protect the ark. I didn't understand what he meant until I discussed it later with Hank. But he said...well, I will let Hank tell you."

"I thought you looked familiar," Hank said. "Weren't you the driver of the truck that tried to run the police barricade near the border?"

"How did you know?"

"I was there. ZZ and I tracked you from the Valley of Elah. Something terrible happened there. Didn't it?"

Abrams cleared his throat. "This is why I asked Hank to be here."

"My friends were murdered. We discovered the ark under the Dome of the Rock and were on our way to the airport, or so we were told, when we were taken to the remote spot you discovered."

"Do you have any idea who killed your friends?"

Scooter looked down at his rough hands and nails underscored with a thin layer of dirt. "An Arab with enough power to convince the Waqf to allow us to dig under the Dome of the Rock."

"That has to be a pretty exclusive club. I believe the map you used to find the ark was the same one stolen from Rabbi Eli Cohen before he died. It appears your Arab's influence extends into Israel."

"Is there anything else you can tell us about this mysterious Arab?" Courtney asked.

The woman sitting across from him could easily grace the cover of *Vogue* or any of the fashion magazines. She was stunning. Who was she?

"My friend Bibi and I were captured by ISIS while trying to evade Shin Bet eight days ago. At least, I think it was Shin Bet. We shared a prison cell with a condemned ISIS soldier. He made a incredible statement that I have no way of verifying, but I believe is true."

"What did he say?" Courtney said leaning across the table.

"That Yasin Mohammed was the former high commander of ISIS."

CHAPTER EIGHTY-ONE

Tehran, April 30

The stakes of Yasin's trip to the Iranian capital could not be higher. Iran was threatening nuclear retaliation against ISIS, unless it retreated from the Golan Heights. The caliphate had invaded the Heights after Iran's crushing defeat.

"I understand you have some influence with Oma-Murshid," said President Vadim of Iran. "If that's true, I urge you to make him realize that unless he withdraws his troops immediately and returns the Golan Heights, Iran will destroy Raqqa and Damascus with nuclear weapons. This is not a bluff. You have 24 hours."

Yasin crossed his legs and leaned back in the over-stuffed chair. The room was ostentatious with large dark furniture trimmed in golden gilt. Vadim was half Iranian and Russian. Not a good combination. His name meant deceiving and unpredictable in Greek, which given his record couldn't more true.

"What is there to return? Your country lost the Heights. You don't have enough tanks and troops left to hold it."

"We have reinforcements on the way."

"The Golan Heights doesn't belong to Iran. Israel captured it from Syria. ISIS has more right to the area than Iran."

Vadim stroked his long gray beard. "More Persian blood has been spilled there than Syrian. We will not back down."

Yasin uncrossed his legs and stared intently at the Iranian President. "How do you know ISIS does not have nuclear weapons?"

President Vadim chuckled. "They wish they did."

Yasin sipped his tea, then returned the cup to its saucer. "The world believes Iran destroyed Chicago, but we both know it wasn't your country."

Vadim shifted in his chair. "How can you be so sure?"

"Because I know who detonated the bomb. If you attack ISIS, you will be destroyed."

"Who's making this threat? ISIS or you?"

Yasin took another sip of tea. It was spicy with a hint of cardamom. Very good. "ISIS now controls part of Pakistan's nuclear arsenal. Those weapons are not aimed at Israel. They are pointed at every nuclear installation and every major city in your country, including Tehran. If you attack ISIS, you won't eliminate it, because its fighters are worldwide. But if the caliphate attacks Iran, your country will become a nuclear wasteland."

Yasin set his cup down again. Vadim's face was as pale as his beard. His left eye twitched. He cleared his throat. "Where did you get this information?"

"Does it matter? What's important is that you believe it. Oma-Murshid will not agree to vacate the Golan Heights, but he will allow your military to retreat with dignity."

"Persians do not retreat." His voice quavered.

Yasin stood and smiled. "You have forgotten your history. Do not make the same mistake Darius made against Alexander. He underestimated his strength and lost."

"How do I know you speak for Oma-Murshid?"

"You don't. But are you willing to gamble?"

CHAPTER EIGHTY-TWO

Jerusalem, May 1

News networks drowned airwaves with reports that the Ark of the Covenant, believed to be a myth, had been discovered by ISIS soldiers near the Sea of Galilee. Scooter sat in front of a computer in the basement of Hebrew University with Abrams and his two friends. He studied the televised images of the engraved sarcophagus containing the ark. The top had been removed to reveal the golden cherubim within. The great earthquake, that had leveled much of northern Israel, had supposedly unearthed an ancient vault containing the ark.

What a sham. The whole discovery had been staged.

Video footage showed fighters encircling the chest with AK47s raised in triumph. The fighting between the Islamic state and what was left of the Iranian army had stopped. ISIS was firmly in control of the Golan Heights and the Sea of Galilee region.

The announcement confirmed Scooter's speculation that Mohammed was the mysterious Arab who had hired him to find the ark. And if ISIS had possession of the ark, it gave validity to the prisoner's claim that the political savant was a former ISIS commander with strong influence over the caliphate.

Scooter looked up from the computer at Hank. "When are you going to run the story on Mohammed?"

The reporter leaned back in his chair and ran his hand through his red curly hair. "With your testimony, we have enough to prove the ark's discovery in Galilee is a hoax, but we still can't prove Mohammed stole the ark, or that he's connected to ISIS, even through it's apparent to us. My editor has confirmed he will print the story on the ark, but not on Mohammed."

"Why not? The bigger story is Mohammed's connection to ISIS. I told you what the prisoner said. Why isn't that enough?" Hank seemed overly cautious. But maybe it was his editor.

Courtney stood up and paced the room. "There has to be some other way to get the truth out." She had let her hair down. It was thick and golden and flowed over her shoulders.

"The evidence we have connecting Mohammed to ISIS is hearsay," Hank said. "I'm hoping this article might encourage someone else to come forward."

Dr. Abrams shook his head. "You realize you are all in great danger once the article is published. Your lives will be in constant peril. Yasin Mohammed will not stop until he finds you." He swept his hand in front of Scooter, Hank, and Courtney. "You won't be able to stay here much longer."

"My life has been in peril ever since I signed up to find the ark," Scooter said.

"And mine, since I agreed to help ZZ find the map," Hank said.

Everyone turned to Courtney who was leaning against the wall and seemed lost in thought. She shook her head. "I always thought I was a good judge of people and that evil people were easy to spot. That was my business. But then I met Yasin. He appeared to be a good and honest man with noble ambitions. It still disturbs me that he was able to deceive me."

"Well, praise be to Jehovah that something good has come from evil," Abrams said. "The earthquake that flattened the Temple Mount would have destroyed the ark if it had not been found. With its discovery, Jews everywhere will cry out for the temple to be rebuilt." He paused. "And Israel controls the Mount."

"But ISIS has the ark and the scrolls," Scooter said. "The heart and soul of the temple."

"I believe they will be returned to Israel," Abrams said.

"Only after you pay a bloody fortune for them," Scooter said. But there was another possibility that he didn't have the heart to say: Mohammed might destroy the artifacts to increase his power within the Arab world.

Courtney said, "What I don't understand is why the CIA won't release the photo of Yasin and Oma-Murshid? They have the evidence to connect him to ISIS. It would expose him as a fraud."

Hank let his chair rock back down and looked up at Courtney. "Mohammed is a very influential man. Who knows what subterfuge is occurring behind the scenes. The CIA may be trying to blackmail him with the photos in hope of turning him into a spy."

Abrams adjusted his large thick glasses. His beard was totally white except for traces of black around his chin. "The discovery of the ark near the Sea of Galilee will stir up great fervor among Muslims throughout the world. There is an Islamic prophecy that connects the ark to the Mahdi."

"What's the Mahdi?" Courtney said.

"The Islamic messiah," Abrams said. "One of the events confirming the identity of the Mahdi is his discovery of the ark and lost books of the Old Testament. Ironically, Mr. Mohammed's first name, Yasin, is also one of the names of the Prophet Mohammed in the Qur'an, and he is allegedly a descendent of Mohammed. All fulfill prophecies about the Mahdi."

Scooter glanced at Courtney who had drifted off again. What was she thinking? All of them in the room with the exception of Abrams had lost so much. But even he had lost the opportunity to pour over the ancient scrolls and kneel before the ark. But Courtney had lost the most. It wasn't just her sister and mother, and friends, but her identity. She seemed fragile, like a piece of fine china with hairline fractures. She had been drawn into the magnetic pull of a rising star that like a black hole swallowed everything in its path.

They all had.

CHAPTER EIGHTY-THREE

Istanbul, May 2

T he deadline for Iran's nuclear ultimatum had passed. World leaders had been holding their breath over the threat of a nuclear attack against ISIS, except Yasin.

He sat across from Abdul Khalid, the first President of the United Middle East. The capitol was temporarily housed in a converted church until a new building could be constructed. But this was more than a church. It was the Hagia Irene, the first church built in Constantinople by Constantine. Historians were appalled at the takeover of the church by the new government, but Yasin assured them it was only temporary. Christians had said little as he expected. Their religion was under siege and the occupation of an old church was the least of their problems.

The church, a beautiful blend of Byzantine and Moorish architecture, had been used primarily for concerts because of its amazing acoustics.

UME President Khalid sat on a gold tufted sofa that strained under the burden. "What did you say to convince President Vadim to withdraw his threat of nuclear retaliation against ISIS?"

Yasin said, "Iran hasn't made any announcement of a change in its position toward ISIS. As far as we know the threat still stands even though the deadline has passed."

"Yes, but they haven't attacked. You must have said something to persuade them."

Yasin sipped his tea. "I appealed to the President's self-preservation. I believe he has no desire to be a martyr."

"You threatened him?"

"I reasoned with him. ISIS has an arsenal of nuclear weapons pointed at every major city and nuclear installation in Iraq."

"Is that true?" Abdul's thick black eyebrows pushed his heavy brow upward.

"It is."

"And how did you learn this?"

"From an inside contact."

"I thought ISIS forbade any contact with outsiders."

The Islamic state had many sympathizers who contributed money and resources but weren't members of the caliphate. The new president had little idea of how ISIS worked, but that was fine. Better to have a president who needed his help than someone who didn't. "I made a friend while I was in prison."

"Humph." Abdul rubbed his hand against his sweating brow. "What's to keep them from pointing their missiles at us? We counted on Pakistan joining the union and acquiring their nuclear arsenal."

"Pakistan will still join. And we might retake the bases ISIS now controls."

"I can't tell if you are naive or an unrealistic," Abdul said frowning. "If the information you received about ISIS's control of Pakistan's nuclear installations is accurate, it's all over. There is nothing to stop them from destroying whom they choose."

Abdul was right about one thing. The world would never be the same. Whoever controlled the new nuclear-armed ISIS, would make the world dance like a marionette.

*　　　*　　　*

As the jet descended over Jerusalem, the devastation of the Temple Mount came into full view. From above it looked as if the earth had swallowed the mosque and shrine. Of course, there was a logical explanation: the honeycombed tunnels beneath the Temple Mount had caved-in during the earthquake, collapsing the foundations of both structures. A ring of Israeli soldiers surrounded the entire 35-acre plat to prevent Arabs or Jews from inspecting the ruins. Israel had taken control of the mount and made clear they would not allow the mosque and shrine to be rebuilt.

The UME had dispatched Yasin to negotiate a settlement with Israel over the rebuilding of the Temple Mount. But the UME had nothing to offer. He, on the other hand, did.

CHAPTER EIGHTY-FOUR

Jerusalem, May 3

"The destruction of the Temple Mount changes everything." Prime Minister Daniel Ben-David removed his glasses and cleaned them. The prime minister had a large head with a high forehead. Wisps of white hair sprung in chaotic Einsteinian directions. "The Al Aqsa Mosque and Dome of the Rock are gone, and we intend for it to remain that way."

Yasin and the Prime Minister sat on the upper patio of his home in the Talbieh district overlooking the Old City. Heavy foliage and trees obscured most of the white limestone house from the street, which looked like many of the other upscale homes along Benjamin Disraeli Street, except for the IDF soldiers posted at the front door. Yasin took a sip of iced tea and glanced out at the flattened Temple Mount.

Ben-David stared at Yasin, his eyes narrowing. "You violated our agreement," he snapped. "We gave you the map so you could find the ark and return it to Israel. The agreement was you would get credit for the discovery, and we would get the ark. Instead, you gave it to ISIS. Why?"

"The ark is safe and will be returned provided we reach an agreement."

The prime minister stood up and walked to the balcony. The fan above whipped his hair into a standing ovation. "We had an agreement. The ark belongs to Israel. I don't know what game you are playing, but be careful Mr. Mohammed."

Yasin brought his hands together and sighed. "The unexpected loss of the shrine and mosque alters matters as does your occupation of the Temple Mount. How could I in good conscience give up the ark now when Islam has lost so much? I would be scorned by every Muslim throughout the world."

Ben-David wheeled around. "What do you want?"

"To rebuild the mosque and shrine and…"

"Out of the question." He interrupted with a dismissive wave of his hand.

"You didn't let me finish. And for Israel to build its temple on the mount."

Ben-David's eyes appeared gray, but perhaps they were light blue and only looked pale against his skin and hair. He looked at a painting on the wall of a night sky and a moon and stars. Geometrical blocks of every color stood in the foreground, which looked like Van Gogh meets Picasso.

"It's the Western Wall at night." The prime minister nudged his head toward the painting. "The Western Wall is all that remains of the second temple, but for centuries it has been enough to give my people hope that someday their temple will rise again. How could I tell them that they will have to share what is rightly theirs with Muslims."

"Tell them the truth. You made a deal to save the ark. Your people will understand and you will have your temple."

"How can you make such a proposal? Do you speak for ISIS?"

"You know I do."

The prime minister snorted and turned back to the balcony. "What about the scrolls? ISIS has reportedly stolen them. We want them as well."

"I've only seen photos, but I understand from an expert who examined them that they are authentic and from the first temple era. But Mr. Prime Minister, surely you realize the scrolls are a separate negotiation."

"What do you want for them?" he said brusquely.

"Peace."

"Who doesn't except for our neighbors who want to annihilate us?"

"I believe the Middle East is ready for peace."

The prime minister turned around and looked perplexed. "Iran and Russia have destroyed our oil facilities in the Golan Heights. ISIS has routed the Persians and Russians and now controls the area. Hamas and Hezbollah have hammered our cities with rockets and you talk of peace? The only thing these murderers have in common is their hatred of Israel. There will never be peace as long as radical Islam continues to infect the minds of Muslims."

"Let me offer a theoretical question. If I can bring peace between the Sunnis and the Shiites, and Israel and its enemies, will you open your border to Palestine and share Jerusalem?"

Ben-David snorted. "You are either an idealist like all the other negotiators before you or you're crazy." He paused. "But if you can bring peace, you're more God than man. Certainly Israel will listen."

"Tell your troops to not attack ISIS. They in turn will not attack you, although they plan to push into southern Lebanon to crush Hezbollah. I plan to meet with Hamas, Hezbollah, and ISIS to forge a new relationship."

"What about Iran? The deadline they gave ISIS has passed, but they have made no announcement. Peace among the other nations is meaningless unless they are a part of it."

"I have already met with them."

"You have? What do you think they will do?"

"We will have to wait and see whether they really want the end of the world."

CHAPTER EIGHTY-FIVE

Jerusalem, May 7

The Gaza strip looked much like the Temple Mount in Jerusalem. Flattened. Few buildings stood. It seemed the historic earthquake had exacted its toll against Israel's enemies while leaving much of Jerusalem and its surrounding cities intact. Yasin asked his driver to stop.

"It's not safe," the driver said, his voice quivering.

"I will be fine. Please, right here."

The black SUV bounced to a halt on the rubble-strewn road as the driver nervously scanned the surrounding area. Yasin stepped from the vehicle. A dirty, brown haze hung over the city. The air tasted of dust. In the distance kids took turns kicking a ball against a large slab of concrete. Twisted rods of rebar protruded from the fallen wall. The boys noticed him and stopped kicking the ball. One of them ran into a nearby skeletal building.

Yasin checked his watch. In a few minutes he would meet with Salaam Nahid, the leader of Hamas's military. The country was destitute and one of the poorest in the world. If it weren't for international relief and support, it would be nothing but a graveyard.

A man emerged from the ruins with a rifle. He lifted it and aimed at Yasin. The driver inside the vehicle rapped frantically at the window before diving out of sight. The soldier held a rifle against his shoulder, peering through the scope, then shouldered it and ran toward him.

Yasin walked toward the man.

"I was worried for a moment," he said as his old friend approached.

Hakim hugged Yasin. "I would know you anywhere, even in a suit." He patted Yasin's arm.

"How is the fight?"

"Block by block. Hamas fighters are tough, but we are winning. The people are ready for change. They will listen to you. Do you know what they are calling you?"

"What?"

"The Mahdi, the savior. They believe you will bring peace and liberate them."

"That's why I came."

*   *   *

Hamas soldiers blindfolded Yasin and led him through a series of turns. Nahid, the commander, was taking no chances. He was the real power behind Hamas, not the President. Nahid controlled the military and whoever controlled it, controlled Hamas. A door opened and Yasin was led inside. An acrid smell of smoke and animal urine permeated the air. He was pushed into a chair as the blindfold was removed.

"I'm curious why the prince of peace has come to Gaza?" Nahid said, squinting as he took a drag on a cigarette. He wore a black patch over his right eye. To his back was a wall lined with maps. He leaned against a worn wooden table as a tabby cat jumped onto it and brushed against the man called *the butcher* by his own people.

"I came to discuss the future of your country."

He chuckled. "We will never have a future until every Jew is dead."

"It appears the Jews aren't your most pressing problem. I understand ISIS is gaining ground against your troops."

Nahid swept the cat off the table and stood, his one good eye glaring. "That's a lie. We are crushing their fighters. Soon, Palestine will be united under Hamas."

"And then what?"

"Then, we will crush Israel."

Yasin smirked. "Your plan has never worked, and it will never work. Israel cannot be conquered from the outside. They could unleash hell against you if they wanted, and destroy every living thing in this godforsaken land."

Nahid leaned back against the table and glanced at the cat weaving itself in between his legs.

"And even if you were to defeat ISIS, how will you lead your people if they will not follow? They are discontented."

"They are always discontented. They always want more food, more gasoline, more of everything."

"Take a minute and consider this," Yasin said. "What if the Middle East were united? Sunnis and Shiites together as brothers. What would the world look like? You're fighting for scraps Nahid, while a feast awaits."

The commander kicked the cat, which shrieked and ran into an adjoining room. He shook his head. "You think you're so smart. You crisscross the Middle East making big speeches. Peace will never be achieved by clever words. In the end, only bullets and bombs matter."

Yasin stood. The Hamas leader had lived with war for so long, he couldn't imagine a world without it. "There has been plenty of killing. The time for healing is at hand. You are either part of the solution or part of the problem. You must decide."

CHAPTER EIGHTY-SIX

Jerusalem, May 8

Hank was anxious, but he wasn't sure about what. It wasn't the article about Yasin. He had finished it, and Goldstein was reviewing it. But it wasn't really anxiety he was feeling. Anticipation would be more accurate. Like what he felt on his wedding day.

He stood up from his desk at *The Times* and looked around the office. Everyone was at work, except him. He couldn't concentrate. He sat down and looked at the article on Mohammed. He reread it. The peacemaker, as many were calling him, was nearly bullet proof. In the last week he had negotiated what seemed impossible: peace between the Sunnis and the Shiites. Iran and ISIS had laid down their arms against each other. The story about the real discovery of the ark beneath the Dome of the Rock and the staged one near the Sea of Galilee seemed pointless now. There was no Dome of the Rock. No reason for Muslims to be upset about someone excavating underneath it.

Could Yasin be the one? The dark king Daniel prophesied about?

An old bent-over man dressed in black stood just beyond Hank's window. His back was turned. Hank stood. "Deena."

She popped up from her desk across the office. "What's up?"

"Do you know this man standing outside?"

She walked to a window and peered out. The man turned around as if he knew he was being watched.

"I've never seen him before."

Hank shuddered. He had. He was the same man he and Kat had seen before their wedding, the same man who appeared at the university and guided ZZ and him toward the Valley of Elah. And here he was again. Why?

His pale skin was glowing as if the sun was shining on him. But it was overcast and muggy. Then, he did something odd. He waved as if he was saying goodbye. It wasn't a sad goodbye but more like I'll see you soon.

A trumpet blared above Hank's head, vibrating through his body. "Did you hear that Deena?" His face felt flush as heat radiated through him.

She pointed at Hank.

"What?"

"My God, you're on fire," Deena screamed. "You're on fire!"

The trumpet resounded again with a deafening boom drowning out Deena's screams. Suddenly, he felt a jolt shake his entire body as if something had seized him. Then, he was weightless as if he were floating. Suddenly, he jettisoned upward, flying at incredible speed. Everything was a blur except the most brilliant light ahead he had ever seen.

CHAPTER EIGHTY-SEVEN

Jerusalem, May 8

Courtney pulled up *The Times* on the computer and searched for Hank's story. The headline was about Yasin's peace deal with the Sunnis and Shiites. Where was the article Hank had written? It should have been published by now. She picked up the phone in the basement of Hebrew University and dialed the newspaper. The line rang but no one answered. No voice mail. She tried again with same result. Strange.

She tried the main number. It was busy.

Scooter rushed into the room. "Did you hear?"

Courtney dropped the phone into the receiver. Her stomach tightened. "What?"

"Millions of people have disappeared all over the world." His face was flush.

"Is this a joke? Now is not a good time." Scooter's corny sense of humor was getting on her nerves. But if it was a prank, it was convincing.

"I'm serious. I just saw a news report. I ran upstairs to see the city. It's crazy out there."

"Okay, you win. Great gag, but now, I have to find Hank." She turned her attention back to the phone and picked it up.

"Courtney, look at me." Scooter walked around in front of her. "I wish it were a joke. But it's not."

His dark brown eyes glistened. She took a deep breath. "You've got my attention. Any explanation?"

"No one knows. It just happened minutes ago."

A sick feeling rumbled in her stomach like sour milk.

"Who were you calling?" Scooter said.

"Hank. The article he wrote about Yasin isn't in the paper. I haven't been able to reach him. I'm worried."

"Do you think…?"

He didn't have to finish his thought.

Courtney jumped up and ran out of the basement to the stairs. She had to see for herself. When she reached the main entrance, in the distance, dark plumes rose across Jerusalem. Sirens wailed.

Scooter rushed to her side and stood silently looking at the city.

A girl sat crying on the cracked and broken steps to the university.

Courtney walked down to her.

She was a kid. Maybe nineteen. "What's wrong honey?"

The girl looked up, her eyes red and blurry. "I saw my boyfriend burst into flames and disintegrate. It was horrifying." She doubled over and wrapped her arms around herself and cried.

Courtney placed her hand on the woman's back and tried to comfort her. But she felt as distressed as the young student. Where was Hank?

CHAPTER EIGHTY-EIGHT

Gaza Strip, May 10

Yasin stood behind a podium in Erdogan Stadium in Gaza. The arena, built by Turkey to provide a modern venue for Palestinian sports, was packed with more than 20,000 people despite its precarious condition. Even the earthquake resistant structure could not completely withstand the impact of the most devastating quake ever recorded in the Middle East. Fissures snaked throughout the stadium's gray skin like a fractured eggshell.

A chant was building in the stadium and Yasin waited for it to reach a crescendo.

People shouted: "Mahdi, Mahdi, Mahdi." They stamped their feet undaunted by the cracks beneath them.

Snipers were posted throughout the stadium, searching for any sign of trouble. Hamas had issued a fatwa against Yasin, calling for his death, because of the peace brokered between the Sunnis and Shiites. His friends had warned him against a public showdown with Hamas, but there was no other way.

Yasin raised his hands as his image looked down from the large jumbotron. "As I drove through Gaza recently, I saw a nation ravaged by war. Its people destitute, eating from garbage dumps. Hamas blames Israel for its destitution, but I say blame your leaders. They have deceived you. What do you have to show for 75 years of struggle? Will the next 75 years be any different? Some may declare: we will die before we ever agree to peace with Israel." He nodded.

"And what will death bring you? Citizens of Palestine, death is not the answer. Life is. You have entrusted your lives to leaders who eat steak while you scrounge for scraps to feed your families."

In the distance a fight broke out. Police rushed to the troublemakers and subdued them.

"I've looked into your eyes and know every one of you wants a different life. A better life. Rise up and claim what is yours and help me tear down Israel's wall."

A roar rose from the crowd as the chant of "Mahdi, Mahdi, Mahdi" began again.

CHAPTER EIGHTY-NINE

Jerusalem, May 10

Courtney glanced at the headlines in the newspaper posted outside *The Jerusalem Times*. *Vaccine Kills Millions*. The Centers for Disease Control had issued a statement that the spontaneous combustion of people across the world was a reaction to the drug that had saved billions from the deadly pandemic four years ago. But not everyone who had been inoculated had died.

She and Scooter walked into the newspaper office. It was empty. "Hello, anyone here?" Courtney said.

A man poked his head from around a corner. "What do want?"

"I'm looking for Hank Jackson."

The man looked at the floor. "He's gone."

Courtney cleared her throat and tried to ignore the hollowness boring into her. "Gone where?"

He looked up, focusing his dark eyes on her. "Where have you been lady? He's dead. Up in flames." He threw his hands into the air.

She buried her head into Scooter's chest and tried to restrain the sudden urge to sob.

"It's going to be okay," Scooter said patting her back.

"No it's not."

A stylishly dressed woman walked forward. "I'm sorry honey. We all miss him. How did you know him?"

Courtney looked up. "We met a few days ago. He interviewed me for an article he was writing."

"Are you Courtney?"

She nodded.

"I'm Deena." She extended her hand.

Courtney shook it. "This is Scooter."

Deena shook his hand.

A man walked toward them. "I'm Goldstein, the editor. Now, might not be the best time to tell you, but I've decided to not publish Hank's article."

"Why not?" Courtney said, her face suddenly feeling flush.

"Mohammed is bringing peace to the Middle East, something no one thought possible. I don't want to be the one to deter this process. I'm not saying I won't publish it, but not now."

Courtney glared at the editor. "That's exactly what you're saying. If Hank were alive, you would publish the article."

Deena's eyes welled up.

"Look, I'm doing you a favor. If that article is published, you're both dead. Mohammed is idolized by millions of Arabs and a negative article like this will incite them."

"He already wants us dead."

CHAPTER NINETY

Jerusalem, May 14

Yasin stood on a podium built over acres of wood covering the entire plat of the Temple Mount. Below the planks, lay the ruins of the collapsed Al Aqsa Mosque and Dome of the Rock. A vast sea of people packed the mount, pressing against a barrier of United Nation soldiers in front of the platform. The dignitaries on stage included presidents from the United Middle East, Iran, and Palestine. Even ISIS had sent a representative but the caliphate's supreme leader was not here. The prime ministers of Britain, France, and Germany's chancellor were all present as well as the President of the United States. Any nation that had ever played a part in the peace process between Israel and Palestine was represented.

Yasin lifted his arms and looked up toward the sun showering him in light. He lowered his gaze to the crowd and smiled. "Today, we mark an historic event: a peace no one thought possible. But today, Sunnis and Shiites, Palestinians and Israelis lay down their arms and unite." He swept his arms over the people. "Let this peace stand for a thousand years."

The crowd of Muslims, Jews, Christians, Sunnis, and Shiites and every race on earth roared their approval.

"We stand on the ruins of the Al Aqsa Mosque and the Dome of the Rock, which I know troubles many of you as it does me. But I have an announcement that will cheer your hearts."

A silence fell over the multitude.

"In the spirit of peace, Israel has agreed to allow Muslims to rebuild their sacred mosque and shrine."

A roar from Muslims rose into the thick air.

"In exchange, Israel will be allowed to build its temple."

Muslims fell silent as Orthodox Jews threw their hats into the air.

"And...the wall between Israel and Palestine will be torn down. Jerusalem will be not only the capital of Israel, but of Palestine."

A deafening tumult shook the platform.

Yasin raised his hands and motioned for quiet. "As you have heard, the Ark of the Covenant has been found. The great earthquake that rocked northern Israel exposed an ancient tomb containing the ark. ISIS soldiers discovered it, and have graciously agreed to give the ark to Israel for its temple. You heard correctly." He nodded. "They have also agreed to turn over ancient scrolls of the Torah that I am told predate the Dead Sea Scrolls by more than 500 years."

A group of Arabs shouted something that sounded inflammatory but was lost in the ambient noise.

Yasin ignored them. "Is this not proof enough that peace has overtaken the Middle East? May the rest of the world follow our example and beat their swords into plowshares, their spears into pruning hooks and never lift arms against a brother, nor learn war anymore."

"And let us not forget to also celebrate the birth of two nations: Israel's birth in 1948, which they celebrate today, and the birth of the United Middle East. Let us always be partners in peace and commerce."

Some Arabs yelled again, this time clear enough to hear: "No peace with Jews. Death to Jews!"

Yasin shot his hand toward the men and pointed at them. "Then move as far away as you can. Because this land is held by those who want peace. Those who don't can leave now."

The men dropped their heads as those around hurled insults at them.

Yasin raised his hands again as a man cried out, "He is the savior, the Mahdi." Another standing nearby yelled, "The prophecy has been fulfilled."

A chant of "Mahdi" began to resound like an echo through the throng.

Yasin turned toward the dignitaries behind him. They seemed confused about what the people were shouting and its connection to him. But he understood. The Mahdi was the guided one prophesied in the Hadith. The one who would discover the Ark of the Covenant and lost scriptures of the Old Testament.

The angel, who called himself *I am,* had promised he would make him great if he worshipped him. He had not failed. And now the whole world would discover *I am* through Yasin. In ancient times, he was Marduk, Ashur, Ra, Zeus, and Jupiter. The early Hebrews called him Baal. People today called him Allah, Brahma, Father, Mother, Eloihim, Christ. But no matter what they called him, he was the same. The great *I am.* And he had chosen Yasin to build a great temple to reveal him to the world.

She was standing close to the front, staring at him. It was her stoicism amid the enthusiastic spectators that caught his attention. She was dressed in a fashionable orange tunic and wore a black hijab that was draped across it. A veil covered her face, exposing only her eyes. But it was enough. The piercing blue eyes were as unmistakable as fingerprints. He glanced at his security team to see if they had noticed the woman in front of him. They hadn't.

Why was she here? He had scoured Jerusalem searching for her. Although unskilled in covert techniques, she had managed to elude a top team of investigators. She had more courage than common sense. But it was such audacity that had attracted him to her. Had she come to stand in silent derision or to taunt him, knowing she would be difficult to track in the sea of people? Or did she come to whisper into the ears of those who would listen that he was a murderer and not to be trusted?

At one time he felt an unexplainable connection between them. Now, he felt nothing. Not hatred, or scorn. Just nothing. No one would believe her story, particularly now. Still, she would have to be contained.

She continued to stare as he spoke. He turned toward another section of the crowd and spoke to them of how peace would change their lives. Then, from the corner of his eye, something swung from beneath her hijab.

A sharp pain exploded in his head as the world spun and the floor struck him in the face. Screams erupted. People bent over him shouting to each other, but he couldn't understand.

CHAPTER NINETY-ONE

Jerusalem, May 14

Scooter stood only a few feet from Courtney. He hadn't recognized her at first behind the veil, but she had an idiosyncrasy of rotating the diamond ring on her right finger when she was nervous. He had observed her do it a number of times in the university's basement. It had to be her. She was fixated on Mohammed and hadn't noticed him. But without the hat, mustache, and jeans, he was almost as unrecognizable as she. He had bought a suit for the occasion. The second one he now owned.

People were packed together, all jostling to get closer to the peacemaker. The world was still trying to figure out how Mohammed had brokered peace between ISIS and its enemies. If only they knew.

Courtney continued to stare at the politician, as if she were in a daze. If he didn't know how much she hated him, he would swear she was still in love with him. Why had she come? Perhaps, the same reason he was here. To witness history. And to look in Mohammed's eyes when he said ISIS had discovered the ark and scrolls. Scooter clenched his fists and fought the anxiety rising within. Mohammed had always been several steps ahead of him.

"Many of you are questioning the disappearance of millions," Mohammed said."

Scooter turned toward the podium.

"You have heard no doubt that their disappearance is because of the rapture. Nonsense, I have many Christian friends, and they are still here." He turned back toward the dignitaries seated behind him. They nodded in agreement. "I met with the scientists at the World Health Organization, and they unanimously agree that the sudden combustion of people across the world was a reaction to the vaccine many received four years ago. One of the reasons I believe this is true, is because very few in the Middle East were inoculated in contrast to the United States where the virus began. As a result, very few of us have suffered the fate of millions of Americans."

There was a flash of clothing to Scooter's right. Then, two loud cracks.

He turned. Smoke hovered around Courtney as people scattered screaming.

Mohammed staggered at the podium and fell forward.

Wails erupted as people attempted to run.

A man on the platform pointed at Courtney who stared catatonically at the fallen leader. He drew a gun from inside his jacket.

Scooter lunged toward her as the man fired.

CHAPTER NINETY-TWO

Jerusalem, May 17

She should have died. She wanted to. But Scooter gave his life for her. Why did he do it? She barely knew him. Courtney sat on the bed and brushed at her eyes, fighting back the tears.

The Israeli cell was clean unlike the Turkish prison. She was the only occupant in the cellblock, which was surely vacated to prevent a riot. There were no windows. Only a bunk, a sink with a small metal mirror above it, toilet, camera in the corner of the room to monitor her every move and concrete gray.

She had expected to feel differently after killing Yasin, as if his death would atone for the many she had caused. But she didn't. The guilt was still there. And with Scooter's death, the burden was even greater. Zoe told her Jesus Christ died to free us from sin and make us free. If only, that were true.

A metal door clunked. There were footsteps. Voices.

A female guard opened her cell door. "Someone is here to see you." Her dark eyes shifted back down the corridor.

"A visitor?"

As the man stepped into her cell, she stumbled into the wall and gasped. She couldn't breathe.

The guard stepped outside.

It isn't possible. You were dead. She had seen the gaping hole in his head, his blank eyes, and a bystander drape a suit jacket over his head. She tried to speak but her throat tightened.

Yasin stood before her with a bandage around his head. His dark eyes bore into her. "What you meant for evil, God meant for good."

"Who...who are you?" she stuttered.

"Muslims will call me the Mahdi. Jews, the Messiah. Others will call me God. For only God can conquer death."

He turned toward the door, then stopped and looked back. "The first time I met you, I felt an unexplainable connection. When you left, I told myself I was mistaken. But when I saw your gun pointed at me, I understood. Every savior has a betrayer. It was your destiny."

He walked out, and the guard shut the door.

Courtney stood trembling and then, for the first time in her life dropped to her knees and prayed. *Oh God, Zoe believed in you. I don't pray for you to save my life, for it is lost. But I pray to know you as she did.*

There was a rap at the cell door. A female guard stood there.

"May I come in?"

Courtney stood up and nodded.

The guard walked in holding a book. "I know this is going to sound crazy coming from a Jew, but I'm also a Christian. I felt compelled a few moments ago, to give you this. She handed the book to her. "It's a Bible."

Courtney took it.

"Read Daniel and Revelation. It will help you understand what's happening. I'll be back from time to time to discuss it with you." The guard walked out and closed the door.

Courtney sat down and opened the Bible. She had never read it. The pages fell open to *Revelation 13*. She looked down and began to read. *And the dragon gave the beast his own power and throne and great authority. I saw that one of the heads of the beast seemed wounded beyond recovery—but the fatal wound was healed. The whole world marveled at this miracle and gave allegiance to the beast.*

Courtney put the Bible down. A book written hundreds of years ago had predicted what happened. Only God could do that. A fog began to lift for the first time in a long time. Yasin said she had fulfilled her destiny. He was wrong. Her mission was just beginning.

Afterword

I want to thank my wife, Holly, for the work she put into the manuscript. Not only did she assist in editing, but she helped shape Courtney's voice. I like short, clipped dialogue, and Holly reminded me, women use a lot words. She also suggested a different ending, which I chose.

Many thanks to my beta readers. Your feedback is invaluable and provides ideas and changes I'm either too blind to see or never even considered. Thank you.

Finally, just a note about the Hebrew letter placed at the beginning of each chapter. The character is beit. It refers to God's dwelling house, which seemed appropriate for the story.

About the Author

D
ave Slade is the author of the popular novel *The Christ Virus*. *Dark Star Rising* is the second book of the trilogy Dark Star Legacy.

He is a graduate of San Jose State University with a Bachelor of Arts in Journalism and the School of Ministry at Calvary Church. He lives in New Mexico with his wife, Holly, and Aussiedoodle Steinbeck.

www.ingramcontent.com/pod-product-compliance
Lightning Source LLC
Chambersburg PA
CBHW071211250626
47159CB00001B/284